PERSONA NON GRATA

A NOVEL BY

P.N. GWYNNE

Amazon Publishing Inc.
for
PNG-RDC(BVBA)

ISBN-13: 978-0-578-90436-8
Library of Congress Control Number: 2021920855

This book is a work of fiction. Any resemblance to any actual persons,
living or dead, is purely coincidental.

Cover design by Matthew Morse at HeyMatthew.com

1994

SMALL FRENCH EMBASSY
SMALL EX-COMMUNIST EAST EUROPEAN COUNTRY
BIG BORDELLE

"Now you listen to me, *petit,* and listen well, so that we have no misunderstanding: I am a *Sergent-Chef* of the *Légion Etrangère, verstehen? A*nd when not sleeping, drinking, fucking or shitting, I kill people. That is my *boulot,* that is what I do.

"*You,* on the other hand, are *sensé* to be a diplomat, however half-arsed, and as such, and to the extent that you have any purpose in this life at all, it is to make *precisely* the kind of call I am hereby ordering you to make, right now. *Compris?* Have I made myself clear?" Michel-Ange's face was blank –whether from paralyzed shock or mere bemusement was unknowable and, in any case, moot.

"*Bon. Execution. Et qu'ça saute.* Hop it, my lad."

(p. 193)

OTHER NOVELS BY P.N. GWYNNE:

Firmly By The Tail
Pushkin Shove
The Bronx Bombing
"Imperialist Warmonger Pig" or An Occurrence At Landing Site-Echo

THIS ONE'S FOR ALSIE.

"I am against all governments, including my own."

— GEORGES CLEMENCEAU *(French President from 1906-1909 and 1917-1920)*

"The job of an ambassador these days is exactly like that of an airline stewardess; you serve a lot of meals and you clean up minor messes."

— HENRY CATTO *(Former U.S. ambassador to The Court of St. James)*

"Diplomats are old women of both sexes fussing around worrying about what the whole world thinks when in fact no one gives a damn."

— ALAN JUDD *(Author and ex-officer in Her Majesty's Secret Service)*

"Diplomacy is not for the proud."

— JAY NORDLINGER *(Author and Senior Editor of NATIONAL REVIEW)*

"Things got bad, and things got worse, I guess you know the tune...."

— JOHN FOGERTY
("Lodi")

"Things arre gonna git worrse, beforre they git even worrserr."

-- (LORD) GEORGE ROBERTSON
(Ex-British Defense Secretary, ex-NATO Secretary General, and a Scotsman)

"Any life when viewed from the inside is simply a series of defeats."

— *GEORGE ORWELL*

MAPS AND DIAGRAM HAND-DRAWN BY MICHEL-ANGE TO SHOW HIS GIRL-FRIEND JENNI-FAIRE.

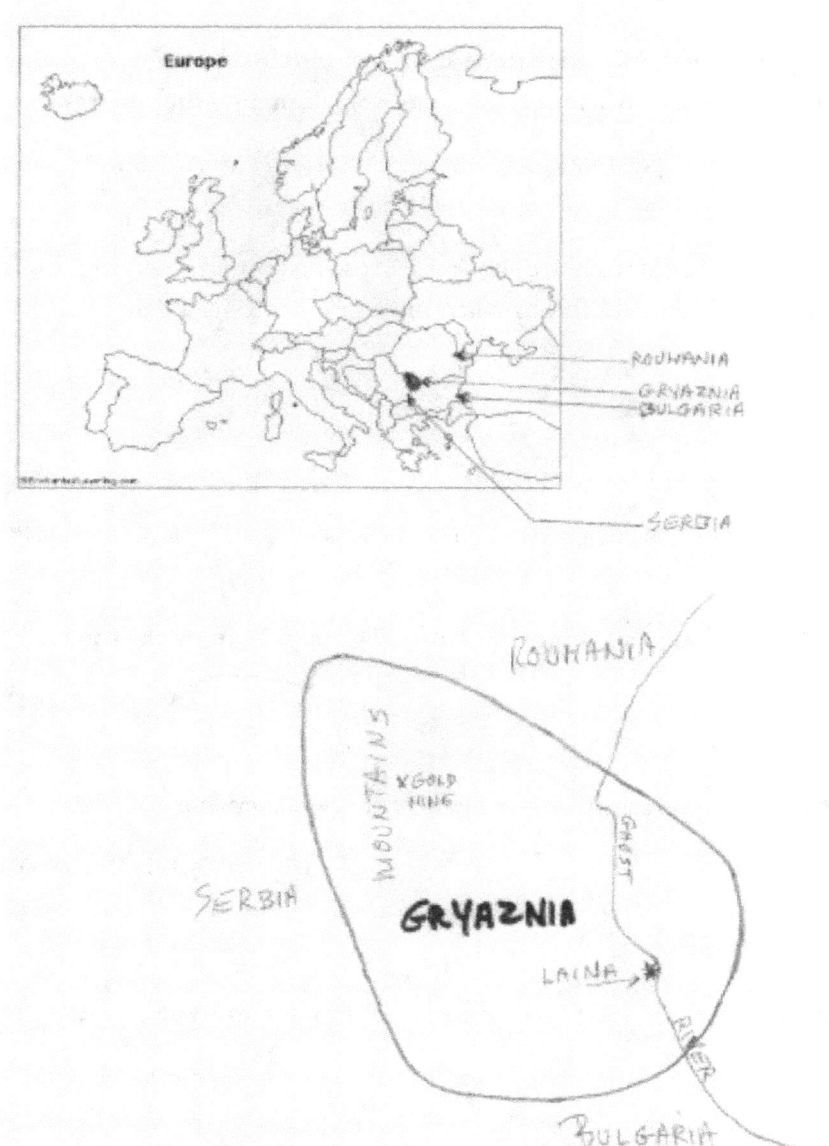

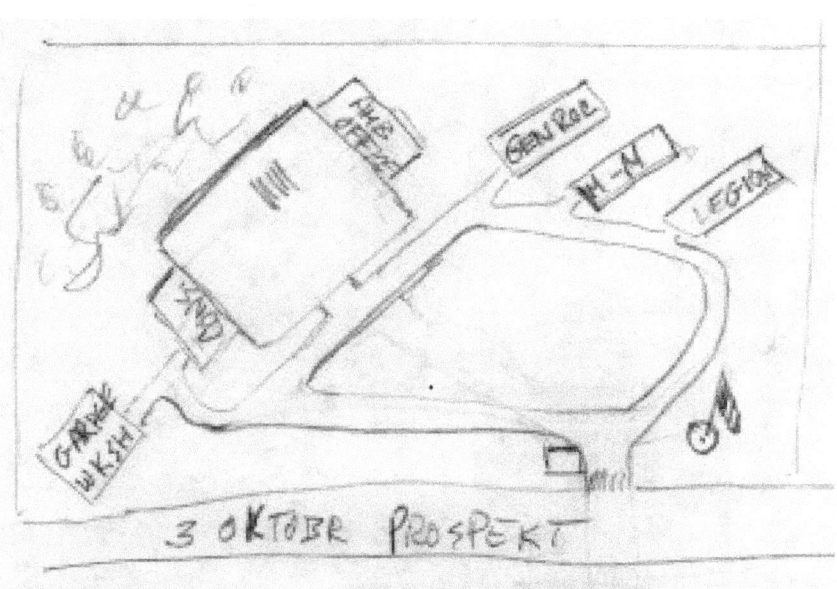

PRINCIPAL CAST OF CHARACTERS

(in order of appearance):

Michel-Ange Grenier de la Fassederad – French Cultural Attaché/Chargé d'Affaires, Laina, Gryaznia

Jennifer MacKoy – American graduate student; Michel-Ange's Californian girlfriend and flat-mate in Paris.

Mademoiselle Bérénice Bergère – Col. Mincemot's assistant, ("Mother Superior")

Col. Bertrand Mincemot – shadowy *"eminence grise"* at the Quai d'Orsay, Paris

Madame Bébette – old lady "librarian" to Col. Mincemot's particular "service"

"Manu" (Emmanuel) – Corsican ex-French soldier and owner of "Le Macaque", Michel-Ange's "local"

Ivan Pomeshanskiy Ivanov – Gryaznian citizen; chauffeur and "go-fer", French Embassy, Laina

Staff Sgt. (*Sergent-Chef*) Wolf Schlechtermann and **Pfc. (*1ère Classe*) Martinho Meiavelha** – French Foreign Legionnaire guards, French Embassy, Laina

Irina Vozhbuzhdena – Gryaznian citizen; receptionist and administrative assistant, French Embassy, Laina

Jean-Loup Moitié – French Consul and Commercial Attaché, Laina, Gryaznia

Clothilde de Brest d'Anjou Duquon-Lajoie ("Clo") - Wife of French Ambassador to Gryaznia

Armand St. Emilion de Pépinière Duquon-Lajoie – French Ambassador to Gryaznia

Vasily Maximovich Pozadnik – Gryaznian Minister of Culture, Sport, the Arts and Other Peculiarities

Major Kiril Nikolaievitch Krivoy – Gryaznian Ministry of Interior, Directorate of State Security, (*"Direktsiya Gosudarstvennuy Bezopasnosti"* – *"DGB"* – *"DéGéBé")*, Diplomatic Liaison Division.

Gerasim Vladimirovich Grib– President of The Republic of Gryaznia

CONTENTS

1

MICHEL-ANGE

Begging your kind attentions, dear readers, I propose herein to guide your good selves through a not un-movemented and at times astonishing tale of surpassing improbability, human folly and karmic randomness.

Although it concerns a young friend who is French, I myself am not – being instead of a nationality which is rather something of an international *bouillabaisse*. And while I am tolerably educated, I cannot claim English as my first tongue, so I will ask in advance for your indulgence if some of the locutions which follow are perhaps of a... well, of a slightly exotic construction. (Indeed, my English was acquired from a grab-bag of sources which included doting parents, dogged teachers, an eclectic diet of books and periodicals, lurid screens both large and small, as well as selected graffiti from the world's walls and bespoke men's room stalls on five continents.)

To proceed, then:

My young friend in question – and the protagonist of this saga – was, in this month of April of *Anno Domini* 1994, 24 years old. Six feet (1.82 metres) tall, fit and wiry, of pleasing if not-completely innocent mien. He kept his dark hair unfashionably longish and it, conforming to the hoary continental *habitude* of not too frequently washing it, tended to look upon him not tremendously unlike as if he had sitting upon his noggin a small, crumpled umbrella.

And while *ho-la-la* was he French, he was, in fact, more than merely French: he was, to his almost-visible bones, a *Parisien*.

But most of *all,* he was an *Enarque*. (True, he had emerged dead last in his graduating class there, but he was an *Enarque* nevertheless. Just.)

Now, a common garden-variety Anglo-Saxon reader, (as you may well be), possibly unfamiliar with the full import of this last datum, would be excused in imagining that an *"Enarque"* might be some species of wild syndico-nihilist-Trotskyite-cobblestone-throwing anarchist, am I not right? After all, what does the word *sound* like? Yes, quite.

But such an Anglo-Saxon reader would not be more arse-backwards in so concluding:

Because an *"Enarque"* turns out to be not a bomb-throwing Marxist, but rather something *quite* different: an *"Enarque"* is a graduate of the cringingly prestigious E.N.A., the *"Ecole Nationale d'Administration"*, an Olympian institution located in the east of the country – in Strasbourg – and which, in France, is the post-graduate equivalent of a theoretical combination of Oxford-Cambridge-Harvard-Yale-Princeton and West Point... and its alumni have been pretty much "running" France (if that is not too ironic a term) since Nappy was a corporal, ... or, well... at least since Yank GIs liberated the place in '44.

And one of the amazing things about the E.N.A. is that it does not discriminate between proclivities of Left or Right, or even Shades-In-Between. All that it requires is that its students work like mad and be dashed brainy to begin with – and that includes even those who end up last in their class (which, as previously mentioned, is what our boy, our protagonist, had, in fact, contrived to do).

Also, however, it must be added that it does not hurt the chances of a prospective *Enarque* if he (or, occasionally, she) is the French version of To the Manner Born. (*"Né à la manière"*? Not too sure about that one....)

Which brings us to the name of the subject of all this introductory faff, viz., one Michel-Ange Grenier de la Fassederad.

High(ish)-born (he had an ancestor who had been one of Cardinal Richelieu's bastard sons, and more recently his *papa* had been Something-Or-Other "important-but-shady" in the long-departed Giscard-d'Estaing *régime*), young Michel-Ange, before busting his arse at the E.N.A. had busted his arse first at the daunting Lycée Janson de Sailly, which is the Parisian version of Eton-Harrow-Deerfield-Choate, and then busted undergraduate arse at the austere, no-nonsense Institute of Political Studies, a.k.a. *"Sciences Po"*.

Although he really didn't need them, he sometimes affected spectacles that he liked to allow to slide down his thin nose – which added an element of innocent bewilderment to the otherwise pleasant and unthreatening demeanor of our young and gay *boulevardier*. Although I suppose I must add that "gay" is used here in its old traditional sense, because whatever other quirks and oddities might pertain to Michel-Ange, sexual ambiguity was not among them.

Au contraire – young Michel-Ange appreciated the ladies with the keenness for which his compatriots are justly reputed. Until fairly recently he had unwisely saddled himself with a haughty and supposedly aristocratic girlfriend, Léonie Chopin-et-Saint Just, but their pairing had foundered, and rather raucously, too. Because Léonie had early-on expressed the desire – demanded, more like – to be beaten. Spanked. A *procédure* which, to his credit, a taken-aback Michel-Ange had never quite managed to get the hang of. Or even *begin* to fathom.

Now safely free of that entanglement, he currently maintained his own flat on the terribly *chic* (except in July and August when it was overrun by all the tourists in the world who were not in Spain, but things were alright for now as it was still April) Rue Mouffetard in the Left Bank's 5th Arrondissement.

And he enjoyed, at least for now, the intimate companionship of a quite fetching dark-tressed, dark-eyed and long-legged American *nana* from "Marin County" (wherever that was – in *la Californie du nord*, he believed), one Jennifer MacKoy. She was some sort of graduate student of something, somewhere (Michel-Ange was not too clear on this – he was vaguely aware that words like "post-modern", "gender", "deconstruction", "studies", "patriarchy", "conflict management", and, was it "intersegmental"? "inter"-something, at any rate, were involved, but he was never sure of their correct order), but regardless of all that, for the time being they were living together in reasonable compatibility. She was clean – certainly more than *he* was – friendly, stylish, reasonably *amusante*, intelligent enough to appreciate and even deploy sarcasm, easy on the eyes and, mercifully, possessed of more of the traditionally-understood sexual tastes than the dangerously unfathomable and unlamented Léonie Chopin-et-Saint Just. Plus, she spoke French. Of a sort. French-*ish*.

They had met – literally bumping into each other – outside the *"Mesdames"* and *"Messieurs"* at *Fouquet's* famed establishment on the Champs Elysées, one Friday lunchtime. She had been washing her hands, (whilst he, shamefully, had not been), and she had said, in "Frenglish", as they'd brushed by, "*Pardon*, hi, hey, say, *chouette rétro* suit – is it Saint-Laurent?"

Michel-Ange, who knew a bit of English, from the movies, principally, had stammered "*Euh,* sorrie, but, euh, *non,* eet eez a razzer éould *démodé* Cardin..."

But that impossibly naff opening had sufficed to permit them to proceed upstairs where they'd invited each other to consume coffees and Calvados-es together. And they'd exchanged phone numbers and very soon after that they'd become, without much ceremony or even apparent effort, something of an "item".

When they weren't bouncing around in his little flat on the Rue Mouffetard, they "hung out" quite pleasantly (sometimes joined by "pals" of hers) at the Café Flore, Les Deux Magots, and the lethal Rhumerie in and about the Boulevard Saint Germain.

So *that* was alright, then.

2

LE TÉLÉPHONE

The problem was, Michel-Ange was technically unemployed. And not just "technically" – *actually* unemployed. For, *"Enarque"* notwithstanding, he had no proper, independent, source of income.

He was currently being bankrolled by his politically-connected *papa* who, it might be argued (despite a discreet divorce from Michel-Ange's *maman* who was now re-married to some species of Sardinian "prince") could well afford it – living, as he did, in quietly understated splendiferousness in an *apartement particulièr* on the "sunny" side of the Avenue Foch. But the reclusive and somewhat austere *paternel* was nevertheless a bit concerned about the future of his *fils*.

And thus *papa* had rung up one evening and said, *"Salut, mon vieux,* but I was just wondering how your career is coming along, which, in fact, you don't, euh, appear yet to have embarked upon, *n'est ce pas?"*

"Well, *papa*, you know that I've applied at the *Quai d'Orsay*, but I have yet to hear from them."

"Yes – how long have they been keeping you waiting?"

"It's like a small eternity. A month, I'd say. More like two, actually."

"What? Has the name Fassederad so quickly evaporated into the ether? Attend a bit – I'll soon sort out that sorry *canaille*. Stay near your *téléphone* for the next few days while I... organize those cretins at the *Quai* – I promise you, you will be hearing from them. And in the meantime, my fond salutations to your *petite amie Américaine.*"

The "Quai d'Orsay" is, in fact, a series of contiguous buildings on the left bank of the Seine which, in their collectivity, constitute the French *Corps Diplomatique*. Their Foreign Service. Their version of what in Washington bears the distinctly more unlovely nickname of "Foggy Bottom" ("Froggie Bottom"?) And all, of course – this being Paris – also very stately and elegant.

But there is a small nuance: whereas in Britain they have a sharp corporeal distinction between MI6 and the Foreign Office, and in America there is no legal confusion between the CIA and the State Department, the French – being French – do it a bit differently: elements of their foreign intelligence service, the DGSE, (whose headquarters are on the Boulevard Mortier in the 20th Arrondissement), also share quarters with the Ministry of Defense in the 14th Arrondissement and with the Ministry of Foreign Affairs on the Quai d'Orsay.

So French cloaks and daggers find themselves intermingling bureaucratically with diplomatic white ties and striped trousers. Much after the fashion of the old Soviet KGB, only (thankfully and usually) in a more civilized fashion.

Thus, it was never exactly clear *who* Mr. de la Fassederad *père* contacted over there at the Quai d'Orsay, but a few days after his telephonic exchange with his *papa*, the landline (Michel Ange refused to carry or even own one of those newfangled cellular telephones) rang at the Rue Mouffetard and was answered by *Mademoiselle* MacKoy.

There ensued a short – but no less incomprehensible and, (towards its end), agitated – exchange, which concluded abruptly with Jennifer shouting, "Michel! *Viens içi!* – there's a most *étrange*... woman on the line. Claiming to want you. Huh, as if. Here – "

Michel-Ange approached the instrument with more trepidation even than usual. *"Allo? Oui?"*

The female voice at the other end addressed him in a tone that managed to sound both bored and stentorian: "Are you Michel-Ange Grenier de la Fassederad?"

"Euh, ... *oui*. I cannot but admit to it. *Madame*."

"Eh bien. In that case please permit me to convey to you my most sincere felicitions – " Michel-Ange wondered if he should interject a perfunctory *politesse* here, but she continued before he could resolve this minor quandary *"Monsieur* de la Fassederad – if that really is your name – I strongly recommend that you pay the strictest and closest attention to what I am about to impart."

"D'accord, madame. But as long as we're becoming, ah, that is to say, acquainted, may I permit myself the temerity of inquiring with whom I have the honor of speaking?"

"Non."

"Non?"

"Non, monsieur."

"Ah."

"I am calling on behalf of a certain Colonel Bertrand Mincemot. who is the Director For Special Projects, Central Europe, at the *Ministère des Affaires Etrangères.* And you are hereby convoked to his office, which situates itself at Quai d'Orsay 24, 2nd *étage*, room 218Z, at 10:30 tomorrow morning. Do not be early, but *certainement* do not be late. And of course do certainly not neglect to bring with you comprehensive identity papers."

"Yes. Certainly. *Madame.*" Michel-Ange scribbled furiously on his palm with a Bic while awkwardly cradling the receiver. "Understood – I think."

"Good. *Au revoir* and *à demain, monsieur.*"

"Yes, well, I will *certainement* be there tomorrow, you may be assured of that. *Merci énormem* – " But she had rung off before he could finish.

Jennifer emerged from what the *Americains* might have called the "kitchen-ette" wearing rubber gloves, and inquired "So, *qui* the fuck was *that*?"

"Someone – some rather terrifying *gonzesse* – finally calling about that possible position at the *Quai*– I have to go around tomorrow morning."

"Well *good* – it's about time you showed the world what you can do."

"*Do?* Oh yes, hah – I get what you mean.... *ouaaiis,* ... tell me again, just what is it that I can 'do'?"

By way of an answer, Jennifer kissed his cheek, briefly grabbed his crotch, and retreated to her culinary *divertissements.* Michel-Ange stood there, hesitant – weighing the advisability of pursuing her....

3

LE QUAI D'ORSAY

The next morning, while listening via France-Inter to the latest enormities emanating from still-*communisant* Serbia, and watching out of one eye with for-the-moment-unrequited desire as *Jenni-faire* dressed herself needlessly (he felt) provocatively as she organized herself for whatever it was that she did, wherever she did it, Michel-Ange busied himself in *le cabinet,* trying to sort out, or at least *flatten*, his unruly hair. He also attended to his *besoins,* showered, shaved, and donned a custom-made *cintré* blue-striped shirt, his *Enarque* tie, a navy Givenchy linen suit, and black tasseled Gucci loafers.

Lastly he brushed his teeth which grimaced whitely at him in the mirror. *Right, tant pis, that's the best I can do,* he decided as he shut off the light and emerged from the bathroom.

In a small whirlwind of *vas et viens,* he and Jennifer kissed and said *"ciao"* to each other, as she swept out in a piquant wake of Guerlain's best. (A gift from him.)

He pocketed his *pièces d'identités* and grabbed the copy of his birth certificate that he dug out of a drawer. When he could come up with no further dilatory reason not to, he reluctantly accepted that he had to proceed.

To which purpose he impelled himself, via a vile-smelling Peugeot diesel taxi whose Algerian driver, giving every impression of being utterly stoned, not to mention deaf and dumb and God help us even blind as well, took a damnably long time in finding the requisite bit of the Quai d'Orsay (or, indeed, any trace of the Quai d'Orsay *at all....*)

But in the end, Michel-Ange got there. And not even, by flexible French bureaucratic standards, late.

He now underwent a dizzyingly elaborate "security" fandango – an almost fairground profusion of double and revolving bullet-proof doors, followed by rote examinations of his *papiers* by convincingly robot-like C.R.S. paramilitaries.

Eventually, however, he was allowed access to a lift and even more eventually he found himself at Room 218Z, into which he was buzzed. To enter an anteroom which was of a fittingly bureaucratic starkness. Only the French *tricolor* standing in a corner disturbed the generally gray aspect of the place. Well, that and the striking presence of a stern but elegant-looking lady "of a certain age": she was still this side, (but within striking distance), of sixty – in a salmon Chanel suit, with a great mane of silver/blonde hair and an unsmiling but classically beautiful face that reminded Michel-Ange of an aging Michèle Morgan.

Putain, dis, thought Michel-Ange as he gazed upon this person, *if she weren't so forbidding this could have been a Meese Monnaie-Pénnie situation even if I am nothing* like *a Jémes Bombe...* Remembering he was no *Jémes Bombe*, he coughed politely and was about to introduce himself when she, putting on the chained spectacles that rested upon her stately chest, observed off-puttingly,

"You're really very young."

Michel-Ange, unsure if a reply was even expected, instinctively thought better of attempting "Only in years, *madame*" and instead ventured a neutral

"In effect. *Madame.*"

"It's *mademoiselle*, actually."

"Ah. *Tres bien.*" That somehow didn't sound *quite* right, but he decided to let it lie and to forge on regardless. "Well, euh, *mademoiselle*, I am de la Fassederad. I believe I have a *rendezvous* with a certain Colonel Mincemot. Euh, might I inquire if you are the person with whom I had the unparalleled *plaisir* of speaking on the *téléphone* yesterday?"

"*Exactement,* young man."

"Well, there we are, then. Enchanted. Would you, euh, perhaps like to verify my documentations?"

This still-*attirante* – but nevertheless forbidding – *présence* (who Michel-Ange did not yet know chose to go by her birth name of Bérénice Bergère) removed her glasses and replied, still with studied *hauteur*,

"*Certainement* not, as that would only be redundant. It's enough that you have them. The fact is that you have been under close surveillance since... since a small time, now. By the way – " and here she produced what she perhaps intended as – and almost was – a smile, "I congratulate you on your *compagne Americaine – très bien.*"

What did one say to such a thing? "Well... *merçi* in her behalf."

At that point a red light flashed on a small console on her desk, and the hint of a smile vanished: "You may go in now. But I warn you, do not sit until and unless you are invited to so do."

"*Merçi encore, mada–mademoiselle.*" He felt a reluctance to leave her strangely reassuring presence but she buzzed him in and thither he found his legs taking him.

The colonel's office was as stark as the blonde *matrone*'s anteroom. The same bureaucratic gray, the same national *tricolor* standing in the same corner – the only immediately apparent difference seemed to be that on the wall behind the desk there were a large, colored map of Europe and, next to it, an inscribed photo of a French army officer in airborne battledress who meant utterly nothing to Michel-Ange, but who was, in fact, the legendary Lt. Gen. Marçel "Bruno" Bigeard.

Behind the desk sat the recipient of that dedicated photo, the extremely scowling, extremely crew-cutted figure of Colonel (*11ème Division Légère d'Intervention*) Bertrand Mincemot, holder of (amongst other gongs) the *Croix De Guerre Des Théatres d'Opérations Extérieures, Avec Palme.*

After having been wounded at Dien Bien Phu and damned near killed in an undercover operation that had gone disastrously free-fire in the *casbah* during the Battle of Algiers, Mincemot had found himself Defense Attaché at the French Embassy in what had become the independent Republic of Djibouti. Following that tour he was appointed as the "Political Officer" in the office of the *Prefet* in the *Département* of *Gouadeloupe.* Following which he had been on "official loan" as "Special Strategic Advisor" to the President of Gabon. And his last job, before this current position as "Director For Special Projects, Central Europe" at the Foreign Ministry, had been to be one of France's "sherpas" who initiated the far-flung and still-ongoing international *palabre* that would eventually (next year) culminate in the Dayton Peace Accords on Bosnia.

But right now he glared at Michel-Ange as if this latter had trodden in some *saletée* in the street and had brought it into the inner sanctum on the sole of his shoe. His general mien was a most off-putting mixture of dislike, dismay, disillusion and fatigue.

Michel-Ange stood there, trying not to visibly quake.

Eventually Mincemot opened the down-turning crack that served as his mouth and, in ominously bass tones, allowed: "Ah, de la Fassedarad. What a pleasure."

"*Merci, mon colonel.* And likewise, *mon colonel.*"

A hint of an upturn now appeared to flicker on that mouth. "De la Fassederad, may I compliment you on the aptness of your surname... while persisting in entertaining a twinge of doubt concerning your given name."

"*Merci encore, mon colonel.*" *I'm not entirely certain I like how this is beginning,*

"Yes. Well. Enough of these politenesses. De la Fassederad, the 'powers that be'," and here he let escape an out-and-out grimace, "have decided, in their ineffable inscrutability, to appoint you as 'Cultural Attaché' at our embassy in Gryaznia. ex-People's Republic of. *La Gryaznie*. In its poxy capital, Laina, to be precise."

Although stunned by this news, Michel-Ange managed "Ah. How... formidable. *Mon colonel*. *Merci* enormously, *mon colonel*."

"Don't thank *me* – hah!, what an idea..." The colonel now rose and, lighting a *Gauloise*, tapped with his lighter the puny little purple blob on the map between yellow Romania, red Serbia and green Bulgaria. "You know where the place is, I trust – you've *heard* of the place, I hope?"

"But of course, mon colonel." (Michel-Ange restrained himself from adding "*Hé!* – E.N.A., remember?")

"Good. *C'est déja ça*. Now listen to this carefully with all your quivering ears: in this job we want you to do as little as possible." *No problem there*, Michel-Ange thought. "While, of course, staying out of trouble." *Now* that *could be a little trickier....* "Of course, perform whatever 'culturalities' –" the colonel pronounced the word as though he'd just tasted a bad mussel, "are strictly necessary, but don't fatigue yourself too much on that stuff. Remember just two things: 1) *Ricains* and 2) No Trouble." *"Ricains"? Leave it for now.*

The colonel returned to his seat. "Now then – you will receive papers to sign, contracts, insurance stuff – that sort of thing – at your *domiçile*. Also a diplomatic passport and a round-trip first-class ticket to Laina, all of which you will duly sign for."

"*Oui, mon colonel. Merçi, mon colonel.*"

"Mother Superior, there – " he gestured vaguely in the direction of the anteroom "will occupy herself with these affairs." *"Mother Superior" – nice.*

"Of course. *Mon colonel.*"

There now ensued a pause which very soon turned uncomfortable – Mince-mot evidently thinking that this particular interview had pretty much reached its natural conclusion. But Michel-Ange mustered the courage to keep it from expiring: *"Mon colonel,* may I only inquire – why Gryaznia?"

At first the colonel seemed taken aback by such a bizarre question, but then he leaned back and decided to become expansive,

"Because those 'powers that be' seem to feel it necessary to beef up our *présence* there, which currently only consists of the Ambassador and a *type* who is both the Consul and also what is rather euphemistically, which is not to say laugh-ably, described as the 'Commercial Attaché' – and I'm not even so sure about the propriety of *that* set-up, sounds like a hell of a potential *pétard* to me, but so far nobody's asked me.... More reassuringly," he continued, "there are also a couple of *Légionnaires* by way of security – *des brave types.* As well as a recep-tionist/secretary lady who is a Gryaznian, as per the local law, and some other local hired help. And that, as far as I am aware, is it. And we, euh, *they,* euh, 'of-ficially' feel that the *Americains* are exercising increasingly excessive influence there. And so you are to be the added 'beef."

Some "beef" thought the colonel as he squinted at Michel-Ange who, he ob-served, now looked as though he wanted to say something, but was holding back.

"Yes?"

But Michel-Ange remained mute. So the colonel persisted, louder now,

"Alors? You wish to say something? Spit it it out, young man."

Michel-Ange felt like one of those WWI *"poilus"* going up "over the top", but eventually ventured: "Well, the thing is, I mean... the *Americains*? Why the Americans? – surely we have more pressing adversaries than them, *non?"*

The colonel pondered this for a second. "No doubt. No doubt. But right now in the ex-Yugoslav *bordelle,* the *Grosses Têtes* are particularly keen to keep it a European show. Which means, I'm afraid, not so much *Yang-qui* go 'ome as

Yang-qui sté *'ome.* Anyway, why? Are you particularly pro-*Amérloque,* by chance?"

"Well, as it happens" continued Michel-Ange, throwing caution aside – *In for a centime, in for a franc. For you, Jenni-Faire!* – "I am, a bit, yes. I was quite unique at the E.N.A. in this regard."

"Yes, I can imagine."

"But I always found them rather *sympathique* – if a bit innocent – and I always liked their films and music. And not to mention, of course, their young ladies…"

"Yes. Well, it happens that I also harbor a doubtless heretical secret admiration for *ces cons de 'Ricains* – and always found them tolerably decent to work with, but *that* – " and here the colonel banged his palms on his desk as if to put the conversational train back on its tracks "is neither here nor there: which was Gryaznia, and, speaking of which, why *not* Gryaznia, anyway, *hein?* Would you perhaps prefer Belgrade? Because we have several openings *there,* I'm reliably informed – in fact Belgrade is, I believe, currently being bombed by Allied air forces on behalf of the ONU *as we speak …*"

"Euh, *non merci beaucoup* and completely, *mon colonel.*"

"No, I rather thought not. Now then, your base salary will be 43,000 francs per month. Plus your lodging and reasonable living expenses will be taken care of by us, but you'll have to *démerde* all that with the Ambassador when you get over there."

"*Merci, mon colonel.*"

"Oh, and how, by the way, are your English and Russian?"

"*Pardon? Mon colonel?*"

"*Anglais et Russe.* Those are the two most functional languages in Gryaznia, where their local *patois* is a kind of *petit nègre* Russian. For sure you can forget French, which will get you nowhere, except perhaps kidnapped."

Michel-Ange pondered this latest data. Eventually he offered "Well, sir, in English I can understand many words used in barroom fights and by GIs in combat, as well the words of most popular music and, ahem, I have also made the happy discovery that I know enough *Anglais* to navigate tolerably well with the fairer sex – I can, for example, say 'I love you, my *chérie*'."

There ensued another pause between them. At least as portentous as the previous ones. The glumness of Mincemot's glare at young Michel-Ange, although difficult to believe possible, actually intensified. The colonel eventually replied,

"Well, in Gryaznia, with a bit of luck, all that *tissue de chiasse* will get you is killed. And your *Russe*?"

Michel-Ange didn't have to consider this overly long – he wouldn't even *recognize* Russian if it were bellowed into his face through a megaphone. So he judged that the least unwise way to answer was, "Well, in truth, it is not *énorme, mon colonel*."

"What does that mean? – that you only know how to say 'I love you *ma chérie*' in Russian? Or not even that?"

"Euh, desolatedly the latter, *mon colonel*."

"Right." Mincemot, his face now set like a reddish brick – an exasperated reddish brick – opened the main drawer of his desk and out from under a pair of handcuffs and a Browning 9mm automatic, he fished out a sheet of official Foreign Ministry stationery, upon which he scribbled something, while averring,

"De la Fassederad, please don't take this overly personally, but permit me to inform you that in my expert opinion you are a *nullité totale*. What we used to call in the Army a 'NAC' – which you should not be enormously surprised to learn stands for *nulle à chier*."

"*Merci, mon colonel*."

"*EBN EL SHAMOOTA!*" cried the colonel, employing an Arabic malediction he'd picked up during his para-military *séjour* in Algeria and whose precise meaning need not detain us here.

Presently Mincemot composed himself. (At least outwardly.)

"Ahem. Please pardon that slip of the tongue. Now look, de la Fassedarad, as you have zero Russian and only three words of English which if you ever have the *temerité* to try out amongst the savage denizens of the Gryaznian *canaille* will, without the slightest doubt, land you in the most enormous mountain of *merde* you could ever imagine, I am therefore giving you this authorization. For you to acquire a crash course in functionally-sufficient elementary Russian and English."

He signed the requisition paper, folded it into an envelope and handed it over to Michel-Ange.

"Here," the colonel continued, "Now, you take this note to an establishment – it's a kind of foreign language *boutique* that we sort of, well, subsidize – called '*Vos Gueules Les Mouettes*', which situates itself on the Quai Saint Michel. Give it to the old lady who runs the place and who calls herself 'Bébette' which, now that I think of it, is rather appropriate, as she is undeniably quite *folle* – and which no doubt explains why she is One Of Us, but... let's not get sidetracked on *that*... So, what she will do is provide you with all the books and tapes and computer stuff – what do they call it? 'software'? something *cinglé* like that – which reminds me: are you, ah, *au courant* with computers? Do you know how to use one?"

"Again, desolately not, *mon colonel.*"

An increasingly nervous Michel-Ange was beginning to wonder how long it would be before his checklist of professional deficiencies would disqualify him from not only this, but, indeed, *any* employment. So he continued,

"I mean, of course I *have* seen them being operated and, indeed, my American lady friend claims to be *une éxperte* on the things. But I have managed to resist applying myself to them so far. *Mon colonel.*" Michel-Ange now decided – he had no idea why, maybe it was an instinctive feeling that this was a make-or-break moment in his young life – to again throw caution to the wind. "I might add, *mon colonel*, by way of justification, that I have been influenced by some words

I encountered during my studies at *lycée* which were from a certain 17th century English *milord* by the name of Lucius Henry Cary, the Third Lord Falkland, whose opinion it was that 'If it is not necessary to change, it is necessary not to change'. I am, I'm afraid, a bit old-fashioned for my relative young age."

Mincemot, was astonished and, despite himself, impressed by Michel-Ange's words. For he harbored the *exact same* aversion to the new technology, not to mention a bedrock kinship with such a manifestly reactionary manifesto as he'd just heard quoted. He now felt somewhat less repelled by what he had, until now, thought to be an irredeemable young dilettante. But of course it would never do to even hint as much, so he grumbled:

"Well that's as may be. There may come a time when we will have no choice but to submit to the inevitable, but for now – regardless of which methods you end up using, you will present this *bon-pour* to old Bébette and she will set you up with whatever is required – Berlitz, Assimil, I don't know what systems they use these days – "

Michel-Ange took the envelope with no comment and tried to deal with the colonel's stare, which continued, laser-like.

"So. You will depart for Gryaznia after a delay not to exceed 21 days." Michel-Ange gulped. "During which time I, we, expect that you will have mastered enough rudimentary English and Russian to not be an obvious danger to yourself as you carry out your official duties, such as they are. So I cannot urge you strongly enough to apply yourself with your utmost assiduity. Perhaps your *copine Américaine* can help with the English. And as for the Russian, well... just fucking *démerde.*" He again smacked both palms down on his desk "Now I believe our affairs are approaching their conclusion, here. Just sign those papers with *Mademoiselle* Bergère out there before you depart us –" *Ah, so Mother Superior has a name....* "and then go keep an eye out for the Americans."

By now Michel-Ange felt courageous enough to venture one final bit of cheek before allowing himself to be shuffled out the door, "But, *mon colonel*, how does your order to, in your own words, 'do as little as possible' conform with 'keeping an eye on the Americans'?"

The colonel's former asperity threatened to return. "*Mais voyons,* it's simple – you contrive to do as little as possible officially, while at the same time watching what the *Ricains* are up to. Just *démerde,* de la Fassederad, *voyons!*"

"Oui, *mon colonel.*"

As Michel-Ange began stuffing the colonel's envelope into his attaché case, Mincemot steepled his fingers, again leaned back in his chair, and now attempted – not terribly convincingly – to convey something approaching playfulness,

"De la Fassederad, I must confess that not tremendously much about you intrigues me, except for one detail: why do you persist in addressing me as '*mon colonel*'?"

Michel-Ange paused and looked up, genuinely surprised. "Because that is what I believed I was meant to call you, *mon,* euh, *colonel.*"

"Whatever gave you such a daft notion? Was I ever your colonel? In any conceivable sense of the word?"

"Euh, *non, mon--*" ATCHOOM! *hell of a moment to sneeze...* "*colonel.*"

"Did you ever serve in the Army, de la Fassederad?"

"You know my record, *mon colonel,* so I take that as a rhetorical question. And as you are also no-doubt aware, the E.N.A. is not an establishment from which emerge a tremendously high proportion of *militaires, mon colonel.* If any at all."

"Yes, quite." Now Mincemot fixed his black eyes on Michel-Ange's. "And in those circumstances I believe it would be best if you ceased immediately from referring to me as 'your *colonel*'. Goddammit. *Enfin.*"

"But then how should I address you?"

"Do you know? I think probably the best would be that you not address me at all. Now, as I intimated earlier," the colonel rose and leaned over his desk to shake hands "I believe our affairs are concluded."

Michel-Ange also rose, shook Mincemot's dry clamp of a hand, turned and, feeling as though he'd just emerged from a tumble-dryer, began to head unsteadily to the door...

... to re-enter the tense and unpredictable force-field of She that he now knew was called *Mlle.* Bergère a.k.a. *La Mère Supèrieure,* which he found most fitting indeed.

As he reached for the door handle, he heard Mincemot call him, in yet a different tone of voice – this one verging on what might be conventionally-understood as "civil":

"De la Fassedard! – attend a second – come back, *jeune homme.*"

Michel-Ange turned and saw that the colonel had lit himself another cig, and was beckoning to him: "Come, resume your seat a second." Michel-Ange did so – *What is it* now? *Had the old pirate decided, at the last minute, that the whole thing's off?*

Mincemot continued. "*Ecoute.* I excuse myself if I've sounded a little hard – and *of course* you should call me 'mon colonel'.... The thing is, though, ... well, not to put too fine a point on it, *petit*... well, it's just a tough *merdier* of a world out there. And *especially* so in a *foutue bordelle* like Gryaznia. Where they fuck their sisters, their mothers and even their *grandmothers*, but they will be only too happy to kill *you* should they catch you so much as looking sideways at their daughters – "

Michel-Ange was trying not to dwell on any of this when it actually got worse...

"And on top of all that, they are all perpetually drunk and, I have reason to believe, occasionally engage in the *eating* of their murder victims – oh yes, they frequently chop each other up with insouciant drunken abandon for little – or even no – reason that is apparent to the outside world... something that they didn't even do in *foutu* Gabon, at least not to my knowledge..."

The colonel trailed off and seemed to muse... before snapping out of it,

"*A*nyway – " he suddenly resumed, absent-mindedly stubbing out his Gauloise on his – *mon Dieu!* – *his fucking palm!* "you appear to me to be nice-enough lad. Indeed, perhaps *too* nice. So remember, not everyone out there is as decent-ly-disposed as you are. Or, heh, even as much as *I* am. So have a care out there, and, ah, try not to neglect to return. *Bonne chance, mon petit,* from an old *schnock* who wishes you well. *Allez*, good *séjour*."

Michel-Ange again stood and again proffered – and this time damn near had crushed to splinters – his hand, and again made his way *Mlle*. Bergère-ward.

Who, once her *fiéf* had been re-entered, abruptly pressed upon him about a half dozen documents to sign. He took them to a coffee table across from her desk and seated himself to address them. One in particular struck him as al-most *purposefully* sinister:

This was a sort of confidential disclaimer/waiver sort of thing, which stated – right there, in black and white – that should he, Michel-Ange Grenier de la Fas-sederad, in case he involved himself in, or with, anyone's death (to include his own), wounding of anyone (also to include himself), or involve himself in any "entanglements" of a legal or otherwise "embarrassing" nature – well, notwith-standing his Diplomatic Status, in the event of any of the above-mentioned "misadventures", the French Government would disavow any knowledge of him. Or of any of his family or heirs. At all. Sign here, please.

Michel-Ange re-read all this to assure himself that he'd seen right. He then cleared his throat and turned to address *Mlle*. Bergère. Tapping his pen on the offending bit of paper, he ventured,

"*Mademoiselle*, euh, surely this rather... morbid document here must be meant for, euh, some other service than, well, than the one I am being invited to enter. Is it not?

"No, *Monsieur* de la Fassederad, I am desolated to confirm that it is not."

"Well, in that case, it cannot possibly mean what it purports to mean, surely..."

"I am desolated to confirm that indeed it does, *Monsieur*."

"But, as I understand it, I am to be a *Cultural* Attaché – what can that possibly have to do with any 'embarrassments', 'woundings', 'entanglements' or, *eventuellement* and, *mon Dieu*, 'deaths'?"

"Ahh," she now seemed to adopt a philosophical manner, "but you know, *Monsieur* Michel-Ange – I hope you don't mind that I address you as Michel-Ange, as I have nephews older than you – life is full of the unforeseen. Not to mention that *la Gryaznie* situates itself in the middle of a zone of war, *désagrément* and mayhem. And," she concluded "in any case, it is standard. So sign."

"So this is all just... *normale*? Everyone signs it?"

"Well, I don't know about *everyone*, but certainly everyone who works for Colonel Mincemot does."

"But if I am killed or wounded or imprisoned, and our gov– or, euh, you, I mean, *he* – disavows all knowledge of me, how would I be represented, or cared for, or – " he searched for another word but could not find one "or, well, ... *be buried*?"

"Such eventualities will – *would* – be taken care of. But anonymously. Discreetly. You may have confidence in that."

"Really?"

"Really. *Parole d'honneur*." She smiled. "And I will assuredly not miss your funeral."

Well, fuck me, thought Michel-Ange, recalling a pungent locution of *Jenni-faire*'s, as he duly applied his *Jean Encoque (still* another *Jenni-faire*-ism) to the dotted line.

When the *paperasse* was completed, he thanked Mother Superior with half-mock/half-serious formality and made to leave. She followed him to the outer door and they faced each other. Michel-Ange bowed slightly and went to shake her hand...

...but instead, she astounded him by grasping his upper arm lightly with her fingertips and half-whispering "Just don't forget to return, Michel-Ange."

(The *second* time he'd heard this off-putting exhortation in less than ten minutes... *merde* alors....)

4

MADAME BÉBETTE

The *"Vos Gueules Les Mouettes"* (literally "Shut Up You Seagulls") bookshop found itself at 115-*bis* Quai Saint Michel – which was not, in fact, *all* that far from 24 Quai d'Orsay, and had he not been feeling, post-"interview", so unsettled and scramble-headed, Michel-Ange would ordinarily have legged it there.

But in the event he decided he'd take a taxi, and, to this end, flagged down *another* old black Peugeot 505 diesel. Its driver was a manifestly African *mec* and his cab stank marginally less than the previous taxi, thanks to a veritable forest of Christmas tree-shaped air-freshener thingies dangling from the rear-view mirror. This was actually to the taxi's credit, after a fashion.

But on the debit side, loud and mindlessly repetitive African guitar music filled the car. It occurred to Michel-Ange to ask the driver fellow to turn it down a bit, but he decided that, inasmuch as the ride should be a short one, such a potentially fraught intervention on his part wasn't worth the candle.

But eventually, amidst the din, it dawned on Michel-Ange that they certainly by now should have reached their destination. He peered out the window – *where the fuck* are *we*?

The driver must be stoned on *ganga* or *khat* or something – which might certainly explain the increasingly nauseating interior smell which in truth, Michel

Ange now realized, bore a closer redolence to the Gare du Nord than to pine trees....

Or else the *con* might actually be *asleep*. (!)

Michel-Ange shouted into the lobotomizing din "*Hé! Mon vieux!* Turn down that *foutue vacarme!*"

No response appeared to be forthcoming, and as the taxi continued its erratic journey into uncharted urban territory, the increasingly alarmed Michel-Ange took the extreme action of tapping on the graying curly-haired conk in front of him.

Without modifying their heedless forward progress in any way, the driver turned and grinned at Michel-Ange – an alarming act in itself, compounded by the jarring revelation of a lack of front teeth.

In return Michel-Ange vigorously mimed a version of turning a radio knob counter-clockwise.

The driver just narrowly averted a head-on obliteration with an oblivious Renault van, as he turned back and complied, radio-wise. Up to a point. But at least the racket was now at a level that permitted conversation.

"*Hé, mon cher chauffeur*, may I ask what is your name?"

"Dieudonné, *patron!*"

"*Oui*. And from where do you emerge, Dieudonné?"

"Ouaga, *patron!*"

Ouagadougou. Just perfect. Michel-Ange decided not to ask the fellow how long he'd been driving in Paris because, in truth, he didn't want to know. Instead he ventured:

"And permit me to inquire, my dear Dieudonné, have you, in fact, got any idea at all where this address on the Quai Saint Michel is?"

"Not *éxactement, patron.*"

Et, bim! "Yes. I got that impression. Do you, in fact, even know where *any* of the Quai Saint Michel is? *Monsieur* Dieudonné?"

"Well, *patron,* I think that it finds itself more or less straight ahead. Do not make yourself worries, *patron.*"

"Right. *D'accord.* But permit me to inform you, my good Dieudonné, that if you continue on this course, even more or less, you will arrive, certainly within even your lifetime, back to Ouagadougou – " *from which,* Michel-Ange uncharitably thought to himself, *one wonders why the putain de merde Those In Charge felt it necessary or even desirable to allow you to emigrate – but let us not permit ourselves to descend into Incorrect Thinking...* so instead he continued,

"So please do not take it amiss if I command you now to make a left *here – yes, now! – HERE! ... Bon...* Now, another left – yes, *here* – I *m'en fous* if it's the wrong way on a one-way street – do as I indicate – no there are no *flics* around, and don't worry in any case, I'm a *diplomate* – there, now around that *rond-point,* and head there – *there!* – and mind those kids – now pull over. *Bordelle.* Jesus Christ."

He felt like an overworked and harassed air traffic controller about to lose his last vestige of cool, as he guided the cheerfully heedless Dieudonné to their destination on the Quai Saint Michel.

As he alighted in front of the bookshop, or whatever it was, Michel-Ange surprised himself by actually adding a nice tip to the fare. *"Now,* Dieudonné, you can continue your journey to Ouagadougou" he told the beaming *zouave,* who seemed overjoyed with his job well done: *"Merçi-merçi, mon bon patron!"*

Shuddering away this latest surreal taxi experience, Michel-Ange now squared his shoulders as he faced this mysterious edifice. Which, after he rang a bell and entered, at first glance seemed more of a *dustshop* than any kind of bookshop. Goodness, what a musty, smoky *merdier....*

He could vaguely, through the hazy darkness, discern racks of what might well have been books, but could also have been something else... containers of some sort? Perhaps made of plastic? Hard to tell – but for sure, there were no actual human beings. Neither customer nor customee.

"Allo?" he called out. Rather more loudly than he'd intended.

From some nether region of this bizarre establishment there came a shouted *"Ouais, j'arrive!"* The voice was almost certainly female but was in a range that sounded ominously to Michel-Ange more baritone even than his own.

He waited. This day was still far from over but already it seemed to him to have lasted the better part of a lifetime.

As he stood there in the sepulchral dimness, surrounded by dust and cobwebs, Michel-Ange noticed a jarring exception to the otherwise pervading gloom: the *parquet* upon which he stood positively *shone* like some kind of oaken skating rink.

Which it more or less turned out to be, as, when the mythical "Madame Bébette" eventually hove to from out of some unseen hole in the wall, she did so by gliding – or more accurately, *swish-swishing* – on a pair of outsized slippers that looked more like little felt water skis than your conventional *pantoufles qua pantoufles.*

But that turned out to be but one of a number of manifest eccentricities which apparently made up the whole Madame Bébette *embalage.* Make no mistake – this was not some sort of demure delicate frail dowager such as, for example, the "old lady" in the Babar books – in fact, rather the opposite. For starters, she had more of a moustache than Michel-Ange could coax if he didn't shave for a week. Moreover, although the day was already well advanced, she wore what looked like a flower-patterned *robe-de-chambre* which, Michel-Ange fervently hoped, (if she ever moved into proper light), was *not* "see-through", although in all the dusty opacity he needn't have worried. Furthermore, she had attached to her lower lip an extinguished cigarette butt which looked Super-Glued there and which gave every impression of having been so for a long time. Years, perhaps.

She almost resembled a ninety-year old Edith Piaf (who always looked ninety years old in any case). To Michel-Ange her whole *présence* fairly screamed "cat lady", and had she suddenly produced and affixed a monocle to herself and started cackling he would not have been the least surprised.

Instead, she squinted at him. And eventually croaked: "Are you him?" All the cigarettes had rendered her voice quite witchy.

Like the imbecile that (he felt) he was sometimes (unwarrantedly) taken for, Michel-Ange reflexively looked behind him to see who she might be referring to, but of course, seeing no one else, turned to re-face this awful person.

"Why, yes, I probably am. Who, actually, did you have in mind?"

"Some *jeune prodige* sent by the Colonel. From the Quai – well, from his... euh, *secteur* of it, anyway."

"Ah, well yes, then – that would be me, alright."

He fished out Mincemot's authorization and handed it over. Without looking at it she tucked it into her robe.

"What kind of computer have you got?" she barked. "Or have access to? Plan to use?"

Uh-oh. "Well, you, euh, see, *Madame*, the thing actually is, d'you see... well, ... well, I don't actually *have* a computer. In fact, I do my utmost to avoid them."

"Really? Is the Colonel *au courant* of this?"

"Yes, I believe I let him know this. And I don't think he found it to be particularly disqualifying – "

Madame Bébette snorted dismissively, "Yes – he's *another* one – he's still nostalgic for cleft sticks and *radio tam-tam*. Anyway," she intensified her gaze at Michel-Ange "so what *do* you have then – you at least have a tape recorder, *non?*"

"Yes, I have one of those. It's old, but it functions."

"Right, well let me put *these* away – " She took a shoe-box full of what they called these days "floppy discs" away with her and *swished-swished* off into the obscurity offstage... to presently re-appear, this time bearing a plastic sac. Which she handed to Michel-Ange, who, peering in, could identify two books and two sets of old-fashioned audio cassettes in neat plastic holders.

Pretty much intuiting what was afoot, here, Michel-Ange nevertheless felt the need to maintain a measure of *correctitude*, so he went through the motions and asked *"Pour moi?"*

"No, they're for my god-daughter Citronelle – what do you think?" Madame Bébette swiped her hands on her bathrobe and observed "I will say this, though – it is purely through the sclerosis of our bureaucracy – our sheer institutional inertia – that we still even have these things around. I would wager, young man, that you will be the last human ever to use these cassette *trucs.*"

"So be it. So, euh... how much do I owe you, *Madame*?"

"Regrettably, nothing. The taxpayers have already paid for them. So don't thank *me*."

"Well, *merçi quand-meme, Madame.*"

He turned and headed with his sac through the gloom towards what he hoped was the door but could just as easily have been towards a hatch that led down to Dante's 12th Circle. But no, it mercifully turned out to be the door, alright, and as he prepared to exit, the old bat Bébette, invisible, called to him:

"*Attend, petit.*" Michel-Ange attended. In his tracks. "Look," she continued, "I've seen better, but I don't remember seeing any younger. So, well... just... endeavor not to fail to return."

Bordelle de merde! Three times, now.

"*B'en... mérçi, Madame.* I will do my utmost to re-emerge, and even in one piece if possible. You are very *aimable.*"

He eased himself out and, deciding that he'd just about had it with taxis and the possibility for further shock to his psychic well-being that they represented, chose instead to walk back to his flat on the Rue Mouffetard. Which...

5

LE MACAQUE

He found to be Jennifer-less. She was off somewhere. *Pas de problème.*

Sitting at the kitchen table, Michel-Ange loosened his tie, poured himself a big glass of his cheap, dishwater-like "Valstar" beer, drank half of it, burped, sighed, and pulled out these books. From this plastic sac. From the *formidable* Madame Bébette. Courtesy of Colonel Mincemot and the French taxpayer. Which would supposedly, magically, in three weeks' time teach him some English that might be more elevated than " 'Allo béby, can I paireps buy you some drinky?". And this Russian which... well, looked like so much bloody Greek to him.

Assimil. "The *Méthode* Assimil" proclaiming "English Without Pain". Already the title was causing him pain.

He opened the English volume to "*Leçon* N° 1". And gaped in mounting incredulity. *Quoi?*

He drained the rest of the Valstar, poured himself another and, in a state of no small agitation, grabbed the other volume, "Russian Without Pain" and went directly to *its* "*Leçon* N° 1"... and stared at *it. Encore, quoi quoi QUOI?*

Non, non, non.

It was suddenly clear to Michel-Ange that if he was expected to deal with these manifest imbecilities that purported to be, you should pardon the expression, teach-yourself-a-foreign-language books, he would damn well be needing something more fortifying than this barely drinkable tepid *foutu* Valstar.

So grabbing his two volumes, he clattered downstairs; (he took the lift, when it was working, *up,* but couldn't be arsed dealing with its ancient clanking lethargies when he was going *down*).

He made a sharp left on the Rue Mouffetard – and promptly crashed into a mini-convention of Oriental tourists who were, for no apparent rhyme or reason, blocking the entirety of the narrow sidewalk. But he was by now possessed, so he put his head down and, rugby-style, bulled his way through, emerging from the camera-bedecked scrum a little askew, to hare off down to his "local" *bistro/tabac, "Le Macaque".*

The *patron,* a laconic chap known universally as "Manu" (for Emmanuel), was wearing his usual apron and disabused air. Acknowledging Michel-Ange's agitated arrival with one raised eyebrow, he said,

"Salut, toi. You look like you're taking a break from the Paris *marathon.* Which doesn't occur for another 2 months. They tell me."

"Stop your *conneries* and deliver a double Cognac-Perrier. *Subittissimo."* Manu was Corsican, and while Michel-Ange's English did not, as has already been established, extend vastly beyond "Yes yes, fuck me fuck me" and his Russian was even *beyond nulle,* he *did* know the odd word of Italian, which he sometimes produced in order to amuse himself with the publican. A sort of verbal badminton.

This *type* Manu was certainly a piece of work. A bit of a human iceberg – the small visible bit hiding a huge history beneath. After flunking his *bac* in high school in Ajaccio, he'd joined the French army at the age of seventeen. His prowess as a soldier had soon gotten him transferred to the elite *1ᵉʳ Régiment de Parachutistes d'Infanterie de Marine* (1ᵉʳ RPIMA), in which he'd served for sixteen proud and valiant (as they say) years. He'd risen through the ranks from a Sub-Nothing to the exalted status of Sergeant-Major, or *"Adjudant-Chef"*.

Suffice to say that being an "Adjudant-Chef" in the 1ᵉʳ RPIMA is no small thing, and *le Chef* Manu had served with distinction (not to say quasi-lunacy) during the First (out of about six, depending on how you counted) Tchad War (*Opération Epervier*), and then later with "Opération Barracuda" in the Central African Republic. Indeed, he is still remembered by many in N'Djamena (which had still been, when he was there, "Fort Lamy") and Bangui (which is still, amazingly, "Bangui"), with a mixture of fondness, terror, fear, love and loathing. In short, his service in Africa had not been unobtrusive.

Now, however, he was retired from all that, and instead owned and ran this bistro in Paris. From which, truth be told, the only real pleasure he ever *really* derived was, from time to time, heaving drunks and miscreants out the door. Literally. And sometimes even horizontally.

But never young Michel-Ange, here, who was a *sympa* enough lad. (Although he wouldn't have lasted ten minutes in the Tchad. Not that that was saying much, really, as there were precious few white men who could last ten minutes in the Tchad. Or *black* men, come to that....)

In any case, the boy seemed, unusually, all *excité* now. When normally he confined his Macaque presence to placidly smiling or occasionally coo-cooing with his leggy American girlfriend. But now he was waving some sort of book in Manu's general direction.

Manu brought over the double Cognac-Perrier, which Michel-Ange quaffed with the speed and enthusiasm not shown by any human since Peter "Aurens" O'Toole led the parched Arab boy to that blessed icy lemonade in the Alexandria Officer's Mess.

"Eh! – ça vas, fiston?"

"Certainement" (gasp) "bloody fucking not. *Encore –* "

Manu delivered another C-P. "Alright... much as I'd prefer not to know, you may as well tell me about it."

"I've got this job – I'm now among the employed."

"Well, nothing *a priori* wrong with that – people *have* been known to survive such calamities."

"Yes, of course – listen, I'm not *débile*, I always knew that sooner or later a job would be my fate. But this one entails my being posted as a – and here I can scarcely believe I am actually pronouncing these words – Cultural Attaché, whatever that may *putain* entail, to *la Gryaznie*. Can you believe such a thing? The Republic of Gryaznia!"

"What? Wait – you're going to represent *us, la France,* somewhere?" Manu allowed a hint of a smile to creep onto his leathery face. "Pardon me, but... *you?*"

"Yes – *me*. A 'Cultural Attaché' – can you credit it? They might as well put me in a colored tunic, a bonnet with bells on it and issue me a stick with a pig's bladder on one end – "

"*Eh bien – décidément...* But be reasonable – a job, even a *diplomatique* one – is not such a bad thing... people have jobs, people work, you know – surely you can do it too."

"Well, I'm not so comfortably confident of even *that*, but in the meantime there's this fucking *langage bordelle!*"

"Go ahead, I'm listening..." Manu had moved off to fulfill some bartender tasks a little further down the *zinc*.

"They tell me I have to learn *Anglais* and *Russe* in three *foutue* weeks. Can you imagine?"

Manu – who in between his sixteen RPIMA years and buying Le Macaque had also spent a couple of years with Bob Denard and his *barbouzes* actually taking over a whole country, The Comoros – could imagine pretty much anything, so he allowed himself:

"So? What's the big *histoire*? Just fake it. *Le bluff. Le 'bullshitte'*, as the *'Ricains* say. That's what any normal *mec* does who's in such a *petrain*..."

Manu, like bartenders immemorial and with Old Testament resignation, was now rinsing beer glasses in dirty water. "I mean, what are they going to do, test you before sending you out there?"

"With that colonel? – I wouldn't put it past them. Anyway, here – listen to what they've given me to deal with, here..."

Manu couldn't think of any further make-work just now, so he reluctantly re-entered Michel-Ange's orbit. *"D'accord.* So tell me. What have they given you, then?"

"Well, I mean to say. I mean... here, take this 'English Without Pain'. My *cul, ouais*? *Here, here* – just their first *leçon* – I ask you: It says 'My tailor is rich'. *'My tailor is rich'*. What kind of *connerie* is that?"

"Stop shouting. You'll frighten the customers."

"What customers? There aren't any – those three idiots don't count, they were here when you bought the place."

"Yes, well... this might be because of your hysterical shouting. Which," he nodded out his front window "can probably be heard on the other side of the Seine. People will think this is an *asile de fous*.... Anyway – and as long as you bring it up – what's so insupportable about 'My tailor is rich'?"

"What's wrong with 'My tailor is rich?' I'll tell you what's wrong with it – it's of no earthly use to anyone anywhere under any conceivable circumstances. In fact," Michel-Ange warmed to his theme, "it so happens that I actually *have* a tailor, and he is indisputably *not* rich. He is, in fact, an illegal no-papers Tunisian who works in a dingy little hovel of an *atelier* up on the second floor above the *boulangerie* over there on the Rue Ortolan. His name is Couscous Alhamdoulilaye, and he is as poor as one of your poorer species of church mice. This is due to the fact that, despite my paying him handsomely to construct my *costumes* and *chemises*, he, in his Islamic lunacy, has chosen to lumber himself with what appears to be *at least* four wives, with whom he has contrived to produce something on the order of a hundred and fifty squalling *marmitons*. So let us be clear in our *propos*: he is not rich – he is poor. And as far as I'm concerned he deserves to remain so. And I will so inform such of the general Gryaznian population as might be interested in such a burning slice of the passing human drama – which, I expect (and fervently hope) will not number very many more than exactly zero!"

"Hmm," nodded Manu, not wanting to provoke his young friend any further, "you perhaps have reason."

"And how. But wait! There is," cried Michel-Ange "if even possible, worse!"

How formidable, thought Manu. "Tell me."

"I will, if you shoot me yet another double cognac-Perrier. Here, and keep the change." Michel-Ange unloaded a small salad of French currency on the *zinc*. And now proceeded to pull out the "Russian Without Pain" volume.

"Now my good Manu," Michel-Ange resumed, "you are a wise, kind, patient and judicious perambulator of the world's boulevards – "

"Well, I wouldn't..."

"No, yes, you are! Or – alright, maybe you're not – *n'importe, laisse tomber.*" Michel-Ange made a gesture as if clearing cobwebs from above his head. "What matters is this – here, listen to this mindless cretinry: *'Ia lioubliou tchai'* – *"Niet, Ia nye lioubliou cacao'*. Do you know what that means, Manu?"

"Euh, *non*, not with immense accuracy, *mon petit*. Something to do with tea and cocoa perhaps. But so what, who cares? It means what it means..."

Michel-Ange persisted, still aggrieved: "The importance of what I am endeavoring to convey, my dear Manu, is that these two, supposedly complementary, phrases translate themselves – according to this *foutue* book and I swear I am not making this up – as 'I like tea' and 'But no, I don't like cocoa'. Did you ever in your life? Can you even begin to imagine such a thing? As representing *la culture Française* to unwashed foreign multitudes I should disport myself thither and yon, *urbi et orbi,* announcing that I prefer tea to cocoa? *Hein?"*

"Eh? Oh! Yes – *yes,* of course, *mon petit."* Manu's attention, it had to be said, had been wandering. But now he renewed his effort to address the *res.* "But look, you know, it's not, in fact, the whole *urbi et orbi* world – in truth, it's just *la* shitty little *Gryaznie* – where there's a good chance no one will notice you *at all* – "

"Hmm, yes, there *is* also that possibility – *encore* you may have reason.... *bon.* in that case, and on that encouraging note, produce another double cognac-Perrier and I'll leave you alone. And keep the change, or did I already mention that?"

He stared, a little goggle-eyed, as Manu picked through the *fric* on the bar. It was unclear if there even would *be* any change... Michel-Ange gulped down this last and utterly superfluous drink. Which would have been superfluous to a water-buffalo. Hell, it would have been superfluous to a *bulldozer.* Let alone skinny young Michel-Ange, here. Who now, phrase books reluctantly in hand, made for the door.

"*Salut,* Manu. Sorry if I was too loud."

"*Héh, petit,* think nothing of it. You know you're at home here." Manu, whose back had been to Michel-Ange, as he re-arranged some bottles, now turned to face the departing lad. "And *éh!* – don't forget to come back, *hein*? *Allez – ciao!"*

Which, Michel-Ange was still conscious enough to realize, made it now *four* times. In the same day. Which was not yet even over....

He felt not entirely unlike a whipped dog as he slunk back to his place. Where, mercifully, the lift appeared not to be, for once, "out of service".

6

JENNI-FAIRE

All this cognac intake resulted of course in an unusually long time for his key to work properly, but eventually he acceded.

"Salut, Chéri," called Jennifer from the bedroom, to where Michel-Ange tottered. He found her on the bed in a provocative state of disattire, directing concentrated female fastidiousness to her toenails. He attempted to kiss her, but was arrested in this *démarche* as she pushed him away.

"Poo! You *pue!*"

"Yes. Well. It's called Life. Or so I am led to understand...."

A still-vaguely pugnacious Michel-Ange sloped back to the "kitchenette", where he drained the dregs of a half-empty glass of red wine. By now Michel-Ange had well and truly achieved the state that they on the other side of the *Manche, les Rosbifs,* like to amuse themselves by euphemistically describing as "tired and emotional".

He staggered into the bedroom and, with his shoes still on, passed out.

Later, at about 2200H, Jennifer, who'd left him to sleep it off and had gone out, let herself back in. And made herself – of all things! – a cup of hot cocoa (*Leçon N° 2: Ona lyubila kakao.*) Which she carried with her into the bathroom, where she performed her usual series of facial and bodily manoeuvres that, whenever Michel-Ange was present to witness them, he always found infinitely mystifying (though not without a certain exotic allure). But in any case he did not figure in the current proceedings.

When she could think of nothing further to apply, massage, tweak or rub, she switched out the lights and aimed herself in the dark to the bed, where she slid in between the sheets, intent upon cuddling up against her little Michel-Ange in the universally-beloved "spoon" fashion.

However, her attitude of tender benevolence abruptly vanished when she discovered that not only was he asleep (nothing, per se, *all* that wrong with that), but that he was doing this *fully clothed*. Even unto his *chaussures*....

"Hé, chéri! Would you mind a terrific amount if you unclothed yourself to better befit a civilized sleeping mode? To include, *mon Dieu* and fer cryin' out loud, your clod-hopping *godasses*?"

Mere prodding wasn't enough – she had to resort to actual punches to waken him... which was no easy feat. But eventually,

"Hé? Wha-? Quoi? Shoes? Clothes? *Ooof! – that's* what this is about? – you don't have to hit me – just mention it... no problem – " He fell out of bed, shed and kicked off the offending apparel, and re-bedded himself.

She was somewhat mollified now, and – speaking of apparel, offending or otherwise – she kindly offered, *"Alors?* You in the mood for some amusement? Because if so, tell me now, and I'll... you know," she was referring to a few bits fetching under-scantiness that she knew delighted him during intimate moments, "but I don't want to have to get up later...".

But he just emitted a half-hearted "Euh, very *chic* of you. But perhaps just not right now, if you don't mind – perhaps in the morning?"

"Hein? Something wrong? Are you *malade,* by chance?" Although not unprecedented, morning *amour,* specially on weekdays, was highly unusual.

"*Non,* not at all... It's just... well, the fact is, *ma chérie,* I had something of a rather, ah, agitated, not to say at times downright enervating, day... which has caused in me certain... well, preoccupations."

"What the hell does that even mean? Jesus, you people – "

She actually meant this more playfully than the words implied – but Michel-Ange still felt like playing along,

"What? Who, what 'people'? – you mean us French?"

"No, you *énarques.* So exquisitely over-educated you can't put one simple word in front of the other."

"But my Jenni-faire – this charge is as unjustified as it is invidious – "

"See what I mean? Anyway, what's with these so-called 'preoccupations'? I've never known you to have any such thing, ever – well, not that you'd notice, anyway...."

"It has to do with *la Gryaznie.*"

"What?"

"The Republic of Gryaznia. The little place between Romania, Bulgaria and Serbia."

"Yes. I've heard of it. So what about it?"

"Hah! You may well ask!"

"Yes. I am. What about it?"

"I'll *tell* you what's about it – " cried a suddenly re-animated Michel-Ange, propping himself up on one elbow, "They're sending me there!"

"*You?*"

"Yes, *moi. Moi,* of all earthly people. To represent France."

"That's absurd. *Who's* sending you? And," she swallowed, "what the hell *for?*"

"Well, that's not entirely clear. At least not to me. I mean, it's the Quai d'Orsay – the Government – the Foreign Ministry... except, not, I suspect, *really* the Foreign Ministry – no, I think that it's rather actually some mysterious *adjunct* of the Quai d'Orsay – maybe the DGSE --"

"Slow down – the *who*?"

"The DGSE – it's our CIA – I think they're the ones who're *really* behind all this, although one can't, of course, be sure. As I know from my papa and further learned at the E.N.A., nobody is ever who they purport to be in the *coulisses* of our *politique étrangère*. Anyway, it's all tied up in the person of a mysterious and rather ferocious colonel – *he's* sending me...." Michel-Ange tailed off, somewhat lamely.

"And these mysterious... *forces* are sending you to Gra – to this place – for *what*, again?" Jennifer was now sitting with her arms akimbo, in the universally-recognized pose signifying I-don't-believe-a-word-of-this-bullshit.

"Ah – *la meilleur*! You'll like this – "

"I'll be the judge of that."

"Yes. Because, d'you see, the thing that they want me to do out in *la Gryaznie* – other than doing nothing, but that's another story – is to be our, that is to say France's, *Attaché Culturel* – "

"*Quoi? You?*"

"Yes. And within three of the merest of weeks. During which, in fact, the colonel in question suggested that you might even be able to help the cause a bit, and perhaps coach me – for example, how would you say in your exquisite Californian surfer *patois* 'Your Excellent Excellency'?"

Jennifer shook her head in disbelief. "I don't think I've ever heard such a pluperfect crock of shit in my whole young life. Let me get this straight – you, *you*, out of, what sixty million French people, have been chosen to represent two thousand years... *of French culture?* To a bunch of recent ex-commies in some benighted eastern shit-hole? I need a drink."

She got up, switched back on the light and nakedly clomped into the kitchen, as Michel-Ange called out after her:

"Look, I don't know what kind of byzantine contrivances my mysterious papa machinated to get me this posting, but be reasonable – a fellow cannot live forever on bread and *baising* alone, even if the *baisee* is such a lovely, creative and, dare I say it, *complaisante*, euh, *spécimène* as your good American self. The point *is*," he upped his volume as she was now making kitchen noises, "that sooner or later, I had to get a job. I mean – quite apart from my *papa* being pretty insistent thereupon – can you think of any other line of work I'm suited for? Particularly?"

"Alright – let's say I grant you all that. *But in fucking Gryaznia?*"

"Well, it was, after all, to the *Foreign* Ministry that I applied, so a foreign posting was rather to be expected. Now of course, perhaps Tahiti or even Bermuda might have been more convivial – but I was emphatically assured that the only alternative currently on offer is Belgrade which is actually, as we speak, being bombed by your American Air Force and even, if I do not *détrompe* myself, our own Mirages, so I thought it prudent not to choose it over the recently-decommunized delights of Gryaznia and its, at least so far, un-bombed capital, Laina. Which reminds me," he lay back down with a sigh, "I know strictly – *mais alors, exactement* zero – about the place... I should probably pick up a *Guide Michelin* on it, if there even *is* such a thing...." he trailed off, really rather pathetically....

But just when it seemed that Michel-Ange was a spent force, he rallied and sprang back to apparent life:

"In fact, if you want to know the truth, a lot of it is *your* fault, *ma chérie*...."

"*Me?*" expostulated the poor girl, from next door, "What on God's green earth do *I* have to do with any of this fucking ridiculousness? – Sorry, don't take it personally, but that's what it seems like to me."

"Well, not *you, qua you*, my *chérie Californiène* – I mean 'you' collectively – you Americans."

"Oh? Do tell."

"Well, as the colonel put it, we – France – have detected an excessive influence by what he calls 'American interests' in Gryaznia...."

"Oh really? Well, I read the papers – probably more closely than you do – and you sure coulda fooled me...."

"Well, as I say, that appears to be the official French view of things, as vouch-safed to me by the colonel – and that to, ahem, keep an eye on this excessive American influence, he wants an extra body at the embassy, i.e., *moi*, and the colonel also says – "

"You wanna know what I think?" She had returned from the kitchen, chewing something, and re-seated herself on her side of the bed.

"But of course, *ma chérie*."

"I think your colonel is a stone raving psycho loonie – a real what they call out on Saint Germain a *fasco-parano* – "

It occurred to Michel-Ange that their conversation had suddenly careened off into a murky vector that was unlikely to prove productive, to put it mildly, so he decided to attempt a re-direction:

"Oh but *ma chérie* you're *so sexy* when you make yourself indignant like this – here, give us a *bisou*...."

But Jennifer was not so easily put off. She gently but deftly pushed him away,

"What – get – get *away* with that – what I don't understand is why they imagine that, of all things, you might be a fitting representative of... *culture?* What cultural insights do they – or you – imagine you're going to bestow on the long-suffering people of... of... this place?"

"Well," attempted Michel-Ange "for a start, in my last year at the E.N.A. we in the Drama Club put on *"Iphigénie"* by *Euripède* in which I played a surprising-ly sprightly, so I was told, Agamemnon – "

"Right. You. Agamemnon. Right. And that's the cultural, ah, nourishment they're crying out for there in war-torn Grungelandia, is it?" She smiled and stroked his face, "Yeah, *that* sounds about right –"

"No, I just mentioned that as a modest cultural *bona fide* and of my possible fitness for this role."

"Yeah, well..." Jennifer now leaned back on the bed, on one elbow – wagging one stupendous leg up and down on her other stupendous leg, which distracted Michel-Ange momentarily but he forced himself to re-focus – what was she saying now? "... I mean, just how does one go about *being* an Attaché of Culture? Have you given *that* any thought? Got a plan? You and your colonel?"

"*Non*. But *voyons* – how hard can it be?"

Truth be told, no he hadn't, and no he didn't. But at her goading, he now gave the matter some thought – an almost physically painful task for Michel-Ange, and one he'd hoped he'd put permanently in his past when he'd mercifully escaped successfully from school.

Now Michel-Ange had never considered himself a particularly political fellow, but neither was he a *naïf* or a dreamer and so the one thing he most decidedly was not was a leftist "true, secular believer" like so many of his class and cohort. Although he knew the type well – arse-achingly well, in fact – and knew *exactly* what kind of "cultural program" would have been chosen by "them", that sainted clerisy that made up *Les Intellectuels de Gauche* (and the august *Académie* that blessed their machinations), if they were given half a chance: That dreary agenda – the Canon of Sartre, de Beauvoir, Godard, Fanon, Rousseau, Althusser, Derrida, Barthès... as the dreaded *Amerloques* said, *ohgodkillmenow....*

But somehow Michel-Ange didn't see Colonel Mincemot signing off on any such tendentious *merdier* of a cultural "program", and Michel-Ange, whose own cultural tastes, such as they were, ran rather to the apolitical, the retro, the *comique populaire* and the outright *"bête et méchant"*, hoped he might be able to push some of his own favorites – Jean Poiret, Michel Serrault, Louis de

Funès, Gerard Oury, Lino Ventura, Bernard Blier, Michel Galabru, the afore-mentioned Jean Anouilh, Jean-Jacques Annaud, Pierre Schoendoerffer, Jean Raspail, Jean-Francois Revel, Michel Sardou...

...and on this tentatively positive note Michel-Ange's internal *récapitulation* sputtered out. But it was *way* too soon to devise any specific cultural "pro-gram" and in any case he was too thoroughly banjaxed by recent roller-coaster events to want to pursue it much further with Jenni-faire just now, so he of-fered as a stop-gap,

"Plan? A *plan*, you say... well, no, not yet. Too soon. And anyway, it's compli-cated – the colonel told me they didn't in truth want me to *do* anything except watch out for you Americans, but should I be called upon to actually intro-duce something 'cultural', I don't know, I might try to put in a call to BHL – he once came and gave a talk to our class, and I managed – "

"Who?"

"Lévi. Bernard-Henri. You know – the *nouveau philosophe.* That guy with the hair, and the shirt opened to his *nombril* – he's always on the teevee. As *préten-tieux* as they get, and as far as I'm concerned largely incomprehensible as well, but at least not a blatant Marxist and, judging from my fellow students, he's very popular. *Tres sexy.* In fact he's just your type, *ma Jenni-faire de mes reves...* " and he lunged at her reclining form, but she, with the deft intervention of an upraised foot, deposited his body with a clunk on the floor beside the bed.

"And," he resumed, picking himself up and resuming his place on the bed be-side her, as though nothing at all had just occurred, "speaking of my E.N.A. class reminds me that one of them is a *pote* of one of the guys in *Les Innocents* – you know that group, non? They're pretty good – maybe I'll see if they might be interested in doing a *tournée* in exciting *folklorique* Laina... so, you'll see, while I have not begun to formulate any kind of program yet, I am not entirely without cultural resources..."

Michel-Ange tailed off, once again into vaguely unsatisfactory vapidity. It oc-curred to him to wonder, *en passant,* if he'd be getting laid tonight...

Jennifer rose and again returned to the "kitchenette" for some more wine, and returned bearing a Parisian specialty that she'd recently acquired through a kind of cultural osmosis – a most expressive pout that she deployed before setting off on a new tack:

"Alright, Michael, look, let's forget about this colonel and your mission and 'culture' and Grizzly-land and all that for the moment. But what about *moi*, then?"

"Hein?"

"Me. What happens to me? Do I stay here? Or what? You wouldn't invite me to come with you, would you?"

Merde! I hadn't thought about that. Hmm. But now that I do think of it ... I'm not sure what to think. Let me think....

He got up and also procured *him*self a spot of *rouge*. "Well, for a start – and I'm thinking out loud, here – I can't see old Colonel Mincemot – "

"That's his *name?* Oh my God you're shi – "

"Yes, that's his name. And I can't exactly see him exploding with enthusiasm over any scheme involving your accompanying me – but nor does it sound as though it would be so hugely enjoyable for *you*, either, *ma chérie* – "

"Hey, I didn't say I *wanted* to go," She sipped her wine *while still pouting* – extraordinary, "I was just wondering what... well, what the deal might be, is all..."

"Well look, here's how I think I see it: I'll go out to Gryaznia alone and investigate the whole *bordelle* out there. See what the situation and conditions are. And if things appear... well, *évolués* enough to warrant it, I shall invite you to come and visit."

She abandoned the pout and pursed her lips. He continued,

"Yes, it's not ideal, but it's a plan. And in the meantime, if you like, you can stay on here. In fact, I very much wish you would," Michel-Ange leaned over and attempted to kiss her neck. He missed his mark, painfully stubbing his lips on her collarbone, but he hoped he got credit for the *galanterie* nevertheless.

He even warmed to his theme, now, "And now that I will have a 'normal' income, I will make arrangements for the rent and *charges* and all that, for while I'm away. You have your key. And you can continue doing... well, ... whatever it is you do – study... thesis... project – that marvelous thing you're working at. And everything can be, as I believe your *Beugs Beunné* says, hunkus dorus!"

"Well," she eventually said, her face back to its default prettiness, "I sup*pose* that could work. For the immediate future, anyway. As long as the electric stays on in this place, and as long as you stay alive in *that* place – and as long as you don't forget to come back – " *Five* times, now. *Et tu, Jenni-faire?*

So there the matter rested: In a state of... mutually acceptable – one might even call it *diplomatic* – concord.

And better yet, a little later – before gratefully surrendering to the welcoming arms of Somnus – they made a kind of semi-frantic love. Far from their most spectacular, to be sure, but definitely passable. (After which Michel-Ange silently congratulated himself on having successfully, under the circumstances, carried the thing off – *at all*....)

7

LES PRÉPARATIFS

The next morning, at the civilized hour of ten o'clock, he got another call from *Mlle.* Bergère.

"Good morning, *Monsieur* Michel-Ange."

"Ah. Ma – " he coughed, "*Mademoiselle* Bergère. Hello again."

She did not dither. "We will be needing four photographs from you. And for official uniformity, please get them from a *Photomaton*. Nothing 'new-tech' or digital."

"Oh. Right. The diplomatic passport. Of course. Well, as soon as I've chased the vultures out of my hair and covered myself suitably I shall get on it. And bring them around to your place, *asappe* – "

"*Pardon?*"

" '*Asappe*' – it's *Américain* – it means *tout de suite* – the colonel will know – "

"No doubt. The photos, please." And she rang off.

Jennifer, who was in the bathroom doing something intricate to her eyebrows, called to him "Who the *merde* was that?"

"That secretary of the colonel. Says I need new passport photos. You wouldn't believe this woman – she's a completely ferocious half-*mémère*/half-*poule-de-luxe* – and still eminently *baise*-able – "

"Don't be a perv," Jennifer said, as she swept out of the bathroom, finished her coffee, grabbed her satchel, and, in a delightful little *tourbillon* of Van Cleef and Arpels, pecked him on the cheek. "OK, Michael, I'm off to the *facultée* – you, don't get into any more trouble – "

"*Ciao,* and yes, *ma chérie,* I will endeavor to follow your wise counsel – which, hah hah, is the same as the colonel's." he called to her as she departed.

He now set about the tedious business of making himself presentable: Shaved. Hammered down the more stubbornly errant eructations of his hair. Teeth. *This thing that Jenni-faire calls le "pitte-stique".*

Now, to dress rather more *soigneusement* than usual – *it's a diplomatic passport, after all: I think this pale blue shirt with the straight-point collar, the old black and yellow "Sciences Po" tie with its discreet little lions and foxes (designed by Christian Dior himself, who, rather amazingly, was a S-P alum), the trusty old double-breasted blazer rather than the single today...* aaaand... *done.*

He took himself to the nearby Place de la Contre-Escarpe, where there was a *Prisunic* which housed a *Photomaton* cabin. Upon whose stool he parked his arse as he plonked in the requisite coins.

He stared at his reflection in the black glass slab and it occurred to him that he looked like nothing so much as a "WANTED" poster for the cartoon cowboy Lucky Luke. And five minutes later he was proved correct in this pessimistic view.

Clutching these four Studies In Enigmatic Discomfort, he *Metro*-ed himself back to Col. Mincemot's office at the *Quai.*

Mlle. Bergère, (who today was wearing a gray Dior – speaking of whom! – outfit) peered at his contribution.

"You look in reality actually better than *this*," she commented, in what Michel-Ange speculated was possibly a stab at kindness.

"Yes, well, one would like only to hope so. But it is indubitably a fact that these were taken less than an hour ago and, as they say, the camera never lies."

"Never mind." She dropped the photos on top of some other official *bumf* in a shallow basket that Michel-Ange noticed was labelled "M-A G DLF/Laina".

"I already have my own basket?"

"*Absolument*. You're one of our group, now," she said, allowing herself a small smile – *my first!* "and *chez nous,* each within the group is autonomous." Michel-Ange would have liked to explore these cryptic words further, but she didn't let him. "We'll get all this *paperasse* to you in the next few days, some of which will be for you to keep, and some which you'll have to sign and bring back to me. In the meantime, *apply yourself to your Assimils.*"

"Right – *that* parade of *Guignoles* –" he muttered as she rose and gently shoved him out the door.

"Apply yourself. We'll call you. *Allez – ouste!*" and she closed the heavy Ministerial door behind him.

Women. The more I know them, the less I know them. This one – Mère Supérieure, mon cul, ouais? – is some numéro... she and the colonel there are some team, aie-yayay – what am I doing in this crowd?... A snatch of song from his favorite musical group, Procol Harum, came to him:

There's too many women and not enough wine,

Too many poets and not enough rhyme,

Too many glasses and not enough time –

So... draw your own conclusions.

He re-*Métro*-ed himself back to Michel-Ange Hqs at the Rue Mouffetard. Jen-ni-faire was still away, doing whatever it was she did. (Michel-Ange truly had no clue, and was more than happy to leave it that way.)

Although her mythical (in his mind) pedagogical skills would be welcome now.... he thought, as he nipped into the kitchen and downed a largish *pastis*... before applying himself to this more-than-a-little *opera buffa* task. The more he gazed at these lunatic language texts, the more they revealed themselves to be even worse imbecilities than he had at first glance intuited.

For example. From the "English" volume:

"Pray, my good sir, can you indicate an installation where I might buy some fresh aubérgines?" Well, thought Michel-Ange, *that* should get me started right smartly in Gryaznia... where I doubt they would know an *aubérgine* if they slipped in one.

Also: *"Excuse me, Mister Conductor, but this seems to be local train to Slough. I appear to have committed an error, having wished, rather, to embark on an express train for my journey to Stoke-upon-Trent."* Fucking useful in suburban Laina... always assuming, of course, that there *was* such a thing as suburban Laina....

And, most intriguingly: *"Please mister, I beg you. Do not nose your thumb at me."* Which, come to think of it, *might* prove useful in a place like Laina after all....

And from the "Russian" volume:

"Pardon me, friend, but do you know where may I discharge myself?" Eh? Well, *that* hardly sounded promising – although with these ex-commies, you never knew... might turn out to be just the ticket....

Also – and most arresting indeed: *"Do not touch me! I am an international!"* Dashed useful. If you were a center-forward for *Paris-St. Germain*....

And, 'allo, 'allo, wot's *this* then? *"Miss, I cannot but admire your extremities."* Well, now *that* could conceivably prove useful – but, see? this was *precisely* the sort of thing upon which one would have wanted some *Jenni-faire*-ian wisdom applied....

Ho, la la, what *spécimens*, he wondered as he fetched himself another *pastis*, could have concocted such a salad of artless trans-national fatuity?

Anyway, he soldiered on until late afternoon, at which time Jennifer returned and, over replenished glasses of, now, *rouge* and fortified with little *saucisson*-and-*gruyère toasts* that she caused to materialize in the kitchen, she did her considerable best to salvage the foundering *S.S. Michel-Ange.*

For example, she introduced "I take no shit" to his repertoire, a phrase which Michel-Ange found so potentially useful that he went and looked it up in Russian. In which, as best he could de-code, it translated into something like *"Ia nié prinimayou gavno!"* As he scribbled it down in his impeccable *lycée*-impressed cursive, he almost couldn't wait to try out in real life.

And so things progressed.

Until four days later, when there occurred a near-catastrophe:

Despite her previously-voiced intention of "calling him", Miss Bergère did no such thing, and instead just one day suddenly appeared *chez Michel-Ange* at the Rue Mouffetard, unannounced, uninvited and certainly unexpected. It was a Saturday morning, when Jennifer was practically guaranteed to be in residence.

Oh la la, quelle histoire...

What happened was: the Mother Superior pitched up in the black Ministerial Peugeot 605, which continued idling as she exited therefrom and commanded the somnolent *concièrge* to buzz upstairs to inform *Monsieur* de la Fassederad that he had *"une visiteuse urgente".*

Michel-Ange had been luxuriating on the crapper – happily perusing *Charlie Hebdo* – so it fell to Jennifer to deal with the *concièrge*. Her permanent American suspicion – what she called her "female intuition" – kicked in and she barked at the intercom to *"attendez"* before giving her consent to buzz anybody in.

And she went to, and peered down out of, their window that gave onto the Rue Mouffetard. To behold the top of a female silver-blonde head and a bird's-eye view of a prominent bosom. Against which were pressed a thin what appeared to be briefcase.

Jennifer turned and yelled, "Michael! Your... Mrs. Robinson from the Ministry is downstairs for you!"

What? "J'arrive – !" Bordelle de chiasse, thought Michel-Ange, as he "arranged" himself in semi-panic. Bursting out of the little w.c., he once again eschewed the snail-paced ancient lift and descended the stairs rather after the fashion of Franz (*"I voz gombledely out von gondrole fram ze top to ze boddom"*) Klammer winning downhill Olympic gold in '76.

He burst onto the Rue Mouffetard and practically crashed into the impatient *Mlle. Bergère,* who was drumming her fingers on the briefcase and giving a good impression of someone who was tired of hanging about. She shoved this briefcase at Michel-Ange and said,

"*Ah – vous voila! Voiçi* all your *paperasses,* including your *passeport diplomatique* – don't forget to sign it – as well as your *lettre de créançe –* "

"*Merde* – do I really need one of those?"

"Of course you do. Without it you are a nobody. At least officially." She looked him over with fresh asperity, "Mind you, even *with* one...."

"But... who do I give it to?"

"*M'enfin!* Wake up! To the authorities – the Gryaznian authorities – down there! Look, the Ambassador – if he's sober – will explain all the protocols and niceties to you. Meanwhile, we seem to be blocking traffic, here – must *file –* " She now squeezed his same upper arm she'd touched before and, as she disappeared into the back of the black Peugeot mini-limo, called to him, "Be alert!" *(Soit vif!)* "The colonel must have seen *something* in you..."

Jennifer, still up at the window, observed this little *entrechat* with mixed emotions. She was glad that Michael was finally being prodded off his *farniente*

ass into something resembling honest remunerated activity, but she also wondered if the "real world" (let alone the Eastern European portion of it) and
Michel-Ange were quite ready for each other. Indeed, if she and Miss Bergère
had been on sharing-a-half-bottle-of-Bordeaux terms, they would have found a
confluence of misgivings as concerned the sometimes-oblivious-seeming object
of their mutual interest.

Said object, upon letting himself back in, saw that Jenni-faire had retreated to
the bedroom and so pulled up a *fauteuil to* address himself to this new dossier
of documents, most of which, with the exception of his handsome new passport, he had difficulty comprehending – not least because much of it appeared
to be written in Cyrillic Gryaznian (in which he could not discern anything
remotely like "Madam, I cannot but admire your extremities").

But the stamp from the French Ministry of Foreign Affairs appeared reassuringly often enough, and he signed his name in the various places that had
thoughtfully been indicated for him, and... *blah blah...* diplomatic protocols...
blah blah... mutual cooperation... *blah blah...* consult annex to plenipotentiary... *skrnxjnk schrmmflx...* he nodded off into a fitful and impromptu nap...
during which he dreamed he was skiing – in total fog, but with supernatural
skill – frightening yet thrilling.

To be awoken some hours later by Jennifer who, amusingly enough, had since
donned a T-shirt that said "No Fear" on it. Michel-Ange, who one second ago
had been *schussing* down a near-cliff, blinked at it in astonishment.

"Wakey-wakey, Michael, I've made us a *goûter* – a dunch."

"A what?"

"Dunch – it's my afternoon version of brunch."

"I don't even know what the *morning* one is..."

"Never mind – come, come over here – "

And she dragged him over to the table where she had, out of seeming nowhere, concocted a steaming *choucroute garni,* a good portion of which a semi-famished Michel-Ange semi-inhaled.

Later that night they again... went at it. So to speak. Two nights in a row was fairly unusual for Michel-Ange (and, he – *ahem* – assumed, for Jenni-faire as well) but all this Mission-To-Gryaznia business seemed to have injected a certain fizz and *élan* to the intimacies of the little MacKoy/de la Fassederad *ménage,* and the frisky *ambiance* had been further enhanced by Jennifer's donning, for the occasion, some of her *oolala* sexy *sous-vêtements. B'en merde, dis, I haven't even been paid yet, and this new job is already paying off....*

A few days later, upon his return from an evening session at *Le Macaque* (still bellyaching to a largely tuned-out Manu about obscure foreign language enormities), Jennifer had greeted Michel-Ange from the bathtub in which she'd been luxuriating, with the words "Hey, your mother-superior" (he'd told her of the nickname) "from the Ministry called – message is by the phone."

Sure enough, in her impeccable handwriting with little circles above the "i"s he read: "Tomorrow night. 1930. The main bar at the Hotel Meurice. Not be late."

So that is precisely where and when Michel-Ange the next evening pitched up, to find Colonel Mincemot in a dark suit, seated discreetly at a corner table in this impossibly sumptuous *bar/salon,* pretending to read *Le Monde* but actually surveying the hushed *vas et viens* around him.

Spying Michel-Ange, he waved his newspaper and with a motion of the head ordered him over.

"What are you taking, my boy?" he said as Michel-Ange sat himself. The colonel saw that the boy was staring at his own green drink. "Mine, here is a *ga-li-gali* – a horrible concoction made of equal parts peppermint liqueur, Scotch whiskey and Coca-Cola which I became very fond of in the *matitis* of the *Oubanqui* and which I *really* don't recommend."

So Michel-Ange settled for his usual, less exotic, cognac-Perrier, and waited for the colonel to speak. Which, as soon as the waiter had shoved off, began briskly enough:

"So, *mon cher jeune homme*, how go the English and Russian lessons, *hein?*"

"Well – "

"Very good, very good. I'm glad to hear it. Now look," the colonel leaned forward and gestured that Michel-Ange should do the same, "I wanted to tell you something *de vive voix* which I'm not even so keen that Her at the office – " *Her at the office?* "should be a party to, so attend closely: the thing is this, and I know I alluded to it at our first meeting, but I want to clarify it further, here: this whole 'Cultural Attaché' *masquerade* is all well and good, but between you and me, it's not the real reason why I'm having you sent out to this Gryaznia place."

"Non?"

"Non. Now listen, I don't know what that Ambassador of ours out there – I forget his name, it's hyphenated, no surprise there – will have in mind for you to do, culture-wise – and of course I want you to keep him as reasonably happy as you can, but, really, don't break your head over any of that culture stuff –

"Your *real* job out there will be to act as my personal seeing-eye dog. I want you to keep me informed about what's going on out there, both inside our Embassy and outside – the Americans, the Russians, the Serbs, the Muslims – all that *racaille*. And I, from time to time, may send you explicit instructions. We've got a specially-installed secure commo system there, somewhere – the Ambassador will fill you in on how it works – and that will be our link to me –

"The point is, *fiston*, that while I want you to remain *correct* with the Ambassador, *I* will remain your real *patron*. Got it? *Pige?*"

Although utterly unversed in bureaucratic infighting, even Michel-Ange could foresee the odd complication arising from the colonel's scenario. But that did not prevent him from declaring, with false pseudo-military bravado, "Absolutely, *monsieur.*"

"Good. Good." The colonel now shook Michel-Ange's hand and gave him a soft paternal pat on the cheek. "Now I think you should *fout-le-camp.* I'll stay on here, a bit. So *merde, merde merde, mon petit. "*

And that had been that, colonel-wise.

As Michel-Ange strode out of the hushed majesty of the Hotel Meurice onto the Rue de Rivoli, he felt a twinge of alarmed apprehension that such an inconsequential person as himself should be considered worthy of *any* responsibility by *La République*'s phantom movers and shakers, much less entrusted with a clandestinity that the colonel seemed to be asking of him here... but... well... *tant pis – either they know what they're doing or it'll be their funeral,* he concluded, and left it at that.

Eventually the daily countdown wound down. No more stupid Assimils, no more fretting, fussing, and generally faffing around. Tomorrow was "Go-Time" – *"Le Jour G"* (for Gryaznia).

"So what time tomorrow?" asked Jennifer.

"D'you know – I can't even remember exactly. *Merde,* I'd better have a look– " and retrieving his Bergère-delivered document-*serviette*, he pulled out his air ticket and itinerary. "Yes. In the morning. Here – " he handed the bumf to Jennifer as he went to pull his battered old Vuitton suitcase from under the bed.

"Well", she observed, "They put you in first class at least, but on the on the other hand it's with something that calls itself 'Balkan Airlines', so I dunno...."

"Yes, I admit, that does sound a bit 'rum' – as that drunken idiot English pal of yours ffoulkes-Pomfret – two effs, none of them capitalized – from *La Rhum-merie,* likes to say..."

"He's a polo player," sniffed Jennifer, as though that explained anything.

Dragging out this Vuitton relic, which was not something he would ever have bought for himself in a million years (it didn't even have any wheels and as far as he could tell the only people who were seen in public with Vuitton luggage any longer were conspicuously from the Orient) but which had been a gift from his *maman* on his 18th birthday, Michel-Ange thought back to one of the lectures that had made the greatest impression on him during his studies: it had been given back in his undergraduate days at *Sciences Po* by the visiting ex-head of the French Foreign Intelligence Service, Count Alexandre de Marenches, who had told them:

"To compete in today's world, you must 1/ scheme like the

Chinese, 2/ plan like the Germans, 3/ dress like the English,

4/ play by Russian rules which means no rules at all, 5/ be

prepared to lie like a Muslim, 6/ be enigmatic as the Japs,

7/ charm like the Italians, 8/ be audacious as the Israelis,

9/ fight like the Koreans, and 10/ use whatever equipment

the Americans are using."

And when one of Michel-Ange's braver colleagues had piped up "And nothing French?" the old aristo-spook had laughed and said "No, nothing – except eat, drink and fuck" (*"Bouffe, boisson, baiser"*)

The old man's Third Edict was all well and good, but Michel-Ange maintained his own idea of elegance – so into the old Vuitton went:

Two gabardine St. Laurent suits, one tan, and the other gray pin-stripe; the double-breasted white linen suit – copied from one of his old Cardins by his previously-evoked bespoke Tunisian tailor, Couscous Alhamdoulilaye; a tweed sport coat from Hackett; some twill slacks with slanted bottoms from NewMan; a half dozen of his custom-made French-cuffed (*poignets mousquetaires*) monogrammed shirts, (white, pale blue and pink, one-each solid and one-each striped); a clutch of ties; and an adequate supply of knee-length black socks and variously-colored boxer shorts (Michel-Ange eschewing the racier type of "slingshot"-type undertrouserings favored by his male *co-çitoyens*); a couple of knit *chemises Lacoste;* his pair of black dress shoes – *and* his ready-to-go *trousse toillette.* Also, more in hope than expectation, his white tennis shorts and sneakers. And, as an afterthought, in a little interior zip pocket he slipped a Polaroid photo of Jenni-faire in her aforementioned saucy undergarments, his Ray-Ban aviator-style sunglasses, and a silver pocket flask which he first topped up with Rémy Martin cognac.

Finally, he set aside what he'd be wearing for the trip: his navy blazer from Hackett (*voila* "dress like the English"!), white shirt with his full initials *"mag-dlf"* monogrammed in gold script on its left breast, the old *Sciences Po* tie, gray gabardine slacks, his pair of boxer shorts in the national tricolor which Jennifer had bought for him, fresh socks, and his dark-brown-almost-black Ferragamo loafers with discreet little tassels on them.

Which left him holding his old Burberry trench coat (so old it dated from when "Burberry" actually meant something)... he wanted to take it with him, but not have to drag it onto the plane, so.... he stuffed it on top of his other *merde* and jumped up and down on the suitcase like Sam from *Yosemité* in the *Beugs Beunné* cartoons, until he managed to clack it shut. And *hop-la!,* he was ready for whatever the wild Gryaznians could throw at him.

Throughout his preparations, Jennifer had hovered over him like a kind of slinky mother hen – unusually for her, whose normal attitude towards him was more one of ironic amusement. But she seemed genuinely sorry to see him go, and he reciprocated with an extra measure of what for him passed for tenderness towards his cherished *Jenni-faire*, (who, it had to be said, he preferred in her more familiar aloof and independent mode).

"Let me know your *co-ordonnés* over there as soon as you have them, okay? I don't want to be getting my news about you from... lurid headlines," she murmured into his neck, at one point.

"But of course, *ma chérie*. And I shall immediately explore, upon my arrival, the possibilities of your coming out there for an eventual visit." he replied, just prior to embracing her... with intent.

All in all, their last night together was certainly satisfactory, but... a bit wistful, actually.

8

THE BALKAN EXPERIENCE

The next morning, *bim!*, at 0815, the ministerial Peugeot pulled up in front of his place and started beeping obnoxiously and repeatedly. Still not quite dressed, Michel-Ange hopped over to the window, opened it and called down *"Ca va, ça va, j'arrive! Merde –!"*

In short order he: brushed his *dents*, perpetrated the necessary in the w.c., completed his *habilement*, swallowed the last of his coffee, threw down a quick shot of *pastis*, embraced his contentedly still-somnoling *Jenni-faire*, grabbed what he by now thought of as his "Mother Superior" *serviette* which contained all his documentary vitalities, threw a last look around, and...

... let himself out. He clattered down the narrow stairs, being more or less dragged down them by his suitcase.

To erupt out onto his Rue Mouffetard and *boingg!* into the back of this sleek conveyance. Which was immediately a different universe – not least because it still bore faint traces of recently-departed Essence of Bérénice Bergère, which was unfortunately being overwhelmed by Fug of *Gauloise*, wafting from up front...

Specifically from the smoking black-*casquette*-ed head of a man in a black suit who, other than a curt "I know" in answer to Michel-Ange's initial "Good morning, sorry if I made you wait – so, it's De Gaulle *Satélite* 2-B", performed the admirable service of remaining completely mute for the entire journey.

Only when they arrived and he was helping Michel-Ange with his case did the chauffeur give voice, and his phlegmatic tone did not disguise the portent of his words:

"So look, if you haven't yet done so, now's the time to put your *flingue* in your checked-in bag, here."

"My what?"

"Your *flingue* -- your *arme.*"

"But I haven't got one."

"Quoi? They didn't give you one? Nothing?"

"Decidedly not. In fact, the subject never even came up." Already Michel-Ange was directing a reproachful thought towards his supposedly *archi*-martial colonel, "Why, do you think I need one?"

"You kidding? There where you're going? You'll be the only one without one, in that whole *bordelle* of drunken *cinglés.* "

"B'en merde – it's a little late now..."

"For sure. Maybe they'll give you something when you get there. If they don't, make sure to ask 'em. I know the neighborhood and, believe me, it's a veritable shooting gallery they've got going on out there – you'll definitely want to be armed. Although – " he slammed the trunk shut, "at least it'll save me the hassle of having to go in there with you and weasel you through security. Well, young man, good luck to you –" he shook Michel-Ange's hand with the Colonel's tell-tale bear-trap grip, "And try to remember to return safely..."

ENCORE!? CA SUFFIT COMME CA!

By now in a not-terribly gruntled mood, Michel-Ange thrust himself into the *Satélite* B-2. In search of this supposed Balkan Airlines....

Which rather quickly proved itself to be elusive. To not say actually illusory. In any case, it proved nowhere to be found. No "Balkan" anywhere.

Formidable.

Instead, after a good bit of peering hither and yon, he eventually spied a well-hidden little "Information" desk, tucked between a *Relais* newsstand and the *"Mesdames"* and *"Messieurs"*. Where, of course, there was a short, but vocal, queue.

First was the inevitable lard-*derrièred* American couple, he in a pair of "work" (otherwise why the great vestigial pockets?) trousers which inexplicably stopped just below his knees, and she in what looked like a track warm-up suit, angrily inquiring why there wasn't a McDonald's in this terminal and no, some "Euro-fake" called "Quick" was "not the goddamn same". But obtaining no satisfactory answer, they eventually slunk off.

No more successful was the next party in line, an equally-preoccupied woman who turned out to be a Bangladeshi, extravagantly draped in gaily-colored layers of what could well have been living room curtains, accompanied by what seemed like a dozen mewling children all appearing to be under the age of ten – how could such a thing even be biologically possible? – who inquired rapidly (though more politely than the Americans) where she might obtain a visa to Italy, which was apparently something she was only just now realizing she required. She received, for her pains, a scrap of paper with the address and phone number of the Italian Consulate in Paris. Shoved through the little gap at the bottom of the bullet-proof glass window. Next?

Michel-Ange approached. *"Euh, pardon,* but... where would Balkan Airlines be hiding itself, then?"

Behind the gap into which he spoke sat, rather to Michel-Ange's surprise, a delightful young black lady with exquisitely fine Guinean features who informed him that through some sort of mutual arrangement between the parties concerned, here at Charles de Gaulle it was SABENA who occupied itself with all matters pertaining to Balkan Airlines, and she was in the middle of gesturing where *they* might be located when Michel-Ange found himself rudely elbowed aside by a hysterical woman demanding in a *Marseillais* accent where the arrivals hall was.

Reluctant to physically scrum to regain his rightful place at the front of the queue, Michel-Ange decided to make do with such info as he'd managed to glean, and eventually located the SABENA transfer desk which, amazingly, really, when one considered how many flights there were between Paris and Brussels, was un-manned. Or, come to that, un-womanned. (Of course, for anyone familiar with the you-should-pardon-the-expression work habits, such as they were, of the Belgians ....)

In lieu of a live human being at the SABENA desk there was one of those vaguely breast-shaped brass bells which, this being SABENA, could well have been a 19th century antique. Michel-Ange banged upon it smartly. When this elicited no discernible response, he resumed banging, only now with more vim. And also repeatedly – causing fellow supplicants at neighboring transfer desks to look upon him with a mixture of alarm and grudging admiration.

After this extended mini-concerto of clarion *bing-bongs*, a result, of sorts, was produced. In the form of a tall, languorous fellow who emerged from the hidden recesses where airline personnel quite justifiably retreat from having to deal with their inevitably outraged newly-dubbed "customers".

This specimen's hair was, if anything, even shorter than Mincemot's, but most certainly unlike the Colonel, he sported an enormous walrus moustache. Bearing SABENA's oddly one-winged insignia upon his narrow chest, he swished towards the counter and addressed Michel-Ange.

"Yaies? Wat eet eez? Eef you so do pleez?"

"Look. I speak *Français*. In fact, I *am Francais*. In *fact, un diplomate Français*," and he plonked down his brand-new diplomatic passport.

"Oooo, but how divine for you," cooed the fellow, who gave every impression of just having emerged from one of those *siestas* that might well have still got him arrested in at least some of the United States.

"Yes, well... that's as may be," replied Michel-Ange using what, for him, passed for a stern voice. "but I am here to check in for Laina."

"Really?" The fellow peered about in what was an excellent impression of genuine confusion, "And where would *she* be, then?"

For a fleeting moment it occurred to Michel-Ange that he might be the victim of one of those hidden "candid camera" televised farces, but he mentally rolled the dice against that possibility and stolidly forged on: "Not a *she* – the city, Laina, the capital of Gryaznia."

The guy, smirking behind his *Dupont/Dupond* ("Thompson/Thomson") facial shrubbery, gave himself a light tap on his forehead and said "Oh but of *course*, yaies, we *do* de-serve *la Gryaznie*, how *bête* of me – but the creative manner in which we do zis is by sub-contracting the work to *Aire Linguis*."

"*Who?*"

"The '*Eye-riche*' – the *Irlandais*. *Who*, by the way, I believe locate themselves at the *Satélite C* – you must take the lift, there – and then walk a small distance. *Bon voyage*, and," smoothing back his non-existent hair, he had the *culot* to add, "Thank you for using SABENA!"

Silently evoking Anglo-Saxon maledictions that he'd picked up from the already-missed *Jenni-faire*, Michel-Ange found a random *chariot* for his wheel-less *putain* of a Vuitton suitcase and hauled himself the "small distance" which of course turned out to be more like 2 kilometers to *Satélite C* and the Aer Lingus transfer desk therein.

Where he was most pleasantly gratified to find an actual human being actually on duty.

The Aer Lingus person – in fact, a comely red-haired and freckle-faced Irish colleen straight out of a tourist brochure – was neck-deep in the impenetrable complexities of trying to sort out the multiple confusions of a pair of manifestly drunk soccer or rugby (it was impossible for non-initiates to divine which) supporters whose team, one could only assume from their over-exuberance, must have won something, somewhere, but whose air tickets, as their fellow-Celt Scots like to say, had somehow "ganged agly". They seemed more pathetic than threatening, although their beer pong was strong enough to be picked up as far as Calais.

The Aer Lingus girl, with a patience that should have merited her immediate Beatitude, eventually organized them seats for Dublin, and they stumbled off, punching each other in jovial imbecility.

It was thus in an atmosphere of blessed relief (for both of them) that she turned to address Michel-Ange, and inspected his ticket and passport.

"Merciful Mary. A diplomat. Gracious. Will ye be stopping all the wars, then?"

"Would that I could, *mademoiselle,* but I fear that such is not very immediately proximate. Indeed," Michel-Ange allowed himself the reckless luxury of attempting expansiveness, "I, as it happens, will be representing 'Culture' which, as far as I can tell, does more to *start* wars than to stop them. Still, I shall do what I can. For, if no other reason, you." And here he coaxed forth a disarming smile.

"Ah, but that's kind of ye, sir. Culture. Hoo... posh. I love a bit of the culture meself, but who has the time, eh? Anyway, here ya go, Mister de la... de la... Faster..." she kept on smiling even as she gave up on Michel-Ange's surname, and – in a flurry of efficiency seldom displayed by anyone, anywhere, at any time in the entire history of airline checking-in – she actually allowed him to check his bag *here*, rather than go to the regular check-in line, and handed him his boarding card.

To top it off, she winked at him as she did so, which not only endeared her to him forever, but when she said *"Bon voyage"* pronouncing it *"Bahn voy-ajie"* and conspicuously did *not* beseech him not to forget to come back, well, ... he could have kissed her on the spot.

Instead he said *"Mademoiselle,* the day is still young but you have already been its undoubted high point – a thousand thank yous," and, bowing slightly, he turned and strode off.

Events continued for a while in this upbeat mode, owing mainly to the happy confluence of his traveling both First Class and on a Diplomatic Passport. Even *"Petit Prince du 16éme"* that he was, he was not really accustomed to being treated like an intimate of Louis the Sun King – as all these sundry air flunkies suddenly appeared happy to do – and although he was fully cognizant of how phonus-balonus it all was, Michel-Ange found that he didn't really mind the treatment all that much.

And certainly here in Aer Lingus' hoity-toity "Gold Circle" First Class Lounge all was utterly hunkus-dorus. After an initial *cognac-Perrier,* Michel-Ange proceeded to consume enough Guinness Stout to knock out a mid-sized gorilla – but he, being actually taller than your average mid-sized gorilla, felt just fine. Finer and finer, in fact.

Eventually his flight was summoned and, fairly bouncing along on his tasseled tootsies he was ushered through a long tube, which deposited him into this Balkanian aircraft, where he was invited to make a sharp left, into its little penned-off First Class ghetto.

Truth be told, when *Mlle.* Bergère had informed him – it seemed years ago, already – that he would be flying on something called Balkan Airlines, he'd laughingly imagined some kind of 1916 Austro-Hungarian *Gotha* bi-plane carrying Saint-Exupéry-type mail-sacks while firing synchronized machine guns through the propeller, with the few "First Class" passengers hunkered down with their carpet-bags up front by the storage compartment....

But he needn't have worried. Because what it was that he had entered was, in fact, something called a TU-154B, apparently the Soviet answer to the Boeing 727, and an aeroplane which, while undoubtedly older than he, Michel-Ange, was, was apparently serviceable enough. Well... serviceab*lish,* certainly. As, in the event, it proved less overpoweringly and comprehensively awful than one might have been excused in imagining it might be.

Indeed, a fair description of the whole "Balkan" Air "Experience" could be summed up in the title of the old Cliff Eastwing movie, "The Good, The Bad, and The Ugly".

The "Good" was the indubitable comeliness of these Balkan Airlines Air Girls, who were not only pretty, but were deployed in seemingly platoon-like numbers.

Now, the dire world-wide Air Stewardess Situation was one of Michel-Ange's lesser, but nagging, preoccupations: he was aware, from photos, films and even a hazy recollection from his own earliest days, that In The Beginning, the job of Air Girl had once been considered highly glamorous, and its practitioners had been akin to starlets and fashion models, albeit with added practical skills.

But then the global nuisance of "political correctness" had grabbed the commercial aviation industry by its shriveled testicles, with the result that now, the job of stewardess – especially in western Europe and America – had become the quasi-exclusive reserve of a scowling phalanx of angry, post-menopausal (that in some cases bordered on the demented), frequently overweight, bossy, unkempt and near-amok grannies-from-hell who managed to combine a hazardous physical kak-handedness with a general neo-fascist attitude. And the whole package gift-wrapped in ill-fitting droopy-arsed trouser-suits.

This development – along with the general cretinization of the passengery – had caused flying, in Michel-Ange's experience (as well as most everyone else's), to become, in the words of the American *boulevardier* Ben Stein (that he'd seen in one of Jenni-faire's magazines), "the closest law-abiding citizens get to being in jail".

But not, apparently, so with this throwback, retro Balkan Airlines, where the Air Girls were still – miraculously – pretty, friendly, indeed downright alluring and just generally a pleasure to behold as they flitted competently about, kitted out in navy mini-skirts (!) and slinky red-and-green silk blouses. And when they reached up to help someone with their overhead encumbrances, or seated themselves facing the passengers upon take-offs and landings, well... just, *bravo!*, Balkan, *bravo!*

Somewhat less *bravo*-ish (and this was the "Bad") proved to be the virtually incessant p.a. announcements that resonated within this long Tupolevian tube: a veritable blizzard of blather, first in a version of "French" which sounded to Michel-Ange's practiced ear not unlike a recording of bad *Québécois* played backwards, "Paul-Is-Dead"-style. Followed by some otherworldly Slavo-Balko confabulation that not only bore no resemblance to any of Michel-Ange's As-simil-Russky, but, indeed, to any known terrestrial tongue. So from beginning to end, he had no idea what he was being told, asked, ordered, or warned of. (But of course as a frequent victim of flying, he had a pretty good idea. *Don't inflate until outside the aircraft....*)

And the worst of it was that it never seemed to end. Even when airborne. Except at random moments when it would be interrupted by a kind of insipid girlie-pop music, also in Foreign, of the kind that might have won the Eurovision Song Contest in 1958.

The only thing that was clear from any of this non-stop racket was that Balkan Airlines definitely did not want its passengers to sleep.

Which was really a shame, because the "Ugly" in this whole setup were Michel-Ange's fellow passengers. Whose baleful presence took the form, most immediately, of what could not be less than 300 pounds (135 kilograms) of smelly, sweaty male Dutchness that huffed and puffed up the aisle just as the doors were about to close, and crammed itself into the what one would have thought ample-enough first-class seat next to Michel-Ange (which he, silly twit, had harbored fond hopes would remain vacated for the duration).

Not only did Michel-Ange's newly-arrived neighbor fill old Comrade Tu-polev's best attempt at luxuriously commodious seating, but he actually managed to overflow his allotted space like a sort of out-of-control cheesy oil spill. Indeed, worse, while commandeering full possession of the dividing arm-console, this humongoid embarked upon an immediate deployment of "lap-top" computer, files, mobile phone *avec* charger, and other new-fangled gadgetry – to such an elaborate degree that it occurred to the appalled Michel-Ange to wonder what, if anything, this fellow might have left behind in his office.

No sooner had all this gear been installed and arrayed around his ample person, than one of the perky Balkan bimbettes came bouncing up to inform the

Dutch blimp that all his clobber would have to be shitcanned ("put some udder place") prior to "off-take".

And also of course, the totally unsatisfactory – if predictable – result of *this* intervention was that by "off-take", most of the Dutchman's crap had been stashed in-and-about *Michel-Ange's* alloted space.

Somewhere in all this strenuous arranging and rearranging, it emerged that his unwelcome traveling companion was one Dr. Hendrik van den Kakhof from Leyden in the Netherlands and that he was a "Special United Nations Ambassador for Humanitarian Affairs", specifically attached to UNESCO, charged with bringing to the children of Gryaznia... well, Michel-Ange was never to fully ascertain the exact details of the cornucopia of earthly delights that Professor/Doktor/Mijneer van den Kakhof would be delivering, because, once having unburdened himself of all this ferkakta communication gear and introduced himself, he swallowed a chubby fistful of pills and almost immediately assumed the comatose mode for pretty much the entire balance of the trip.

But no situation is so bad that it can't be made worse, a truism that was confirmed in the *rest* of the TU-154's already not vast – indeed, it consisted of only eight seats, two rows of two seats on each side – First Class section, which was filled with what looked like an African poobah of some kind and his family: two (apparent) wives and three children, 2 boys and a girl.

A diplomatic (small "d") inquiry on his, Michel-Ange's, part revealed this group to be the Ambassador of the People's Democratic Republic of Malaria, that nominally Marxist-Leninist little kakocracy that located itself north and east of the two Congos, and his "immediate" – as opposed to extended – family, who were returning to Laina after a month of *vacances*.

Well, how even *more* delightfully *formidable*.

Actually, to be fair to what appeared to be the long-suffering gentleman, the Ambassador himself seemed blameless enough in Michel-Ange's eyes, as, except for the occasional murmur, he gave a convincing picture of one *who had nothing at all to do with* the noisy little crowd that unaccountably attached itself to him.

However, his two wives, on the other hand, (one conspicuously older than the other), obliviously maintained throughout the entire journey a non-stop yammering, jabbering over-talking dialogue with each other, about God-only-knew-what, at max decibels, without ever seeming to pause for breath. (If Michel-Ange hadn't witnessed it first-hand he wouldn't have thought such a thing possible.)

And, as a bonus, the two ladies came equipped with vast quantities of string-tied, overflowing, and sometimes even leaking (!) Louis Vuitton (!!) "hand" luggage, which required constant visiting and which thus very soon got deployed, half-opened, all over the forward portion of the plane.

Their three kids – an unlovely mini-riot of vicious little snot-nosed brutes, all appearing to be in the 8-10 years-old range – yelling, crying, fighting, laughing, shouting, jumping, and (Michel-Ange strongly suspected) pissing and shitting all over the seats, into which the harassed Balkan air girls tried, with only indifferent success, to, from time to time, re-afix them.

Thus, the brutal bottom line (as Jenni-faire would have said) was that this single VIP Malarian family had quickly managed to transform the theoretically snooty First Class area into an instant Third World slum – a hellish Hieronymous Bosch-ian cross between Paris' *Gare du Nord* and the Central Market in Kinshasa.

In short, this was no fit *habitation,* however temporary, for a finely brought-up *Petit Prince Du 16ème...*

So, after being airborne for a suitably insupportable length of time, and after a couple of restorative glasses of Bulgarian champagne (which, despite their being served to him with most enticing glimpses of Balkan *décolletage,* tasted vaguely like fish paste that had been left out in the tropical sun too long), Michel-Ange un-clicked himself, extricated himself from the somnolent encroachments of Mijneer-Captain-Engineer-Ambassador-Admiral van den Kakhof, here, and his laboriously arrayed and re-arrayed electro/cyber manifestations – and stepped into the aisle. Ostensibly to "stretch his legs", but, in truth, in desperate search of some kind of escape. Literally.

To this end, he (as they said in his beloved old cowboy movies) "moseyed on back", stepping gingerly over, around and through this pre-teen African civil war being enacted with frightening precocity in the aisle, smiling fixedly all around, *"Pardon, pardon, merci, merci,* hah hah", pulled aside the curtain, and beheld the, er, "aft" section.

And it was here that he beheld a bonus "Good". For this section of the plane – about 85% of the Tupolevian total, in fact, and the part that *Jenni-faire* referred to as "toilet class" – was practically empty. Indeed, just about the only paying passengers appeared to be: seated amidships, by the wing, a group of seedy and disheveled male alcoholics who could not have been anything but international journalists. And *way* in the back, just forward of the actual *toilettes,* was an aged *baboushka,* dressed (more like encased) in a sort of black sack, either passed out or *actually dead...* and it occurred to a slightly alarmed Michel-Ange that, if indeed she was alive, she might have left Laina, bound for Paris to (perhaps) visit relatives, fallen stone asleep, neglected to wake up during the Paris stop-over, and now would be re-deposited back in Laina, in a state of utter cluelessness.

Still, the old lady was of no particular concern of his. Nor, apparently, was she to the bevy of Balkan Airlines beauties who congregated in the aft galley, chatting merrily in their impenetrable para-Russian dialect and, in at least two cases, doing their nails.

Surveying this near-empty aft-section situation, Michel-Ange, no dummy he, mused (accurately) on how the world was not exactly teeming, at the moment, with candidates eager to visit the current multi-ethnic shooting gallery of the Balkans generally, and the dreary little tentatively-post-commie backwater of Gryaznia in particular.

Well, the Balkans' (and their airline's) loss was Michel-Ange's gain, and he glided into the first available row of three empty seats, lifted the arm rests, gratefully arrayed his skinny frame thereupon, and allowed the relatively soothing thrum of the engines masking the endless blah blah from the p.a. system, to ease him into blessed unconsciousness.

This flight from Paris to Laina lasting a mere three hours, he was only awakened twice. The first time was to be served "luncheon" which (at least here in toilet class) consisted of a kind of stew in beet sauce, which Michel-Ange managed to get down with the aid of a can of Bulgarian "Astika" beer – which went some way to mask the beet sauce but which, in the end, tasted pretty much as its name suggested.

And the second time was when one of the Balkan dollies tapped him on the shoulder to offer him a cutesy Balkan Airlines key-chain – a little green rubber bird – which she seemed to think he was terribly in need of. He was so astonished to be woken for such a thing that he accepted it with bewildered gratitude.

Laina International Airport is, in fact, an old converted Warsaw Pact air base that had been originally placed, for defensive purposes, in a dry river-valley outside of town, so that its approach is one of the diciest in the world.

In any case, when the pilot suddenly started his Stuka-like dive, it occurred to Michel-Ange that he didn't want to get off the plane *behind* that African moblet up in first class, so he reluctantly unbuckled himself and staggered forward to reclaim his seat up there. Where he had to cram himself into the tiny space left unoccupied by the by-now utterly splayed Mijneer/Emperor/Santa Claus/Commander/Secretary-General van den Kakhof, who was being near-slapped to consciousness by one of the more athletic Balkan girls.

Smart move on his part, because even allowing for a little impromptu mini-ceremony of lingering (on his part) *mwa-mwa-mwa* goodbye kisses with the assembled already-regretted Balkan Air Girls by the exit door, he managed to leave the fat Dutchman and the Malarian Ambassador and his impossible family in his wake and de-ass (as he had once heard Lee Marvin say in a war film) the Balkan Experience before anyone else. Leading his own parade, (so to speak).

9

WELCOME TO GRYAZNIA

Michel-Ange emerged into an ominously dark and gloomy Laina International Arrivals Hall where he had to squint to make out what was what.

In the residual Stalinist murk he could discern four queues, all of them for the moment, mercifully, empty: One for "Gryaznian Nationals", another for "Strangers", one for "Crews" and one for (believe it or not) "Diplomats and Peoples of International Importance".

Michel-Ange, armed with his still-virginal Diplomatic Passport was damned if he wasn't a P of I-I, so it was into this station that he directed himself. (Glancing quickly behind him, he could see the exemplar of human dilapidation that was the Malarian family galumphing his way, followed by the bedraggled mini-gaggle of international journalists, with the fat-headed Dutchman bringing up the rear – no sign, alas, of the poor, ancient *baboushka* – would she be flying back to Paris shortly? Good luck to her. Michel-Ange again congratulated himself for his prescience in getting off the plane first....)

Although the immigration officers seated at the three other desks appeared to be *compos* and variously preparing their stamps and reference ledgers and whatnot, (priming themselves for... not much, really, unless further impending flights were expected), the young officer assigned to "Diplomats and Persons of International Importance" was... *don't tell me... merde... asleep*. Stone *out*,

"*Ka-oh*". In fact, he was actually *snoring*, and a bit of drool even appeared to be leaking onto his blotting pad. (Which was, when you thought of it, what a blotting pad was *for*, really, but still....)

Michel-Ange gazed upon an abundance of tousled black hair – not, come to think of it, *all* that unlike his own – in some perplexity. An AK-47 with a 30-round magazine in it hung prominently from a hook in the fellow's booth, and Michel-Ange did not feel like doing anything rash so soon in his nascent career. So his very first act as a diplomat was to clear his throat. Diplomatically. *So* diplomatically, in fact, that it produced no result whatsoever. Awkward, this. In a rather less diplomatic escalation, he took his blue diplomatic passport and, with its bound corner, tapped the blotter sharply about a millimeter from the fellow's nose....

Now this *did* deliver the goods:

The young Gryaznian border guard sprang to alarmed life, rather after the fashion of a prodded sleeping crocodile. Fumblingly adjusting a peaked *casquette* adorned by the flamboyant post-communist white-green-and-red eagle emblem of the new Gryaznia on his aforementioned tousled conk, the poor fellow fairly shouted *"Chto?"*

"Chto?" was something Michel-Ange was reasonably confident he could handle. Indeed, one of the things he clearly remembered from his exhausting trek through the supremely mis-named "Russian Without Pain" odyssey was that *"chto?"* meant "what?" in Russian, and, thus, was probably similar in Gryaznian.

And even more miraculously, he was pretty sure he had a reply ready, which he delivered with a tinge of pride:

"Euh, d'aubry diéne, mon cher grajdanin – Ya diplomatt françouseki, y votte moii diplomatischesky passeport!", which was supposed to mean, more or less, "Euh, good day my good citizen – I am a French diplomat and here is my diplomatic passport". Apparently enough of this cod "Frussian" penetrated the

consciousness of this still half-asleep flower of youthful Gryaznian profession-alism to cause him to take up Michel-Ange's documentation and frown at it.

Presently the fellow – abjuring French altogether – barked at him in ur-English "You bringk nefa?"

Nefa? Who the hell might *she* be, now? Michel-Ange turned to see if there might be some woman in the immediate environs who might plausibly answer to "Nefa" but all he saw was the motley African contingent pulling up, so he again dug deep into his hazy recollection of Painful Russian and came up with:

"Niet, ya, euh, poutchestovatte vodinochkou. Y ya nié znayou nobodé nasvanyé Nefa." – which he hoped meant something like "No, I travel alone. I don't know anybody named Nefa."

The face of the young border guard – who had just glanced over Michel-Ange's shoulder to behold the Africans awaiting him – now became clouded with consternated frustration. *"Niet, niet"* he said, now rubbing his thumb against his forefinger knowingly, "Nefa, nefa!"

Ah!, merde! suddenly remembered Michel-Ange – the "nef" was the name of what passed for local currency, and "nefa" would be its plural. Well, not only did he not have any, he'd yet never even so much as *seen* any. For that matter, he didn't even have a clue what the damned things might be *worth*. If anything. In white man's money, that was. But at least now he could riposte:

"Ah!, nefa, of course, *bien sur,* nefa – *your* estimatedly honorable *monnaie.* *Euh, niet* – I desolatedly have but none."

"Den wat," the fellow persisted, continuing to rub thumb and forefinger, but now tapping his neb with his other forefinger, "you hev?"

"Ah. *Et bien.* I have these *francs Frantsouskis* – " and with a twinge of residual national pride he produced from his inside blazer pocket a wad which turned out to be the hefty sum of FF12,820. These were meticulously counted out by the Gryaznian and 11,820 of them were returned with (Michel-Ange couldn't help noticing) a certain reluctance. Leaving two 500-franc notes conspicuously lying there on the still-moist blotter...

Affairs now seemed to have reached an uncomfortable hiatus. Which Michel-Ange eventually attempted to re-animate:

"Euh, izvinitié, but I believe that you have dropped those two there – " he said, pointing to the two lonely-looking 500s.

The young border guard stared at the bills as though they were alien objects (which, of course, they technically were) that he was just now seeing for the first time – like perhaps bits of colored plaster that might have just fallen from the ceiling (a common enough occurrence under communism, and not yet rectified in the five years since its supposed disappearance).

But the lad snapped out of his reverie and announced: "No, *niet.* Zees – " he tapped the bills "eez tex! Hairport tex!" He then swished away the thousand francs into an open drawer under his counter, from where he then briskly extracted a wondrous assortment of stamping devices with which, having now gathered up Michel-Ange's passport and other documents, proceeded with a great flurry of *biff bing bang bong*-ing to legitimize and, indeed finalize their mutual dealings.

"Bolshoye spassibo! I ham very hopping ve are again meeting!" the young *mec* beamed at Michel-Ange. But then his smile vanished as he turned his attention and gestured to the Malarian Ambassador to approach, with his brood.

Michel-Ange knew he must move away from the booth, but a residual twinge of outrage nagged at him to hang about a second: "Yes, that's all well and good, but... I mean, I'll be needing a receipt for this, for this, 'airport tax' – "

"Chto takoye?"

"A receipt. A... a... a... how would you say it – a, a *confirmation,* that's it – a confirmation – con-fir-ma-tion – " and he made a scribbling motion and pointed in the direction of the vanished francs "that I have paid this 'airport tax' – " *I can't believe I'm even saying the words "airport tax" – an "airport tax"... to enter a* foutue *country? Would anybody back home ever* believe *such a thing? (Much less reimburse me for it?)*

"Ah, da, da, qvitantsya! Daytye minya – " the young border guard's sudden smile indicated that he might have understood Michel-Ange's request, but instead of producing a justificatory receipt – a "qvitantsya" – he reached out of his booth and snatched Michel-Ange's passport. He found one of his recently-bonked stamps in it, and appended thereupon a little squiggle with his ball-point pen.

"YEST vot qvitantsya!" Apparently that squiggle constituted a receipt in Gryaznia. "So! Egaine, koot pie!"

This last was delivered with such finality, (and one of the Malarian Ambassador's wives was, in fact, beginning to actually shove Michel-Ange aside), that Michel-Ange had no choice but to swallow his aggrieved gobsmackedness. And move on.

Which he did, passing through a series of dark tunnels to emerge into a large, and seemingly empty, "receiving hall", in which one of four baggage carousels was squeakily operational.

As he stood wondering in some bemusement how the Central Africans, fat Dutchman and drunken international-journalists behind him were coping with the, hah hah "hairport tex", he eventually espied, among the trundling tied-together bundles-of-*merde* appurtenances of the Africans, his *maman's* Louis Vuitton case, rolling sedately, upright, sticking out like the proverbial sore thumb... *actually,* it stuck out like something else: once, after they'd seen the old American comic film at a "Féstival of the '30's" starring a funny fellow called W. C. Fields who used the expression "like an Ethiopian in the fuel supply", he'd asked Jenni-faire and she'd explained what it scandalously meant, and to Michel-Ange now, that was *exactly* how his suitcase looked, amidst all other detritus on this slowly-bouncing conveyor-belt.

He grabbed the thing and proceeded to, *dum-dum, dum-dum, dum-dum,* the "Customs and Importations" choke-point.

Which Michel-Ange approached, he thought, well prepared for: one of his mates back at *Sciences Po* had had a father who was a big *fromage* in the French Department of Customs and (delightful euphemism!) Indirect Taxes, and this fellow had reported that, according to his dad, the one absolutely sure-fire way to get oneself flagged by a customs inspector anywhere in the world was to allow oneself to make eye-contact with that official – so Michel-Ange now fixedly stared at his feet as he sought to pass before this cordon of dangerously under-employed-looking Gryaznian customs officials.

He could have spared himself the tactic, because not two steps into this mis-labeled "Green Lane", he was flagged down. By a woman customs officer. Well, "woman"... the painful fact was that she looked more like a Kodiak she-bear who might have just emerged from a Kodiak bear beauty parlor, than a human woman. She was about the stature – seriously – of one of your medium-sized professional wrestlers, and her black mustache just served to highlight the brightness of her crimson lips. Draped in an olive drab jacket and a tan skirt voluminous enough to serve as a 2-man pup-tent, she now grimaced at him and, waggling a sharp red-tipped finger, she spoke the two most dreaded syllables east of Vienna: "You! Kom!"

So, he "kom"-ed. And what the hell, he had nothing to hide – plus, he was a diplomat, right? *Exactement.* He heaved his suitcase onto a low table in front of the woman, and smiled at her. Diplomatically.

So did she. "Smiled", that is. Showing an expanse of gold teeth which caused Michel-Ange to want to don his sunglasses. But of course he was a diplomat, so he refrained.

"Hopen!" she barked.

He complied, whereupon she systematically unfolded and generally buggered up every one of his meticulously-stowed belongings. Finding nothing immediately objectionable, she unzipped the side-pocket and fished out the Polaroid snap of Jenni-faire posed enticingly in her racy and gartered unmentionables. You would have thought this Gryaznian Rosa Klebb had discovered a hidden microfiche of purloined atomic secrets, the way she held it up and scrutinized it:

"Kto eto? Who *dis*?"

"Oh. Haha! That is my young lady friend. *Fiancée* of me. Euh, *drooga minia*." and he even found himself fatuously pointing to a non-existent engagement ring on his finger.

"Ah, *Tvoya devushka* – girl-frent fram you! Oo-la-la, Kriézy Harse Sialoon! Placea Pigallé! I like ziss!" and she turned and showed the suddenly porn-ified Jennifer to her male colleagues, telling them in Gryaznian, "Check out this Frog's whore – not bad, eh?"

And now a half dozen Gryaznian customs officials gathered around Michel-Ange – who could *feel* his ears turning red – to congratulate him, shake his hand and pat him on the back. As though he had just won the lottery.

Ho-la-la my poor Jenni-faire, Dieu-merci you're not here at this moment....

Replacing the photo, now this customs-lady-from-hell pulled out his flask of cognac, opened it, took a taste, and pronounced it *"Da!, da!* Goot! Goot *Frantsous* visky!" and *it* got passed around his new circle of Gryaznian customs friends, who all took a taste.

A veritable little fête we suddenly have going, here....

When his cognac had completed its round, the customs lady put the now-practically empty flask back in the suitcase. But the wretched woman was not yet through with her mischief: now unzipping his toilet kit, she fished out his little bottle of Monsieur Rochas eau de cologne, opened it, sniffed, and pronounced *it* also "Goot!", splashed some behind her cauliflower ears, and declared:

"Hokays! Ent dis far mi! I keep! You giff! Far mi! Tenk you, tenk you, *merci Moo-sié!*" She slipped his *flacon* of Rochas after-shave into her uniform jacket pocket, and – *what is she doing?* – stepped out from behind her low table and – *NO! NO! this is* not *happening!* – planted a horrible great smooch right on his (what Jenni-faire called) kisser. *Plein le bec.* "Velcome to Gryaznia, *Moo-sié!*" Michel-Ange thought he might pass out from all this.

But he didn't. Instead, they together squashed his now-thoroughly jumbled and banjaxed suitcase shut, and she and her customs colleagues gestured and ushered Michel-Ange triumphantly through the green line and into the arrivals halls, practically as though he were some kind of returning national hero:

"Come égaine, any times, delighted to hef you!" – *Mon Dieu. Quel histoire. Quel bordelle. What a strange business this Diplomacy wheeze is so quickly proving to be.*

The actual dimensions of this "arrivals halls" were difficult to ascertain because the whole place was befogged by the smoke from just about everybody he could see inside here, who was smoking – (so *this* was where smoking had gone, since it had been practically banned in the West....)

Plowing through this indoor smog, searching for, well, he wasn't sure *what*, exactly, but eventually he spotted someone that brought him up short, rather:

A seriously mustachioed (the Full Stalin, here – none of your "wispy female Border Guard") giant of a fellow in what arguably *might* be called a uniform: a white peaked *casquette* like those the ticket-takers on the old Paris Metro used to wear, a black double-breasted tuxedo jacket over a maroon shirt that looked like it might be made of vinyl, topping a pair of Roumanian jeans and sandals worn over gray socks...

A get-up that Michel-Ange might have been prepared to appreciate with what he liked to think of as his trademark cosmopolitan equanimity had the whacking great fool not been holding a piece of shirt-cardboard upon which had been written, in bold black Magic Marker:

MICHELANGELO

OF THE FACE OF THE RAT

Horrified beyond restraint, Michel-Ange rushed – to the extent he could, schlepping his wheel-less suitcase – up to this horrible manifestation and cried,

"Vuy Ambassade Française?"

"Da! Da!" the chap replied, with an innocent enthusiasm which Michel-Ange did not (then) know was, in fact, vodka-fueled.

"Well, give. Me. That – *foutue* thing!" and Michel-Ange snatched the offending sign from the giant's unresisting hands, ripped it into as small bits as he could and dropped the resulting confetti underfoot. He'd had to endure some of this same sort of thing in school, but he certainly hadn't expected it *here*, of all places.

Erecting himself as much as he could (which brought him up to about the level of the fellow's Adam's apple), Michel-Ange continued,

"Now look here, *mon vieux*. I should like, before anything else, to make one thing perfectly, crystallinely clear. My name is Michel-Ange Grenier de la Fassederad. *Not* 'Face of the fucking rat', for Christ's fucking sake. Got that? You *pige? Ponimayetyé"*

"Da!, da!" the fellow agreed, grinning, "You him! You har him! You har him who is ném 'De face of de rat'! *Horosho!* Is goot! Ve go. Yes?"

"No! Not yet, *putain!* Not until we get this straight! Now, once again, I am 'de la Fassederad' – not bloody 'the face of the rat'. *De la Fassederad* – in fact, it may interest you to learn that we are, indeed, descended from Richelieu – do you, my dear fellow, in fact know who Richelieu is? Or was, rather?"

The fellow just stared at him, blankly.

"Alright, better let's forget Richelieu. Let's start again – " By now Michel-Ange was standing with his legs apart, hands on hips, in a rather farcically challenging stance before this behemoth. "Now, *mon brave,* I know it couldn't have been you – so be so kind as to tell me who it was who instructed you to write 'the Face Of The Rat' on this *carton*."

Rather to his surprise, here the fellow actually seemed to catch Michel-Ange's drift. He replied. "It vass He who iss de Boss – de *Pataronne*."

"What? – you mean the Ambassador?"

"*Kto? Him*? Heh heh. Vat kind idee is dis? *Niet* – de *boss* – *Mwa-tee-eh.*"

"What? Who?"

"*Mwa-tee-eh, Mwa-tee-eh – Konsul – y* de *Komertzialny!*"

"Aaaaah, *Moitié....*" Michel-Ange remembered from one of the colonel's briefings – or was it *Mlle.* Bergère's – that the French Embassy in Laina came equipped with a Consul fellow who went by the name of Jean-Loup Moitié and who doubled as a "Commercial Attaché". It was *him,* then.... In any case, Michel-Ange figured there was not much more to be gained by further berating this poor fellow, so he closed his eyes for a second, exhaled, and adopted a different tone:

"Alright, listen. My dear *monsieur.* As long as we are becoming acquainted, here, may I ask you, euh, well, ... may I ask... *who exactly are you?*"

"Ah! *Da! Moi. Ich. Ia* Ivan Pomeshanskiy Ivanov."

"Excellent. Excellent. Ivan. Well, how do you do, Ivan, I am ravished to have the pleasure of, euh, yes, all that... and I, as you now know, am *Monsieur* Michel-Ange de, de, ... well let's not go through all *that* again – you can address me as *Monsieur* Michel-Ange – "

"*Da!* Michelangelo!"

"*D'accord*, why not. Anyway, my dear Ivan, let me ask you something else... what, exactly, is your role?"

The fellow, who just smiled impassively, gave no indication that he realized that a question had been put to him. *Ho la la...* In fact, the giant seemed keen to grab the Vuitton and get the show *en route,* but Michel-Ange stood his ground and pressed his point,

"Wait – what is your job, Ivan? What. Do. You. Do?"

"Ah, 'do'! *Da, da,* I do – ent how do *you* do?"

Bon Dieu, give me strength – "No, what do you do for a living?"

Ivan appeared eager to get into the swing of things: "*Da*, yes, I leaf pretty goot. Not byad. No complaininks. Tenk you, *spassibo...*"

Michel-Ange again consulted the recess of his brain reserved for "Russian-Without-Pain" matters and managed, *"Vot... vuy... rabota?"*

"Ah! *Da!, rabota ti muy!* Now *ia ponimaiou*. Onderstand! Vell! I – " and now he seemed to get stuck just as he was getting started. "I... I... vell, I... I do... *oll tinks* far Iembassy Frantsous. Oll tinks," and there he would have been happy to leave matters, but judging from Michel-Ange's frown, he could see that more was required, so he attempted to accommodate,

"*Viéry, viéry* match oll tinks. Vat *Moosié* ent *Madame poslanets* – Iambassador – esk me, I do. Vat *Moosié* Mwa-tee-eh esk me, I do. Vat *soldati légionari* esk me, I do. I do oll Frantsous tinks! I vill do olso, now, oll tinks far you! Far you, Michelangelo *kulturni!*"

Well, alright then. Despite everything, and despite the unmistakable burlesque quality of their colloquy thus far, Michel-Ange decided he liked this apparent *homme-à-tout-faire* Ivan Ivanov. As *La Mère* Thatcher had not all that long ago observed of Mikhail Splotch-head, he sensed that here was a man he could do business with.

"Well, my old, this is just splendid," Michel-Ange declared, as he reached up to clap Ivan Ivanov on the back. "So what now?"

"Now? Ah, now ve are talk potatoes! Now ve go Iembassay Frantsous!"

Ivan clapped and rubbed his hands together, picked up the Vuitton suitcase and, Michel-Ange trotting behind, strode out of the gloomy, smoky murk of Laina International's Arrivals Hall, to rather recklessly cross the anarchy of the drop-off ramp, and, pointing in the direction of an adjacent car park, proudly announced: "Dere! Dere your car!"

10

IVAN POMESHANSKIY IVANOV

What he was pointing to eventually revealed itself to be a large shapeless metal mass that was so devoid of any identifiable color that at first it had seemed invisible to Michel-Ange. But as they approached the thing, he was able to focus on it and as he did its total hideousness became better defined. Brick-shaped, perched on four thin wheels, it looked about the size of a smallish, rolling warehouse, and was about as square.

"Tam! Dere! Is nineteen-heighty Volga!" Ivan Ivanov pronounced it "Wolga" and he sounded as proud as a horse trainer with a winner. "Honly 300,000 kilos! Strong like tenk!" This made him guffaw. "Honly two fram six cyilyinders is operatingk, but still go goot! – vell, goot enuff!" and here he waggled his hands in the universal sign for *comme çi – comme ça* "More den less. Makes much smoke, but dis hokays – prove de tink workingk!"

Bordelle de merde, thought Michel-Ange, as Ivan loaded his case into a trunk commodious enough to hold two or maybe even three trussed-up KGB "subjects of interest". Michel-Ange entered the co-pilot seat of this misbegotten relic from the ramshackle "glory days" of the sclerotic joke that had been the Soviet "industrial revolution".

"How *splendide,*" is what Michel-Ange *wanted* to say but, confident that Ivan Ivanov was beyond sarcasm, he contented himself with "So what's this Moitié fellow been given to drive, then?"

"Mwa-tee-eh? De grate *Konsul-Komertzialny?* He hev Lada. Not so olt like dis Wolga – I tink heightey-height – but more smoll ent honly is working one cy-ilyinder. Fram four. Bot is strange tingk – von day is working *dis* cyilyinder, ent udder day is working *dat* cyilyinder – bot oll times honly vun! Is ironic, no?"

Michel-Ange had been watching, fascinated, the fellow's accompanying hand gestures which, in truth, resembled a man milking a cow. "Without a doubt."

"*Da,* de Mwa-tee-eh Lada not so olt like dis Wolga but olso go slow, makes *bik* noise like smoll Ilyushin. Ent *olso* makes much smoke."

"I see. So am I to understand, then, that this superior... *Wolga* will be my as-signed car?"

"*Da!* Far you!"

"And do I further understand that it is – that you consider it – better than the car assigned to Monsieur Moitié of the... '*komertzialny'*?"

"*Da, da.* Niattingk to compare. Dis more bietter."

"Well that's formidable. But may I ask how this happy, if somewhat surprising, state of affairs came about?"

And Ivan Ivanov proceeded to impart to Michel-Ange a convoluted but still mostly coherent explanation of how this Volga had, until this very day, in fact been his, Ivan's, personal property, but that, in anticipation of Michel-Ange's arrival he had convinced the Ambassador to buy it from him at a "*viery* goot price" – *good for who?* wondered Michel-Ange....

"And what will *you* be using now, that you've sold us your car?"

"Oh, dunt vorry of me, heh heh heh, I... vill *miénage*... dis ent det. Dunt vorry of me!"

The traffic – which, except for the very occasional AudiMercedesBMW, was mostly shabby old Russian trucks and shabby old Russian cars, including shabby old Russian FIATs – got heavier and slower as they approached their exit from the Laina Ring Road, and Michel-Ange felt the fetid interior fug of this definitely well-lived-in conveyance rather catch up with him. So he went to roll down his window only to find that the handle was missing – there was just a gaping great hole in the door-plastic with an iron rod visible inside it.

"Euh, *Monsieur* Ivan – I don't know the situation inside *Monsieur* Moitié's car, but inside mine, here, the fucking window *manivelle* appears to be missing."

"Ah! – hah hah hah' *Da!* Hiere! Tek diss!" And he yanked off *his* window-crank and handed it to Michel-Ange. "Is *sém*! Use!" Michel-Ange complied and sure enough, it popped right on, and did the trick. Down came the window.

Well, why not?

"And what," resumed Michel-Ange, his elbow now sticking out the window and welcoming the nice, polluted springtime Gryaznian air on his face, "does the Ambassador drive?"

"Aaah... hmmm... Vell, he hef *ofitzialny* bleck Citroën, most late madiéle, XM-Turbo, viss enti-booliet vindows – booliet-proof! *Viéry* fancy, *viéry* oo-la-la, bot... he dunt use it so match."

"Oh really? And why is that?"

"Vell, becos he hef udder car, hees *own* car – even *more* fency ent oo-la-la. Iss olt femily praparty, belongk in femily long time – is like Fabergé eck viss veels – 1957 Facel-Vega cabriolette, viss DeSoto V-eight motor. *Fantasticheskiy!*"

"A what?"

"Facel-Vega. Dunt exist no more. Too costing match, even far *kepitelistiy*. Bot bee-*yoo*-tifool car! – bee-*yoo*-tiffool! Bleck ent yellow. Ent oll eight cyilyinders is vorkingk – fast like MiG-29! Ent – " and here he turned and looked at Michel-Ange reproachfully "iss, or vass, *Frantsous* car! *You* – fram oll pipples! – Attaché fram de *Kulturni*, should knaw of it!"

"Well, I never heard of such a *bagnole*." Michel-Ange pouted. "Before my time, and anyway I'm not such an automobile aficionado. But, so – what, the Citroën just... *sits* there, then?"

"Niet. Miénié miénié times *Madame* Vife fram de Iambassador is usingk – I drive far her if she is eskingk. Ent udder times, vell..." and here he turned a little coy "is me usingk. *Viery* useful far de *ofitzialny* Iembassy affairs, you are understandingk...."

"Oh yes. I am understanding." What Michel-Ange was in fact beginning to understand was that the daily workings of the French Embassy in Laina depended to a not-inconsiderable extent on the resourceful energies of one Ivan Pomeshanskiy Ivanov. "So is that it? Or does the Embassy own any other vehicles?"

"Haf corse! Poojo P4 'jip' of de *Léjionari* – *Frantsous Armia* four-pie-four – "

Of course! The two Legionnaires. Michel-Ange had forgotten about the Embassy's two Legionnaires, who, he now remembered the colonel telling him, were on a kind of indeterminate loan from their parent unit, the airborne (*Parachuté*) task force that was France's Bulgaria-based contribution to NATO's "Operation Deliberate Force".

"But dey dunt's lets me to tatch it. Dunt's lets *nobodies* to tatch it. *Shtrengt verboten!*"

"You speak German, Ivan Ivanov?"

"Leettle. Smoll. *Ein beeschen.* Is common lengvich in dese parts of worldt," he ended, rather enigmatically.

Having, it seemed to him, rather exhausted the multiple but not-unlimited fascinations of his new embassy's motor-pool, Michel-Ange now endeavored to learn a bit more about this increasingly intriguing *mec,* Ivan Pomeshanskiy Ivanov himself.

"So for how long have you worked for us, then, Ivan? For *Frantsous posolstvo?*"

"Aaaah, *etwa...*" again he waggled a hand, *mas-o-menos*-y "Fife years – since fall-ingk of Olt Régime. In Olt Régime I voss tenk driver/meccano, T-72, Gryaznia *Pipples Armia – kapral*. But ven komt de nieuw régime, now oll ievrybawdié is suppose be *kapitalisiy*, ent *pouf!* oll Armia *guiniralny* soddenly be *directoryie na kampaniye,* ent, *heh, viéry* strange, is no more mah-nié for *Armia – no mah-nié! –* so miénié of us are qvitted out. Bye-bye *merde-gavno Armia!* Houra! Houra! – now evriebodié is civilist, now evriebodié is free far to mék mah-nié!"

"I see – but how did you end up specifically with *us, les Frantsous?*"

"Ah, dis iss tenks fram my dear fodder-by-laws."

"Ah, *le papa* of your *Madame* Ivanov – I mean, Ivanov-na?"

"Da. Vife. Viery nice, strongk cahntry girl."

"Sorry?"

"*Cahn*try, cahntry – fram de *cahn*try – her fodder in olt régime voss miénager off calliéctive diéry farm, next to hour tenk base – det how I meeted Grasha – my *Madama* – Ivanovna – her fodder voss Party miember."

"Were you a Party member in the old régime, Ivan? Just curious."

"*Niet.* Vass not *mnié-mnié-mnié*-mendatorié far *soldati* – or even *kapralni* – be Party miémber – honly for *serzhanti* ent *ofitzialni.* Enyveys – " he interrupted himself, re-lighting a pestiferous old half-smoked cigarette that he fished out of the Volga's commodious ashtray, using a primitive rope lighter of a kind that Michel-Ange had only ever seen used by Portuguese migrant workers, in his childhood. A few puffs and Ivan continued with renewed enthusiasm,

" – so, fodder-in-laws fram me, now in nieuw régime, viss diéry farm, vell, diss diéry farm dunt hev so goot re-*mnié-mnié-mnié*-re-*fridgeratsia,* ya? Olt, bed eqvipment. So, match meelk – *maloko* – is goingk bed, rottingk. Oy, vot do?, vot do? Oll pipples dey is tell him must trow meelk evéy, trow evéy meelk or vill mekingk ievrybawdié sick. But he say *niet,* he hev idee – *beek* idee! – Mék chizzes fram rotten *maloko*! Diss his idee! Ent he do! He mék! He mék beek steenkingk chizzes. In begin, nawbadié is vanting, ievrybawdié is tellingk him nawbodié is vanting hees steenkingk chizzes – "

This seems like a pretty damn convoluted answer to my question of whether he was ever a Party member...

" – but den in Laina, von day, in wisit to GLUM diépartimient store to try sell chizz, he bump into olt Iambassador Frantsous – ent diss olt Frantsous men he smell piéckage under harm of fodder-in-laws ent sayz *'Oh la la*, wat ess dees nice smellingk?' Ent he is to itt a leetle piss von diss steenking chizz, ent he like it *viééééééry* match, ent he tell fodder-in-laws he like diss chizz ent so dey mék more friendlié *palaber*, ent den he signingk contracti viss Frantsous Iambassy. Ent sints den fodder-in-laws hev goot chizz biziness in oll Laina – first he sell chizz to oll iembassies fram odder cahntries, den in oll Gryaznia! Ent det how I meet pipples from Frantsous Iambassy, ent dey gif me job! Ent *vwala!*"

"So your father-in-law is the... Big Cheese, *hein?*"

"Hah hah hah, iss goot choke, *Moosié* Michelangelo! I hem likingk you, *Moosié* Michelangelo, you iss viéry ironic – is goot."

Well, "goot", then. Alright. *Tres bien.* So Michel-Ange had now appeared to have made his first Gryaznian *copain*. Progress seemed to be occurring here, as they entered downtown Laina proper....

The Volga's two working cylinders farted rudely as Ivan Ivanov downshifted onto the *Boulevard of The Grand Revitalization* (which had been, just five years ago, the *Boulevard Fidel Castro*). And *paf! bing!* into a most horrendous near-stationary traffic jam. Of, as previously-noted, smoke-belching Russian military-style trucks, quivering little Lada/FIATs, and more than the odd braying and shitting donkey-cart.

Putain, thought Michel-Ange, how could they have traffic jams... *in Gryaznia?* Where he had more or less imagined that people got around, if at all, in, yes, donkey carts. Which, he noted in some alarm, he might be reduced to if this much-abused Volga clutch and three-speed manual transmission decided one day that they'd endured just one traffic jam too many....

Eventually, after about an hour of stalled, suffocating, eye-tearing be-smogged horn-beeping bedlam, (during which, for a five-French franc coin – having not yet had a chance to acquire any of these alleged local nefa – he grossly overpaid, from a smiling and be-grimed urchin who approached his open window, for a kind of sesame-seed covered bread thing which he shared with the beaming Ivan Ivanov), they eventually turned onto a broad avenue called "3 Oktobr Prospekt".

In fact, "broad" did not really do this thoroughfare justice, as it seemed almost as wide as a soccer-football pitch. This was due to the fact (which Michel-Ange had already learned at the Lyçée Janson de Sailly) that Stalin, aping Napoleon before him, had a strong penchant for extremely wide arteries in Soviet cities – and those cities which he appropriated into the Soviet Union's orbit. And this requirement, by both those famous philistines, had nothing to do with city-planning aesthetics, but rather with the physical practicalities of crowd suppression – specifically, Napoleon had wanted avenues wide enough to allow horse-drawn cannon to be able to turn around quickly (in order that the cannon barrels should point, ahem, in the "right" direction), and later Stalin insisted on the same amplitude for his T-34 tanks.

So this explained the enormous avenues and boulevards of little Laina, (more firmly appropriated into the Stalinian orbit than which no city had ever been), and specifically its imposing "3 Oktobr Prospekt", the street address of the sprawling French Embassy, at whose front gate the farting, smoking "Wolga" now pulled up.

11

THE FRENCH EMBASSY COMPOUND, LAINA

The French Embassy in Laina turned out to be more than just a single building – in fact it was a group of them, hence "compound".

Which began at a massive iron gate, giving out on a graveled driveway that diverged, with one branch circling around to the left towards a deceptively large

garage/workshop, after which stood the imposing old 3- (really 2 ½-) storey *chateau* that served as both the French Embassy and Ambassador's Residence – and on either side of which were attached two wings, (which made the old *chateau* look like it had two giant prefab ears), one of which housed Moitié's Consular office, and the other the Ambassador's actual office. The other branch of the driveway circled around to the right, towards three parallel single-storey rectangular residential/admin bungalows.

The two branches of the driveway in effect enclosed a fairly large (about 600 square meters), rhomboid/parallelogram lawn. On one corner of which (the corner nearest the gate) was planted an imposing flagpole flying the French tricolor. And in the middle of the lawn, a croquet set – the full *panoplie*: hoops, wickets and all – was elegantly, if quaintly, laid out.

Back at the gate – indeed right next to it – there stood a sturdy and commodious grey-painted "guard house" that looked, in fact, like a section of a toll station from the A-6 *autoroute* that might have been transported here intact, London Bridge-like.

From which now emerged a wiry little *métisse* (*café au lait*) French Foreign Legionnaire, in white *képi* and "parade" battle dress with the distinctive if incongruous red-tasseled epaulets, a fully-loaded black FAMAS automatic rifle slung across his back and a MAC-50 9mm automatic holstered at his hip, who represented ½ of the Embassy's security detail.

This was was Private First Class Martinho Meiavelha, who was born in Mozambique of a Portuguese father who'd been an alcoholic mechanic at the local Toyota franchise but had since died, and a mother who was a local Mozambican girl – now lady – who still worked in a pharmacy in Maputo (which had still been "Lourenço Marques" when little Martinho had been born there.)

This pleasant and obviously fit-looking fellow saluted them and indicated with a nod and a flick of the hand that Ivan Ivanov should shut down the Volga. A process which, while fairly uncomplicated and even rudimentary in most cars, proved more problematic in this case – indeed, it took the old "Wolga" almost a full minute of wheezing, hiccuping, farting, trembling, and generally making a whole metallic meal of the thing, before finally giving up the ghost with a melodramatic *"wssshhhhh-pop-krunk"*

During which performance, after acknowledging Ivan Ivanov ("Re-*ciao*, Ivan") he went around and addressed Michel-Ange through his open window,

"Bonjour Monsieur – So you are the new *patron* of the Culture? The guy Moitié told us about? – I believe your name has something of the rat – "

"Non, non, non – nothing to do with a rat – or rats. Nothing to do *at all*. This *Monsieur* Moitié seems to have been woefully misinformed. But by the way, a cordial *bonjour* to you, *Monsieur* Private First Class *euh, euh...*" Michel-Ange could proceed no further as, unlike their other comrades-in-arms in the French military, Legionnaires did not wear name tags – in fact, names *qua* names were

pretty much mere notional formalities in the Legion – even when in cases such as Embassy duty, where they might have come in handy.

"Meiavelha, Martinho, at your service, *monsieur*, but everyone calls me Martin. Or better yet, Meia. Can I see your relevant *paperasse justificative*, please?" Michel-Ange handed over his bumf.

"Ah yes – de la Fassederad – yes... not rat... that Moitié!... Anyway, welcome to our little happy family, hah hah, *n'est ce pas*, Ivan? Hah. Have you been briefed on where you'll be bunking, *Monsieur* de la Faisan – ?"

"Fassederad – *de la Fassedard*."

"*Compris!* – Fassederad! Got it! *Bon*, Ivan, you know where the *Monsieur* goes, right? That's right, *chez* Moitié – and I'm pretty sure his half is clear of all, euh, evidence of previous *habitacion... Monsieur!*" With that, Légionnaire Meiavelha saluted, went to unlock and pull open the gate, and disappeared into his toll collector's guard house. While Ivan began the laborious process of re-starting this "Wolga". During this process, a suddenly suspicious Michel-Ange put it to his new colleague/*copain*,

"Eh, Ivan, what did he mean that he's 'pretty sure' that my, *euh*, lodgings are 'clear' of previous... whatever? Who else resides here, other than their Excellencies *Monsieur* and *Madame*, and this *type* Moitié?"

"Ah! Hah hah! I vill 'splain to you. Iss a *beetchen*, how say, a leettle beet, *mnié mnié mnié – delikatniye....*" By now he had re-coaxed the Volga back to noisy life, and he advanced about twenty five meters on the right fork of the driveway and pulled over, letting the engine idle (if you could call the pained clattering "idling").

"*Mnié mnié mnié*, you see," continued Ivan Ivanov, "here iss de tingk: you are seeingk over dere bik buildingk, beeyootiful *chateau* buldingk? Yes?" *Yes*, agreed Michel-Ange. "So, det iss Iembassié ent olso Iembassié *reszidentura*, ya? Da?" *Yes*, agreed Michel-Ange.

"Now, over dere," Ivan pointed to the three longish parallel rectangular single-storey buildings off to the right, "is tree houses for the *cadres*, de, *mnié mnié mnié* personnels. So, de first van, dere, de van most close to us, is vere lives *Legioneriye*. Ent de mittle van iss vere is livingk *Konsul/Komerzialniye* Mwa-tee-eh in de vun haff, ent, until you comingk today, udder haff voss empty. Now, vill be far you, bot before, voss empty. *Vershteh? Ponyat? Compristo?*

"I think so, yes. But what was the Legionnaire fellow referring to when he said that my, er, part of the house should now be 'clear'?"

"I kom now to ziss. Ziss iss *delikatnyie* part. *Eh,* iss not so issy to say, bot I vill do best, becoss I em tinkingk det I am likingk you, *Moosié* Fassrat – *Moosié Kulturniy*."

"Yes, yes, I'm all hears, sorry, ears –" *Mon Dieu, what can be so horrible that this fellow is making such a pig's ear of telling me?*

"So, hiere it iss: hiss Excellentzia Moosié de Iambassador heff so viery laffly beeyootiful *oo-la-la Madame* Iambassadovna vife, bott – ent hier is de bott – like oll mens, he iss olso likingk a *beetchen*, a little beet of oo-la-la on de side, *da?* – *nalevo* ve say it—means 'to de left', heh heh heh. Ent in case of Moosié de Iambassador, de most simple *nalevo* iss sometimes my, ehhh, my *mnié mnié mnié, kollegua...* Irina...."

"Who?"

"Irina. Irina Vozhbuzhdena. Yongk lady who iss vorking here as Iambassador's *secretaria* ent ollso far Mwa-tee-eh – she iss Iembassié *récépziya-priyemnoy* ent *gieneralniy administratzia*."

"Yes, I've been told of the existence of this person."

"Da, *kollegua menia* – togezzer ve kip Iembassié goingk, heh heh – she iss viéry pritty ent, eh, *simpaticheskiye,* bot sometimes ken be, howyousay, *mnié mnié mnié, temperamentniye* – get qvickly excited. But *viéry* nice – "

"Right, got it, I *pige* – so this young lady, in addition to being a charming, excitable personal assistant to everybody – " *will that include me, I wonder?* "also provides, shall we say, aid and comfort to our hard-working Ambassador. And what about *Madame* the *Ambassadrice?* Is one to assume that she is sophisticatedly okey-dokey, as they say, with this situation? Or are things rather more old-fashioned and is she kept in the dark by all concerned? One – meaning I – should, I believe, be made aware of the state of play, here, lest one puts one's foot egregiously into something... untoward..."

It was unclear just how much, if any, of this rambling question Ivan Ivanov understood, but he nevertheless ventured:

"Ah, *da*, de *Madama* de *Iambassadorina* – her. *Da*. Vell, she iss – like I sayingk before – bee-yoo-tiful. Bot ollso kamplicated. I dunt know if she iss knowingk about Irina. Bot probably, maybe, yes. Vimen is ollvays knowingk about every tings. *Alvays. Knowingk* – dunt know how – but dey hev de six sensingks, like miégic. Bléck miégic. Vich iss vy iss alvays such priablems for us mans. But," he brightened, "you must not trabble yourself about *Madama* – I hem sure det she vill be likingk you – like vill Irina!"

"Well, how reassuringly French this all sounds – even to charmingly and internationally include your own rather *raffiné*, if I may so say, attitude, *mon cher* Ivan."

"*Da, da* – oll viery goot far iévrybodié, bot now I em guessingk det dey, *Moosié* de Iambassador ent Irina, now dat you har arrived, dey must be moving deir... deir 'aid ent kamfortings' to... vell, I dunt know far ciertain bot guessingk vill be movingk now to *Komunalniye Recreatziy* House...."

"The what?"

"De turd house – dere, de one most close to Iembassié. Iss place *rieservalny* far *gueneralny mnié mnié mnié recreatsiy* of oll iembassié pipples, vich minns *légionariy*, Mwa-tee-eh, ent av course sometimes Iembassador heemself – viss Irina... ent," Ivan's eyes turned down for a rare abashed moment, "sometimes ollso me."

"You! Well, who would have thought! You!" Sarcasm did not come naturally to Michel-Ange, but after only a couple of hours in this *foutue* place, he found himself quickly becoming more comfortable with it – despite his certainty that it would land stillborn, "And how does *that* happy circumstance come about?"

"*Veeeell*, you must be understandingks," Ivan continued in his role of louche Man Of The World, "I em livingk outside fram Laina *centralnyi*. On udder side of olt Lenin Ring Road – sarry, now 9 *Naviémbre* Ring Road – een smoll flet. Sometimes iss no *electricitesche*, place hot – or kolt! – miény times smellingk bad, ent miény times vife, *zhenschina*, Grasha iss in bied mood – *soooooo*, den Ivan vantingk to stay someplace udder, someplace more, *mnié mnié mnié*, *gemütlich*, so I ollso come hier. To relex!" Ivan now in a slightly alarming music-hall fashion elbowed Michel-Ange in the ribs and concluded exuberantly, "Ent, now, *you* may be usingk! Iss nice place – you vill like!"

"No doubt." Michel-Ange returned to a previous nagging thought, "But if where I am to stay has recently been, er, *stayed* in, who, if anybody – " and he found himself turning rather uncharacteristically fastidious, "is responsible for, you know, I don't know, well ... *cleaning* the place?"

"Hah, *da* – dis iss bizness fram Irina – ez head fram *administratzia*, she hef team of yongk girls who do diss vork, klin oll iembassié buildingks – viery *mnié mnié mnié*, ie*ffi*cient!"

"Again, no doubt. Alright," Michel-Ange suddenly realized he'd had more than enough of this Volga's fetid interior, "So! What do you suggest? Should I go first to present myself to the Ambassador, or better first to let me investigate my living quarters?"

"I tink first you go your house, ent I vill tell Irina to tell Iambassador det you arrive. Niever goot idee to mék sarprise far Iambassador – viss heem you are niever knowingk *reactzia....*"

So they drove the short distance to this middle bungalow, and, while the Volga again went into its wheezing and shuddering shut-down ritual, they de-arsed the blessed thing.

"De Mwa-tee-eh Lada not hier, he gung somevere – he hev *miénié commertzialniy* affiairs – *Konsularniy, ech!*, not so match – " Ivan said as he pulled from his tuxedo-jacket pocket an envelope containing five individually-marked – but in Cyrillic! – loose keys, which he gave to Michel-Ange,

"Dese far you – diss van key iss far hier, yore housings, diss van iss far houtside guétte, if far sam reason Légionaryi not dere. Diss van iss far Iembassié frant door, diss van iss far *Recreatsiy* house, over dere – " he indicated with his chin the bungalow next to them, "ent *finalnyie,* diss van iss far frigo in de *Recreatsiy* house. So. Plizz. *Nat to loose* – most difficult far de *duplicatsia.*"

"Goodness. And with the key to this Volga, here, that will make six. *Eh bien!* And regard! – " cried Michel-Ange with genuine delight, "look!, I have just the thing for them!" and he produced his little green rubber Balkan bird key chain. *Et voila!*

Ivan now produced from his blue-jean hip pocked a jumble – about the size of his head – of his *own* keys, from which he chose one and he unlocked the Moité bungalow, which would henceforth be the *Moitié/de le Fassederad* bungalow.

Ivan switched on a light as they entered a small central ante-room, with a mirror and small table against the opposite wall, from which two discrete little studio apartments gave off, to the left and right. As Ivan opened the door to the one on the right – the non-Moitié side – and deposited the Vuitton suitcase inside, something suddenly occurred to Michel-Ange:

"Eh, would you mind, Ivan, if before you leave and I get settled in here, if we went and had a quick look inside that... recreation villa, there?"

So they did. The went over and had what Jenni-Faire's English pals called a "shufti" at this little French embassy oasis of R+R.

And, truth be told, it revealed itself to be not all that awful. Indeed, at first glance, it looked rather reminiscent, (if slightly less opulently so), of the recently-enjoyed comforts of the Aer Lingus' "Gold Circle" First Class Lounge back at Charles De Gaulle. The unforgettable line by Slam Pickers in "Dr. Strangelove" (one of the many films which had helped to form whatever English Michel-Ange commanded), uttered upon inspecting his Air Force survival kit:

"Shoot! A fella could have a pretty good weekend in Vegas with all that stuff" sprang to Michel-Ange's racing mind.

Instead of dividing the space into two separate smaller flats like his and Moitié's, this whole "recreation" bungalow was laid out like a single well-appointed (as envisaged by a *bourgeois* bachelor) living space, with at one end a full bathroom (tub/shower and w.c.), and at the other end what appeared to be a complete kitchen.

In addition to what one would normally find in a living room, such as sofas (one of which pulled out to make a bed), chairs, coffee table, bookshelves, TV, hi-fi, and even a not-all-that-smallish bar with a couple of upright bar stools, there was, squarely plonked down at the bathroom end, one of those miniature soccer table games that the French called a *baby-foot* and the Anglos rather mysteriously knew as a *"fusbol"*. Oh, and a jarringly un-French dart board adorned the wall against the bar.

The other wall decorations seemed more haphazard than "co-ordinated", and consisted mostly of framed posters – viz., Alain Prost in his F-1 Williams-Renault at Magny-Court; the 1992 French national rugby team; Johnny Halliday at the *Olympia;* a copy of the famous painting of Catherine Deneuve as "Marianne"; and Gérard Depardieux as Obélix from the film *"Astérix le Gaulois"*. There was also an Alpine ski poster from the tourist board of Haute Savoie; a photo of General Leclerc leading some Free French Sherman tanks down the Champs-Élysées at the liberation of Paris in '44; as well as the inevitable, if practically life-size, image of Brigitte Bardot wearing not very much. And finally a plaque of appreciation for something-or-other from the Franco-Gryaznian Cooperation Society.

As Michel-Ange took all this in, Ivan Ivanov scurried about like a kind of semi-demented salesman, pointing out all the earthly delights of this hedonistic hideaway. Starting with the bottles standing behind the bar,

"Look, here you are findingk de finest of *internatzionalnyi* alcoholics – viskies fram England, Amierika, China, ent gin fram Italia, ent wodka fram Bulgaria, rom fram Venezuela – "

"And what's this?" asked Michel-Ange, pointing to a rather dodgy-looking olive-colored bottle with a label saying, simply, "Glüüt".

"Oh, det – " Ivan Ivanov stuck out his tongue and made a face, "Is alcoholics make fram *asparzha... asp... asparaguznyi,* fram Albania, taste like *merde,* sam girl giff to *Légionari* Martinho, *bleuh!* – bat kam, look hier! – " and he dragged Michel-Ange to the fridge which he unlocked with one of his *miénie miénie* keys,

"Look! – full fram bier!, Stella, Saint Pauli, ent, av corse, de best Gryaznyi pils, *Polarnia!* – oll dese tingks putted here by cleaningk girls fram Irina – "

Now he was presenting the television set, as though this were 1879 and he was unveiling the light bulb:

"Ent in de *televizyia,* hev de most *moderniy* cassette Vee Hash Ess machine, ken vatch notty-notty veedéos fram Roumania, (Légionari dey hev!), ent on kabel Tévé ken get *miénié miénié kanalnyie* – de two Gryaznia State *kanalnyie,* ORT fram Moskva, Beebeebceeb fram Ooo-Kah, ent haff corse, Frantsous Internationalnyi. Ollso CNN, ent – " and here he made the universal gesture of "oo-la-las" with his two cupped hands hefting something invisible in front of his chest, "even samtimes, ven you are luckies, ken gettingk RAI fram Italia, vich is alvays hevingk de gurlies viss de oo-la-las ent vearingk no clotheses! – "

With this happy news Michel-Ange felt that his quick survey had more than sufficed, but the good Ivan was not so easily deterred – as he now directed them to the bathroom area, and specifically the *douche*:

"Far de hot vater, iou most turningk dis smoll tingk here, ent turn off ven finitsh – sém tingk viss your douche in your *apartamient* – "

"Yes, *merçi* infinitely, Ivan, this is all splendid – but please, let us now go back to this place of 'mine', I've seen enough here – very *magnifique* indeed – *trés* Club Med! *Allez...*"

And so they regained the Moitié/de la Fassederad *résidence.*

The set-up therein was fairly spartan but definitely functional – the furnishings and *décor* being what you might call " '70s American Motel With Brezhnevian Touches":

The two identical "studios" contained: A double bed, a round table with 4 chairs, a sofa, a coffee table, an *armoire*, a chest of drawers, a mirror, a kitchenette with sink, coffee machine and small fridge in one corner, and a plastic enclosure with w.c., and shower in the other corner. And a couple of lamps and a waste-basket rounded out the *ameublement*.

The only apparent difference between the two little flats appeared at first glance to be that Moitié had a picture of a beach scene in Tahiti on the wall behind his sofa, while Michel-Ange had picture of what looked like the Bolivian Andes, or Peruvian – anyway, one of those places where the local women liked to wear bowler hats.

Figuring it was alright because Ivan was there as cover, Michel-Ange ventured into Moitié's half, where he immediately thought he detected the tell-tale tangy trace of marijuana-air, but he couldn't be certain – he wasn't *that* much of an expert in that department.

Moitié might be absent for the moment, but his existence *qua* existence was nevertheless most definitely in evidence – with his shirts, socks and *(phwah!)* y-fronts scattered about; what appeared to be a Gryaznian empty pizza box on his bed, and a mini-mountain of dirty dishes in his sink. The vision of Moitié's haphazardly discarded "smalls" prompted to Michel-Ange to ask,

"Eh, Ivan – is there any kind of laundry *sérvice* available, or do I wash my laundry in the sink, here? Or what?"

"Ah, *da* – I voss forgettingk – every Manday marningk, you liv diérty clotheses on biéd, ent Irina girls vill ték – bringk bek sém night. Goot, yah? Ent sém viss garbages – dey ték, Manday marningk!"

"Excellent. But another thing, before you disappear – " something was niggling Michel-Ange as he surveyed his new "home", "What's the situation of

the *téléphone* in this *barraque*? I only have one telephone number, and it's for the Embassy itself – "

"Ah, *da*, de *téléfon*...." Ivan, seated at the flat's table, suddenly got cagey. "Iss *complicatzia*.... in olt régime, voss easy – *téléfon* dunt exist – honly de *Douchka* hev téléfon – "

"The who?"

"*Douchka* – de Gryaznia *KaGéBé* here iss koll *DéGéBé*– smoll far *Direktsiya Gosudarstvennuy Bezopasnosti,* dey kip olt ném, bot ve say *Douchka* – enyvey, under olt régime, *niet, nitchevo* téléfon far *nobodié*. But den, viss new régime, sodden koms téléfon – houra! houra! – everybodié so heppy, everybodié iss now on téléfon, neeeeever stop tokkingk – *blieh blieh blieh, tok tok tok,* far couple of yiers. Bot den," now Ivan threw his arms in the air, miming an explosion, "*Pam!* – since lest year, *kaput*, téléfons dunt vork. De new 'pablic-privat' hah hah dunt mék me laff! téléfon kiampanié kém to ték oll fones evéy far *reparatzia,* dey say, dey say *reparatzia*, bot – *niever kom back! Pouf!* Nabadié hév téléfon no more! So now, here, ve only still hev *originalniye* téléfon fram de Iembassié, ent det nomber iss still vorkingk, ent..."

And now Ivan tapped his nose in a gesture which Michel-Ange understood was meant to convey something devious but whose exact coded relevance to the current situation evaded him,

" – ollso, Mwa-tee-eh hev van of dese new, *mnié mnié mnié, cellularniye* télé-fons. How he get dis I dunt know – nabodié know, bot I sink fram Péris – but he hev. Are you hevingk?"

"No, *mon Dieu,* no." *I'm putting off the inevitable as long as I can.* "But don't the people here have those cellular things? In Paris everyone does – except me."

"Hier? Niet. Hier, awnly *gengksteri* ent *Douchka* hev. Ent even gengksteri begin to get rid – chipper to hev beek tattu on far-head det say 'I hem gengksteri'! – ent ollso dunt vant pipples tink dey *Douchiski*!"

Michel-Ange, who didn't much care either for technology *or* telephones, lost what little interest he'd had in the matter, took a deep breath and said, *"Bon.* Well, I think that's about it, for now, I think I can take it from here – you've been an absolute *champion*, my dear Ivan, and I thank you infinitely."

"Da, hokays – it vas most *plaissir* to receivingk you, *Moosié* Michelangelo – ent ve vill see itch odder most frequentlisch, I em olvays around Iembassié ent I em olvays et your siérvices...." and they shook hands. As he walked out the door, Ivan called back,

"Keys in Wolga – ent de car peppers is in de back – if you hev trahble, kom see me – I fix! *Au ra-vwa!"*

Michel-Ange closed the door and took stock of his new lodgings. Taken altogether, there certainly wasn't much in this bungalow of "his" and Moitié's to cheer the spirit or ennoble the soul, (and Michel-Ange shuddered at the fairly surreal thought of introducing Jenni-faire into such a living arrangement), but as a student Michel-Ange had happily survived worse, and this would certainly do as accommodation for a, ahem, *célibataire* such as he was. Once again.

12

IRINA VOZHBUZHDENA

It was now five p.m. On this day, which, it seemed to Michel-Ange, had started about 10 years ago, and in another galaxy. But he resisted the urge to flop down and try out this new bed for a quick sieste. He had, euh, Official Business to attend to.

But even before that, he needed to re-become presentable, so he "sorted himself out", after his fashion: brushed teeth, tried to hammer down his hair, pitsticked his pits... the minimum, perhaps, but the normal. *The minimum normal.* Availed himself of the w.c. – well, *that* worked, at least. Good good good – (*without* that *working, you're sunk before you even start....*)

He took awhile to find the right key with which to lock his new home, but eventually he was, in the words of Jenni-faire, "good to go". He set out on foot to the Embassy/residence/*chateau*, about thirty meters along the driveway.

The imposing gray stone *chateau* had once belonged to an old aristocratic Gryaznian family, the last scion of which, an old duffer called Count Igor Dubbelhof, had been interrupted and shot dead as he pottered in his garden (the area now over-grown by ash trees behind the Embassy) by those... "social reformers" of the original *Douchka* in 1946, when Soviet T-34 tanks were pretty much the only traffic on the streets of Laina, and Gryaznia was becoming a "People's Republic of". The count's family had been arrested and the countess had been raped in jail and died there from "internal complications", while the two children had grown to adulthood at hard labor until freed and exiled to Austria in 1956 when the briefly-successful Hungarian uprising had temporarily panicked the Gryaznian communist regime into partially emptying its own little gulag.

(Back in Paris the Quai d'Orsay harbored an ongoing, if low-priority, apprehension that the Dubblehof heirs would one day emerge from the ether of exile to claim back their *chateau,* but so far this hadn't happened, and the French Government continued to quietly occupy the premises while paying a derisory rent to the Laina City Government. The rent was derisory because at the time of the country's unexpected de-communization five years previously, amid the administrative chaos that engulfed the relevant department of that Laina City Government, the one and only thing it remained clear on was its strong desire to avoid at all costs the litigation of its pre-communist property).

Michel-Ange had been vaguely informed of all this by the Colonel and *Mlle.* Bergère, and as he approached this stately old stone rebuke to history he mused,

Pfff... Communism – what a thing, eh? Fucking shambles. What was that expression of Manu's? – "Encore une affaire qui marche" I've only just got here and already "history" and "progress" are beginning to depress the merde out of me... freaking me out, *as Jenni-faire says...*

He mounted the Embassy's front door steps and pressed the doorbell. Nothing. Tried again. Still nothing. So he fished out the relevant key from those Ivan had given him, and let himself in.

And, of course, he found himself immediately standing in the Great Entrance Hall of the *chateau* itself. All marble underfoot and dark wood paneling all around; smelling pleasantly of perfume and furniture polish. His footfalls echoed as the strode about, wondering if anyone was *in camera*, so to speak.

He called, in a tone that he hoped sounded diplomatic, *"Allo?"* and opened a door and beheld the book-shelved walls of a library, and almost immediately bumped into a pneumatic female form, which had evidently just roused itself from the library's leather couch and was hastily attempting to exit.

Thus did he become acquainted with the nubile, to not say winsomely zaftig, if reputedly not-uncomplicated, Irina Vozhbuzhdena, Ivan Ivanov's colleague, and "General Administrative Associate" ("GAA" in French bureaucratese) of the *Ambassade Française à Laina.*

About 30-ish in age, the first two things that struck one (or at least which stuck Michel-Ange) about Irina Vozhbuzhdena, were 1/ her Jessica Rabbit-like curvaciousness and 2/ her voluminous hair, which was of the garishly un-natural burgundy wine color that only seems to be found on women in ex-Soviet Bloc countries – a color which cannot be said to be soothing on the eye but which is undeniably arresting. The combined effect of 1 and 2, indeed, was so overpowering, that it rather distracted one from the essential prettiness of her face. All in all, she was, undeniably, quite the *nana.*

She was wearing a short, pale-blue dress decorated with purple flowers (and not, it seemed, much else, save a pair of quite high heels), and she'd been in the process of smoothing and pulling it demurely down – it having hitched up during her just-interrupted nap – when she'd collided with Michel-Ange at the library door.

Her momentary discomfiture did not, however, deter her from seizing the initiative. "So! Iss you?" she demanded.

Attempting a smile, Michel-Ange replied "Well, if you're meaning the newly-appointed Attaché for Cultural Affairs Michel-Ange Grenier de la Fassederad, then I'm happy to confirm you in your *perspicacitée, mademoiselle."*

"Ah! Otchen horrosho!" she cried, and now embraced him, planting three big wet *mwa mwa mwa* smackeroos (as they said in old Jimmy Stewart movies) all over his stunned face.

"Euh, spassibo, euh, énormément," he stammered, "absolutely ravished to be here, and to meet you.... But where, if I may ask, would the Ambassador be, would you have any idea?"

"Ah, pfouah!" She flipped up both hands in disdaining dismissal.

"Pardon?"

"You me heerd – His *Eggzelentzia* is *viéry* biezié – he is evéy playingk de britch vis his frent, Breeteesh *Eggzelentzia* Saire Bazil Knott-Protheroe – " Amazingly, she managed a decent approximation of the British Ambassador's actual name, but for the rest, *mon Dieu!*, Michel-Ange noted with alarm that her accent was of the same "Boris and Natasha Badonov" impenetrability as Ivan Ivanov's.

He ventured, "*Britch?* You mean the card game, bridge?"

"Da, da, de guémme. Guémme of carts, most *tiérrible* deeficulties far playingk dis guémme, he try titch me van time! – only can be vinningk iff completeliy ent totalniye cheatingks – so is par-*fecte* far diplomati. You are playingk viss dis guémme?"

"Euh, no, thankfully not. And what about *Madame? Madame* the *Ambassadrice?"*

Irina made a face. "Iss still slippingk. Olvays iss still slippingk. Ontil de night times, ven she diésapeer. *Viééééry* straynche vomans. I strongkly riéccament you not be bozzeringk viss her – more bedder you bozzer viss me!"

"Ah – hah hah, yes, no doubt!" Michel-Ange laughed a touch nervously. "Well, then, what about the other fellow, my house-mate *mec,* Moitié, I believe is his name – would you know of *his* whereabouts?"

It occurred to Michel-Ange that, although perhaps not strictly according to protocol, it might be tactically a smarter move on his part to first get to meet this mysterious, this apparent man-about-town, Moitié – and leave the Ambassador, whose game of bridge he could always say, if so pressed, he had not wanted to *dérange* – for later.

"Mwa-tee-eh? Dunt know if he dere now, bot he iss beingk more times den iss, *mnié mnié mnié, normalniye* far eemportant *diplomatishskiye Consulatniki* piérsonalitié, een place colt, excuse mi pliss, "Post-Liénin Baccarat Café". If you ken belief such a ném-ingk of such place. *Pfouah!"*

Again with the *pfouah!* But, more to the point, this "Post-Lenin Baccarat Café" sounded intriguing. To a degree.

"Hmm. And where does this Café place find itself? I might like to venture a voyage there and meet this *Monsieur* Moitié – please explain to me where it is – "

"You?! By yourselfs – alone? You who hes niever been inside ceetié Laina? Hah hah hah, mék me laughing. You vill gettingk losted – or arriested – or kilt! – far sure nawbodié vill niever findingk you égain – ent den how ve explain to your Mama, eh?" She then, of all things, slapped his shoulder, "No! – you vait here fife *minutiye*, I fix me hup a leetle beet – put on smoll lipstickingks – ent I kom viss iou!"

"Well, *b'en, merçi, alors.* I shall remain rooted to this spot, faithfully awaiting your return."

"Vat?"

"Never mind – just go. I wait. *Bolshoye spassibo.*"

13

MOITIÉ

Eventually she reappeared – with her lips now the same alarming color as her hair – and, flapping her arms like a young, rather racy mother hen, willed them both out the door and towards the Volga.

"Have you a car, Irina?" Michel-Ange ventured, going for what he thought might be anodyne small-talk.

"*Da,* hev – olt Moskvitch," and apparently to prove this she abruptly pulled a pair of windshield wipers from her voluminous fake-Gucci handbag and waved them in his startled face "bot iss today een garatch – I kip dese so garatch robbers dunt ték! Now –" she pushed him towards the Volga's driver's door "drive. Ent I vill show you. Ent be carefuls, dunt hit pipples."

The Volga wheezed itself to life, and he adjusted the mirrors – an operation that unexpectedly proved athletically demanding as he kept having to jump out and run forward to adjust the side-views which were, unaccountably, mounted on the fenders above the headlights.

It took a couple of violently abrupt stall-outs before he got the hang of the clutch, but eventually Irina guided Michel-Ange out the gate, where he stalled again, but this time because he'd been put off by Pfc. Meiavelha's salute – was it intended as friendly mockery, and if so, was it in fact all that "friendly"? Or was it, rather, the correct protocol? And if *so,* how was he supposed – expected – to respond? (Michel-Ange had never actually "saluted" anyone in his life... not even Colonel Mincemot....)

In the event, he sort of waved wanly at the Legionnaire and he tentatively lurched out onto this 3 Oktobr Prospekt. That proved to be one vast slow-moving traffic jam, oozing forward like a jerky lava flow – trucks, vans, Ladas, trams, all tormented by a plague of scooters and motorbikes darting demoniacally in and out of the pollution and racket.

As Irina, her animated face about six inches from his, "guided" him in a series of drill sergeant barks that would have warmed old Mincemot's heart, Michel-Ange got the feel of this old Volga... which drove unlike any vehicle he'd ever handled before. It felt as though he were at the wheel of a large motorized mattress, whose external contours he could only vaguely apprehend – that reluctantly responded to every command, whether from pedals or steering wheel, a half-second or so *after* he'd given it. Unnerving wasn't the word for it.

Eventually they mercifully left the choked and choking 3 Oktobr Prospekt and effected a series of manoeuvres in unlovely downtown Laina, (which appeared to be, at least at first glance, little more than an undifferentiated agglomeration of gray, boxy, crumbling Stalinist concrete). Their progress involved, at one point, a hair-raising U-turn, but she finally guided him to a *Put* (Avenue) Georgi Antonescu and ordered him to park at the only space "available" – which meant half the Volga protruding into an intersection. "Dunt vorries – dunt farget, you hev *diplmatiskiye* namber pléttes – ken park verever!"

They found the "Post-Lenin Baccarat Café" about half a block down on Georgi Antonescu, and entered through a saloon-style set of swinging doors.

The place was got up to resemble a wild Gryaznian approximation of an American diner, and was thus, beneath a profusion of garish tubular neon, configured into separate booths, each with its own little retro jukebox. (Amusingly enough, Pink Floyd's "Wish You Were Here" was thumping through the establishment's sound system.) And along one entire side, instead of an American diner's lunch counter, there ran a long bar – of the alcoholic kind. Behind which a large, bald, but heavily mustachioed fellow who looked like he could have just stepped out of a vodka ad was slicing lemons. Irina and Michel-Ange greeted him with a nod as they entered, and he unsmilingly nodded back.

Moitié was not difficult to identify, inasmuch as he appeared to be the only patron. (The place technically considered itself a night spot, and it was still only late afternoon.)   Moitié was seated at a booth near the back, seemingly engrossed in tapping into his then-relatively novel, black, brick-like "cellular" telephone.

Young – he appeared to be about Michel-Ange's age – with a blank, expression-less, roundish face, Jean-Loup Moitié was, (also like Michel-Ange), a fit-looking fellow, though a good two inches (five cms) shorter, with haphazardly-cropped blond hair brushed all together to form a little quiff above his forehead. He was nattily got up in a tweed sports jacket over a maroon turtle-necked shirt, and sand-colored corduroy trousers. And suede desert boots on his feet. Al-together, he could have, at a stretch, passed for a real-life Tintin, albeit an up-to-date 1994 model (and thus without the old-fashioned golfing plus-fours). And, at the moment, an uncharacteristically aggravated Tintin, as he could be seen frowning and jabbing at his apparently unresponsive phone-device with increasing belligerence.

As Irina and Michel-Ange approached his booth, he sensed the presence of intruders and ceased his fruitless ministrations. He put down the phone, took a long swallow from the bottle of Polarnia beer that he had before him, and looked up, his face back to its normal blank expression.

Irina kicked things off: "Zhan-loo!, *bon-zhoo* – I'm sarry to destierbe, but I bringingk for you to meet your new *callegua,* new *Kulturniye* attaché, Michel-angelo de, de – "

"That's alright, thank you Irina – how do you do, *Monsieur* Moitié, I am de la Fassederad – just arrived."

Moitié permitted himself a small smile, "Oh, *that*'s the name – "

"Oui. Exactement." Michel-Ange, exercising, he thought, exemplary – even extreme – diplomacy, decided not to belabor that defamatory sign Ivan Ivanov had been holding for him at Laina International this very morning.

"Eh bien... take seats – " said Moitié, with an attempt at affability.

Moitié could (and often did) give off an aura of impatience, truculence and arrogance – indeed, he was generally possessed of what *les Americains* would call "an attitude" – but at heart he was not a bad sort. For he could also be amusing, brave, loyal (as opposed to trustworthy), and, above all, endlessly resourceful. In fact, if you caught him at the right time and in the right circumstances, (Michel-Ange would learn), this *type* Moitié could even verge on the *"sympa"*.

Over the next few days, Michel-Ange would sporadically glean the following intel about his young colleague (and, eventually, collaborator – if that was the word):

He came from Grasse, a town a little to the north of Cannes. Well, more to the point, his family did. No, sorry, his *papa* did. (His *maman,* a very nice and blameless lady, came from the Auvèrgne.)

Now, the thing – indeed, the *only* thing – about Grasse that is worth knowing is that approximately 99.98% of all the perfume in the universe is made there. (The 0.02% that is *not* made there reportedly emanates from clandestine shed and cave "labs" in Belarus, Moldova, Kazakhstan and other sundry "-stans", from ingredients which are mostly mixtures of farm animal fluids and purloined MiG jet fuel, and about which, rest assured, the less said the better).

Incidentally, one would imagine – indeed, one certainly would be justified in imagining – that the town that produces All The Perfume In The World would, perhaps, if nothing else, enjoy a pleasantly fragrant air quality, *non? Mais non, mon chèr,* or as Jennifer might have said, not in your bippy: for the rude fact is that the process of producing perfume is one that results in the most unholy pong this side of whisky-distilling.

So the town of Grasse (which literally means, interestingly, something approximating "fat lady", a datum which also does not bear too much pondering) *pue*-ed. Stank. And tourists who make the mistake of visiting there should not blame the natives – it's not, *contra indicia, they personally* who are responsible. Still, one must wonder to what extent living in a town which is permanently engulfed in such a *gershtunk* might not have negatively effected the sensibilities of its denizens as they perambulate through life...

... such as, for example, Jean-Loup's *papa* who had been an accountant at one of the local perfume sub-contracting laboratories. A hard-eyed, laconic sort, his main *divertissement* – other than his losing battle to try to interest his son in his passion for rugby, which the latter considered a load of pointless inanity – had been a card-and-dice game called *quatre vingt et un ("421")*

Moitié's *papa* devoted his Wednesday evenings at his "local" – an unlovely, if not downright sordid bistro/"tabac" called *"Le Coup De Foudre"* ("Love At First Sight"), where he played the arcane "421" with a regular band of fellow accountants from competing perfume establishments. It was all pretty raucus and freewheeling, and when they weren't winning and losing each others' money, they'd exchange professional secrets of each others' double-dealings, double-bookkeeping, double-dipping and general fiscal diddling. All to great *bonhomie,* if of a rather cynical kind.

It was thus that, at one of these smokey evening sessions back in the mid-'60s, one of *Papa* Moitié's colleagues let drop, *comme-ça, par hasard*, the little mini-bombshell of "insider info" that plans were afoot by a certain consortium to launch a gigantic multi-brand perfume "supermarket" on the Champs Elysées in Paris, (a mere stone's throw, coincidentally, from the famed *Fouquet's* where, as we previously learned, Michel-Ange and his Jenni-faire first met), that would be called *"Le Parfumarché"*. While his colleagues expressed predictably dour doubts about the *rentabilité* of such unseemly *"anglo-saxon, cowboy*-style" ambitions, Moitié Senior was more cannily visionary, and later duly sought out, in the greatest secrecy, the principals of this venture. Who he managed to talk into accepting him as a founding investor, to the tune of about half of all of M. Moitié's unofficial savings (the "official" savings, i.e., those known to *Madame* Moitié, remaining untouched).

And so, when, some ten years later, *Le Parfumarché* proved to be a smashing success and was going great guns, M. Moitié found himself *considerably*, if discreetly, wealthy.

That said, M. Moitié wanted, above all else – and wisely so! – not to alert the tax vultures at the government *Fisc,* and so he stayed on discreetly and frugally in Grasse, at his old accountant's job. But his financial double-life in Paris had led him to make... let's just call them certain useful *connections*. Which permitted him, (much in the same manner as de la Fassedard Senior – at roughly the same time, although of course utterly unbeknownst to each other), to give a little boost to his then wheel-spinning son.

For the terminally-bored young Jean-Loup had been finishing out his last year at the *Ecole Normale de Grasse,* from the last row of whose dusty classrooms he would keep himself awake by launching wadded-up spitballs. The intended target of these was always, of course, the hapless nattering *prof* up front, but his range was not always up to the task and thus his missiles would often land on the backs of his mates' heads and necks. Which of course endeared him not at *all* to his less-than-tolerant school chums, at whose hands an actual lynching had, by graduation time, become a distinct possibility.

But Jean-Loup was to be miraculously whisked away from all that tedium and incipient delinquency by his papa's timely intercession. Which had consisted of a few well-placed phone calls to ex-members of the socialist Mitterand government. (Which illustrated the main difference between the Moitié and de la Fassederad family approaches: Moitié, for all his opportunistic "capitalist" *behavior*, could never budge from his inherited, sentimental socialism – while the semi-aristocrat de la Fassederad was and remained a visceral anti-socialist).

So *Papa Moitié*'s interverntion had resulted in: 1/ a couple of rather pro-forma interviews of the professionally-coached and cleaned-up-for-the-occasion Jean-Loup with mid-level flunkies at the Quai d'Orsay – most emphatically *not* Col Mincemot or anyone even remotely of his ilk; 2/ four weeks of international and economic "orientation" at the *Centre d'Etudes Diplomatiques et Stratégiques* on the Boulevard Murat in the 16th Arondissement in Paris (again coincidentally, not *all* that far from de la Fassederad Senior's opulent flat on the Avenue Foch); and 3/ *pouf!* Jena-Loup Moitié found himself appointed as Commercial Attaché at the French Embassy in Laina, *République de la Gryaznie....*

Where he had been for about ten months, now, beavering away at... well, nobody, either in Paris or here in Laina, was too sure at *what*, exactly, but at least... well, he was *à votre sérvice... Usually* he was, that was... when he was around...

... as he was now, blank-faced before Michel-Ange and Irina. In his hangout, this Post-Lenin Baccarat Café.

Although Moitié was quite sure he hadn't invited anyone – indeed, *he* was the one who'd been importuned and interrupted in the middle of navigating his cellular phone device – nevertheless some unspoken, residual sense of decorum nagged at him that he was supposed to be in some way the "host" of this suddenly-contrived meeting, so he again forced himself into affability and asked,

"You'll join me, then? *Ça va* with beers? Irina? – Fassederad?"

Irina smiled a *"Da"* and Michel-Ange said "Good idea – and call me Michel-Ange – or just Michel – "

To this last Moitié just said "We'll see...." and ordered another round. When the new beers were brought, Michel-Ange found himself making the fatuously empty (as he in fact had not yet acquired any Gryaznian nefa) attempt to pay, but Moitié grandly waved him away with the dismissive " *'Commerce'* – that's me."

Michel-Ange attempted to take back the initiative: "Well, the brave Ivan Ivanov has admirably delivered me to my new *locaux*, contiguous, as you know, to yours, Jean-Loup – can I call you Jean-Loup? – "

"Moitié suits me alright."

"*Ca vas*. Anyway, he gave me keys and a general picture of the state of affairs – "

"Have you used any hot water in there yet? *Douche? Lavabo?*"

"No, not yet – hah hah, although I should not delay that activity much longer, hah hah – "

"Well, when you do, make sure you turn on the little black *bidule* on the pipe at the bottom and – most important – turn it off when you're done. The plumbing's still completely antediluvian around here."

"Yes, Ivan mentioned that to me. No problem. So what, if you don't mind my asking, are the commercial possibilities here? Are there any French companies here that require your intercession? How do you mostly occupy your time?"

Moitié pondered this last question for a second, wondering whether to reply "That's a bit personal, *non?*", but decided to let it drop,

"Well... the car and gas companies are here – but they were here before I arrived and were – and continue to be – doing just fine without me or any – " he produced a smirk, " 'intercession' on my part. To tell you the truth, such interactions as they require with their home bases in Paris they're capable of performing perfectly themselves, *merçi beaucoup.* Which is fine with me. In the meantime I occupy myself with smaller *besognes....* "he tailed off vaguely, before brightening and blurting "In *fact,* my biggest 'commerce' over here is with the sale of visas – I *am* also the Consul, remember?"

"Really?" *Did I just hear that correctly?*

"*Mais non!* – I was joking! Who would ever do such a thing? Eh, Irina?

Hah hah – "

"Heh heh, goot qvestion" ventured Irina, her eyes downcast and reddening a bit.

"And what about you, then," resumed Moitié, " 'culture' – what the hell form will *that* take, *hein?* What's the deal, exactly, with culture? Are we buying or selling? I don't quite get it – but maybe that's just me. What's the angle? How's it going to work, Fassederad?"

"Well, nothing firm yet. We have some ideas – but I'll certainly keep you *au courant* as things develop...."

"*Ouais, c'est ça* – you do that. We could certainly use a bit of *divertissement* around here... isn't that right, Irina? *Hein?*"

Again she mumbled, a small abashed smile on her red lips, "Viss-out doubts."

Moitié drained his beer, suppressed a belch, patted his flat stomach, stretched, looked around, clapped his palms down on the table and announced,

"*Bon!* Well, my friends, if you don't terribly mind, I am desolated but I'm afraid I must resume my duties, here..." and he waggled his cellular phone at them.

And with a remarkable lack of further – or, *any* – concluding niceties or salutations by anyone, Irina was bundling hereself and Michel-Ange out of the Post-Lenin Baccarat Café and back into his homely Volga.

"So what now? Do you think?" asked Michel-Ange.

"Bek to Iembassié. I sink you ken be needingk paireheps a restingk. Or, if Moosié Iembassidaor – or even Madama – is bek, iou ken do yore *introductzia* – *normalniye* should be doingk before Moitié...."

And as they got in, she unaccountably kissed him on the cheek. He turned and looked at her, obviously surprised, but said nothing. For her part, she smiled and said, simply, "I hem heppy you are here, Michelangelo!"

As they made their way back to 3 Oktobr Prospekt, Michel-Ange noticed that he'd be needing gas soon, which reminded him that he still had no local *fric,* so he asked,

"Listen, I don't suppose my *Carte Bleu* credit card will work over here – "

"*Such Frantsous criedit cart?* Hah hah hah! Dunt mék me laff! Ah, no. – Hiere in Gryaznia, honly Wisa – you use Iembassié Wisa criedit cart."

"Right, but I'll still need to change some francs for some nefa – where do I do that?"

"*Normalniye* you do viss Moitié – Consulate siervice, afficial rét of exchientch... but iff you dunt vant he knowingk yore bizinesses, ent you vant *bietter* rét of exchientch, den you ken do viss Ivan Ivanov – he viery *discretzia* ent mek *viéry* goot exchientch *calculatzia!*"

"Right, *merçi bien*. Ivan will be my man, then...."

14

THEIR EXCELLENCIES

Arriving at the Embassy compound, they were saluted in, this time by Legionnaire Staff Sergeant Wolf Schlechtermann, who'd replaced his junior colleague-in-arms Pfc. Meiavelha, at the gate.

Wolf – not short for "Wolfgang", not short for anything, "Wolf" *tout court* – Schlechtermann was a blond, set-jawed "force of nature" originally from the western side of the village of Mödlareuth, which had straddled the old East/West German border, and, in truth, he bore a more unnerving resemblance to Hardy Kruger in "The Wild Geese" than to a soldier in the French army.

Displaying no apparent curiosity regarding Michel-Ange, he waved the Volga through, and it pulled right up to the Embassy/residence proper, next to the official Citroën, besides which stood, apparently waiting, Ivan Ivanov – as threadbare-smart as he could be in his half tuxedo/half Paris Métro conductor's get-up.

"Hmm," allowed Irina "it sims *sam*badié ees een."

Leaving the Volga to shudder and wheeze itself off, Michel-Ange walked over to Ivan and said,

"Ivan, *mon cher*, Irina tells me you could change me some francs for your nefa – and I'll be needing, oh, at least nine or ten thousand nefa, can you...?"

"*Da, da*, ken do, far certain," and he pulled out a breadloaf-sized wad of greasy, faded nefa from his jeans arse pocket and was about to start pealing some off when... a loud slam was heard from the Embassy's massive front door.

Uh-oh – it was, apparently, *Madame l'Ambassadrice* exiting the premises, and she appeared in quite a purposeful hurry. Ivan Ivanov looked at her in alarm and re-faced Michel-Ange – a suddenly changed man,

"*Oich!* Ve finitch lader – far now, here, ték edvence, *dva* towsant nefa – I trast you!" and he pressed some of the nefa notes into Michel-Ange's paw, before assuming his version of standing to attention.

Madame l'Ambassadrice was, in fact, *Madame* Clothilde de Brest d'Anjou Duquon-Lajoie, known to her intimates as "Clo", (though the *hauteur*, not to say *froideur*, that she radiated rendered the very notion of her having "intimates" a rather remote one).

For a lady of her age (which Michel-Ange, who was really quite preternaturally handy at the arcane art of lady-age-guessing, made out to be mid-50s – in the *Mlle.* Bergère range, actually, although both ladies were thoroughbred mares from *very* different stables) she wore an all-black outfit that was remarkably provocative. To such an extent that Michel-Ange was (momentarily) at a loss as to where to look. *B'en merde alors:* extremely low-cut mid-calf-length form-fitting black satin dress with a slit on the side that went up God-knew *how* far, over seamed Dior *collants* and ankle-strapped high-heeled footgear of the kind that he had once heard Jenni-faire dismiss as "fuck-me shoes".

And this exotic packaging was rendered all the more remarkable by the fact that she emerged from one of the most blue-blooded families of Orléans, and had a *diplôme* from the Sorbonne in *philosophie,* so she was at least hypothetically not stupid... in fact, experience had taught Michel-Ange that such women were most definitely *not* stupid. Complicated, for sure. Dangerous, almost certainly. But stupid? *Jamais de la vie...*

In any case, this provocatively elegant *poule de luxe d'un certain age* was clearly On A Mission of some sort as she *clack-clacked* down the stone steps leading from the door to the driveway.

As she swept by them, she cast what one is led to understand is known in the trade as a "withering glare" in the direction of Irina, before turning her suddenly smiling attention to Michel-Ange, and to whom she directed the only words she would ever utter to him, to wit, *"Bonjour, jeune homme. Et au revoir."*

After Ivan open and closed the boot/trunk to satisfy her of its contents, she eased herself into the back seat of the Citroën, displaying a goodish expanse of thigh before pulling in her still-splendiferous legs.

Throughout this whole little *pièce de théatre* the semi-agog Michel-Ange hadn't said a word – and nor, for that matter, had Irina, who'd (again) kept her eyes lowered. But now, as Ivan Ivanov drove Her Excellency away Irina muttered, "So. Now you hev sin de *Madama*. Is goot, you thinkingk?"

What Michel-Ange was *thinking* was the French equivalent of *Holy shit! – what was* that *all about? – Now that's a damn handy project for* some*body...!*, but what he actually replied was a non-committal *"Effectivement...* undoubtedly, euh, a *présence."*

"Pfouah! Dunt know how okeh she iss in bet, but far sure she is not so okeh in de hed – ent olso not even, iff you iss eskingk me, so *oolala* lookingk as she *tink* she iss – but kom, let us find poor *durak* who iss married viss her – "

And she led him into the wood-paneled Bosnian-carpeted darkness of the Residence, with its fake Louis XV furniture and grandly-framed prints of Seurat and David on the high walls. Michel-Ange's first, previous glimpse of the place had been hurried and partial, but now he took the place in a bit more comprehensively:

For example, although he'd originally encountered Irina napping in the library, she actually commanded a surprisingly functional reception desk/console, right here, by the main door. Warsaw Pact "high tech" – which was to say, it had a touch-tone telephone with what appeared to be several buttons for branch lines. And what looked like a computer.

"So, this is your *bureau*, is it?"

"*Da, da* – fram dat chiair I hem boss off oll Iembassy."

"Glad to hear it – I see a computer. *Formidable.* Does it work? Do you know how to use it?"

"*Da,* it work... work okeh – " She made a face which cast doubt on how just "okeh" this might be "*Frantsous* 'Minitel' systiéma iss okeh – bat awnly prablie-ma iss viss canniection – samtimes-*da*, miénié times-*niet.*"

She deposited her sleek rump onto her rolling chair, and looking very much in charge, pushed a button on her phone.

"Iexcellence? *Da,* iss me, Irina – *da* I hem downstiairss, bot *niet,* I hem nawt alone – in fect, I hev hiere de new *Culturnyie* Attaché – *da, Moosié* Fass – Fass – *Moosié* Michelangelo, *da* – ken kom hup now? Da? *Tres bien, moosié!*"Then, pressing her lips close to the receiver, she tried to add *sub rosa* "Later, *mon séri* – " but Michel-Ange heard anyway...

Later, mon séri?

He was happy to disregard this last rather remarkable post-scripted transmission, and she was once again on her feet, pushing him towards the grand and winding staircase:

"Go hup! He iss expect! Ent dunt vorry about heem, de great Frantsous Iem-bassador – he iss olt poossiékiette!"

Once upstairs (which he had ascended at what could only be described as freight-elevator speed), he found himself facing a corridor on one side of which was a door with a little oval plaque on it that said "W.C.", and on the other side was one with a somewhat larger plaque which said "République Française". Fighting the temptation to enter the first, he knocked on the second. From which came:

"Ouai? – entrez, de Dieu!"

At this less-than-reassuring invitation Michel-Ange entered what turned out to be a quite trim office-type room, which Michel-Ange could see, (as the connecting doors were open) led to the actual Ambassadorial bedroom and bathroom and dressing room. So in addition to his official office downstairs, the Ambassador also maintained this other, quite practical, working area up here, with a massive pine-wood desk right next to his personal apartment. *Pratique.*

Son Excellence Armand St. Emilion de Pépinière Duquon-Lajoie, holder (somehow) of the *Légion d'Honneur,* turned out to have a long aristocratic face beneath receding hair, not unlike the distinguished French actor Jean-Pierre Marielle, though with rather more of a distracted air: Debonair yet vaguely harassed. The French have a word for this muddled, worldly languor that Duquon-Lajoie exuded: *désabusé.*

Now he surveyed Michel-Ange's tentative presence, raised an eyebrow, and smiling slightly – or was it a grimace? – lit a small cigar.

"Take a seat, my boy."

Problem was, there didn't appear to *be* any seat to take. As Michel-Ange looked around in search of some way to accommodate this latest preposterous thing he was being ordered to do, he heard,

"That's alright, don't bother. *I'll* sit, instead. You can remain standing, if you like." *Eh? That's certainly a new one for me....* And then, exhaling smoke as he leaned back in his Ambassadorial *fauteuil,* Duquon-Lajoie proceeded, pleasantly enough,

"So you are the new... 'cultural' type, are you?"

"Indeed so, *Monsieur l'Ambassadeur.*"

"Good. Good. I take it you've got all your requisite *paperasse* with you?"

"Yes *Monsieur.* I believe I need to still present myself to the Gryaznian Ministry of... of... excuse me, but I can't seem to remember its exact full name – "

"Yes, me neither... These people. Ridiculous title, I know, but 'Culture' is in there somewhere... along with a lot of other inscrutably extraneous *conneries* – but let's not bother with that now, Irina will take you there in good time. She knows those people – they're hers, after all. I take it you've already met Irina?"

"Absolutely, *Monsieur*. Her, and so far, in chronological order, *Monsieur* Ivan-ov, one of the *Légionnaires* – the Portuguese one, then *Monsieur* Moitié, then the other Legionanire, the sergeant, and then briefly, just now as she was de-parting, *Madame* the Ambassadress. But most *definitely* Irina, yes *Monsieur,* and most helpful indeed she is proving to be, if I may say so. *Monsieur.* "

"And she will find you a place for you to install yourself, downstairs. From which you will be able to conduct your... culturalities."

"Without doubt, *Monsieur*. I can assure you, *Monsieur,* I am not a complicat-ed person."

"I am delighted to hear it, de la Fassederad. And in fact, my boy, you will find that I also, within certain parameters, am not a complicated person. And if all goes well – and please do not take this personally amiss in the slightest – you and I should have only... tangential contact with each other. I am a strong be-liever in the Talleyrandian *'Surtout pas de zèle'* school of diplomacy.

"But having said that, as concerns our working circumstances within this Em-bassy, I have one advice to give you, and one instruction to give you:

"The advice is: be wary of young Moitié, there – I should endeavor to not mix yourself with his... affairs, if I were you."

"D'a-- d'aaaaacord" said Michel-Ange cautiously "I'm pretty confident I can accomplish that – but may I inquire why you counsel this? *Monsieur?"*

"Because he's fucking dangerous, that's why." The Ambassador saw Mi-chel-Ange's eyebrows rise at this, so he added "Just... trust me, he is."

"Alright, *monsieur,* understood. I had no intention of meddling in his affairs in any case – scarcely know the fellow! – but I'm surprised to learn that someone who is not apparently military or outwardly at least connected to intelligence should be 'dangerous'...."

"De la Fassederad, do us all a favor: don't ask. Just stick to your onions and leave Moitié alone. Hmm? Good."

The Ambassador decided he'd finished his little cigar, sighed, stubbed it out, and wondered why that mysterious interloper "Colonel Mincemot" hadn't warned him of this new lad's innocence – in the one curt, official message he'd received announcing this latest posting. But, *tant pis* – as an old bridge player he'd long since resigned himself to playing the cards he was dealt. He continued,

"So that was my one advice. As for my one instruction, it is this: Do not mess with – do not *tripotte* – Irina. Do not even *touch* her. In fact, do not even *think* about touching her."

While uncertain that he'd even heard this latest bit of gratuitous outlandishness correctly, it occurred to the alarmed Michel-Ange that he'd *already* touched the Irina in question. Or, rather, that *she* had touched *him*. And rather unrestrainedly, at that....

But even as he approached Jenni-faire's "freakout-mode" he was still instinctively compos enough to keep this datum to himself. Instead he attempted,

"Very good, *Monsieur,* understood. But may I venture to ask – why not? Is she... well, *malade* or something?"

"Certainly not! What an idea. No, my dear young *gaillard,* the reason is because *she is mine.* Do you understand? *Mine.*"

Ho-la-la, la-la, where the putain de merde *are we going with this?*

Things had so brusquely taken such a surreal turn that Michel-Ange (as though he were watching, in disinterested fascination, a Fellini film or something like that) now heard himself suicidally saying:

"Alright, *Monsieur*, I certainly also understand that. But as long as we are being so, ah, candid with each other... euh... may I venture to inquire where that leaves the, euh, the, euh, *status*... of your lady wife *Madame l'Ambassadrice?*"

Ambassador Armand St. Emilion de Pépinière Duquon-Lajoie now glared at Michel-Ange for several long seconds. Then he said, with cold deliberation,

"You know what? Here's what: *you* can have her. If you want – or, more to the point, if she'll want *you* – though God knows she's not too choosy. But be warned – and I tell you this with all friendly, perhaps even avuncular, intent – she has an aura. *An aura*, my lad, which can – indeed, has been known to – kill. *Kill. From a distance of as far as ten paces.*"

He stopped to gauge the effect of this on the young fellow before him – which appeared, judging from the latter's bulging eyes, to be not negligible. The Ambassador lit another *petit cigare* and continued, now in a somewhat more placid manner, as though none of the preceding had occurred,

"But please – " puff, puff, "just be, for the love of God, quiet. About all of this. Remain above all discreet – we are, after all, diplomats, *n'est ce pas?* Hah hah. So be a team player and you'll do fine, here – and I'm sure I have no reason to believe that you and I shall not get along famously...

"Now, I think that will be all. I am *en retard* for my *sièste--*" *Sièste?* wondered the near shell-shocked Michel-Ange, *it's almost dinner time.* "Irina – whom, as we have just agreed, you will not touch – will take you, I believe tomorrow, to the relevant Ministry. And so, all other eventualities going as planned – and why, hah hah, should they not?, hah hah – I trust I'll not be seeing or even hearing overly much of or from you for the duration of your *séjour* with us. So, the very best of good luck to you, *mon fils.*"

With that, the Ambassador stood and shook Michel-Ange's suddenly lifeless hand and fairly shoved him out the door.

On rubbery legs Michel-Ange wobbled down the stairs – during which he found himself briefly but terribly missing Jenni-faire – to be, of all things, embraced at the bottom by Irina, (who'd quickly put away her nail file when she heard his descending clatterings).

"Listen!" blurted Michel-Ange, "First of all we are not to be touching. And certainly not *here*. Or, indeed, if I understood correctly, *at all.*"

"*Vat?* Who is tellingk you dis? Heem?" and she nodded upstairs.

"*Exactement.* And, if you must know, he seemed rather emphatic on the subject."

"*Feh!* He iss olt fool!"

"Is that so? Well, he seemed to indicate that, your little *cinéma* here and elsewhere notwithstanding, you and he are, in reality, having – how-can-I-put-this? – a little personal *oo-la-la* lovey-dovey *'je t'aime, moi non plus' malinky* kissy-kiss *shkandal* going on between the two of you... In *fact* – " Michel-Ange now seemed to hesitate, "he says that you... 'belong' to him."

"Ent you are believingk dis? Shém from you – he iss awnly diairty olt dreamer. Me, belongk to *heem?* Vat krézy idee – I belongk to *nawbadié!*"

The two stared into each others' eyes in something of a stand-off. Then Michel-Ange blinked and, looking down, said,

"Alright, look – I seem to be about as introduced to this place – " he waved his hands about to indicate the whole French Embassy implantation in Laina "as I feel I can stand, at this point. And I think I'd like to go back to, er... my place... and unpack. And things. You'll be taking me to their *Ministère* tomorrow, I believe?"

He disengaged from her gaze and headed for the Residence's main front door. She followed him out.

"*Da.*" she said as they regained "his" Volga. "Hev méd far you *rend'-vous* at nine. Bim! Vell, bim-*ish*. Fonctionaries samtimes slow to beginingk in marningk...."

The Volga farted them the short distance to his and Moitié's bungalow, (from which Moitié's Lada was still conspicuously absent). As they pulled up, Michel-Ange was mulling over asking Irina at what point she expected to *fous le camp* and leave him to get on with things on his own – but she gave no indication of having any schedule of her own, and instead piped up,

"You mawst be hangrish – ent is niattingk in your *frigo*. Ent miéby it not so goot idee you steal fuds fram Mwa-tee-eh."

"This is most certainly true – hard to know what I'm more, famished or *crèved* with fatigue..."

"So – you like pitza? Av corse, *ie*verybadié like de pitza! Kam – ve go get, iss place not far, get *benzin* et sem time! Sem place! Ivan giff you nefa, you can now pay!" She exclaimed this last bit as though it was meant to be a blast of huge good news to Michel-Ange.

In the event, they again passed out through the barrior, Legionnaire Meiavelha back on duty, with whom Irina exchanged a few words that Michel-Ange did't catch. They motored less than a kilometer down 3 Oktobr Prospekt and pulled into a "*Gryazmaslo*" filling station, to which was attached a garish shack below a stuttering green neon sign about the size of a soccer goal which proclaimed

"РОКЫ БАЛБАО! КАМПИОН ПИЗЗА!"

("Roky Balbao! Campion Pizza!")

While Michel-Ange filled the Volga with Russian gasoline for, it had to be said, shockingly little money (about a fifth of its Parisian price), Irina entered the pizzeria. By the time he'd joined her she was already in possession of a large boxed pizza, and a little paper bag to go with it. She opened the steaming box to reveal the usual confection, dotted with red circular toppings.

"Yum. What's that you got there? *Saucisse?*"

"*Niet* – iss Albanian *spetzialitié* – dis place owner *Albanskyie* – dese tings iss *svekla*, eh, *mnié mnié mnié*, what you callingk in Frantsous, eh, *betteraves!*"

"Beets?" *Beets?* "*Beurk!* On *pizza?* Are you people *cinglés?*" Unlike most of his countrymen Michel-Ange was not finicky about his food, having somewhere acquired a veritable Anglo-Saxon culinary insouciance. But beets on pizza was, surely, a barbarity too far. But Irina was adamant,

"*Phouah!* Wat you knaw? You are new – knaw niattingk of goot Gryaznia fud!"

"I thought you said it was Albanian."

"*Albanskyie* people like leetle *brat* far Gryaznians – leetle brodder. In oldt days, Gryaznia vass awnlié cahntry to *riekognatzia* Albahnia. *Albanskyie* mans iss hokays – dey genksters – " she winked at the impassive pizza-wallah "but *hokay* genksters. Now péy nice *Albanskyie* men!"

He did so and they Volga-ed back to Michel-Ange's lodgings, stopping first to hand over the little paper bag to the beaming Legionnaire Meiavelha.

"Dis iss goot ting vat you are doingk," Irina informed Michel-Ange as they shut off the Volga and entered his and Moitié's "barracks".

"What? Of what do you speak now, my *chérie?*"

"Dat – dat vass prachuto-calzion vat you chust give to Martinho, dere – he vill now loff you *viééééry* match, ent he vill safe your life if dere is anti-Frantsous *demonstratzia* or trabble!"

Michel-Ange smiled, "Well, in that case that was money certainly well-spent – so here we are, then...."

Entering his abode, Michel-Ange was about to turn to bid *bonsoir* to Irina, but she pushed by him and entered, switching on the light as she did so. He followed, dumbly, vaguely wondering if somewhere along the line he'd acquired a wife without anyone telling him. Glancing to his left into Moitié's "flat" he saw again the empty pizza box.

"Ah, I now see where Moitié gets his nourishment."

"*Da. Albanskyie* Roky pitza *viéry popularniye* – heh heh, kip Frantsous Iémbassié alife! Kom, tsit!"

They installed themselves on "his" sofa and each consumed a slice of this passable pizza utterly ruined by, *ack!,* beets.

Michel-Ange realized quite how exhausted he was, in these waning hours of this, what had without doubt been the longest day of his young life. (And even if he hadn't been, he would have feigned it – to divest himself of Irina...)

"Irina, I am *crevé* – dead. I am now going to wish you a most sincere *bonsoir* and *merci* and – "

"Are you vant I should stay viss you? Ken do! I dunt need go home, ken stay!"

A vision of an amok Ambassador Duquon-Lajoie, brandishing his *Legion d'Honneur* sword in one hand and clutching his crotch with the other swam into Michel-Ange's febrile mind, and, trying to mask his desperation, he stammered,

"Non, merçi, ma chérie – perhaps some other time. I'm sure it would be *délicieux,* but trust me, in my current state of desuetude I would be rotten company, anyway."

"Hollright, I get miéssage," she pouted. But at least she now stood and, clutching her fake-Gucci carry-all, finally made to vacate the premises. Yet, insanely, for some reason – was he again acting suicidal? – Michel-Ange found himself asking,

"Euh, how will you get home? Shall I drive you?" Realizing his peril too late, he almost fainted with relief when Irina – not for the first time, and certainly not the last – surprised him: instead of throwing herself at him in the fashion which his short but intense exposure to this creature had already taught him to expect, she smiled sweetly, almost maternally, and tousled his already-tousled hair,

"Niet, chéri – you vould niever in million yierss fint your vey beck to hiere – I tek trem, iss issy far me." And with that she kissed him lightly on the lips and, as she was letting herself out, turned and said,

"I kam in marningk – eight-tirdy, exact! Be priepiéred to go. Rend'vous viss Mienestier et nine. He may be létte, bot ve ken not be. *Ciao, Michelangelo....*" and the door closed behind her.

The ensuing silence seemed suddenly almost monastic to the grateful Michel-Ange, who now set about:

1/ Cramming the box with his remaining beet-pizza into his tiny fridge, practically folding it in half to do so. Maybe that might improve its taste – certainly couldn't hurt. In any case, it would be his breakfast in the morning.

2/ Kicking off his loafers and shedding his trousers, jacket and necktie.

3/ Digging out his toilet *trousse* and brushing his teeth.

4/ Setting the alarm *bidule* on his watch for 7:30.

5/ Switching off the light.

and finally,

6/ crashing on this foreign, but not uninviting, bed.

At some point in the night he actually got under the covers. And dreamed he was sitting alone in a Ferris Wheel. Although Jenni-faire had paid for his ticket, she had declined to enter the ride with him. As the wheel ascended, Michel-Ange could see that he was, in fact, in some wondrous and beautiful sunlit fairyland, but he couldn't enjoy the vista because... right in the row in front of him sat Colonel Mincemot, who was – *what the hell?* – laughing and sharing an ice cream cone... *with Irina*. What a terrible dream. He willed it away, and started over....

15

THE MINISTRY OF CULTURE, SPORTS, THE ARTS AND OTHER PECULIARITIES

Beep beep beep. *Merde.* Click.

The first thing he noticed, (once he'd taken a full ten seconds to remember where the hell he was), was that Moitié had not returned in the night. Or at any rate, that the premises were still conspicuously Moitié-less. As he began going through his matutinal *procédures*, Michel-Ange speculated not so much on *whether* whatever Moitié might be off currently doing was illegal, but just *how* illegal it might be....

And speaking of Moitié and illegalities, Michel-Ange, having scanned the barrenness of his own "kitchen" and attendant shelves, decided to live a little dangerously and so wandered over to his neighbor's quarters where he helped himself to the instant coffee to be found there – "Picorico" brand, from Bulgaria. He organized it on Moitié's hot-water-maker and was careful to cover his traces when he was through – God knows what payment Moitié would extract for this petty larceny if he found him out – Michel-Ange doubted it would come gratis.

Returning to his side, he pulled out yesterday's "Roky Balbao" beet-za from his little *frigo*, and it unfolded before him like some gigantic, horrible doughy venus fly-trap. *Ooof!* He took a few bites, by way of *petit déjeuner*. *Hmmm*, the flavor of this confection had neither improved *nor* deteriorated overnight, but rather *metamorphosed* – indeed, it seemed to have somehow acquired a cheesy *soupçon* to it... not so much *bleuh* as *bleu*... The words "sketchy" and "botulin" briefly passed his mind.

He left his yesterday's laundry in a hopeful little pile on his un-made bed for Irina's as-yet-unseen cleaning girls, as he now spiffed himself out in a fresh *costume* – the grey pinstripe – with blue shirt and *Enarque* tie, which, he felt, ought to pass muster with whatever body of Gryaznian bureaucratic stolidity he might encounter. On this (as he looked out his window) bright spring day.

And on the dot of 0830 Irina appeared on his doorstep – she, also freshly got-up, now in a gray mini-skirt, pink blouse, and a black bolero-type jacket that appeared to be made of suede. As fetching – if not more so – as yesterday, and even (if one discounted the mini-ness of the skirt) arguably "business-like". Her burgundy lipstick again exactly matched the arresting color of her hair, and she now transferred a bit of it onto Michel-Ange's cheek as she *bise*-ed him good morning.

"*Bonzou'*, my *chéri* – ready? Do you hef oll your *identitatzias* ent letters off credibilitié?"

Michel-Ange waggled his "Mother Superior *serviette*" at her, and they were off. He drove, she guided.

Inside the coughing Volga, Michel-Ange made a stab at preparatory elucidation,

"This Ministry, then, it's –?"

"Da – de Mienestrié av *Kulturnyie*, Arts, Spoart ent Udder Peculieritiés – iss on Baba Paraskieva Boulevard, I show you – "

"*A propos* – my dearest Irina, euh, are you able to enlighten me as to just what, euh... those 'Other Peculiarities' might be?"

"*Heh!* Who knows? Esk dem. Enyvey, dey will not be tellingk you. Ollso enyvey, I belif you are not vanting to know. Uzeless – dey are oll complétte uzeless. Samsingk to do viss 'Nationalniye Chiérecter'. *Phouah!* – netionalniye *stupiditiés*, is vat...."

"I see. And the actual Minister will be there?"

"*Da*. His Honorabilitié ex-Comrade Vasily Maximovich Pozadnik. He iss, how ken say, *mnié mnié mnié* – " she decided to go for emphatic ambiguity, "*moodié* man."

As opposed to whom, around here? "Well, no problem – we shall just have to charm him, *n'est ce pas*?"

She guided him through a series of convolutions around the clogged and pot-holed "thoroughfares" of downtown Laina (one almost certainly involving going the wrong way on a one-way street). Before eventually pulling up at what, for a place purporting to be the National Headquarters of Culture, the Arts, Sport and Ineffable Whimsical Whatnots, turned out to be a virtually window-less 5-storey brown block of remarkable dourness. Definitely of the "Early Penal" socialist school of architecture.

"Park here," she pointed, but Michel-Ange could see no parking space.

"Where?"

"Dere... *Dere.*"

"*There? Here?* But that's on the *foutu* sidewalk!"

"*Da*. Are ve diplomets or are ve not? Dis Wolga may be shit car but steal hev *diplomtnyie* number plettes! Park hiere – do vat Irina is tellingk you, *durak!*" He complied, feeling like a felon.

They entered, presenting IDs to Kalashnikoved soldiers, who scowled at them and their belongings. Visitors' tags were slung around necks. *"Hokays – ken go hup".*

The Minister's *suite* was on the top floor. They stepped out of the lift into a garishly opulent waiting room – all tubular frames and leather – which was empty, save for a ancient *babushka* cleaning lady who was emptying ashtrays. Upon the arrivals of these visitors she ceased her labors, pushed a button next to what was clearly the Minister's door, and shrank away through a scarcely-visible *cul de sac* in one of the corners.

Irina and Michel-Ange took seats, and he gazed upon the reading matter on offer on the glass coffee table: fresh copies of "Laina-Pravda" as well as variously out-of-date editions of "Gryaznia Bulletin" (in English), "Russia Today" (ditto), "The Economist", "Jeune Afrique" and something rather surreal apparently published by the North Koreans called "Joguk" that Michel-Ange was about to dive into, when a green light went on above the minister's door. The door itself simultaneously clicked and swung open, seemingly of its own volition, and a great cheery bellow came from the ministerial sanctum that sounded like *"VLEZ! VLEZ! VUVETYE, VOYTI! VLEZ!"*

Irina needlessly poked the already-startled Michel-Ange "Det's far us! Kom!" *This guy sounds not unlike* our own *putain of an Ambassador...* "Ent try to be not stupit – in fect, iss bietter iff you be charmingk – " this last bit muttered at him as she fairly pushed him through the open door.

The 50-ish Minister of All Those Things turned out to be, (almost inevitably), short, fat, and blessed with a great pile of black hair the jumbled haphazardness of which surpassed even Michel-Ange's in its creative anarchy.

He was got up in a brown double-breasted suit, a dark gray shirt, and a tie that was either maroon or also brown, but which in any case, was "tied", if you could use that word, in such a confabulated fashion that it actually half-resembled a noose. With one collar-tip looking like it was threatening to fly away, a betting sort would have gotten short odds that this was a fellow who'd just rolled out of bed having slept with his clothes on.

Which was not to suggest, however, that conviviality was not the order of the day in the office of Gryaznian Minister for the Arts, Sport, Culture, and Other Peculiarities Vasily Maximovich Pozadnik. Upon whose desk, at 9 a.m. on this weekday morning, tellingly stood an open, half-filled 1.75-litre bottle of "Balkovskaya"-brand vodka.

He greeted Irina with a beaming, expansive cordiality that suggested prior... at the very least... er, *acquaintanceship.* When he released her from his Sumo-like embrace he faced Michel-Ange with arms outstretched,

"So! Iz you de great *novoyie Kulturnyie* man fram Frantsous!"

"Well, your Honor – euh – *Honorabilité,* euh, *oui,* I suppose I am."

"So! Ve tost! Iz voidka goot?"

Pardon? What the hell's the correct diplomatic protocol, here? Indeed, what would Mincemot make of these tomatoes? Hell, forget Mincemot – what am I going to say, anyway? "Non"? Sure I am....:

"*B'en...* why not? With pleasure, *Monsieur le Ministre...*"

"Ent far *grazhdanka* Irina?"

"Vell... paireheps smoll. *Bolshoie spassibo.*"

The Honorable ex-Comrade Minister Pozadnik produced, from a desk drawer, a set of 4 crystal tumblers which were clearly marked with the Czech Airlines logo, and he embarked upon an extended session of Pouring and Toasting and Down The Hatch.

"TO THE REPUBLIC OF GRYAZNIA! – *nazdrovya!*"

"TO THE *REPUBLIQUE FRANCAISE*! – *a vos souhaits!*"

"TO FRANCO-GRYAZNIAN FRIENDSHIP AND COOPERATION! – *tzeers!*"

"TO CULTURE! – *houra! youpiii!*"

Michel-Ange's eyes were beginning to water and Irina had developed a definite rosiness of cheek... but the Minister's ebullient enthusiasm carried on – fortified, even.

"So!" he roared, while still grinning (not easily accomplished simultaneously, but Pozadnik had not become a Minister without possessing certain... skills), "You hef de *offitzialnyie akreditylnyia? Frantsous pisma* – peppers? *Papee-eh?"*

"Absolument, mon cher Monsieur le Ministre – voila!"

Michel-Ange handed over his sheaf of official Miss Bergère-generated bumf, which the Minister attacked with an even more impressive variety of governmental stamps than the fellow back at the airport – *biff!, bang!, bonk! bonk!* – and then he pulled out a pre-drafted Cyrillic document which he signed and handed to Michel-Ange,

"Dere! Now, ess you say in your beeyootifuls Kieneda – " *Quoi?* – Canada, now? " *'Mi casa es su casa'!* You now hef *diplomaticheski* license – you are free ess birt!"

Michel-Ange peered at this document and saw near the top **Мишел-Анж де ла Фасдерат** which his basic Cyrillic told him was... him. He stuffed the paper in his Mother Superior-case.

"So, now, tiell me about your *Frantsous pragrama* far *culturnyie* tings!"

Well alright, then.

Even though Colonel Mincemot had instructed him to, in effect, "do fuck-all down there, except keep an eye out for the Americans", Michel-Ange had taken that for a bit of Mincemot-ian hyperbole and had, regardless, done some rudimentary preparation for this very moment. It was thus in something approaching a gung-ho spirit that he now opened his mouth and began unloading:

"Eh bien, Monsieur le Ministre, on behalf of the French people, whose government has given much strategic thought and planning to the particular character and culture of the great Gryaznian people, and *conforme* to the aspirations

of Franco-Gryaznian amity and cooperation, I have the honor to announce to you that we have confected a detailed and expansive plan to – ”

“To do exiéctlié niattingk. Niattingk.”

Hein? Comment? Michel-Ange nudged Irina and hissed “*What'd* he just say?”

Her eyes were down, directed at the hands in her lap. “Niattingk. He is sayingk you vill do niattingk.”

Michel-Ange stared back at this personage – who was beaming absurdly at him. Presently he stammered,

“*Mais, mais,* I don't understand – I was sent here to – ”

“My frent!, my frent! – *mon ami!*” the Minister stopped him, raising his hands, “Izz no miatter – izz no miatter vat porpoise dey sendingk you – ve izz not vantingk, ent ve izz not needingk, *kulturniye* pragriama fram Frantsous. No tenk iou, *non mérçi.*”

“*Mais –*”

“*Mais* niattingk. Look, *vuijete,* if you miébbe bringingk plen far buildingk Plé-boy Miension in Laina, *could* be interiest…. or, *mnié mnié mnié,* if you bringingk pragriama far build Clab Miéd beth-ent-spahz deluxe resort kemps, den ve *miébbe* talk… bot… *izz* you bringk Plé-boy Mension far Laina? Eh? *Izz* you bringk Clab Miéd spahz-ent-deluxe resort kemps far Gryaznia? Eh, mine boy-chick? I dunt sink so!”

????? Mais qu'est *ce que c'est que cette foutaise?* «*Mine boychick*»?

Michel-Ange just stared back, speechless but slightly shaking his head – though whether in answer to the Minister or in simple, ongoing disbelief, was unclear even to himself. He found himself mumbling,

“…but we have – had – developed a comprehensive and integrated plan for… for….”

Seeing the lad in a state of apparent shock, Minister Pozadnik again cut in, but now adopting what he thought was a conciliatory tone:

"Egaine, look, *vuijete* – far me, you are lookingk like nice boy, not like odder olt diplomati who is oll full fram *gavno,* how you say, *merde* – bot here in Gryaznia, oll radio, *televisiya,* kinema, priess, média – oll iz belongk to ahss, to Stét. Ent iff ve need *teknisheskyie* help, or *finantzia* help, ve ken get, fram Russkiye, or fram Sierbska – saw no needingk help fram Frantsous. Ve dunt need, ent ve dunt vant."

Did that philistine Mincemot have a secret "hot-line" to this Gryaznian min-isterial spécimen? Surely not... or was such a thing possible? Still, Michel-Ange, seemingly on autopilot, felt he had to lodge *some* official demurral, however lame:

"But..."

"Bot vat? Vat? You tink ve dunt hev in Gryaznia, *mnié mnié mnié,* writers? You iz niever hearingk of Boris Grumbich ar Dmitri Bychkov? *Musicalniye* campozitors? – You iz niever hearingk of Vladimir Gachski? Apera singingk – Nadezhda Formicovna? Pop eedol – You niever hearingk of *internationalniya* super-star Sasha Glavinsky ent hees grupa 'Overkill'?"

Michel-Ange had, needless to say, never heard of any of these people, but he just stared back, fearing to say so. The Minister went on, relentless,

"Ent *folkloriki* singingk ent dencingk – *oy,* de *folkloriki* siningk ent dencingk! – ve hevingk dis kamming out fram our *hears* – from, how is you sayingk in yore Kiéneda," *Why – on top of everything else – does this deranged lunatic persist in thinking that I have anything to do with* Canada, *of all places?* "out fram of our holes in *ess!* Ve iss tryingk to *export* our *folkloriki* singingk ent dencingk *troupi* – de *lest* tingk ve are vantingk iz to import *more!* Ent fram *Frantsous!* – oy!"

Michel-Ange would have been happy to continue saying and doing nothing, but he found himself again leaning over and whispering into Irina's ear, "Is this possible? Is he serious?"

And she muttered softly, with her eyes still downcast, "*Da*. I varned you – moodié men."

Well, Michel-Ange remembered someone, from the depths of his extensive schooling, once saying "If you've got no options, you've got no problem", so he faced the still-grinning – his default mode appeared to be a grin – Minister Pozadnik and said,

"Alright, I think I apprehend your drift, *Monsieur le Ministre*. But now – and I appreciate that this might not be actually a direct or even proximate concern of yours – what do you suggest I do with myself? During my *séjour* here?"

The Minister of This That and The Other, seeing that this young French dip-lo-pup was now a spent force, came quick with his reply:

"Vell, naw prabliema! Dere iz *miééénié, miééénié* tingks vat you ken do! – Far start, weezit hour laffly ceetié Laina, vich is kampletlié fool aff *interiestniye, mnié mnié mnié* invitalitis ent – Irina, vat is karriekt vort?"

"Peculiarities, *gaspadin*," she replied, still softly, still not looking at anyone.

"*Da, da*, de teepeek Gryaznia peculiaritiés, saw *miéénié, miéénié* – ent dis re-mint me! – iz you miérrid? Hev vife?"

"*Euh, non*. Why?"

"You can mék diskaver off oll *miénié, miénié* beautifools Gryaznia vimens! Dis iss alvays goot ting far yongk men like you to doingk – start here viss Irina! She iss beautifools like Meess Gryaznia, ent *viérié* frentlié – saw I hem hearingk – you shoult spendingk your time viss herr – iss goot plen!" And the still-grin-ning Minister Pozadnik proceeded to actually wink at him....

It occurred to the near-shell-shocked Michel-Ange that this was the second time in less than twelve hours – since that surreal session with the Ambassador – that he'd been gratuitously invited to take liberties with the (as far as he, at least, was concerned) entirely blameless Irina. He looked over at her, and, sure enough, her still-downturned countenance seemed close to tears. *Well, who wouldn't be?* Indignation began bubbling in his nether regions, and as it grew it displaced the shock that had been benumbing him since the first ministerial "niattingk".

And although not a particularly decisive fellow, even Michel-Ange could see that there was nothing further to be gained by extending this Kafka-like *mise-en-scène*.

But the Minister gave every impression of wanting to keep the party going:

"So! Now det ve hef goot understandingk betveen us, *alles gut!*, ess ve say een Kiéneda!" *It's 'we', now?* "Ve trink égaine to hiéppy Franco/Kiéneda-Gryaznia *cooperatzia!*"

Feeling a bit like the condemned man being given a last cigarette by the firing-squad commander, Michel-Ange watched dumbly as all three of their tumblers were re-filled, and when it was his turn again to "tost!", he mustered whatever Spirit of Resistance he could and declared, in French,

"Here's to us, and death to assholes!" (*"Vive nous, et mort aux cons!"*)

"Vell!" shouted the Minister, clapping his hands, "So, det is concludingk aff hour biéznesses here todé, so tenk you too match ent goot-pie plizz! You go now, ent I hem viéry match hopingk det pairheps ve iz not seeingk ich udder ever égaine! *Moo-sié --* " he shook Michel-Ange's hand, " *Grazhdanka Vozhbuzhdena –* ", and he kissed Irina four times on her cheeks.

And so down the lift and dump the ID necklaces and out the door. Breathing some bracing fresh air. In this world in which suddenly Everything had Changed. At least for Michel-Ange.

As they trudged to the Volga, Irina took a tissue out of a pocket of her bolero jacket and wiped some tears, still not looking at him, said, "I hem *saw* sarrié, Michelangelo."

"Yes, well, one must admit, *that* certainly could have been a bit more *agréable*. But never mind. And there's nothing for *you* to feel sorry for – this is hardly *your* fault – Here, come on, please, don't cry, things will be alright, you'll see." *N'importe-quoi....*

Sniff, sniff. "Ve must be goingk to tell de Iambassador off dis new news, no?"

"No doubt. But it can wait."

It wasn't so much the feckless Duquon-Lajoie that Michel-Ange was contemplating, but rather the figure of Colonel Mincemot – *who'll no doubt be delighted* by this turn of events, which under normal circumstances could not be viewed as anything but disastrous.

"Look, Irina, would it *dérange* you terribly if you went back to the Embassy alone? Go ahead, here are the keys, take the Volga and go back. You have no doubt other affairs to occupy you. I'll be fine – I just want to walk a bit, clear my head."

"But – " She appeared to have stopped actually crying, which at least was a relief.

"No, you go. I'll get a taxi back, don't worry about me, I'll be fine. *Allez –*" He kissed her on the cheek – so recently visited by the repellent Minister Pozadnik – and shoved her into the Volga.

As she started the engine – *oogh-oogh-oogh-oogh, koff, skwaark, bang* – she handed him a card through the window, "Tek diss, *idiota, durak –* "

"Qu'est ce que c'est?"

"My cart – it hév Iembiassié address – show to téxi driver."

16

WALKABOUT

So there he stood. Four (or had it been five?) large vodkas already to the good and it was not yet eleven a.m. *B'en mon p'tit con – at least they'd be proud of me back at Le Macaque....*

But more to the point – there he stood... *with my entire mission seemingly now gone completely* pffft! *before it's even been taken out of the box and deployed... what'll Jenni-faire think? Or Papa? Or, for that matter, that putain of a Mincemot – sure he wants me to do nothing, but will he be happy to hear that the locals feel the same way? None of it bears thinking about....*

Instead, Michel-Ange was content to just amble off into this ugly gray – but above all anonymous – concrete shambles that was "downtown", just-barely ex-Communist, Laina.

Actually, "content" was hardly the word – but he did feel rather strongly that he suddenly wanted to put the frustrations of officialdom aside for just a bit.

Although... He looked down these drab, unpromising streets. *Hmmm – was I* peut-etre *a bit hasty in cavalierly – not to say half-drunkenly – sending Irina off like that?*

Michel-Ange's two glimpses of "Laina life" thus far had been The Post-Lenin Baccarat Café and the Roky Balbao Pizza, two establishments which, while perhaps not exactly the Blue Bay in Monte Carlo or the Ritz back at the old Place Vendôme, came, if nothing else, equipped with colored electrical lights and at least notional indoor plumbing – intimations of civilization which were less than obviously on offer when one came into actual contact with the dreary, bedraggled spectacle this recent post-communism really presented, once one got on the other side of the car-window glass: Just a vast profusion of poured Brezhnevian concrete, all chipped right angles and crumbling façades – and a lot of it in vomit yellow, to boot.

Michel-Ange started to wander aimlessly down increasingly insalubrious streets. On a surprisingly chilly day for this time of year – gray above, and gray-brown-yellow-*bleuagh* below.

It had been over five years since communism had gone *phut!*, vanished like some kind of murderous conjuror's trick in a Gogol-ian nightmare, but one wouldn't have immediately known it from lethargic, threadbare 1994 Laina, which still looked – and acted – miserably, stubbornly, commie.

A city of barely half a million people, with no metro/underground system and, until just the day before yesterday, virtually no private cars, Laina relied – for such vitality as it could muster – on its network of trams and buses. One of whose "shelters" now stood, blocking most of the sidewalk, just in front of Michel-Ange.

And tied to one leg of this shelter was a motley collection of dogs and cats – everything from puppies and kittens to one-eyed toms and flea-bitten old towzers. *Oh how quaint*, at first thought Miche-Ange, *a little* ad hoc, al fresco *pet shop* – until he realized with horror (the unshaven lowlife manning the show should have been a giveaway) that this was no open-air pet shop, but rather an exchange where people could buy and sell animals *for food*. This was confirmed when he watched an old man hand the spiv a little mutt in exchange for some ratty nefa notes – and the unspeakable *mec,* addressing this freshly-arrived well-dressed and obviously foreign witness, actually leered at Michel-Ange, "You vant? Far itt! Iz goot!"

Mais ça vas pas, non? Michel-Ange shivered involuntarily, shook his head and moved on.

He turned onto a street larger than the others called **улица жертва**, which he knew, thanks to *Madame* Bébette, meant "Sacrifice Street": a clamorous thoroughfare for the apparently exclusive use of street vendors – of every conceivable thing under the sun (or rather, gray sky) – from turnips to obsolete Gryaznian military uniforms and gear. Little piles of chipped crockery. Canned fish. Piles of beets. Bicycle pumps. 78rpm records. Old samovars and hookah pipes. Used clothing (that had already looked used when it was new). Decks of playing cards and tarot cards. Old paperbacks and textbooks. Framed pictures of Karl Marx. Empty jerrycans and detached windshield wipers.

A flea market, in short, but in this Gryaznian version the *trottoire* bazaar was rather more redolent of domestic desperation than the cosmopolitan enthusiasm that normally suffused such affairs. "Sacrifice Street" – well, somebody somewhere had a sense of humor – or rather "irony" as they called it in this part of the world. (Michel-Ange remembered being told somewhere along the line that there was no word in Russian for "humor" – which hadn't, of course, prevented the extraordinary profusion of sick jokes during the *ancien régime*.)

In any case, most of such commerce as was actually transacted on old Sacrifice Street *appeared to be between the stall-holders themselves.* Certainly, there didn't look to be many, if any, "outsiders" – no obvious foreigners, let alone tourists. Other than this young French diplomat, of course.

Which reminds me – Mincemot wants me to keep an eye on "The Americans" – Hah! that's a good one! Americans? – I don't think I'll bump into any here, that's for sure… but maybe the colonel would like one of these handsome Gryaznian Army casquettes with the old hammer and sickle? Get a grip, Michel-Ange, you're delireating… in fact, what in the name of God is that, now?…

What indeed? For, wending her wobbly way towards him down this Sacrifice Street there now came a headscarved-and-aproned old woman leading two goats on two strings held in one hand and carrying a knapsack, which had a small milking stool tied to it, in the other.

Michel-Ange made the (border-guard) mistake of establishing eye contact with the old babushka, who as a result halted in front of him, seated herself and, extracting a plastic cup from a tube of them in her knapsack, proceeded to milk these goats, right there and then.

Michel-Ange, whose grasp of zoology and animal husbandry was at best hazy, could only hope that the goats were female, otherwise this whole Breughelian scene would be even more bizarre... *but wait – it was – it did!* – it got even more hellish, ... because now, keeping the goats anchored by stamping on their strings with a slippered foot, she wordlessly pulled out, also from her knapsack, a bottle of pungent home-brewed alcohol of some kind, which she poured into the goat milk. And which now, unbidden, she pressed upon Michel-Ange, putting up two fingers that at first he took for the universal "get stuffed" sign (which he found, in the circs, a bit incongruous, but in this unreal setting everything was possible) but which pretty quickly and pretty clearly turned out to mean not two, but twenty. Nefa.

He handed over the required, and – stifling the desire to ask her if she didn't, by any chance, have any ice – quaffed this old woman's dicey concoction in one go – *cul sec!* – (he wanted to taste it as little as possible). Handing back her plastic cup, she stuffed in her knapsack and, nodding approvingly, she gathered herself up and, with her little flock in tow, ambled away.

He stood there blinking, as this latest infusion of alien alcohol had its effect on his innards. His eyes were actually beginning to water. Still, there was nothing for it – he resumed his way down this kaleidoscopic street. Of not so much "sacrifice" as sad surprise.

All of the stuff for sale appeared as worthless as it was astonishing. *Tiens! look there* – a set of American presidential *matrioshka* dolls, with all of them going back to Nixon arrayed beside the bowling pin-shaped Bill Clinton – *would that amuse Mincemot? Not likely. Jenni-faire? Even less....*

A little further on he came across a fellow selling.... *AK-47s.* A cardboard sign said "US $50". *Can they even be real, at that price? Probably locally made – or Albanian... Hmm, I wonder what the post-communist gun laws are around here... Putain de merde! – 50 US dollars? – that's not much more than dinner with Jenni-faire.... Would this be of interest to Mincemot? Perhaps... (make a note...)*

Moving on. A young girl behind a pyramid of strange pink-ish root-like vegetables. Or tubers of some kind. Michel-Ange had never seen anything like them, and wasn't even sure they were edible – they might well be medicinal, in some strange folky "old wives remedy" way. In any case, the girl wanted two nefa apiece for them, three nefa for five. Michel-Ange smiled and passed.

But then he came across something that really brought him up short:

Across the street from the girl and her roots, a little further along, was a lone, extremely sickly-looking – she was actually *yellowish* – old *babushka*. She was plonked on a wooden chair, behind a large upturned cardboard box, to which had been taped an old magazine photo of Todor Makarov, the last of the Gryaznian commie leaders, (who'd been strung up by his goolies, Mussolini-style, along with his hated wife Tamara, three years previously by revenge-bent celebrating mobs of Gryaznian citizens in the soon-to-be-renamed Lenin Park). Which was ominous enough, but worse:

On top of the box sat that which she was trying to sell. Which turned out to be... a shoe. A single shoe. A filthy brown mud-encrusted worn-out sort of (male) farmer's boot, to be more precise. A left-footed one, to... boot. And next to this mute mini-monument to be-*merded* misery, had been scribbled "Ⓗ*10*" the circled H being the symbol for nefa.

Well, this was one enormity too far for Michel-Ange, who tottered over to the nearest kiosk where he motioned for, received, and drained in a damned quickish fashion a Polarnia beer. (Which, as it happened, cost 10 nefa.) As he pondered this latest human disaster. A single, used shoe for sale for one US greenback, or six French *balles,* might only be a *small* disaster, admittedly, but even small disasters were disasters. For *someone....*

Fully fortified, (by five previous vodkas, one recent goats-milk-and-something-no doubt-100 proof-and-kerosene-based, and now this latest beer), he decided upon action.

He strode purposefully, if a bit unsteadily – booze exacerbated the unrepaired pavement – back to the old crone, whose lone bit of footgear remained, not too surprisingly, unsold... and, smiling broadly at her, handed over a 20 nefa note.

She smiled back, revealing an alarming but no longer surprising lack of teeth, and started to scrabble around for some change (nefa-pennies were known as *trochkas,* and Michel-Ange noticed approvingly that they had holes in them), but he raised his palms and, still smiling, spoke a rare phrase he remembered from his Russian tapes, "Keep the change." (*"Sdachi ne nado"*)

She also kept smiling (they were like two grinning idiots, here) and handed him the revolting shoe-boot. Which he, hands still up, pushed back at her – *I don't know what I'd rather have less – this damn old shoe or two slugs in the back of the head* – assuring her through his straining grin, *"Niet niet,* you keep, *sdachi!"*

Merde. Wrong move, Michel-Ange....

Because at this, she abruptly flew into full Gryaznian-bonkers mode. Her face was now a mask of Munschian dementia and she grabbed his 20-nefa note, crumpled it in front of his face and hurled it at his startled head. And unburdened herself in the most voluble fashion imaginable of a torrent of Gryaznian execrations and imprecations, including obsolete scurrilities and ancient curses such as might have reddened the face of the most hardened reprobate.

Not for the first time that day the crestfallen Michel-Ange slunk away. He *hoped* with dignity but in *fact,* not unlike the proverbial whipped dog. He certainly didn't bother to pick up the crumpled 20-nefa note.

Bordelle de putain de bordelle de merde.... what a country....

He wandered away from this misbegotten Sacrifice Street – neither knowing nor caring where. Just... away.

He allowed gravity to pull him down descending streets until he found himself by the warehouses, quays, cranes and industrial work-sites on the banks of Laina's river, The **призрак река**, The "Ghost River" (its recently-restored name, after being known as the Peace River for the last half century). He bumped up against a rusty railing and stared gloomily at the brown water. Watched a desultory barge chug by. Otherwise, nothing much was happening on this aptly-named "Ghost River".

What a morning. So where do I stand now? Should I accept being a 'non-person' in this place? Do I even have a choice? And if so, what might that be?

Despite it being late-spring, a cold stiff breeze blew at him from the river, forcing him to squint.

He turned to reluctantly face the bedraggled gray-brown mess that was Old Laina, as though its ugliness might throw off a clue.

Well, mon vieux, you're not having the most brilliant start to this so-called career of yours, are you – I wonder if you're really cut out for this... Hell, I wonder if you're really cut out for anything....

Then, as though out of nowhere, yet another *babushka* appeared. At his elbow, no less. Wizened, toothless, headscarved old *babushkas* were clearly one commodity (if that was the word for them) that Gryaznia produced in over-abundance. This one peered earnestly into Michel-Ange's face.

"Zashto tuy plachesh, sinko?"

The startled Michel-Ange could decipher just enough of this.

"Crying? I'm not crying.... Go away, please, I'm fine, thank you, no, please..."

"Da, da, plach – "

"*Non, niet,* I tell you – it's not tears – it's the drink, it's the wind, it's the..." *ho, la la* "I assure you, I never cry – "

But the old woman persevered and, pulling an unspeakable rag out from her frayed jacket cuff, attempted to dab his eyes. This proved too much for Michel-Ange, who extricated himself from this importuning old woman and the riverbank railing against which he was pressed by grasping and pushing her firmly but gently by the shoulders, and easing her to one side,

"Grandmother, I pray you, you are most amiable but I am perfectly well and in no need of your kind assistance."

And, upon releasing her, he himself passed a finger reflexively across the corner of one eye. The desire struck him to press a coin upon her for her kindly intentions, but by now he was so wary of the volatility of these *babushkas* that he dismissed the inclination with an inward shudder and instead just strode away.

How the devil do I find a taxi in this merdier? The only vehicles I see are trucks, vans, the occasional tram and the even more occasional private Lada, Fiat or, God help me, Trabant....

Michel-Ange then remembered someone – Irina? naa, someone else – telling him that in recently-freed eastern Europe, to fill the taxi shortage, the owner/drivers of private vehicles were offering themselves up for *ad hoc* taxiing services, to augment their newly-unsubsidized incomes. So, feeling suddenly rather American, Michel-Ange did something he'd never done before – he waggled his thumb at the next passing conveyance.

Which turned out to be a GAZ "Gazelle" van whose lettering on the door identified it as belonging to the Laina Municipal Bureau of Sanitation and Water-Works. Its driver was a cheerful young *mec* in blue overalls with a blue Bic held by one ear and a yellow *papirosi* cigarette stuck in his mouth.

He skidded to a stop and leaned over to open the passenger door for Michel-Ange, who showed the fellow Irina's business card, causing him to nod and say *"Da, da – sorok-pyat."* Michel-Ange knew this meant forty-five, to which he readily agreed, making a mental note that on top of everything else, he'd be needing to complete that nefa transaction with Ivan Ivanov pretty damn soon.

This skiving young municipal worker – who struck Michel-Ange as strangely Parisian in his professional insouciance – proved so enthusiastic and good-humored (at one point declaring "I loff Johnnie Halliday!" *Hey,* there's *some Culture!*) that, in the not terribly long drive back to the French compound, he actually managed to buck up Michel-Ange's sagging spirits. (Somewhat, anyway.)

Indeed, when asked by an inventively gesticulating Michel-Ange whether he would not be missed from urgent municipal duties at the Laina Water-Works *Directorate,* the fellow clapped Michel-Ange on his back and cried "Ah! Hah hah hah! I like you! You are *viérié viérié goot Frantsous comique!* 'Dey vill mee-iss me' – hah hah hah!"

17

"LE ROUGE"

Well, this fine young product of Laina's municipal bureaucracy successfully negotiated that city's ongoing automotive tauromachy and delivered his new friend the French *comique* back to the Embassy, where Michel-Ange exchanged "fraternal" nods with the now-on-duty Sgt. Schlechtermann, who raised a Jeeves-like eyebrow at Michel-Ange's mode of conveyance but snapped him off a salute nevertheless. (Michel-Ange, walking along the driveway to the Residence, noted how quickly one could get used to this novel kind of greeting).

Irina was at her receptionist desk, and she rose to *mwa-mwa* Michel-Ange, who was already looking towards the staircase.

"Is the Ambassador in?"

"*Da* – chust. So, how vass your tourism?"

"Later, *ma chérie* – "

As he legged it up to the second floor she called out to him "I not tell him nassingk!" He knocked on the Ambassador's half-opened door.

"*Oui?*"

"It is *moi,* de la Fassederad, Mister Ambassador. I am desolated but I have a small problem. *We* have a small problem. Otherwise I would not be deranging you."

"Enter, enter. Tell me, I'm listening, that's what I'm paid for – I'm fairly certain, at any rate... by the way, how did it go with your Minister – who is, in fact, my *good friend* the Minister?"

"Well *justement* – it turns out he had some rather astonishing news to convey to me. To us, actually – "

"Go ahead."

"May I take a seat?"

"But of course my dear fellow, make yourself at home."

"Thank you, *monsieur.* Well, to put it as succinctly as I know how, he invited me – no, he *ordered* me – to do fu- well, to do eff-all. *'Nitattingk'* was, I believe, his very word."

"Hmm. Interesting. Nothing, eh? Do *nothing?* He has no desire for you to bring some of our world-appreciated *culture Française* to his lovely *bléd*? Did he intimate why?"

"No, not even. Well, not *really,* anyway. He was quite rude, actually, behind all his smiling and toasting. Basically, he just seemed to emphatically believe that ... well, that they have all the culture they need. And certainly have no need for any of ours."

"He made no mention of the Americans, then?"

Him too? What is it with these so-called superiors of mine that they are so borné *on Americans? Either real or imagined?*

"*Euh, non,* as a matter of fact. He said that although they had all the culture they need – and then some! – that if they ever felt an urgent requirement for some *more,* that they'd turn to their friends the Russians. Or Serbs. But certainly not us. And the Americans never came up at all."

"*Et bien.* Well, *that* certainly seems to put a crimp in your plans, *hein*? A bit awkward...." Michel-Ange was not sure he liked this tricky bastard's use of "your", here, and nor did the Ambassador strike him as distressed by the news from "his friend" the Minister of This That And The Other as one would think a normal French ambassador *would* or *should* be. His Excellency continued,

"Well, so where does that leave you – sorry, us? Did he at least accept your *lettres de créances*?"

"Oh yes, he accepted those alright. For what they're worth." Michel-Ange allowing a *soupçon* of bitterness to creep in.

"Well so there you are, then. It appears that you'll be having some extra time on your hands. Whilst you sojourn here with us. Where, I felicitate myself to assure you, you are, of course, most welcome – *surtout* as we are so few. Did our friend," "*our*" *friend now...* "Minister Pozadnik have any suggestions about any possible new directions for... your attentions?"

"Hah! As a matter of fact, yes he did! Shameless. He had the effrontery to suggest that I investigate the local pulchritude – even had the *culot* to suggest I interest myself in ... in..." the Ambassador's previous injunction re Irina was still branded on his brain, but he decided to be reckless nevertheless, "our poor innocent Irina, down below...."

"Ah yes, of course, *l'innocente.*" At this point the Ambassador opened a drawer in his magisterial desk and pulled out a medium-sized bottle of Grand Marnier "A little drop? *Une larme?*"

Michel-Ange needed this like a third eye, but... *no, yes I do need it*: "*Eh bien,* why not, *Monsieur l'Ambassadeur?*"

From out of the same drawer now came two plastic Air France cups. Grog rations were duly apportioned, and Duquon-Lajoie continued "*A la nôtre!* Yes, well, not for the first time, the *modalités protocolaire* of our Gryaznian hosts leave something to be desired, but my previous order regarding you and *Mademoiselle* Vozhbuzhdena still stands – you will occupy yourself otherwise."

It was not often in his young life that Michel-Ange had found himself the "grown-up in the room", but at the moment he most indubitably did not want to dwell on the irrelevant complication of Irina to the matter at hand, viz., his newly-acquired redundancy. Let alone listen to any further Irina-related loucheries from this apparently sexually incontinent goat of an Ambassador. So he changed the subject,

"Well, all of that notwithstanding, it seems to me that I should contact my *patron* in Paris about this *désobligeant* development AVQP", (the French equivalent of ASAP, *"aussi vite que possible"*, pronounced *"avkupe"*).

"Are you referring to MAF," (the *Ministre des Affaires Etrangères*) "or to that knuckle-dragging *barbouze* who announced to me of your posting here?"

"Colonel Mincemot, yes, exactly – him."

"*Au fait* – how did a lad like you ever get involved with such a brute? In fact, who is he, anyway? Who does he work for? – certainly not *us*...."

"I have no more idea than you have, *monsieur l'Ambassadeur* – but I judge it prudent not to vex or even irritate him needlessly – it'll be interesting to hear his reaction to my news today...." The Ambassador appeared to have nothing further to contribute, so Michel-Ange pressed on, "So, euh, if we can perhaps address ourselves to what they call in American gangster films the 'brass tits' – how would you suggest I – ?"

"The brass whats?"

"What? Oh – brass tits."

"I believe the expression is *tacks* – brass *tacks*."

"Really? *Tiens.* Alright, as you wish. In any case, I believe I need to speak to him. Of urgency. How do you suggest I best proceed? I don't suppose I could use *your* phone here, could I? – or I suppose I could ask Moitié to borrow *his gadget,* but he seems in any case to be rather permanently elsewhere, and, as I say, this is not a matter which I wish to allow to *traine*...."

"M'ouaaaais...." the Ambassador steepled his fingers, leaned back in his chair and looked at the ceiling *"Non, non,* you don't want to be using a regular phone or Moitié's thing – insecure, for sure... *non,* we actually *do,* here at our little establishment, have a special system which can be used for communications of a confidential nature," and he now leaned forward to fix Michel-Ange with a conspiratorial gaze, "which I will now explain to you. Incidentally, it was installed by the *Légionnaires,* and Moitié, naturally, knows about it and probably Irina does as well, although she's technically not supposed to... and I regretfully have to inform you that *Madame l'Ambassadrice* also knows of it, as she is forever using it – " and here he made quotation marks with his fingers, " 'to call her children', and multitudinous lawyers..."

Duquon-Lajoie went into, and almost as quickly snapped out of, a pained reverie at this mention of his wife and her phone calls,

"Yes, so the thing, do you see, the thing about this secure communication system is... that it's located in the garage."

"The garage. You mean that building out there beyond Moitié's notional Consulate – you mean Ivan's workshop?"

"The very one. Now then, in that building, in addition to Brother Ivanovich's collection of greasy *patatras,* resides my beloved Facel-Vega. 1957. An unparalleled *triomphe de la téchnique Française* – although, admittedly, with eight American DeSoto cylinders. Black and gold. *Cabriolet,* for when one is in a *sportif* mood. A sublime machine. It was bought by my fa – "

"Fascinating – *passionnant* – Ivan already mentioned it to me. But – ?"

"I'm getting there, don't be so impatient, my boy, we have time – in fact *you,* of all people, suddenly have more on your hands than most.... Anyway, where was I? Yes, it was bought by my father because back in 1957 it was the fastest production car available in the world – 253 kph – In fact, in all of Paris, only Rubirosa had a faster car, and his Ferrari was not a 'production' car...."

He seemed to mentally drift off again, so Michel-Ange brought him back to life by indicating that he might not be averse to another shot of Grand Marnier –

he was beyond caring how little good this would do him... and it *did* snap the Ambassador out of it, as he did the honors and continued,

"So this delectable car, this Facel-Vega, normally sits in the garage. And here, by the way, is the key to that garage," and he opened a drawer, pulled out a single key attached to a large 18kt gold paper clip and handed it over to Michel-Ange, "that I'll thank you to return to me personally when you're done. So, as I was saying, the Facel – which, I may have forgotten to mention, I *and only I* ever drive – has pride of place in the garage. My *official* car is that horrible high-tech Citroën which I can only be induced to enter under the most dire of official circumstances and it can sit out in the rain for all I care. It's mostly in any case only used by *Madame.* For purposes which I could, of course, ascertain if I were to lean on *le brave* Ivanov, but of which for legal reasons I prefer to remain ignorant... "

Michel-Ange, who was fast running out of stratagems to keep the maddeningly meandering Ambassador on topic, now feigned a coughing fit, which of course turned into a real one – damned near blowing out his larynx...

"There there, here, take another drink," *dop-dop-dop* "There, that better? Right, so, to return to this garage *affaire* – the thing about it, do you see, is that underneath the old Facel, after you've wheeled it out, you will discover that on the floor there is a trap door leading to a cavity ostensibly for mechanics to use to work on the underside of a car, but it's been enlarged by our sturdy *Légionnaires* to acquire the proportion of a smallish subterranean sort of *cave* – and it is in *there* that we have installed our supposedly secure communications 'system'. I say well – 'supposedly'."

"Aha!" assented Michel-Ange, to whom these fresh infusions of Grand Marnier were actually inducing something resembling a renewed will to live. "And down in there I will find the solution to my urgent commo requirement?"

"*Exactement.* For in that underground *oubliette,* in one corner, a red telephone finds itself. Which, I am assured by the installing *Légionnaires,* as confirmed by Moitié who witnessed its implantation and who has a certain... *affinity* for these matters, provides a 'secure' line, supposedly invulnerable to the still-rather primitive Gryaznian '60s-era KGB-surplus eavesdropping equipment. I'm afraid there's a bit of an echo and also an annoying delay – a matter of a second or two – involved, but I am assured that that is only the 'scrambler'," (he used the mining term *"broyeur"*) "doing its job."

"Well that sounds sensational. More or less. May I have a go at it? Now?"

"I don't see why not." Ambassador Duquon-Lajoie rose to escort Michel-Ange out of his office. "In fact, you'll find the whole *concept* down there *passionnant* – it's actually quite pleasant, once you've successfully negotiated access. There's a chair, and the boys were obliging enough to *branche* an electrical outlet into their implantations so there is also an electric fan and even, courtesy of Motié, a small fridge – to which everyone using the apparatus in question – we call it *'le rouge'* – is encouraged to contribute something, as it is not serviced by the regular Embassy cleaning staff."

Michel-Ange paused at this, by the door – "But I have nothing to contribute – I've had no chance to go shopping, yet."

"Pas de probleme!" The Ambassador went back and retrieved the half-filled bottle of Grand Marnier and handed it over. "Here! – take this – I'm happy to re-contribute... now then, where was I – ?" They were standing at the top of the stairs, at this point. "Yes, I mentioned 'negotiating access' – now, of course, that involves backing the Facel-Vega out of the garage, an operation to which – and I pray you, pay attention to this – I attach *much* more concern than any *foutu* conversation anyone might care to have on any damn *telephone rouge* – so here's the *astuce:* There are two keys to the *engin* – one of course is always with me, but the spare I keep in the toe of my left riding boot – I keep a pair in a corner of the garage – you can't miss them."

"You go riding? Here in Laina? Where do you keep your horse? Or find any that aren't destined for the butcher shop?" *Is this me talking, or is it the Grand Marnier?*

"No no, I never even use the damn things – the boots. Although I *do* occasionally tell *Madame* that I go to play polo. Complete *foutaise*, of course – I *did* play back in *la métropole*, mind you, but I highly doubt they even know what polo *is* in a lost *bléd* like this – something that my wife could easily ascertain for herself if she wanted, but she chooses instead to believe me – heh, she has her reasons. Now, Moitié knows where the spare key is, but as far as I know, nobody else does. But I am not completely *con,* and wouldn't be surprised to learn that *everyone* else knows – in any case it doesn't matter – our *modus operandi* has so far proved satisfactory. One final note, and in many ways the most important one – " and here the Ambassador dropped his posture of disinterested amusement and became personally invested, *"No one* is permitted to drive the Facel – just back it out of the garage and back in, *c'est tout* – I take note of the exact *kilométrage* and if the odometer moves up a hundred meters in the process of backing out-and-in, I notice. Abuse of this no-drive policy results in loss of red-phone privileges. Oh, and be attentive with the clutch – it is *very* delicate and nervous."

The Ambassador now smiled, clapped his hands, clapped Michel-Ange on the back, and made to re-enter his inner sanctum, "And now, *mon petit*, I need to prepare myself for..." he mumbled something unintelligible "but I wish you the best of good luck and, should you get through, give them my fond regards in Paris." *Clack* went the door and that was it for the Ambassador.

All in all, Michel-Ange found Duquon-Lajoie's attitude preternaturally complacent, but on the other hand it was expressed with such apparently cheerful insouciance that it was difficult to take it amiss. In any case, he had more pressing things to attend to, now, as he bounded down the stairs. Irina was still in her receptionist's turret – legs fetchingly crossed and examining her nails.

"Saw? How it vass?"

"Splendid. Delightful."

Michel-Ange searched among all his bumf in his *sérviette* for the business cards that had been pressed upon him back at the Quai d'Orsay – ah, there they were, one each for *Mlle.* Bergère and the colonel – both mini-masterpieces of obfuscatory misdirection, he now realized: **General Administrator, Ministry of Foreign Affairs"** for the former, and "Di-

`rector, Plans and Special Projects, Ministry of Foreign Affairs`" for the latter. But more to the point, only the Mother Superior's contained a number for *"à domicile"*, and looking at his Tissot, he noted that it was getting on to being about that time that those *farniente* bureaucrats knocked off, back in Paris – not that Mincemot was any such thing, mind, and anyway Michel-Ange knew him well enough by now to know that he operated in a world beyond normal "office hours".

He was about to head to the garage – still clutching the Grand Marnier – when it occurred to him that here as well, it was not far from closing time, and he turned back,

"So look, Irina, I'm off to use the, you know, *kraznoye téléphone*, I don't know how long I'll be. So..."

"*Da,* you go, you do – you hev oll keys ent flet *informatzias* you are now needingk. I too, I sink, I go hom – see you een marningk!" and she *mwa*-ed a big kiss at him, making her look for a second not unlike an exotic Disney lady-blowfish.

So now Michel-Ange clattered out of the embassy/residence and trotted over to Ivan Ivanov's garage, to attend to this next bizarre *tache*.

18

ALLO? ALLO?

Using this latest key, he pulled up the wide roll-up door, and entered the garage, which bore the universal garage-smell of turpentine and motor oil. He flicked on an overhead fluorescent light and beheld the gleaming black and gold *bolide*.

Putain, it undoubtedly radiates cachet, this 1957 Facel-Vega cabrio – oh *yes, I could definitely see myself swanning about in* this *thing*....

He retrieved the key from the boot (*boot*-boot, of course – not car boot) and entered the superb machine's laquered-mahogany-and-tan-leather interior. Once idling, the thing rumbled like a low-flying WWII bomber, but he managed to ease it out onto the driveway without untoward incident. The car's door closed with a solid 16-ton *thunk*.

Re-entering the garage and remembering to pull the door down behind him, he approached the oil-stained now-vacant cement floor, in the middle of which was a worn wooden slab, a little more than 1 square meter, with a smallish hole at one end. He looked around and, sure enough, hanging from the pushbar of what might well have been the World's First Assisted Lawnmower he found a nasty-looking S-shaped hook-type tool. *Just* the thing.

He heaved the trap door up and flipped it onto its back with an impressive thump. Peering down he saw a primitive and extremely steep – *just* short of vertical – set of stairs which very quickly disappeared into dank darkness. (The garage's fluorescent bulb did not extend very far, and certainly not into the hole).

Hmmm... Right, well, there's nothing for it.... Allez, vas-y, con que tu est....

Wishing very much that he had a flashlight, Michel-Ange descended. Gingerly. He found himself counting the steps – why, he had no idea – nine, it turned out. At the bottom, he took a few halting steps with his arms held out, like a patomime *fantôme.* A cold, coily metallic thing brushed against his face, damn near giving him a heart *infarctus* – not since something cold and wet had smacked his horrified 10-year old face on the Ghost Train at the *Foire du Trône* at the Place de la Nation had he felt such a thing. Wildly waving his hands about his head, they encountered a beaded chain, which he pulled and a light came on. *Dieu mérçi.*

From a single 25-watt bulb, it wasn't *much* of a light, but it would do. Barely. To illuminate... what, in the end? Not all that much, it turned out. Of course, one expected secret commo rooms to be rather on the minimalist side, and in that regard this particular extended cubbyhole did not disappoint:

The whole thing was about 2 meters by 2 1/2. And off at one end was a small table which looked as though it had begun its life beside a bed – upon which sat an old-fashioned rotary-dial telephone, red, complete with the ancient supplementary *écouteur* hooked to its back. Next to it were helpfully placed a steno-pad, two pencils, and even a small pencil sharpener in the shape of the Arc de Triomphe. And in a rather quaint gesture, someone had seen fit to place the two-volume (white pages and yellow) Paris phone *bottin* underneath, on the floor. This little setup was attended by a footstool, to be used for the reposing of one's arse when using the apparatus.

And at the other end of the commo room/cave sat a small white Philips fridge, purring away like a great friendly pussycat, next to a rather ratty and mildewed armchair.

Stooping involuntarily (it was unclear if he could stand erect in there without bumping his head, and he was disinclined just now to test the proposition) Michel-Ange placed the Ambassadorial cognac on the floor next to the fridge, and helped himself to a can of graciously-Moitié-provided Polarnia beer which he took with him as he squatted down on this little Snow White And The Seven Dwarves seating arrangement.

He picked up the phone and dialed Mincemot's number at the Quai d'Orsay. There ensued a wondrous series of electronic noises only normally heard in science fiction films – *ping ping ping* – but eventually the old familiar ring tone kicked in... only to result in a recorded announcement (by a woman other than Miss Bergère) that the office of the Directorate of Special Projects was closed and to please leave a message.

Well, stuff that – Michel-Ange pulled out Mother Superior's card and called her *à domicile:*

"*Allo oui?*"

"*Mlle.* Bergère! It's *moi*, de la Fassederad! Calling from the Ambassador's garage in Gryaznia!"

"Mich– you! But *mon Dieu! Where* did you say you are?"

"It's in a... sort of... *place* – hard to explain, really – a secure hole in the ground in the garage at the Embassy in Laina – it's a bit *compliqué* – "

"Yes, *bien sur*. Well, one is always ravished to hear from you, of course – but... why, euh, are you in fact calling?"

"Well, *Mademoiselle* Bergère, the thing is, well, the thing is that... well, things... do not, in fact, appear to have gotten off, here, as, euh, as smoothly as one might have hoped to expect...."

"Young man, I beg you, speak like a normal human being. What is it you want or need of me...or us?"

"*Bon*. What I'm afraid I need is the Colonel's home number. There has occurred something which he should be made aware of."

Miss Bergère now adopted a slightly but discernibly more engaged tone,

"Weeell, I *do* have it, and I *could* give it to you – but have you any idea how... *unhappy* it would render him to be deranged at home, after hours?"

"Yes. I can readily imagine," *and I can, too* "and believe me when I assure you that there are *immensely* more things that I would prefer to do than to call him just now – but something has occurred which I feel would derange the colonel even more should I *not* inform him of it... and rather *rapidement* – "

"What is it that's causing you such *inquiétude?* Perhaps I can intervene."

"You're very *aimable*, but.... oh, alright – here's the thing: when I went to present my... myself... to the relevant ministry, I was told I was not required – no, not just not required, but not *desired!*"

"Really? *Eh bien* – by whom? – who told you this?"

"The minister himself – that blithering cretin – "

"*Effectivement* – this appears to be more than passingly awkward, and I believe it surpasses my competences – you do need to speak to the colonel and I'll give you his private number, but as it doesn't conform to his protocols I'll have to alert him first. So wait five minutes after we hang up before you call – to give me time to alert him – it will mitigate the trauma of getting a call from you on his private phone in the middle of the night," *Middle of the night? Come on, Mémère Supérieure, I thought you rough-tough spook-types wiped your arses with horaires....* "so, are you ready to copy?"

After *Mlle.* Bergère had give him the colonel's number and rung off – not without leaving him with a gloriously gratuitous exhortation that he endeavor to, of all things, "up his game" (*"enfin – assumez, jeune homme!"*) – Michel-Ange sat on his little stool, wondering how to occupy himself for five minutes, and of course deciding that the best way to do that was to go for another Polarnia from Moitié's little fridge. *Aaahh.*

But now, with two minutes still in hand, he had to *pipi.*

Where to go? Even Michel-Ange shrank from the idea, briefly entertained, of pissing in one of the corners, down here, perhaps behind the fridge... and there was no time to *traine* himself all the way out of this hole to go behind the garage somewhere...

So he solved his small emergency by – carefully and gingerly – aiming his *bite* into the popped-open top of the first, empty Polarnia, and, as *les Breeteesh* liked to say, *voila,* Robert was one's uncle. He briefly admired his skill at not making any mess in this delicate manoeuvre before returning to the other matter at hand. He dialed and it picked up.

"Euh, euh, good evening, *mon colonel.*"

Michel-Ange could hear classical music playing softly in the background... so soothing... in such contrast to the barked

"De la Fassederad – I must confess I had not expected to hear from you so soon – and certainly not *chez moi. La Supérieure*'s already tipped me off – now look, can't the Ambassador deal with this? That's what he's fucking there for,"

"Well, it was he who advised me to take the matter up with you, rather..."

At this the colonel mumbled something – more, it seemed, directed to himself than to Michel-Ange – about "that worthless inbred Duquon-Lajoie, not fit to change urinal cakes in a men's *pissoire*" – before resuming "Alright, *petit,* tell me, calmly, what happened. By the way – you're not drunk, are you by any chance?"

The truthful answer, of course, would have been, "Weeell, ... kind of," but instead Michel-Ange cried *"Mon colonel,* certainly not – *quelle idée –* "

The colonel sighed. "Alright... *vas-y, crache –* "

"Well, so, I went around earlier today, this morning, to the Ministry of Culture, Arts, Sports and the Many Miscellanies, as I was instructed to do,"

"Yes, yes – get *on* with it, boy."

"*Bon.* So in the shell of the nut... the minister, a rather unhinged-seeming *type,* if I might be permitted to say so, duly stamped and validated all my *paperasse* in good order... But then he commanded me... euh,... to get lost. To *fous le camp.* In effect, to do nothing – " It occurred to Michel-Ange that this had been the colonel's very instruction to him right from the start, so he improvised a little frantically, "but not, I hasten to add, your own *constructive* 'do nothing while keeping eyes open for Americans', *non* – this was insulting 'do nothing' – do nothing about *anything.* And *least of all* about any French culture. They simply don't want to know."

Ominous silence. Eventually, the Colonel came back, in a measured tone, "Nothing, *hein?*"

"Nothing. He even had the effrontery to tell me I should occupy myself with chasing the local girls. *Mon colonel.*"

"Did the *con* give you any indication why? What their problem is?" And then, without waiting for an answer, "The Americans – it can only be the Americans...."

"I... *écoutez, mon colonel...* with respect, I really don't think it's anything to *do* with the Americans... who don't, in fact, appear to be so thick on the ground, around here, as perhaps you imagine. Rather, it's the Russians and the Serbs who seem to be making all the running with these Gryaznians – which should not be surprising, after all, inasmuch as, as you know, all three are allies in the Bosnian *merdier* – but as far as our French culture is concerned, *prrrrrp!, que dalle.*"

"Fassederad," the colonel now sounded menacing, "How did you so quickly and comprehensively manage to fuck things up over there?"

Michel-Ange, down in his hole, a thousand kilometers away, had no way of knowing that Mincemot, contrary to how he sounded, was delivering this last bit rather *pro forma.* For the fact of the matter was that – as he'd made clear to the lad at their first meeting – not only did he not give much of a damn whether or not Michel-Ange delivered any "French culture" in that shit-hole, but on the contrary – if he were prevented from doing so it would free him up to do what the colonel was *really* interested in, viz., *finding out who was up to what, in particular the Americans* – and, while he was not prepared yet to accept the boy's verdict that the Americans were, in fact, up to nothing, if it turned out the boy was right, then... *why were they not?* Up to anything? ... The Americans, after all, were everywhere – and if they were not "in" Gryaznia, Mincemot wanted to know *what do they know about the place that we don't?*

But Michel-Ange was in a too-enervated state to grasp the tactical possibilities of his altered status, and the colonel heard him now protesting,

"But *mon colonel,* I did strictly nothing – in fact I scarcely managed to utter more than my name and deliver my salutations when I was told, *prrroup!,* that my services were not required – "

The colonel cut him off, "Alright, listen – it's not possible to pass me the Ambassador, is it?"

"I'm afraid that's not an option, down here where I am." *To put it mildly.*

"Or the other imbecile, the Consul *mec,* Moitié?"

"Nor, I'm afraid, him. Even less so." Michel-Ange thought it diplomatic to not expand on this.

"Alright, *petit,* let's leave things till tomorrow. Let me give this some thought, and maybe make a call or two – this isn't, after all, exactly a national emergency – I imagine the *République* – and even you – will survive. But let me be certain of one thing – despite telling you they didn't want any of our culture, they *did* accept your credentials, *n'est ce pas?* You *are* duly accredited, right? I mean, we don't have to pull you out or anything, do we?"

"Yes – *non* – yes, they did stamp and accept everything. At least that."

"Alright... so there's no need to panic. You can stay on down there as Culture Attaché, and do... other things. Or we could revise your appointment. Could make you a 'Political Officer', although we prefer not to use that in *coco* or ex-*coco* countries... maybe 'Admin Officer'... or 'Co-Operation', except we do even less *coopération* over there than we do culture... or, heh, perhaps 'Public Information'..."

" *'Public Information'*? But, *mon colonel*, I know nothing. About anything."

"Heh, *justement*. Or perhaps we'll just leave things in *status quo*. Let me think about it. But for now, don't lose too much sleep over this. Might even work out for the best – if you don't have to waste your time with concerts and literary conferences and such *merde*, it could free you up... We'll see. So call me tomorrow afternoon. But in the office this time. *Allez, à demain*, young man." *Clack. ping...ping...*

Ouff! What a business. Michel-Ange stood up and, seeking relief from all this crouching like a kindergartner, unthinkingly raised his arms to stretch – only to scrape the backs of fingers on the rough cement ceiling, actually drawing blood.

Putain de chiasse de merde!... and he couldn't even wipe the blood off on his trousers – well he *could,* but he damn well didn't feel like doing so. But there was nothing else useful down here... except this stupid steno pad, from which he now ripped a few pages, but that just served to spread the blood around.

The bloody bits of paper only served to remind him that he was – what with his can of Polarnia beer full of his own piss, and the other empty – beginning to collect an impressive little pile of rubbish down here... which was not *even* to mention that common civility dictated that he should replace *asappe* the consumed beer... which in turn reminded him that he needed soon, pronto, pretty damned *vite* to get to a grocery store and buy himself some provisions... which *itself* only reminded him that he needed to complete his money-change deal with Ivan Ivanov.... which, finally, reminded him that he still owed Ivan some francs to complete the *first* part of their deal....

Ho la la, this diplomatic life is so far not panning out in the slightest *as I'd imagined... Well, tant pis, rien à faire,... Allez, Michel-Ange, pull yourself together, get a grip, and... get your* cul *the hell out of this hole....*

So he gathered up the cans, careful to not to spill the one full of *pipi*, pulled the light chain with his teeth and in total darkness shuffled the few centimeters to the foot of the nearly vertical stairs, up which he laboriously trudged.

Out the top, *hop-la,* cans into a large rubber *poubelle* by the door, replace the heavy trap door – *ker-plouff!* – fetch the Facel-Vega (*care-ful!* not to get any bloody blood onto the mahogany or creamy leather) and ease it back into place, close the garage door, and...

Voila! Finito, basta cosi – as, according to Minister Pozadnik (encountered, it seemed, *ages* ago – although it was, incredibly, just this morning), they said in Canada.

19

A BEUMP IN THE NIGHT

It was by now 2030H and he trudged by the Embassy/Residence, in which lights still appeared to be on, on both floors, but he had no desire to re-enter – not to see if Irina was still there, and re-engage with her and all the *patatras* that would inevitably entail – or for any other reason.

Rather, he felt drained, *creuvé*, and looked forward to retreating to his (and Moitié's) bungalow. Where there was still no sign of his fellow lodger... *and that arranges me just fine.*

Michel-Ange realized that he was famished, so as soon as he'd switched on the light, thrown off his jacket and kicked off his shoes, he attacked the last of Roky Balbao's pizza, which certainly hadn't improved with age, chewing as little and as perfunctorily as possible – for if that last slice had not yet started to turn green, it would certainly not *tarde* in doing so.

When this, not surprisingly, failed to fully satisfy, he wandered over into Moitié's side of their dwelling and peered into *his* fridge. ("In for a nef, in for a shit-load of nefas" – wasn't that the saying?) But there didn't seem to be much in *there* that might be immediately useful to Michel-Ange, either – some old-looking butter, a jar of even *older*-looking mayo, a jar of sour pickles, more cans of Polarnia, the bony remnants of a pre-cooked chicken – and, *aha! allo, allo,* what's this? – most of a large, brown sausage of what appeared to be of local provenance. *Chouette!* In Michel-Ange's considerable experience, one could never go wrong with a *saucisson,* no matter what kind, no matter where.... So he cut himself off a goodish chunk of that, helped himself to one of these pickles, here, and wandered back, munching, into his own territory... making a mental note to add this small *restauration* to the total, when he eventually made restitution to Moitié for the underground beers... not forgetting the francs he also owed Ivan...

But first he needed some sleep. Badly. So he stripped to his boxers, brushed his teeth, flicked off the light, and shuffled gingerly to his bed. Upon which he now with immense gratefulness flopped.

It was a quiet night – although his bed was not all that far from a main thoroughfare (the good old "3 Октября Проспект"), this being socialism-strapped Gryaznia, traffic was very light and so not much motorized noise came from that direction. The last thing he heard was faint music – *pasodoble?* – drifting from what might well have been the Residence...

...Michel-Ange was dreaming: The usual inchoate jumble of illogicalities – *he was on an airliner... except now it suddenly wasn't an airliner anymore, but rather some kind of lounge, from which a grinning Minister Pozadnik was, with much pomp and flourishes, noisily departing – pushing a cart piled impossibly high with luggage... and for some reason Michel-Ange and Irina and Jennifer were following him, now up an escalator which, of course, the Minister's cart couldn't properly negotiate so the luggage came toppling over, on top of them,* crash bang boom –

CRASH BANG BOOM! – hey! that *was no dream, that was for* real...

Michel-Ange sat up at a right angle, propping himself up on his fists like a stick figure.

Although somewhat muffled by distance, the *crash bang boom*-ing came distinctly from the direction of the Residence, and was immediately followed by an unholy series of howls and cries that were as alarming as they were sustained.

All Michel-Ange could think of was one of Macaque-Manu's favorite exclamations: *"Quoi, le quoi, de quoi-quoi-quoi?!"*

What the suffering shitcakes was going on in the Residence? His Tissot had luminous numbers – it was one in the *foutu* morning!

The howling continued – sounded almost stereophonic – two voices?

Well, he damn well couldn't sleep through *this* bloody *vacarme*, that was for sure – and things *did* sound pretty dire over there, so... there was nothing for it....

He bounded out of bed, switched on the light – *still* no Moitié, by the way – and quickly slipped on shirt, trousers and loafers (no socks) – but instead of his jacket he threw on his trench coat (*bigger pockets – you never know*). It occurred to him that a weapon of some sort would not be amiss – (he thought briefly but with considerable rue back to that Ministry chauffeur who'd taken him to the airport and his astonishment at their not having given Michel-Ange an *arme* of some sort) – and scanned his immediate vicinity: there was the odd kitchen knife, but without an accompanying sheath he reckoned it would be a greater danger to himself than to any possible malefactor, and instead pocketed a screwdriver he found in the cabinet under the sink.

He arrived at the still-ominously clamorous Residence and reached for the front door – only to see the thing open, seemingly by itself... But no, it was Irina who'd opened it, and she, obviously hell-bent on a rapid egress from the premises...

...immediately flew into Michel-Ange. Practically into his arms – full frontal (as it were), like two bumping cars – even bouncing off each other, as two such cars would.

There she stood, disarranged and generally hysterical. She was dressed (if you could call it that – the garment in question was hanging off one shoulder) in a short pinkish terry-cloth "robe" (jacket, more like). And as howls of pain still reverberated from somewhere in the darker recesses behind her, she managed to blub through a mixture of tears and mucus,

"He fall! – *bee-hee-hee* – he – !"

"*Who?*" demanded Michel-Ange, trying to steady her by the shoulders,

"Ar-*mant!* Stupit Iambassador! Dranken *idiota-durak!* – I tell him not dis night, I hem hevingk vomans bizness, dunt vant – *bee-hee-hee* – bot he say no, he say tonight eez goot becoss hees stupit vife gone – !"

Michel-Ange knew there were more pressing matters just now – not least the undiminished caterwauling from within – but he nevertheless found himself interrupting her thus,

"Is this a regular thing? Between you and him?"

"*Vatt?*"

"You and the Ambassador – is it a... *regular* thing? – were you *d'accord* with... it? With this... *behavior?* Or did he attack you?"

Inapt as they might otherwise be, Michel-Ange's words at least had the effect of bringing a brusque stop to her crying and emoting, and she instead looked at him with undisguised Slavic scorn:

"Vatt difference? Iz *normalnyie* – mans, vomans – *etteck*, vat mins? Dis iss stupit tok – hef no minningk – *phwaah!,* dunt tok diss!"

Seeing that Michel-Ange was taken aback by this outburst, she now switched gears and softened, "Vat eess more *impartantnyie*, ees he foll, brek stupit nieck, or – nat nieck, brek stupit legck! Kam, look – !" and she grabbed his trench coat.

"But – " he protested, although he allowed himself to be pulled along, "where were you going when you banged into me just now?"

"To get *you!*" Michel-Ange had his doubts about this, but... no matter....

At the back of the Residence's ground floor, by the bottom of the stairs, they found the source of the ongoing clamor: Ambassador Armand St. Emilion de Pépinière Duquon-Lajoie, crumpled in a pathetic heap. Whose sustained yowls of pain now, as he noticed two pairs of legs approaching him, were modulated somewhat to lower-decibeled moaning and whimpering.

Mon Dieu, how the Mighty have Fallen. Literally.

Prior to their being capped by his magnificent, improvised and just-executed, four-point arse-over-apex descent of the staircase, the apparent evening's festivities had begun with the Ambassador, clad in a maroon silk Sulka dressing gown which covered a pair of gold and black-striped (also) silk undershorts from Moschino, and... nothing else, save for a pair of felt *pantoufles* with the *Père Noel* motif on the toes that slid around with the ease of miniature hovercrafts. (These slippers had been an imbecilic souvenir from a long-ago trip to Lapland and the Ambassador liked to wear them when he was feeling particularly goatish – which apparently had been the case tonight....)

And it was that thus clad that he'd commenced his *chute,* insouciantly cradling a *ballon* of Rémy Martin's Louis XIII best (no more of that pedestrian Grand Marnier stuff, which he kept merely for office visitors like Michel-Ange). And it was from *that* now-smashed libation that potentially-lethal glass shards currently sprinkled the scene of the catastrophe.

Which had probably (if it had been properly investigated forensically) been caused by those treacherously slippery slippers, as he'd heedlessly pursued the coy Irina Vozhbuzhdena who'd decided tonight to – for once! – go through the motions of resisting his version of what Procol Harum, in their "Grand Hotel", rather fancifully described as the "Continental slip and slide, Early morning pinch and bite".

In any case, having completed his superb, if involuntary, double-reverse, now-tuck, now-pike, now-layout crash-bang bippity-bop-boom bounce bounce bounce *aie aie aie mygodwillthiseverstop?* descent to the *rez de chausée,* Ambassador Duquon-Lajoie presented a decidedly pitiful sight: mostly-undressed, lying on his side (vaguely but gruesomely describing the letter S), his right hand covered in blood (his bleeding exacerbated by all the alcohol, of course), and his left leg manifestly broken in two places (from one of which the tibia protruded through the skin).

Michel-Ange was not at all sure, to put it mildly, how best to address the situation. But he decided on a positive approach.

"Eh bien, mon cher monsieur–" He realized he'd have to speak louder if he was going to penetrate the persistent Ambassadorial wall of lamentation – *really,* it was all a bit unseemly: the fellow was clearly in pain but nevertheless one would have hoped that a *mec* of his standing and upbringing might have shown a bit more *sang-froid...* not to mention dignity... But there it was – one never knew, did one, how a fellow would react under stress until the *merde* hit the *ventilateur....* So Michel-Ange was forced to speak a little louder, *"Eh bien,* my dear sir – you seem to have fallen... down... rather..."

The stricken Ambassador looked up at him and cried *"You!* You – you cretin! This is all your fault!"

"Me? What on earth did *I* have to do with it?"

"Yes you! Ever since you showed your ridiculous self here Irina has not been the same – she's suddenly become all reluctant and *difficile* – playing hard to get – silly little *connasse* caused me to trip down these stairs – *now* look at me!..."

Irina had been listening to this and not liking the tone of what she was hearing. At all. Indeed, she knew enough French to *pige* that if this babbling Ambassador were allowed to continue unchecked, she'd end up being identified as more of a catalyst to the present calamity than, ahem, she cared to be. So, determined to re-direct the narrative, and speaking over the Ambassador, she piped up briskly about the need to call for a *"niémiergencié niembulance",* to which end she now proposed to call "van two trié" (123), the apparent Gryaznian SOS number.

Michel-Ange instinctively recoiled from this move – he wasn't sure *why,* exactly, but something told him that once one became engulfed in whatever dog's breakfast (*panier de crabes*) passed for the Gryaznian "emergency" bureaucracy, extraction therefrom might not be such a straightforward matter.

On the other hand, he also instinctively knew that it would be a bad idea if he tried to administer any kind of first-aid to this inert (though still loud) specimen, or attempt to move him in any way, so instead he ordered Irina,

"No, no, no, don't do that, please. Not just now, anyway. Rather go to the bathroom and bring a wet towel – we've got to stop the bleeding of his hand, here..."

As she pirouetted off to do this, the two Legionnaires miraculously materialized. *Pouf!*, just like that, out of seeming nowhere.

And while both of them were, as always, (with their white *képis* and red shoulder tassels), quite nattily got up, only Sgt. Schlechtermann was wearing his bloused khaki trousers – while Pfc. Meiavelha, who'd clearly been off-duty, was still in his rather racy *slip*. Although, to his credit, he *had* brought the rest of his uniform, into which he now hopped around, now on this leg, now on that one – pulling himself into *presentabilité*.

Michel-Ange greeted their arrival with almost physical relief. Although after his initial *"Ah!* Thank God!*"*, it did occur to him to ask, "But what about the gate?"

Sgt. Schlechtermann answered simply, "Locked."

Then, squinting at the twisted and still-complaining heap that had been his Ambassador, and then turning to watch Irina re-join them bearing a wet towel and washcloth, Schlechtermann observed,

"Et bien mon fieux!, what the fiddly fuck has been transpiring *here?"*

"Funny you should ask – " began Michel-Ange....

20

MÉDÉVAQUE

Michel-Ange's recitation wasn't, in fact, all that long, and the Legionnaires, being well and truly Men Of The World, *piged* the situation pretty quickly.

Schlechtermann again looked down at Duquon-Lajoie and, almost (but not quite) seeming to enjoy himself, said "Well, *Monsieur l'Ambassadeur,* what a story, *hein?* So how are we feeling?"

"I'm dead," came the croaked reply.

"Not yet," the Sgt. replied, while Meiavelha muttered "If only – " behind his hand.

Irina knelt down to apply the wet toweling to the Ambassador's lacerated hand, but this only set off fresh howling, so she turned and addressed the Legionnaire Sgt., who seemed tacitly to have taken over from Michel-Ange as being In Charge of Things, at least *dans l'immédiat....*

"I vanted to koll de nemiergencié niembulence, but Michelangelo say no, bietter nat – "

"Well, he was right – you were right." the Sgt. acknowledged Michel-Ange with an upward nod. "We don't need any of *that merdier...*"

But Irina's inner Florence McNightingshades seemed to continue to grip her, and she now said, "Poor men, he iss safferingk tiérrible! – I knaw vaire iss *Madame* keepingk hair paine-kiellers, de pills, I ken go get!"

"*Non,* don't bother with that either," said the Sgt., "Rather you – " he indicated his Pfc. "go get the first aid *merde* – and include the kits for the litter, the one for splints and that bag with the morphine *syrettes* – you know – "

Meiavelha ran off to their bungalow, while Schlechtermann helped Irina up and said to her, "*Ca va* for the moment, *Irène,* just stand by here and... a bit of *calme,* I pray you. *Tranquilita.*" And he turned his attention back to Michel-Ange:

"OK, you – even though you're here for... 'culture' – " he spat it out in the Germanic "*kultur*", "I believe your contact at the Quai is a military *type* – "

"Weeeell... of a sort..." *How the hell does he know?*

"Don't argue. I know – we know. So look, we need to organize a *médévaque* out of here. I don't know from exactly where – maybe Zagreb, maybe Sarajevo – maybe even Ljubljana – depends on where our airmobile elements are at the moment, but it doesn't matter – I can manage all that, but first we need to get it authorized at a higher level, which is where you come in."

"Really? I do? You think so?" Once again, Michel-Ange was not entirely comfortable with where this conversation appeared to be heading....

"*Exactement* – You're *just* the *mec* to procure the authorization – so get on your blower – " he used the phrase *souffleur* but in his Hessian accent it came out like cauliflower, *choux-fleur,* "and *execution – illico presto.*"

Michel-Ange couldn't tear the image of a re-enraged Mincemot from the front of his brain, and despite himself he heard come out of his mouth "But *monsieur, sergent,* do you not think that perhaps, as this is a technical, *euh,* para-military-ish matter, it would be *you* who would, in fact, be better advised to make the call?"

As Michel-Ange had been talking, Schlechtermann – who, at forty-one, was not *quite* old enough to be our hero's father, but was nevertheless plenty imposing enough – had approached him so that now, when he drew himself up in order to interrupt, his stony face was about five millimeters from Michel-Ange's:

"Now you listen to me, *petit,* and listen well, so that we have no misunderstanding: I am a *Sergent-Chef* of the *Légion Etrangère, verstehen? A*nd when not sleeping, drinking, fucking or shitting, I kill people. That is my *boulot,* that is what I do.

"*You,* on the other hand, are *sensé* to be a diplomat, however half-arsed, and as such, and to the extent that you have any purpose in this life at all, it is to make *precisely* the kind of call I am hereby ordering you to make, right now. *Compris?* Have I made myself clear?" Michel-Ange's face was blank – whether from paralyzed shock or mere bemusement was unknowable and, in any case, moot. "*Bon. Execution. Et qu'ça saute.* Hop it, *mon gars.*"

Alright, there's nothing for it – both the guy there *and the guy* here *are gonna have my ass on a* tartine, *so either way I'm toast, but at least there's some physical distance between me and the guy* there... *so... no choice, really....*

"Right. *Monsieur – sergent.*"

"*Chef!*"

"*Chef.*"

"That's more like it. That's the spirit, *petit.* Now look – " And now, Schlechtermann pulled out a pocket notebook and started to scribble, "you're likely to need this – I'm sure they've got our location on their maps, but just for the record, these are our *exact* coordinates – for the front lawn, which is, *naturellement,* what I'm designating as the LZ – and, here, *most important of all,* is Meiavelha's and my radio frequency that we constantly monitor and that they must use to contact us AVQP – " He tore off the page and handed it to Michel-Ange. "Got it? *Allez, fiston,* use your initiative and under no circumstances must you fuck this up – do *not* come back empty-handed!" And with that, the Legionnaire sergeant all but kicked Michel-Ange in his *cul* to propel him towards the front door of the Residence.

Where he had to make way for Pfc. Meiavelha who, just then, came tearing in, bearing the relevant medical gear. Which (as Michel-Ange disappeared into the darkness outside) the young half-Portuguese half-Mozambican French soldier now presented to his sergeant.

Schlechtermann took out one of their thirty five-milligram morphine syrettes, that looked a bit like a tube of SuperGlue with a longish needle sticking out of it, from its plastic container and approached the Ambassador, whose crying had by now exhausted itself to a whimper but whose face seemed to be turning puce.

"OK, *Excellence,* hang on to yourself – this should noticeably improve your *train de vie* – ", and, jamming the needle as far as he prudently could into the stricken Ambassadorial thigh, he squeezed out the morphine. (Lovely stuff – Schlechtermann had been given some himself when he'd received a spear – yes, a spear – through the upper arm in Kolwezi in '78… that had been 16 years ago, when he was still a young private, but he remembered *la morph* vividly – and warmly….)

Then, as Irina hovered and flustered around like a kind of preoccupied cross between Tinkerbelle and a queen bee, the two Legionnaires knelt down and gingerly tried to nudge the grotesquely askew lower leg into something approaching its original alignment, without having the jagged broken bones – including the one whose tip protruded through the skin like a tiny periscope – cause even further damage.

Despite the recently-administered morphine, even these minor manoeuvres made the Ambassador seize up in such agony that they didn't *insiste,* and instead deployed and applied the inflatable splint to the decidedly dodgy-looking leg.

That done, they pulled out the retractable poles on their collapsible litter, and set about the task of shifting the broken Ambassador onto it. At this, Irina finally ceased her fussing and contributed by steadying the litter beneath them, all the while muttering – as though the Ambassador couldn't hear her, *"Muy Bog, my Got, dis vill fienesh bedlié for Irina!, Bozhe, pomogi mne!"*

Schlechtermann ignored her, but little Meiavelha couldn't resist nodding and smiling at her, "Don't work yourself up, *'La Perla',*" he said, using the Legionnaires' nickname for her, from her preferred brand of undergarments – an appellation she did not, in fact, discourage, "this will be nothing more than a mere *contretemps administratif,*" and now, lowering his face towards Duquon-Lajoie's, *"N'est-ce pas, Excellence?"*

To which the Ambassador merely grunted again, "I'm dead." Which, noted Schlechtermann, had actually been the only words the man had uttered since they'd arrived on this unhappy scene.

Meanwhile, Michel-Ange again went through the whole garage-and-Facel-Vega drill, (though not before first having another small piss on the lawn – he damn well didn't want to get caught short down there *again*), descended into the commo pit, and again Assumed The (undignified) Position before *le Rouge*.

He inhaled deeply... and dialed. This time it rang so long that it clicked over onto the answering machine, before a groggy but still menacing voice demanded:

"Ouais? 'C'que s'est?, putain –"

"It is again but I, *mon Colonel – de la Fassederad –*", and when this produced nothing but silence, he added "again, *moi,* from Laina...."

"You! But what the fucking hell is it encore?" Then, ominously, there was the sound of a phone falling and crashing about... before the voice resumed with an even more heartfelt *"Bordelle de chiasse! –"* followed by yet another silence. Presently a slightly more composed Mincemot came back on, to start again:

"Alright, *petit,* I assume that if you're calling me at this hour there must be a reason. At least there had better be, because although you have not quite managed to waken *Madame la Colonel* who, mercifully for all of us, is quite *soporifique,* you *have* disturbed the dog, which verges on the impermissible – So, as I said, there had *better* be a reason. And a good one. So go ahead, *tire:* I'm listening."

"Right. Right. Well, you see, it... it concerns His Excellency. The Ambassador."

"Well, what about him. Parenthetically, a fucking fool, but *passons.*"

"Yes. Yes. Well, what has happened is that he seems to have fallen down his *escaliers.* And, I am desolated to have to report, in the process of which he has done himself quite a damage. Mostly to his left leg, which is broken in at least two places – and broken 'compoundedly' according to the Legionnaires – and, although it is in the process of being immobilized by these said Legionnaires, I can report that the leg now presents itself in a most piteously mis-shapen condition."

"Pute-borne! How did this happen? And in the middle of the night? Were you there? – did you have a hand in this, young Face of Rat?"

"I beg of you, *mon colonel!* – assuredly not. I was sagely in the arms of Somnus when it occurred, and was only roused by the frightful *vacarme* – "

"Then what happened? What the hell was he doing *traine*-ing around at this hour of the night? Was he drunk? Is everyone drunk down there? Was there a *nana* involved? From what I understand about this *espèce de connard,* there must have been some *pouffiasse* involved... who is not his wife – which reminds me, what about his wife? What does *she* have to say for herself?"

"Ah well. You have asked many things, there. Starting with the last, the fact of the matter is, *Madame l'Ambassadrice* is nowhere in the environs. At all. *Ffft* – she is gone with the wind, as they say. Which, I believe, is the normal state of affairs, in that *ménage.* But as for another woman possibly being involved, I'm really not current about such matters – "

"Stop it – don't blow smoke up my ass – bunch of inbred *précieux decadents* in this *foutu* so-called diplomatic service. And speaking of which, what about that other idiot, the Consul-Commercial *type* – is *he* around? Is he implicated at all in this *histoire?* – Can I talk to him?"

"Also nowhere to be found. Which is *also*, I have *constaté,* not an uncommon state of affairs – "

"*C'est bon* – I get the picture. Most reassuring, I must say. Anyway, so what do you want of me. As if I couldn't guess – "

"Precisely, *mon Colonel* – the Legionnaires, who, if I may be permitted the observation, appear to have the situation admirably in hand, are of the firm opinion that the local emergency services are to be avoided at all costs and that a heliported medical evacuation is the urgent order of the day. To which end they have charged me to alert you, and to impart to you the following informations...." and Michel-Ange read off the stuff Schlechtermann had given him.

"Right. *C'est tout?*"

"Yes, *mon Colonel.*"

There was no immediate response to this, but after awhile, a bone-weary sigh *did* come from the colonel, followed by,

"Alright. Here's what's going to happen: Me, I will proceed to make some telephone calls. You, you will call me back at exactly 02:30 – no, make it 3, to be certain. In the meantime, you will clear away that fucking *foutu* croquet set from that parade ground in front of the residence – whose idea was that, anyway? Not yours, I trust?"

"*Mais enfin! Mon colonel,* I supplicate you – most absolutely and assuredly not – in any case, I only just got here – haven't had time to shit, if you'll pardon the expression – much less install a croquet set – not that I'd even know how if I *did* have the time...."

"Alright, *ça vas,* don't fuss your feathers. So it wasn't you – but lose the fucking thing anyway, can't have all that *merde* flying into the rotors of the *foutu helico* – "

"Certainly not, *mon colonel.*" But Michel-Ange wasn't *so* out of it that a niggling little thing didn't occur to him: "But, euh, how, if I may presume to ask, did you know they – we – had a croquet set on their – our – front *gazon?*"

"Satellite images. Amazing stuff. We can even tell if the gutters on the residence need cleaning out. Which, I note, they do."

"Ah. Well. But we have actually other priorities just at the moment."

"*Exactement* – so *fous* me in peace to get on with it! – Til later, then – no wait! One last thing: keep trying to get hold of that useless cretin of a Consul. And if and when you get him, drag his *cul* to this phone. He is, after all, supposed to be in charge... rather than you... Alright, that's it for now – *terminé.*"

Michel-Ange hopped it out of the underground commo station – but not before popping and quaffing yet another of Moitié's beers (and adding it to his growing butcher's bill). Thumping the heavy wooden hatch shut, he wondered briefly whether to go through the bother of replacing the Facel-Vega and decided – the way his luck was going recently – that, yes, it would probably be wise to do so. So, *vroom* – and *voila.*

Re-entering the Embassy, he found that the stricken Duquon-Lajoie had lapsed into a sort of morphine-induced quietus, and that the Legionnaires and Irina were sipping *tchaï* and nibbling Gryaznian butter biscuits that she'd rustled up from the recesses of her *kukhnya.*

"You vantingk *tchaï,* Michelangelo?"

"*Merçi,* you are too amiable, *ma chérie.*"

While she went off to sort that out, PFC Meiavelha spoke for both himself and his sergeant, "*Eh alors?* Did you raise your *patron?* Someone gonna be coming to pick up the rubbish here?"

"Well..." Amazingly, Michel-Ange realized he couldn't even answer *that* – which was only the most basic of all the questions facing them at the moment. "I can't say for certain... not yet, anyway... I *think* so... he didn't say *no,* at least."

"Well what did he say – *exactly*?" This from Schlechtermann.

"Two things, actually. No, three. First, is to try to get hold of Moitié – Irina, can you get on that? Call him on that cellular phone contraption of his... Second – to call him, the colonel, back at three a.m. to get further instructions. And finally, to clear away the damned croquet set."

"*Putain,* that's right – can't have *that connerie* fucking up the operation – well, young *Monsieur,* that's something you can do to make yourself useful."

"Me?" asked Michel-Ange, attempting but not really managing to sound indignant. In any case, neither Legionnaire even deigned to respond – they just smiled at him (and Meiavelha even winked). *"Bon, bon, ça va,* I'll go," Michel-Ange groused, but he added "Who the hell's idea *was* that ridiculous thing, anyway? The colonel even had the *culot* to blame it on *me....*"

"*Pfff!* That was Clo's idea – she mistakes this shit-hole for *'L'Année Dernière à Marienbad'* – " the Pfc. was of course referring to *Madame* the *Ambassadrice,* Clothilde de Brest d'Anjou Duquon-Lajoie, but mention of her name suddenly brought him up short: "Oh, *merde, dit* – just by the fucking way – *where the fuck is she?*" He looked around at his sergeant, Irina – even Michel-Ange. "Where's *la folle?!*"

Sgt. Schlechtermann made a "close-it" gesture with his hand indicating that his Pfc. should mind his tongue, and he knelt down and asked the ambassador,

"*Monsieur l'Ambassadeur,* do you have any idea where *Madame* is?"

The groggy fellow actually almost smiled as he mumbled, "No earthly idea. She'd 'be out for some time', is all she said – which is why I thought the moment *propice* to enjoy the company of – "

"Holright, det's enoff!" interjected Irina, and then she addressed her three un-wounded colleagues in a tentative tone, as she was unsure whether it was entirely prudent that what followed should be heard by the Ambassador, "I hem knowingk vere iss *Madame* – she iss et hairport, Ivan Ivanov ték her, in Ceetroon."

"*Quoi?*"ejaculated Michel-Ange, as the Legionnaires shook their heads and smiled. "Is she leaving? Flying somewhere? Making a *rendez-vous*? Or what?"

"Dunt know. Could be any of dese passibielietiés."

"*Main enfin!* – I mean, here we're about to put her husband on a flight to God-knows-where, for God-knows-how-long – the least we should do is put his fucking wife in the picture, *non?*"

Sgt. Schlecthermann, clearly the Voice of Experience and even Calm in their little group, said,

"Don't sweat it, *petit*. She'll *démerde* herself just fine. And the *last* thing this poor *spécimen* – "he jutted his chin at the recumbent Ambassador "will want hovering about him as he fends off disobliging questions of an official nature is *la folle* Clo-clo – " and now he clapped Michel-Ange on the back, "So you, go occupy yourself with that croquet set, and Meia and I'll gather from upstairs whatever shit *le vieux*, there, will need for travel."

"Alright. *Irina!* – " Michel-Ange called to her, as, having unloaded her mini-bombshell about Madame and the airport, she was again back in the kitchenette messing about, "come give me a hand with the croquet – "

"*Non,*" intervened Sgt. Schlechtermann, "we'll need her to help with the Ambassador's papers and crap. Here, take this instead – " and he unhooked the flashlight he wore by his collarbone and flipped it to Michel-Ange "*et ça s'appelle revient –* "

So the Legionnaires and Irina traipsed upstairs to collect the Ambassadorial passport and wallet with credit cards, as well as toiletries and a variety of changes of clothing – all of which they threw into a large gym bag – naturally a *chic* blue-gray job designed by Ted Lapidus, with the *croix-fleur-de-lys* logo of *Le Racing Club De France* (of which Michel-Ange was also a member, but only for the tennis) – that they found in one of his closets. They reached a snag when they came upon the Ambassador's key to the Ambassadorial safe; (Moitié had a smaller, Consular safe).

"This key's useless without the combination, which only he knows. Or knew..." said Meiavelha, "Unless *you* do as well?", this he directed at Irina.

"Mawst campliétlié *niatt!* Vott you sink? You sink I hem *spy?*"

"Mais non, my *cocotte,"* Schlechtermann was unused to the role of pacifier, but he did his clumsy best to unruffle Ms. Vozhbuzhdena. "Anyway, whether he comes back here himself, or gives the code to someone else – a technician of some kind, or his successor – they'll need the damn key here – so I'll hang onto it for now." and he dropped it into one of his voluminous breast pockets. (The *pocket* was voluminous, not his breast. Sheesh, this writing thing...)

Meanwhile, Michel-Ange was faffing and verblungering around out in that extensive lawn that Mincemot chose to call "the parade ground", trying to turn it from a croquet pitch to a helicopter landing site.

Shining the Legionnaire flashlight about, he spied one of the rubberized wire hoops, which he plucked, like a weed. Truth be told, he had no idea how many of these made up your standard croquet *panoplie,* and after a good half-hour of intense scrutiny of every blessed blade of grass out there, (and its brother), he fervently hoped the number in question was not more than six (plus one sturdy, multi-colored post), as that was all he managed to find. Because of course he very ardently did *not* desire to be the cause of a fatal heliported horripilation... anyway, eventually he concluded that he was fucked if he could find any more. *Fini.*

He regained the Residence and dumped the croquet clobber on the floor by Irina's reception desk – to find the others, even including the partially revitalized Ambassador, in an almost festive state. They'd liberated and brought down with them *yet another* bottle of Ambassadorial cognac, with Irina doing the honors from little tumblers she'd produced from that magical little galley/*kitchenette* that she maintained under the staircase (the Embassy's main kitchen was in the back), including even giving Duquon-Lajoie a small sip – which, mixed with the morphine, no doubt was responsible for what some might have called his beatific smile (but which Jennifer would have called a "shit-eating grin").

"You vant, Michelangelo?"

"Alright, *merçi*, although I'd better go *mollo* – I don't want to sound complete-ly *schlaff* when I speak to the *patron* again – by the way, any luck getting hold of Moitié?"

"Oh! I fargiet! In oll *konfuzia*, I fargiet! *Izvinitsye, excusez-moi* – I try now."

"*Alors?*" asked Schlechtermann, turning his attention to Michel-Ange, "You cleared it all, *fiston?*"

"Done and done, *Chef.*" Michel-Ange settled into the one free armchair in the "lounge" part of the Embassy/Residence's reception area – Meiavelha being seated in the other one and Schlechterman having more or less appropriated the *divan*. The Ambassador lay inert but at least more or less quiet on his col-lapsible litter, while Irina was at her reception desk, on the phone alternately to the airport, trying, with so-far no joy, to get them to page Ivan Ivanov – and trying to track down the errant Moitié.

As Michel-Ange settled himself as best he could, he asked the others, "Eh, you, *les militaires,* if I drowse off please make sure to wake me at quarter of three."

In the event, he didn't know if he nodded off or not, but it seemed to get to quarter of three pretty damn quick, and as he now rose to head garage-wards, Meiavelha tooted the refrain from "The Ride of the Valkyries" at him.

Before exiting, Michel-Ange turned and called to Irina, who was once again in her kitchenette,

"Irina, any luck raising Moitié?"

"*Niet!* Alvays biésié, I leef miessatch – I tell heem he mawst koll to hier, viss *urgenzia!*"

Back in his by-now familiar commo pit, and fortified (as if he needed it) with that fresh infusion of the Ambassador's 5-star cognac, Michel-Ange again raised Col. Mincemot. Who was, this time, all briskness and business – no gra-tuitous personal disobligements:

"*Pil!*, on time. That's good. So now listen up well with all your ears, my boy: after much at-times agitated and even surreal discussion at the highest levels of the Ministries of Foreign Affairs, Defense, *la Présidence* and the DGSE – levels that, take my word for it, are not enamored with being woken in the middle of the night and that have included 'Himself' himself who, I may add, *en passant,* was *also* not at home when eventually reached, *mais passons* – anyway, the upshot of all this exceedingly intense *vas-et-viens* is..." and here the colonel paused to inhale, "that at first light, which, I am informed by la *méteo* will be, in Laina, on or about 06:21 this morning, your front lawn – from which has been banished all croquet-related encumbrances, am I correct?"

"*Absolument, mon colonel.*"

"*Bon.* Well, at that time and in that place will be arriving one of our SA330 Puma "Super-Etrangleur" air-rescue helicopters, radio call-sign Blue Félix One, arriving from NATO 'Camp Eirene' in Dubrovnik. Now, Blue Félix One, who, you'll be pleased to hear, will be operating on your – the Legionnaires' – frequency, so you don't have to worry about *that* – will not tarry long, so be prepared to deliver the package immediately. For the record, they, the *hélico* and the package, will then proceed to our Franco-German military hospital in Müllheim, in case anyone wants to know. Like that *putain* of a wife of his, for example, if she ever deigns to show her face.... Fassedarad, are you there?"

"Yes, *mon colonel*, I'm *encaisse*-ing all this. No problem."

"Good, now one more thing. No, two more. First, as soon as you hang up you must *vite vite vite, mais alors* like a fucking *flash*, together with that local Gryaznian talent, that girl we've spoken of – "

"*Mademoiselle* Vozhbuzhdena, *mon colonel* – Irina – "

"Right, *her* – get *her* to get hold of the requisite Gryaznian diplomatic-liaison *zouave-fonctionnaire* to dispatch an official witness to the landing, pickup and departure of both Blue Félix One and the ambassadorial package – otherwise we may well find ourselves officially at war with Gryaznia which – and again, I cannot stress this too strongly – will *not* go down well with the aforementioned highest levels here. Got that?"

"Yes... I think so... yes."

"Look, you've got to do it because in the absence of that *con* of a Consul, Moitié – he's still AWOL, is that right?"

"Completely. Not a trace."

"Well, in his absence, you appear to be our senior diplomatic – hell, forget senior, our *only* diplomatic – presence there at the moment, so, ... *faute de mieux*... you're *it, mon vieux*. And secondly, as soon as this whole operation is over, and the Ambassador has been evacuated – duly witnessed and confirmed *in writing* by a representative of the Republic of Gryaznia – I want you to come back here on the horn to confirm it to *me* – and at that time I want you to bring one of the Legionnaires with you."

"Oh yes? *Mon colonel*?"

"Yes, I will be imparting a further something to you which will require an official French witness. And again, *faute de mieux,* in this case one of the Legionnaires will have to do."

Michel-Ange suddenly found himself wanting some elucidation of this last item.

"Euh – ?"

"Execution! Face of Rat! You have no time to lose! Or waste! Get the hell off this blower – *fous l'camp, petit!* Out." *Click. ping... ping... ping...*

Michel-Ange stared dumbly at the empty receiver for a second... and then snapped out of it – slamming it back and clattering up the narrow and almost vertical steps, again heaving the "trap" top shut, but this time not bothering to replace the Facel-Vega, as he knew he'd be back soon enough.

As he trotted once again back to the Residence, he thought of Mincemot's words: "...the requisite Gryaznian diplomatic-liaison *zouave-fonctionnaire...*" – what the hell form did *that* take?... when it was at home...?

21

BLUE FÉLIX ONE

"Irina!," he cried as he raced in, *"Reveille* yourself! What can you tell me about any official 'diplomatic-liaison' people? – quickly!"

Irina had long since given up trying to get hold of either Ivan Ivanov at the airport *or* Moitié, and had returned to her default project – her nails – but now she looked up, happy for some new action. *"Vy you vant knaw dis?"*

"Becau – "

"Alors, are we on? *C'est* 'go'?" Schlechtermann had never been reluctant to interrupt those he considered his inferiors which, to be honest, was just about everyone.

"What? Oh – yes. *Yes!* – a Puma SA-3-something *Super-Etranger* – "

"Etrangleur – Super-Etrangleur – a nickname."

"Well, one of those is coming in at dawn. Our dawn, here – which I'm told will be about 6:20, so I'd say you – we – should have the Ambassador out there on the grass, ready to go, at, say 6. His call sign is Blue Félix One, he's coming from Camp Eirene in Dubrovnik and will be taking him – " Michel-Ange vaguely indicated the direction to Germany with a very Legionnaire-like gesture of his chin, "to a military hospital in Müllheim – "

"Hah! I know the place, *verdammt*! – I was once a client... well, a patient – there, stayed longer than I needed to – there was a nurse called Yolande – "

"Yes, well, that's as may be – " interrupted Michel-Ange in turn, "but you should be apprised that this Blue Félix One *Super-Etrangleur* will be operating on your own radio frequency, and does not intend to hang around, once he gets here.

"But before *any* of that is allowed to transpire – " he returned to Irina, "we have a crucial bit of business to see to, involving the participation of a still-to-be-identified member of the Gryaznian bureaucracy – Irina, we need, like *immédiatement, subito* – to find, alert – indeed, no doubt *wake up* – and enlist the active personal attendance of a functionary. Of, as I just mentioned, some kind of 'diplomatic-liaison' *zouave* – my *patron*'s choice of word. In short, we need a guy from the government here to witness and sign-off on this violation of Gryaznian air space and, indeed, territory, and subsequent evacuation thence, or else our two countries will apparently find themselves Officially At War – something my *patron very much* does not want."

Pfc. Meiavelha interjected "What the fuck – can't our Ministry of Defense just inform their Ministry of Defense that we have a medical emergency and that a *hélico*'s coming in to sort it out? *Ou est le problème, gars?... merde* – "

"I asked the same thing. The answer, apparently, is that the Gryaznians need to satisfy themselves that the mission was *in fact* what we said it was going to be, otherwise war gets declared – I agree, it's a great system. But hence the need for some fucking *fonctionnaire* – *alors,* Irina? What d'you say?"

Michel-Ange's uncharacteristic assumption of decisiveness surprised even himself, never mind the others. The Legionnaires for once had no ironic comment to make and at least for now *shtoomed* themselves, while a re-galvanized Irina pulled out and consulted an address *agenda,* before answering Michel-Ange,

"Saw, here iss *sittyatsya:* Ve vill be needingk to vake up, een order: Gryaznian Miénistrié off Ientierior, den *Direktsiya* off Stét Siécuriétié vot I tell you about before hiere kolt *DéGéBé,* 'Douchka'. Ent ienside *det giganskiye direktsiya* iss

'Dieplomietic Liaison Divisia' – ent de guy I hem working viss dere is hokay guy, Kiril Krivoy – saw," she seated herself and as she picked up her phone, she looked up, "eeff sambadié gets me more *tchai,* I vill begin to iectiviate dese *duraki....*"

Meiavelha said "I know where the tea *merde* is, I'll get it", and Michel-Ange nodded to Irina, *"Merci, Irène* – and remember, we're pressed for time."

So while the Legionnaires, joined by Michel-Ange, redundantly finished off the bottle of cognac and even more misguidedly discussed the advisability of going upstairs to find yet another one (with Meiavelha in fact being dispatched to do just that), Irina embarked on a fierce telephonic exchange of Slavic vituperations with a succession of irritated, outraged and in all cases groggy mid/upper-level drones in the Gryaznian military/foreign/security bureaucracy, in which *vertolet* ("helicopter") and *pomoschiy* ("emergency") and above all *subudi li se chuka* ("wake up you fucking cretin") figured prominently. In short, cages were vigorously rattled and chains were unambiguously yanked.

Eventually she slammed down the phone, rose and announced,

"Saw! Is goot – ieveryting iss ien order – more den less! Kiril say he hiss hokays, but needingk first pepper – "

Pepper? They stared at her, momentarily struck dumb.

"*Pepper! Pah-pee-yay* een yore *Frantsous."*

"Ah, of course – sorry," Michel-Ange snapped out of it, "a little slow on the uptake, there..."

"*Lee-sten*! – liésten viss oll your hears – " *she's channeling the colonel, now?* "my frent Kiril fram *Douchka,* he iss hokay to vitness *evacuatsyia,* bot needs pepper – ve must calliékt far him dis pepper et DéGéBé *buro* ent tek to heem et hees hom – kam, Michelangelo, ve go."

"Me? Why am I needed?"

"Becoss needingk *Frantsous* diéplomiét for signingk pratakol – ent you are honly deéplomiét I hem seeingk hier – heh, Marteen-oh, iss you diéplomiét?"

By way of answer, Meiavelha grabbed his genitals and offered *"Non, ma chérie, I am the Prince-Héritier* of São Tomé – "

Sgt. Schlechtermann rather more sedately nodded to Michel-Ange and murmured *"Vas-y*, kid, go ahead. Deal with it. And – " he glanced out a window "make it s*chnell*-ish."

As Michel-Ange moved towards Irina to join her on this latest quest, she pushed him back, saying,

"Vaite! Fierst, go hup ent get oll hees – " she looked over at Duquon-Lajoie who continued to lie there with a strangely euphoric look on his *tronche "offit- zialniye* stemps, to stemp on your *podpis –* "

"My *what?"*

"Podpis – how you say, *mnié mnié mnié –* " she made a scribbling motion with her thumb and two first fingers, as though she were asking a waiter for the bill.

"Oh! – right – to stamp over my signature – right, *je pige – attends!"* He scrambled up the by-now infamous stairs to once again semi-ransack the Ambassador's private office, this time in search of official rubber stamps. He found and grabbed a couple in one of the desk drawers... he wasn't overly picky but he *did* reject one that appeared to be of the actual Duquon-Lajoie family coat of arms (!), and clattered back down.

He and Irina again cranked up the Volga and, once Meiavelha had sprinted ahead to let them through the gate and shouted at them "And *démerde* your asses – remember, at dawn we all turn into *citrouilles!*", they shot down the nearly-deserted 3 Oktobr Prospekt, with Irina at the wheel.

Their first destination was a sinister-looking and nearly window-less concrete block down by the Ghost River (not far from where not even 24 hours ago the old *baboushka* had brushed what might or might not have been a tear from Michel-Ange's cheek), which was, according to Irina, one of many of the *Douch-*

ka buildings in the city. This one apparently housed, among much else, the "*Diplomiétic-Liaisonburo*".

For once, the bureaucratic problem was not *too many* people, but rather the opposite – finding the requisite bodies, and then rousing those they did find…. But eventually, 25 minutes later, after much voice-raising and (largely bogus) invocation of "higher-ups", they emerged from the building with a signed (by a mid-level Interior Ministry factotum) and witnessed (by Michel-Ange for the French Ambassador) Gryaznian Ministry of Interior "protocol" authorizing one Major Kiril Nikolaievitch Krivoy to "witness and report on events at or on the premises of the French Embassy compound, Laina, on this date".

And now Irina, still at the wheel, took them to an, if possible, even *more* grim and dreary concrete-scape of a "residential area", on the outskirts of the city – that reminded Michel-Ange, at least in its stark minimalism, of some of Paris' more insalubrious *banlieus,* but which Irina assured him was a "nice" area where "*DéGéBé* ent odder *boo-jwa* pipples is livingk hier! Longk vaitingk leest for get apartmient een diss zone".

Among these fortunates figured Maj. Krivoy and, (it turned out), his young family. Irina and Michel-Ange were buzzed in, and, the lift being on the fritz, they had to ascend three piss-smelling concrete flights of stairs to reach the Krivoy flat that, once they were let into, turned out to be over-heated to *cuisson* level.

The *Douchka* Major in question who greeted them with a nod and a grunt was a strikingly handsome (not unlike the early Alain Delon) young man in what looked like his early thirties, who'd been at that moment seated on his couch in this tiny flat wearing (for today) the shirt and tie of an officer in the Gryaznian Border Guards and… his underpants. *(Much like Pfc. Meiavelha not all that long ago….)*

The poor fellow appeared to be still half asleep, but Irina was having none of it, and they had a brisk exchange in Gryaznian – well, brisk from *her* side, as she cajoled and fussed and mothered (*going, I can't help noticing, so far as kissing his brow*), as well as kicked him in the shin – while he just mostly grunted and moaned. Whatever constituted his "young family" was mercifully out of sight – doubtless in another room, (which itself was proof of their "boo-jwa"-ness....)

Irina turned to Michel-Ange and said, "Now – you mast pé hiem."

Pay him? He *utterly* hadn't seen this coming, but, he immediately realized, that was really just unpardonable naiveté on his part – *of course* he'd need to pay him. The only question was....

"Ah. *Bien sur.* How much?"

"How match you hev?"

Is this how these things are supposed to work? Michel-Ange turned and surreptitiously peered at these greasy and still-unfamiliar notes – the depleted remnants of that hurried and half-arsed "transaction" with Ivan Ivanov... which *still* hadn't been completed.... Looking back over his shoulder at her, he muttered, with notable lack of enthusiasm, "Euh, about fifteen hundred nefa – "

She made a face. "Hal-right – vill hev to do – giff!"

"*What?* But then I'll be *fauché* – !"

"*Giff!*" and she actually stamped her foot. She snatched the money from Michel-Ange, counted out about half and handed that to the still-seated Maj. Krivoy, saying something further to him in Gryaznian to which he nodded in assent. They both then tucked away their portions, he in his uniform shirt pocket and she in her faux-Gucci bag, and she then pushed Michel-Ange out the door,

"Ve leaf him put on *pantaloons*. Kom, ve vaite outside."

"Alright... but what's that game with the money, Irina?"

"He get hef now, ent odder hef iefter the *operatzia* iss finitch."

Normally it was not in Michel-Ange's nature to easily feel aggrieved, but he found that he did, a bit, now: "You and pretty-boy have a nice little *racquette* going, here, haven't you, *ma cherie*?"

"Vat you tok! *Pfah!* Iss *normalniye* to pé – he iss do *beek* faveur to *Frantsous Résplublik*, iz *narmalnye* iexpect to get, *minié mnié mnié, baksheesh!*"

Michel-Ange supposed that, by their benighted lights, she was probably right. But still, the thing rankled... but *that* was probably also almost certainly because the *connard* looked like the young Alain Delon.... *Come on, what am I, some jealous 13-year-old ninny? – allez, Michel-Ange, we have other poissons to fry...*

And thus they waited outside in uncomfortable silence for young Maj. Krivoy to organize himself – the three of them needed to be together to get him past the Legionnaires at the gate. Eventually Irina, ostensibly to "moof heem", went back into his flat... while Michel-Ange, peevishly unhappy at the thought of those two alone together, however briefly, sat and dozed in the "Wolga".

But presently they got their two-car (Krivoy drove a battered old Romanian Dacia that, to Michel-Ange's practiced eye, looked very much like a copy of the already-eminently crappy Renault 5) show on the (empty) road, and drove back to the Embassy Compound as fast as their collectively few wheezing cylinders could manage.

They had to beep repeatedly to get a Legionnaire to open the gate, and in Laina's pre-dawn emptiness, the Volga's industrial-strength horn sounded like an air-raid alert.

"*Ca vas, ca vas, j'arrive* – " Meiavelha hove-to, again at a sprint, and as he opened up, he addressed Michel-Ange, nodding at Krivoy's Dacia behind, "That the government *mec*? To verify?"

"Affirmative" said Michel-Ange "*A propos*, how's the old *con*?"

"Still alive. Happy, even – Wolf gave him a second shot – the guy's *ravi* as a baby on a tit."

"Still no sign of *Madame*? Or, for that matter, Ivan? Or Moitié?"

The Portuguese snorted "Nothing – I personally think Clo's already on a plane to somewhere, and if Ivan's as smart as I know he is, he's grabbing a quick siesta – and Moitié? Probably best we don't know...."

By now the Legionnaires had brought out the litter-bound Ambassador (who was currently, as Meiavelha had reported, happily in la-la-ville, humming softly and unintelligibly) to the edge of the great lawn. Sgt. Schlechtermann approached the three latest arrivals.

"This the *zouave*? The spook who'll assure the *regime* that this is all kosher?"

"*Da*" supplied Irina, "Serzhant-Chief Volf – *DéGéBé* Major Krivoy – " The two military guys saluted each other and shook hands, wordlessly. Pfc Meihalvelha joined them, also saluting, still at a trot, and Irina went off to peer at Duquon-Lajoie. Michel-Ange stood there, scratching his *derrière,* briefly enjoying the pre-dawn breeze, and consulted his watch. 05:55.

Now all six (well, all five – as the Ambassador was facing the wrong way) searched the gradually-lightening sky above the Laina rooftops for the French army's SA-330 "Super-Etrangleur" flying behemoth, code-named "Blue Félix One".

Ah... *there* it came.... and moving at a fair clip, too.... sounding like all the broken washing machines in the world, all set on "HI"....

Most people – and certainly most civilians – have never been on the receiving end, so to speak, of a descending 4,000-kilogram air-rescue helicopter, and thus it is difficult for them to fully appreciate the sensations such a cataclysmic *bouleversement* creates: until and unless the pilot chooses to power down a bit (if and when he does), it is, indeed, so loud that the *cliché* "you can't hear yourself *think*" (never mind speak) takes on vivid new meaning. The descending craft creates an instant mini-tornado which turns anything in its considerable radius into a hopeless tossed-salad... *certainly* including croquet hoops which, had not Michel-Ange been as, ahem, meticulous as he had, would have instantly become deadly flying missiles.

And on top of everything else, the thing came in blasting them with a million-lumen searchlight from its undercarriage that lit up the scene like some "Close Encounters" extravaganza.

In short, a most unsettling catastrification upon all one's senses. (And that was even with*out* door-gunners doing any firing....)

But the pilot did, in fact, humanely crank things down a touch, once the 18-meters-long behemoth's eight wheels were safely resting on the erstwhile croquet pitch, allowing the buffeted, waiting group to push through the maelstrom. They approached the helmeted and still-busy pilot first, but he shrugged, waved a gloved thumb over his shoulder and shouted out his open window,

"See the *paperasse* with my crew chief, Doudou, in back – !"

So they humped the Ambassador's litter the few meters to the rear, where half the helicopter's side stood gapingly open for them.

The crew chief, Adjudant-Chef Denis "Doudou" Donnadieu, a beaming pitch-black young giant from Guadeloupe, received them clutching in a massive fist a clip-board holding a half-dozen official forms which, after a certain amount of awkward "after you, Gaston" *vas-et-viens* between Michel-Ange and Sgt. Schlechtermann ("*Mais putain*, how many times must I tell you – I'm not a diplomat, you are!"), Michel-Ange signed... and then Doudou counter-signed – and then Maj. Krivoy was pushed forward and *he* witnessed and signed, here... and here... and, finally, here... and then Doudou, with a great flourish amidst the still-rampaging noise and wind, gave Michel-Ange a clutch of copies – like a FNAC clerk handing a receipt to a customer... in a force-ten gale.

On his litter, the stricken Ambassador feebly raised a hand and said something to the roof of the helicopter. His words were utterly drowned out by the racket, and neither Doudou or the guys on the ground paid any notice. (Just as well, because what he said was "Don't anyone drive my Facel!")

Rather, the still-crouching Doudou pointed Michel-Ange, Krivoy and the Legionnaires back towards the pilot, to whom they duly returned. The pilot had his half-glass door open and held a radio mike out to Krivoy. The pilot shouted, in fractured "Frabalklish",

"Here, *maïor,* talk – *gavaryat* – to the *tour* – *kontrole* – Laina. Give OK! Give OK, so is safe we go!"

Krivoy took the handset and jabbered a bit in Gryaznian, presumably to the Gryaznian air defense *kommissars,* assuring them of the kosher-ness of the proceedings – again, to keep the whole farrago from getting shot out of the sky. With a final, *"Da, da, kanyechna – dobre e, dobre e – da."* Krivoy handed back to the pilot, who closed his door.

Bon. All the bureaucratic niceties had now been dealt with. His diminished Excellency Armand St. Emilion de Pépinière Duquon-Lajoie had now been safely heaved on board, from where he waved wanly at his depleted "staff".

Michel-Ange and Irina made sure that *Adjudant-Chef* Doudou was apprised of, and in firm possession of, the Ambassador's passport and vital personal stuff, while Schlechtermann went back to exchange final pleasantries with the pilot, a senior lieutenant who was just now putting on his sunglasses to face the rising dawn and who shouted/asked the Legionnaire:

"What the hell went down here, *Chef?* Is your guy wounded? This gonna become another hostile zone?"

"Don't ask. Sir. And no – just a domestic accident – trust me, you don't want to know. What about you-all – things hot where you are?"

"Croatia? Naaa – *de la tarte!* But things are ugly in Bosnia – one section of Sarajevo's a fucking *charnier* – never saw such a butchery, not even in Mogadiscio – talk about 'you don't want to know' – "

"Merde."

"Ouais." A yellow light flashed above the helicopter's windscreen "OK, Doudou seems to be done – *on fous l'camp* – we're fucking off to Müllheim – then back to Dubrovnik – you hang in here, *Chef!"*

"Well, thanks for stopping by, *mon lieutenant,* and thanks for the *coup de main. Ciao, sichere Fahrt* and go well – "

The two saluted and the pilot went back to work – which meant that the almighty roar, clatter, whirlwind and general uproar resumed and, gathering itself with surprising gentleness – bordering on clumsy dignity – Blue Félix One lifted off, leaned forward, and headed off into the rising sun.

22

RE-ASSIGNMENT

The tumult of the departing Puma "Super-Etrangleur" had been such that its sudden absence made the ensuing silence seem all the more notable, almost magic. A void in which our remaining party could discern discreet sounds, like a passing early motorist out on 3 Oktobr Prospekt, and even the rather hysterical clicking of some hardy surviving crickets on the disturbed lawn, no doubt scratching their heads with their six legs wondering what the hell had just befallen them.

Although hardly beloved of – or, to be truthful, even liked by – them, the sudden removal of their Ambassador seemed to cast a sobering pall on the small, exhausted and rather forlorn-looking assemblage that passed for the residual Embassy staff. They weren't quite sure if they felt relieved... or, somehow, bereft.

But Pfc. Meihavelha and Michel-Ange, each in his own way, took it upon himself to break the not-entirely healthy spell:

The Legionnaire by producing, from seeming nowhere (actually, from next to the bottom step to the Residence's front door, where he'd left it, in the dark), the still-1/3 full bottle of Duquon-Lajoie's finest 5-star cognac, and, after taking a glug himself, passing it on to the others....

...and Michel-Ange, who cleared his throat and announced, not *too* unsteadily,

"Right... well... here are we then. Still no sign of Moitié, *hein?*" he looked at Irina.

"*Niet. Nichevo. Nicht.* He biézié, biézié man. He biéziness man. Hah! Dunt naw vat biéziness, bot – "

"Alright, that'll do," and he made the duck-billed "shut it" gesture with his hand that he'd picked up from Schlechtermann. "OK, now look – all of us – including I don't mind confessing, me – are *creuvé* and could use some shut-eye, but before we can get to that there are still, regrettably, affairs to occupy us –

"First, Irina, let's dispense with the good Major, here, if we can – is he done, here? Was everything to his satisfaction? Have we, through his good offices, managed to avert a God-help-us Franco-Gryaznian war? Good – then why don't you pay him the rest of his, euh, fee – and let him be on his way – "

After a quick muttered exchange in Gryaznian, she came back, "*Da,* everyting goot. But I vill go beck to his house – pé heem dere. Iss biétter."

Michel-Ange most emphatically didn't see why this should be "biétter", but he didn't feel like arguing – especially as a more pertinent, if related, aspect to the situation was nagging him:

"*Daccord,* but look, when you, euh, that is to say, euh, are, euh, *fini* with the Major, and unless you have more pressing duties *chez vous,* can I suggest you return here? And that for the foreseeable future you should sort of park your... your good self here, in the Residence? Because I have a strong feeling that your services will be increasingly required before this current, what? crisis? – well, perhaps not *crisis* exactly, but certainly *dérangement* – is finally sorted out...."

"Hokays – bot vere? Vere you vant Irina 'park', as you sayink, her *cul* – yes, I naw *Frantsous* vord *cul* –? Vere I slip?"

"Well, why don't you move into the ambassadorial *apartement*? *Madame* seems to have permanently flown the coop – and should she ever decide to rematerialize, you could always in turn *fous l'camp* quickly enough – and *merde*, it's not as though you're unfamiliar with the *parages*, are you, *hein*?" He nodded to the two Legionnaires, "Do any of you *messieurs* see any *invonvénient* if Irina moves in, here, at Hqs?"

The two shrugged their assent, with Schlechtermann offering "*Et, finalement, pourquois pas?* – for sure she'll be useful and she's more pleasant to have around than either of those two ambassadorial, *excusez-moi*, wankers" (*branleurs*) "so... sure."

"*Bon*. So that's settled. Now – next thing – look, *Chef*, I'm afraid I shall be asking you to accompany me for this next call to Paris – "

"*Moi*? What for?"

"I'm not sure what for, to tell you the truth, but the colonel – that's my contact at the Quai d'Orsay – the 'power behind the throne' *mec* – you and he'd probably get along famously, now that I think of it – anyway, he specifically told me that if Moitié continued to be absent, I should bring with me a French official – excuse me for asking, but... you *are* French, aren't you?"

Schlechtermann laughed, "Heh – *mas o menos, ungefähr* – close enough. Not sure if I qualify as an 'official', though – "

"What? Oh. Well, as you say, close enough. All around. Anyway, so, yes, he wants there to be another Frenchman there – we'll find out why soon enough.... So let's you and I go to the garage, and you, Legionnaire Martinho, better resume duty at the gate – and if anyone shows up for the Consul, just take his particulars – we'll unload it on Moitié if we ever see him again – "

"You kidding?" laughed Meiavelha "What d'you think we do, here, all day? You should see the pile of messages we've *already* got for Consul-*con* – *putain*!"

So with those bits of business settled, they all – including Major Krivoy – finished the cognac. And then the Gryaznian intel officer shook the three Frenchmen's hands, after which all dispersed.

Michel-Ange could hear his Volga farting into life behind him as he and Sgt. Schlechtermann trudged over to the garage.

"Are you familiar with this rather peculiar commo set-up, down in this hole?" Michel-Ange asked as they passed the already-extracted Facel-Vega.

"Sure. Unofficially, of course, but... yes. We're not total imbeciles."

"*Non – bien sur*," Michel-Ange felt compelled to express this reassurance, but he meant, it in any case – the fact was that he was immensely grateful for the assured presence of the two Legionnaires, and, indeed, didn't care to imagine how events might be unfolding without them.

Schlechtermann pulled open the lid and peered into the pit with distaste. "Do you need me down there with you?"

"No, I don't think that's necessary – for now – let's see first what the old *emmerdeur* wants – "

So Michel-Ange again descended into what he by-now regarded as "his" private little command-center, as the Legionnaire looked down from the edge, arms akimbo.

Daylight had pretty much arrived by now, so it was arguably "the next morning" and thus not really an excuse for Mincemot to be so grouchy anymore, but... that didn't prevent him from being so.

"Yes, I'm listening. As though I don't know who this is. Go ahead, Fassederad."

"Yes, *bonjour mon colonel* – well, we have successfully sent the Ambassador off on, ...on, ... on Blue Fanfare Whatever, and – "

"Yes, we know all about that – we've had the pilot on the horn and the extraction seems to have been in order. Tell me about the government rep that you apparently managed to unearth – did *that* all go *correctement*? We've seen no signs of any scrambled Gryaznian MiGs, so we must suppose so, *hein*?"

"Yes. Though not without it costing me a *baksheesh* to the *sacré* fellow – "

"That's what you're paid for, Fassederad."

"Hah, except that I'm not – not for *that,* anyway. As a result of which, as it happens, I'm now actually *fauché* – at least until I can again catch up with my you-should-pardon-the-expression banker, who so far in my *séjour* has consisted exclusively of the excellent but only haphazardly-present chauffeur Ivanov, one of several supposed adjuncts to this Embassy who seem to be in at least semi-permanent states of Absence Without Leave. Or, in the case of *Madame l'Ambassadrice*, actual Desertion – "

"Oh stop moaning, Fassedard. Your job is to *démerde*. You're young. Resilient. *Créative* – hell, to have lasted as long as you did in life without a proper job you *must* be. Anyway, I'm told it's a land of crooks out there – so do as the Romans do. *Allez* – and, speaking of land of crooks – do I take it that there is still no sign of the Commercial-Consul fellow, Moitié?"

"Regrettably not, *mon colonel.*"

"*Bon* – so listen up, my boy, I asked you to bring to this telephonic meeting another French *ressortissant* – have you done this?"

"Yes, *mon colonel* – the senior Legionnaire – a most excellent, if I may say so, element – " he motioned to Schlechtermann to join him and the Sgt. clomped on down, creating an instant crowd in the cubbyhole. Michel-Ange handed him the receiver and retreated to the back wall, beside Moitié's little fridge.

"*Monsieur! Sergent-Chef* Wolf Shlechtermann, *2ᵉᵐᵉ Régiment Etranger Parachuté*, detached, and attached to the Ministry of Defense Protocol Division, *à vos ordres. Monsieur!*"

"*C'est bon*, at ease, *Chef*. I'm Colonel – well, never mind, I'm sure Fassederad's told you who I am. It may amuse you to learn – " it didn't, actually, "that I still owe your commanding officer some money – he and I play cards, occasionally, at the *Cercle* – anyway, where were we? – Right, couple of things, *Chef:* first, fill me in a bit on the circumstances of the Ambassador's injury – I asked Fassederad if it involved a *gonzesse* and he played dumb. Or is dumb – it doesn't matter. What the devil was going on there? Was it a pussy *histoire* or what?"

"Well, I'm not in a position to confirm anything precisely, *Monsieur,* but I'd agree that your conjecture is probably not too off-target," his face suddenly softened into something resembling a smile, "It might help if I put it this way – you surely know the old *blague* about the new lieutenant at Sidi and the Sheikh's harem – "

"Right, got it, *compris.* So, the old *chaud-lapin* was serving himself on the side – with who? That Gryaznian *nana* that works there? Or some outsider? Could we be lucky enough that it was *une Americaine*?"

"Well, again, I can't certify – "

"*Ouais, ouais,* spare me the disclaimers – you're not at a tribunal, here."

"Well, in that case, *Monsieur,* then I'd say that your first supposition was probably the right one."

"Aha! I knew it. What a *bordelle chinois*" (Chinese whorehouse) "Not a soul in this damn administration can keep it in his pants. *Enfin.* So what's the status on this girl, then – she a security risk?"

"I wouldn't have thought so, *Monsieur* – in fact, if I may say, rather the opposite – so far she's been comporting herself admirably and is even proving to be something of an asset... in the current, euh... situation."

"Well. There's at least that. *Bon. Chef,* one last thing – "

"*Monsieur!*"

"The Americans – do you have any idea what they're up to there? What's the scuttlebutt on them?"

"Not much, *Monsieur.* In fact, *que dalle, Monsieur.* You know, Pfc. Meiavelha and I don't *promène* ourselves around much, here – the defense of the compound is pretty much our sole preoccupation."

"Alright – as you were, then, *Chef* – and now please pass me back the kid – sorry, the Cultural Attaché."

Schlechtermann and Michel-Ange had another little "Laurel and Hardy in a revolving door" shuffle before the latter resumed his place on the stool and took up the receiver.

"I'm listening, *mon colonel*."

"*Bon.* Now, the reason I wanted another French *ressortissant* to be present is because what I am now about to impart to you might otherwise seem so implausible – indeed, so absurd – as to require corroboration. Until such time as we can get you hard documented proof..."

While the colonel was speaking, Schlechtermann had helped himself to one of Moitié's waning beers, popped the top, and was now clomping back out of the hole.

"What's that I hear? Is that you, *Chef,* leaving?"

Putain, dis, the old bastard has the ears of a bat! Michel-Ange reassured him, "No, *mon Colonel*, he is just moving to a more comfortable position – "

"So can he – can you – still hear me? *Chef?*"

"Four-by-five, *Monsieur!*" Schlechtermann called from his resumed perch on the edge.

"*Daccord.* Alright, well, not to piss around the bushes any further, Fassederad, it is my dubious honor to announce to you that the Powers That Be – and that includes not only that, excuse me, blithering ignoramus of a Foreign Minister but even the President of the Republic himself who, because this otherwise *minuscule* non-matter somehow, I am told, comes under an obscure rubric known as 'Extraordinary Exigencies Of State', had to be roused in order to append to it his scratched approval – "he paused for breath "have decided to appoint you, Michel-Ange Grenier de la Fassederad, as – and I can still scarcely believe I am uttering these words – *Chargé d'Affaires Par Interim* of France to the Government of the Republic of Gryaznia. Commencing immediately – well, actually, commencing about an hour ago – "

"Quoi?" Michel-Ange fairly yelled, "But, *mon colonel,* this is madness!" He could hear Sgt. Schlechterman chuckling softly above him, which only amplified the surrealism of these suddenly off-the-rails proceedings.

"I am entirely *d'accord,* Fassederad, but what can we do? We are faced with certain ineluctable facts – "

"But I only just got here! I'm just entering my third day and I have no idea of what's going on here! I haven't even been able to properly change money yet – !"

"What? Will you finally shut the bloody hell up about changing money?" Mincemot again sounded apoplectic, "The Government of France wipes its arse with your personal *bureau de change* problems! – *Mais c'est pas vrai!* – Anyway, use the Embassy credit card – forge the signature, they don't even have a proper alphabet down there, *merde,* my *dog* could do it! Meanwhile, just... *démerde.* Tighten your belt. Get a grip. Be a man. In any case, as I say, we have no choice."

"But what about Moitié? Admittedly, he's not here at the moment, but – "

"That's just it – he's not there. Indeed, he *never* seems to be there, which is *another* problem... which we'll have to deal with, but in due course, not just now – *at this moment* – when we have other priorities – such as getting you accredited – *re*-accredited, *putain.* First thing is to get you your Letter of Appointment. You'll get it by fax in a few hours. But the original will come on tomorrow's Balkan flight, in the diplomatic pouch – "

" *'Diplomatic pouch'?"* cried Michel-Ange. "Something *else* I know nothing about – !"

"Ivanov knows – he'll take care of it." Schlechtermann called down, loudly for the benefit of Mincemot, "the *homme-à-tout-faire."* And he added, he thought *sotto voce* for the benefit of Michel-Ange, "It's where we all get our *cloppes,* and that lovely *cognac* we were just having for our early breakfast – "

"It's alright, Chef – " Mincemot interjected – *Meeeeeerde!* – again, *the bat-like hearing!* "whose office d'you think charges itself with *sending* you that stuff?"

The colonel resumed, "So, Fassederad, you'll be wanting to get that Embassy *nana,* the ex-inamorata of our unlamented *Duquon-de-mes-Fesses* – "

"Irina. Irina Vozhbu – "

"The very one. So you'll crank her up again, and have her organize the requisite meeting. *Illico.* Normally, you'd have to go through the Foreign Minister, but you never know – a *douteux* semi-dictatorship like yours over there, you might catch a break and go directly to the President himself – "

"Hah!" remonstrated Michel-Ange, "my one experience with 'presenting credentials', as you so lightly put it, resulted in my being ordered to go home and sit on my *cul* and do *que dalle* – *we*ll, to go play with girls, to be precise – so how will they react when I re-apppear now – *with an upgrade*? When they stop laughing, I wouldn't be surprised if they dropped me into one of their dungeons – which, *entre nous,* I've *no* doubt they've got –"

"You're making yourself bad blood for nothing, my boy – as *Chargé* you'll have the full force of the French State behind you."

"Oh well! – that changes *ev*erything!"

"Fassederad, sarcasm is unbecoming a Chargé d'Affaires. *Allez-allez* – *un peu de tenu,* I pray you – look, I assured the Ministers and the Crisis Committee – " *Crisis Committee?* "that you had the nerves and *couilles* for the job, so don't let your country down – and don't let *me* down, or I'll come down there and... well, you don't want to know what I'll do... *Vu?*"

"But – what if Moitié objects – he is, after all, senior to me – what if he doesn't accept my, euh, authority?"

"If he gives you any lip, just let me know – and I'll have his *cul* out of there faster than he can say 'the Consulate is closed today' – the skyving *enculé*... don't worry, don't think I'm not keeping on eye on the affairs of *that* young *con,* believe me.... *Non,* if he utters the slightest objection, bring him to this phone – "

"Daccord, but... for how long will this appointment be? Surely, no matter how much *confiance* you say the government – *hah!,* I can't even believe I'm saying

this – has in me, such a charade cannot be maintained for very long – have you got a replacement in line for Monsieur Duquon-Lajoie?"

There was a short, but ominous pause at the other end. Presently Mincemot resumed,

"*Ouaaaaais,* well, it seems that things aren't so entirely simple in this regard. The Ambassador *blessé* was what they call a political appointment, and the fact that his something of a live grenade of a wife seems to be loose, not unlike an unguided missile – you still haven't located her, have you?"

"*Non, mon Colonel* – the consensus – " *Consensus?* That's *a laugh – more like a couple of uninformed guesses* "is that she's flown away to somewhere, but we must await the re-emergence of the chauffeur to attempt to shed a bit of light on her destination – "

"*Oui, et b'en voila* – that's why we can't be too hasty in deciding if the Duquon-Lajoies will be returning to Laina or not, never mind who might eventually replace him/them. As though this whole farce couldn't get any more absurd, it seems that *Madame* is something of what they call a *Bolchevique Bollinger* and a substantial financial supporter of the Party – " (the Socialists of then-governing President Mitterand) "and so we just can't *fous* them in the *poubelle* like an old pair of socks – we shall have to be patient – *diplomatique,* if you'll pardon the expression, and see how this plays out. Do you *pige?*"

"Yes, *mon colonel.* It just gets better and better, doesn't it?"

"That's as may be. Again, we have no choice – you're it, *fiston.* So, get cracking with your new accreditation. And call me afterwards, I'll want to know how it went. *Allez – execo!*"

"*Oui, mon col* –" but Mincemot had clicked off before Michel-Ange could even finish the word.

He clambered up and out, Schlechtermann slammed shut the top, and together they set about replacing the Facel-Vega. The Sgt. had never been inside it, so

Michel-Ange tossed him the keys and guided him the few meters as he eased the monster back in place.

"*Sacré bolide* – that's some fucking *engin* – " agreed Schlechtermann.

As they directed themselves back to the Residence, they encountered the Ambassadorial Citroën coming up the driveway. Ivan Ivanov stopped and got out. Both Michel-Ange and Schlechtermann were dying to find out the whereabouts of Madame, but, first they had to fill Ivanov in on all the recent drama. The fellow, whose extra-effusive conviviality again suggested to Michel-Ange that he was drunk – or rather, *still* drunk – at first had difficulty being convinced that the Ambassador was well and truly "*foutu*-the-*camp*", but once that had sunk in, he was duly impressed:

"*Vaow, vaow, vaow* – vat fockingk *bardak* – vat *merde bordelle,* eh? Hooo hah hah! – ent you iz now new boss-man, *felicitatzya, Moosié* Michelangelo!"

Michel-Ange pushed up his palms in the universal "*calma!*" gesture. "Yes, well, we'll see about all that in due course – meanwhile, *mon brave* Ivan, kindly bring us up to speed on *Madame* the *Ambassadrice* – *where the fucking hell is she?*"

"She ték hairoplane to Athena. *Griekenlant.* She appear viéry, viéry.... *mnié mnié mnié... agitatzyia, énérvatskaya* – she yellingk, say viéry bed vords to hairline girls – if she not diplamat, no *vey* she giet on hairoplane!"

Schlechtermann snickered knowingly at this news, but Michel-Ange just blinked and took a moment before offering,

"Well, I can't wait to hear how delighted the colonel will be to hear *that...*" But then he changed tack entirely "*Chef*, I'm sure you and Meia need to zonk" ("*piaule*") "so I'll let you work out with him who goes first and who stays at the gate – meanwhile – " he grabbed Ivanov by the elbow, "good citizen Ivan here and I have some unfinished business together that requires urgent – "

So Sgt. Schlechtermann strode off towards the gate, while Michel-Ange and Ivan Ivanov squared off.

"Now, my *cher ami*, first off, let us recapitulate what I still owe you – and then I hope you will be able to conjure up enough nefa to change for me the sum of...." and as he mentally calculated how many francs he still had with him in cash, he added "and I will almost certainly be asking you to accept a personal cheque for the sum of...."

Ivan Ivanov's eyes had never sparkled more brightly: "Tell me, my frent – "

Fifteen minutes later Michel-Ange's head was spinning from the just-concluded (half on the bonnet of the Citroën, half out of its boot) series of transactions with Ivan Ivanov – *"new math" mon cul* – that had been, in truth, more prestidigitation than a currency-exchange, and of which the only thing he was entirely certain was that the de la Fassederad/Ivanov net-pecunity ratio had just shifted – by stealth, perhaps, but perceptibly nonetheless – in the latter's favor.

Never mind... the cost of doing business... the important thing was that he was now in possession of an operational amount of greasy Gryaznian nefa banknotes, and... if their acquisition had required a punitive "cost of doing business", so be it... because there were now more pressing matters on his mind.

Such as, ... go back to the Residence – he required an urgent word with Irina....

But when he got there the place appeared to be empty. No Irina. And the old rotary telephone on her receptionist's desk reminded him of another lingering... *emmerdement*: Moitié. Or, rather, the absence of any Moitiés.

He fished out of his jacket pocket the number that somewhere along the line Irina had given him for the errant fellow's cellular phone. Dialed – and got a weird local Gryaznian ring tone – *aie,* it sounded, in fact, not unlike the shifting of his Volga's groaning gears – and then, in French:

"This is the number for J-L Moitié, Consul and Commercial Attaché of France. Please leave name and number and you will be recalled." *You will be recalled? I have to hand it to the con, he's not lacking in irony...*

"Euh, look here, Moitié, this is de la Fassederad, the new *type* at the Embassy – we met the other day at your Post-Lenin Café place. Anyway, look, *mon vieux*, there have been some fairly dramatic, euh... events, here, recently, at the Embassy, in your absence, and I think it would be best if you, euh, well, materialized – that you should, you know, *fait surface*. In other words, kindly get over here. Back to the Embassy, that is. Bon – see you soon, I hope. *A bientot.* ”

Well, at least he was now on the record as having, well, done something. (Although it occurred to him – what "record"? He'd just spoken into a "cellphone" – who the hell knew how those things worked, *hein*? *Pffff....*)

Bon, what now?

He ambled down the driveway to join the Legionnaires, from whom he learned that Irina had, indeed, gone home to "giet piersonal tingks", preparatory to following Michel-Ange's kind suggestion that, for everyone's convenience, she move into – at least temporarily – the Ambassadorial living quarters. *Hmmm... how interesting... well, it was my idea in the first place, so why am I only processing this development now?*

Michel-Ange suddenly realized that he was so tired that he was actually self-hypnotizing – and tried to snap out of it, physically, by blinking like an idiot....

It was Sgt. Schlechtermann who, not for the first time, decided what would happen next: "Look, why don't you go get some shut-eye, kid... *Monsieur le Chargé d'Affaires.* You look *creuvé.* There's nothing for any of us to do, for the moment. Go ahead. Either Meia or I will maintain things here."

23

CHARGÉ D'AFFAIRES
PAR INTÉRIM

Thank you, Chef.

He regained "his" quarters – "his" because, (as previously noted), they continued to conspicuously remain unpopulated by any Moitiés. (Although he was already well into his third day here, it occurred to Michel-Ange that he had yet to see Jean-Loup Moitié *à domicile*, so to speak.) *Tant mieux* – more for me he thought as he nipped into Moitié's half of the bungalow for a lightning raid – grabbing another of Moitié's Polarnia beers, a blackening banana and a couple of slices of hardening bread before crashing, clothed but at least jacket- and shoe-less, onto his bed.

He was as exhausted as he ever remembered being, but his mind was such a jumble that he was horrified to discover that he couldn't sleep. In the confabulation of thoughts that roiled between his two ears, indignation kept threatening to bubble to the surface –

Of course *I shouldn't be Chargé d'Affaires of a French Embassy, no matter how small and insignificant –* merde, *I shouldn't be Chargé of any damn thing.... but equally of course, they're right – who the hell else is there? But how can they have been such a short-sighted bunch of imbeciles as to leave a post such as this so criminally understaffed? Because, when you think of it, it's not that unimportant a place – it's not an ex-colonial backwater, after all, not fucking Nouakchott or New Caledonia – this is the putain Balkans, than which there is no hotter neighborhood on the planet, in this year of 1994.... And that old lunatic Mincemot is worried about some...* imagined American activity? Mais ça vas pas, non? *They're all out of their tiny brains....Me, Chargé d'Affaires? I mean, I'm as much of a team player as the next mec, but... please, let's not exaggerate....*

Michel-Ange tossed and fussed on this still-unfamiliar bed, trying various unsatisfactory options with the pillow. Although not yet seven in the morning, it was already light... *I wish I'd kept that eye-mask from Balkan Airlines....*

After about fifteen minutes of this bed-bound thrashing, he gave up. Taking what Sgt. Schlechtermann would have called "a command decision", he threw off the cover, brushed his teeth, re-donned his jacket and shoes, and once again *evacué*-ed his *lieus.*

If he was henceforth to be the *grand fromage* around here, he was going to damn well be it in the *Grand Fromagerie:* The Residence....

... where there might at least be some actual *fromage* in Irina's *frigo.* To which he now directed himself, having entered the Residence via the unlocked (!) front door and where he found, right on the counter in Irina's below-stairs kitchenette, not even in the fridge – as if providentially laid out just for him – a block of Emmental, a box of Melba toast, and yet another still-mostly-full bottle of the Ambassador's best 5-star cognac. Yum yum, glug glug.

Michel-Ange was not (yet) a full-blown alcoholic, (being, after all, still only 24), but he had enough experience with the stuff to recognize its schizophrenic qualities – the professional chin-pullers never ceased to tell you what a *dépressif* booze was, and he was familiar with the sentimentality it could treacherously bring on if not guarded against. But he also knew that it was capable of giving one a jolt of irrational optimism and even reckless *audace* (that the English rather high-handedly called "Dutch courage") – which is exactly what these latest two healthy shots of brandy provided him now –

They want me to be in charge, here? Fine, I'll be in charge – in charge of just what, *exactly, is another matter,* mais passons – Allez, *what was it* Les Woo *sang, "Here's to the new boss – same as the old boss – !"*

And with a fresh booze-fueled spring in his step he ascended the now-mythical stairs two at a time. The door to the master bedroom was closed, but he eased it open and peered in....

Irina was asleep, arrayed on the bed, on her side, looking almost story-book princess-like with one hand daintily hanging off the edge, in an innocent, beckoning gesture. She had conked out much as he had done – fully-clothed but shoe-less – although rather than the flailing flurry of frustration that he'd been, she described a large, graceful letter "S" on this great soft cloud of a bed.... *his* damn bed, it occurred to the cognac-buzzed Michel-Ange.

Mine? Yes, mine. Nevertheless, he saw a red suitcase, clearly Irina's, sitting on an oak chest against the wall facing the bed... And the *apartement particulier* was now suffused with, as another song put it, "the smell of sweet perfume" so that it now *pue*-ed a good bit more fragrantly – to not say piquantly – than it had scant hours before, under its previous tenancy. ... *Hmm, perhaps I didn't think this thing entirely through when I invited her to make herself at home, here... hmm, I believe these are what they call 'uncharted waters'....*

Still, not knowing what else to do, exactly, he decided to... well, to resume his original mission: so he once more lost his loafers and jacket, and made to un-obtrusively lie down next to Irina, perhaps to attempt once more to re-gain the welcoming, if elusive, arms of Somnus...

But no such luck. He pricked up his ears as she shifted and murmured,

"Mmm, Zhan-loo?... is det you?... mmm, Kiril?... *eto tuy?*... mmm...."

What the foutue merde *was* this? He prodded her foot with his...

"Mmm, Armand?... is det you, *séri?*"

"Zhan-loo"? – that swine Moitié! – and "Kiril", that damn "Douchka" pretty-boy! – and now "Armand", of all wretched people, that con *of an Ambassador – !*

Michel-Ange wondered whether he had a right to feel aggrieved... and decided that, on the basis of her earlier kisses and calling him *"mon chéri"* and whatnot, not to mention her currently being in what had now been officially (no less!) designated (even if by only himself) *his* bed... yes, he did. A bit.

So he prodded her on her shoulder: *"Hé, Camarade Irène,* wake up – before you go through your whole list of *conquêtes* – "

She turned to face him – and surprised him with a beautiful smile. "Ah, Mi-chelangelo, *dorogoychik – mon séri –"* She started to scuttle over to where he was parked, over there on the other side of the bed, but he stopped her with a raised palm.

"*Pap-pap-pap* – not so fast, *mademoiselle.* I'm here on business... *non, pardon,* I mis-speak – I am *in fact* here to attain some desperately-needed repose, but before applying myself to that, I must inform you of, euh, latest developments."

"Mmm, *chto?...*" she'd by now reached Michel-Ange and was nibbling his neck and unbuttoning his shirt, but he soldiered on,

"And that is – they are – well, no, let me start again: in the current and sudden absence of your Ambassador Armand, the *patrons* in Paris have decided to make me *Chargé,* so ... in the immortal words of the American Secretary of State General Alistair Vaig, after they tried to assassinate *le brave Président Ré-gane,* 'I am in charge here!' – "

This got her attention, and she ceased her canoodling. *"Chto?* Vat? Not Zhan-loo?"

"Non. Nitchevo."

"Bot, vy? He iss more *seniorniye* den little you..."

"Yes, but as I'm sure you've noticed – as certainly the *patrons* in Paris have no-ticed – your 'Zhan-loo' seems to be rather persistently *absentniye....*"

"*Da – ollso* kiénat be diénided – enyvey, is goot – my Michelangelo iss more mmmm *mignonne....*" and she resumed her tactical reconnaissance of the Body

236

Fassederad – who, for his part, gamely trying to carry on with his small bit of his nation's business, rather found himself caught up in an increasingly invasive bout of what Jenni-faire (of rather shamefully, if temporarily, eclipsed memory) liked to call "suck-face".

"As" *(mwa)* "much as I indubitably agree with you" *(mwa)* "about who is more, euh, *mignon,* that does not obscure the fact that we nevertheless have" *(mwa)* "work to do, i.e. most pressingly" *(mwa)* "to organize a meeting with the Foreign Minister to present" *(mwa)* " – *arrète* for a second, I beg you – my new credentials – "

She laughed into his ear "*Niet,* nat Fahren Miénester – *Priésidient – !*"

"Are you sure?"

"Da – here in Gryaznia iss Priésidient who recieff oll new, *mnié mnié mnié* votkoll, *tchef dé missione* – nat dranken fool Farhren Miénester – I hem knowingk dis bicoss I did *afitzialnye introductzia* viss Armand – "

"*De Dieu...*" The exhaustion that had originally brought him over to the Residence suddenly re-appeared, and he flopped his head down on the pillow, in abject surrender.

"*Niet* prabliém – I vill mék arrange vid Spétzial Pratacol Divizya, hev frent dere – you vill like Priésidient, he iss *ollso* beeg poossiékette – *oll* régime mens iss poossiékettes! – vill be goot far you, my *petit* Michelangelo – you har bik boss men naow, bik *pataronne* – !" and she divested him of his socks and trousers.

If he's anything like the last *enculé of a "poossiékette", the one who told me to fuck off and disappear, this "bik pataronne" will again be in the merde....*

Somehow – without knowing *exactly* how – he very soon thereafter found himself totally desnuded, and Irina in similar mode. Under the cloud-like covers, they embraced and kissed and so on.

Presently she reached out and fumbled in her bag which was on the Ambassadorial night table, and brought back a little dark something.

"Hier – put on."

"What is this, a *capotte?*" *No, you imbecile, it's an inner tube – get a bloody grip...*

"Da – fram Roumania – dey mék de biest dere – not *merde,* viss holes, like Bulgarskiye ent Russkiye!"

"Well, that's useful to know..." But something nagged him. "Yes, but – I mean, look, aren't you on the, you know... pill? *Pilule?*"

"Yes, but nat your beezniess. Anyway, I dunt knaw you – does I knaws you? Niet – nat yet. So put on."

He sighed and decided not to embark on an argument he could only lose but of course there then ensued the inevitable burlesque scene in which he had trouble getting the damn thing onto the reluctant "Petit Michel-Ange", with Irina having to come to the rescue and briskly whip things into shape and get everyone and everything once again properly ready for parade.

During which exercise – which might have been embarrassing to one less enervated than Michel-Ange – he managed to catch quite a glimpse, down in that sub-duvet murk, of her truly exceptional curvitude – even more astonishing *a poil* than covered up – before they fell to grappling and manoeuvering – with, it had to be said, Irina pretty much guiding the way.

So... *hop, hop, et hop,* a bit of this *here*, a bit of that *there*, a little more *hop* and *hop,* let's show a touch more urgency, *now ... et...* come on, come on... *et... voila!*

In the event, the whole business went off in an efficient, if rather perfunctory, no-frills, manner – although, given his advanced level of *débilitude, (same, come to think of it, as that last time with Jenni-faire – I should try this thing again, when sober, some time – I seem to remember it was even better that way....),* the wonder was that he managed it at all. Pleasantly surprised himself, rather, as he pondered his handiwork. (*Chapeau, vieux...*) And it even seemed to pass muster with Irina which, after all, was the crucial thing in these matters. Though she was quick enough to return now to practicalities:

"Trow det in *poubellni* in bessroom –" she ordered, pointing to the disgusting thing dangling from the now-at ease "Petit Michel-Ange".

As he hopped-to (literally), he noticed her go nakedly to her valise, pull out a largish pink bottle, and walk around the room spritzing yet more perfume, randomly, in the air.

"*Hé*, what're you *foute*-ing? This place smelled OK enough already, and you're just wasting that stuff."

"Dunt vorry – hef *bookoo, bookoo* av diss – Jhan-loo giff me ollvays parfium – he hev so match... he hev... he hev...." her usual volubility was for once having trouble describing the vastness of the quantities of French perfume Moitié apparently had at his liberal disposal.

"*Pfff* – easy for him – he comes from the place where they *fabricate* the stuff – his *papa* swims in it."

"So? So vat? Vat *your papa* svim in, eh Michelangelo?"

"Leave my *papa* out of it... actually, my *papa* got me this fool's errand of a job, if you must know," but by now they'd both re-gained the bed. Into which he re-flopped.

And *this* time, he fell asleep without the slightest hesitation or problem. *Waf!* – *lights out, baby, out for the count,* as they said in Michel-Ange's beloved American movies... It was eight in the morning.

Some six hours later (14:05), the little cream-colored "internal" phone – little more than an intercom, really – on the bedside table buzzed obnoxiously – *PUTE-merde!*

Michel-Ange, still mentally ten thousand leagues away, somewhere in the ether, was startled as though electrocuted. He frantically waved about for the infernal instrument (it struck him that this was exactly what he'd done to Mincemot, and not all that long ago, either) and finally grasped it: *"Ouai?"* (*Yes,* exactly *the word and intonation of the poor colonel... Karma...*)

Well, what it turned out to be was Pfc. Meiavelha calling from the guard house at the gate, warning him of "Consular business that I can't turn away – they've been here before, and are now threatening to squat the guardhouse," it seemed that three French "tourists" were missing their passports, which was sad enough, but sadder still, "so I'm sending them in – they're on their way – "

Bon Dieu de merde, what do I do with this, *now? "Bon Dieu de merde*, what do I do with *this*, now?" he asked Irina.

She, utterly unperturbed, was sitting at "Clo" 's "vanity desk" brushing her hair, and, thanks to the speaker-phone which for some reason had been on, had heard Meiavelha.

"Dunt vorry, I vill shaw you – chust dresst yourself ent come down qviklish to Mwa-tee-éh kansuliét office – I vill ték care ontil you come – "

"Merçi, ma chérie – once again, I owe you."

"Heh, da! – you tink I dunt knaw?"

So presently they all found themselves in the Consular Office. This Nissen Hut-like structure which, like its identical twin on the other side of the original Chateau, (the Ambassador's office), had been added to either side of the Embassy, like a pair of monstrous architectural ears. The supposed lair of the increasingly notional (as it certainly seemed to Michel-Ange) Consul/Commercial Attaché J-L Moitié.

He, the spanking-new Chargé d'Affaires – (he'd snatched the nominating fax from Paris out of the machine on his way past Irina's work-space and plonked it on top of the copying machine to be dealt with later) – now deposited his bony arse on Moitié's chair and gazed glumly at these three "tourists":

"Tourists", *mon cul – s'il te plait...* Some «tourists». What they *in fact* turned out to be were "backpacker/trekkers" – two scruffy, bearded young *cons* and a skinny mousy girl with greasy-looking hair, all about Michel-Ange's age and from Paris, but there all similarities pretty much ended. Not only physically but spiritually/mentally as well, for they appeared to be so... terribly *earnest....*

Real, what old Manu called *"knapsacks-for-peace"*-types, (*"les sac-à-dos-de-la-paix"*) straight from the CGT *"comités de soutiens"*, the communes of the 11th Arrondissement, the *"Fete de l'Humanité"* and all the rest of the leftist-*fanfarade... not*, in short, Michel-Ange's crowd – but nevertheless it was his job to listen to their *doléances*.

That turned out to be a tale of woe which seemed to have begun as a "sabbatical" Paris-to-Istanbul slog in a dilapidated old Renault-4 windowed *"Fourgonnette"*, but which had gotten quite dramatically held up by "some *sauvage* militia-types" in the Serbia-Croatia border area ("the actual *frontière* was unclear..." ... that *I can well believe....*), whose *affreux* and drunken members had initially expressed the desire to rape the girl and kill the two men, but who'd been dissuaded from the first by, in the girl's words, "making myself *trés* unattractive" (words which brought Michel-Ange, who'd been struggling to maintain interest, up short – *Eh? Did I hear that right? Sorry, my dear, but now you're pushing this into parody...)* and from the second by "buying back" their lives with their stash of hash and their three passports – "They didn't want our francs, only US dollars, but we had none – and they didn't want our car either, saying it was worthless *merde* – so thank God they *did* have use for *la dope* and our passports, otherwise... *couiic!* – ", this last being a throat-cutting gesture.

Yes, thank God, thought Michel-Ange uncharitably, but he limited his comments to the pedantic "Yes, well, there *is*, after all, a war going on in this neighborhood of ours.... four, in fact, or *five* – if you count the Greek-Macedonian catfight – "

"Exactly why we made a sharp detour into Gryaznia – there are no hostilities here, *n'est ce pas?*"

"No – not *international* ones, anyway. Yet. That we know of...."

In the event, not only could Michel-Ange not provide these three human toothaches with proper replacement passports, he couldn't even issue them temporary six-month ones either because *those* blank forms were locked away in Moitié's little safe, here, and the last thing Michel-Ange wanted was this trio camped out in the Legionnaires' guardhouse *ad infinitum*, or at least *ad Moitié veniat* – and in any case between the five of them present they didn't have the wherewithal to produce the requisite photos, so... Michel-Ange, showing his first burst of freshly-empowered Chargé d'Affaires initiative, found himself typing out – actually painfully *banging* out – on this sluggish old "Minitel" word-processor here that Irina showed him how to turn on, "Declaration of Loss" certificates of ninety-days' validity, which he signed, embossed and stamped with as much official adornment as he could inventively pull together in this sketchy, semi-locked-up Consulate.

"Et voila! – these should see you through to our Consulate in Istanbul."

"You sure these things will suffice?" The least pleasant of the three, a skinny youth whose wispy chin growths evoked the young Ho Chi Minh, made a dubious face. Michel-Ange was tempted to snatch it back from him and tell him to go try the Vietnamese Consulate, but he banished the unkind thought and continued on in his new-found flow:

"Oh *absolument!* – and if anyone causes you any *ennuis*, then have them call me here –" and he wrote down the "official" Embassy number on another piece of embossed Embassy stationery for them. *And good luck with* that, *mes petits....*

Now the girl piped up: "I hope we don't owe you anything for this... *sérvice*, because we are really short of funds – "

Michel-Ange had no doubt at all that the money-magnet Moitié had some menu of relevant charges somewhere, but in the over-riding interest of becoming once again *touristes*-free, he magnanimously threw his hands in the air and beamed,

"Bah! of nothing, of nothing! I am ravished to be able to lend you dear folks *un coup de main* – " and he ushered them out the Consulate's door onto the driveway, adding, with stupefying redundancy "and I will alert the guard to assist your *départ* – good bye, good bye, thanks so much for dropping in..."

"Ouf!" he exhaled to Irina, as he flopped back down on Moitié's rolling chair, "Now please buzz Martinho that they're coming through, with my blessings."

He sat there, watching Irina as she got cracking on the phone, thinking he should:

1/ make copies of his Official Appointment-fax,

2/ get Irina to set up an appointment with the blasted President,

and *(sigh)*

3/ try *again* to contact Moitié,

... when he became aware that she had finished on the phone and was now addressing him:

"... de Martinho iss saying det *anodder* piérson is comingk for Mwa-tee-éh biézniéss – "

"*Quoi?* What d'you mean 'Moitié business'? What d'you mean 'coming'?"

"*Da...* Yongk man fram TOTAL – he say iss piérsonal biézniéss far heess boss, *pataronne* fram TOTAL..."

Elbows on Moitié's desk, head in hands, Michel-Ange moaned "Is it always like this? I don't remember any business for Moitié *all day* yesterday – what's going on?"

"Nat ollvays like diss – samtimes niattingk, ent den odder times, *vlatch!*, comes *miénié, miénié* pipples far *Consularniye* biézniéss – it like *avtobooss*, samtimes dunt comes, den comes *miénié miénié* vun efter odder...."

"Well, hold him here, while I go *pipi* –" Actually, he didn't need to go *pipi* at all, but what he needed was to nip back through the door behind the Consul's desk and into the Residence, to leg it two-at-a-time upstairs into the still fabulous-smelling bedroom, where he found and snatched up the bottle of cognac. *Gloo gloo. Aaaahhh, ... Dieu merci... I feel better already... Gloo... bon, that'll do... Right, deep breath... one last little gloo... Right! – now, let's get back to see what this latest enormity is all about... but first, mind these stairs, don't want to pull a Duquon-Lajoie, here....*

243

He re-entered the Consular office to find a seriously-dressed (navy pin-striped suit) balding, slightly pot-bellied middle-aged man of world-weary mien waiting for him.

Irina opened her mouth, preparing to introduce him, but this new fellow cut her off – not rudely, but with gentle assuredness,

" – that's alright, *mademoiselle* – *Bonjour, monsieur*, we've not met – the lady tells me you're new – but I am Philippe Lemartin, private secretary to M. Roger Pavillon, the *pédégé* of TOTAL-Gryaznie S.A., and I am here on a personal *commission* for *Monsieur* Pavillon – actually, for *Madame* Pavillon...."

And he plonked down a couple of Polaroid photos for Michel-Ange's persusal. At first glance it appeared to Michel-Ange that they depicted some kind of war crime; (this *was* the Balkans, after all). But no, peering closer, it now looked like a sow with a brood of suckling piglets...

"Euh, *s'il vous plait*... just...what am I looking at, here?"

"That is Loulou Pavillon...."

"I'm sorry – Loulou Pavillon?"

"Yes, Loulou, the Pavillon family chihuahua."

Michel-Ange squinted at the Polaroids. *"That's a chihuahua?* Looks more like a cross between a giant caterpillar and the Number 38 Bus on my street – than any chihuahua *I've* ever seen – "

"Well, it's a close-up; not very flattering. And yes, Loulou had attained, ah, robust proportions by the time she delivered her six, euh, *progénitures* that you see there: Lolita, Léo, Lala, Ludo, Lupe and Libélule, the runt of the litter that the Pavillon children have already nicknamed *Cendrillon* – the day before yesterday at the Pavillon family residence at the TOTAL compound, out by the airport, which I don't believe you have had a chance yet to visit, *Monsieur* de la Fassedrad, although we have on multiple occasions had the pleasure of receiving his Excellency the apparently recently-departed Ambassador and certainly your colleague *Monsieur* Moitié, who I note is also absent...."

Michel-Ange wondered if he should have been writing all or even any of this down. Then he wondered whether he could plausibly nip back out again for another hit at that cognac… *non* and *non*…. So in lieu of either, he decided to proceed with caution,

"*Ouiiis—oui-oui-oui* – well, this is most gratifying for all concerned, I'm sure. But how – mmm, how can I best put this? – how, *exactly,* does this happy event, euh, concern *me*? 'Me' as in 'us' – *La République Française?*"

"Aha! Well that's just it, do you see," and the good *Monsieur* Lemartin now pulled out a folder which contained a half dozen similar official-looking papers: "these are the birth certificates for the newborns – "

"*Birth* certificates? For *puppies*?"

"*Exactement* – Loulou has a long – and, I might add, extremely expensively-maintained – pedigree."

"Is it *correcte* to even ask who is the *papa*?"

"It is certainly not beyond the bounds of decency to ask, but trust me, the answer is complicated – involving a male chihuahua of also high birth, but – and you can take my word for this – decidedly *sale caractère,* belonging to the Japanese Ambassador – believe me, it's better if you do not know – "

"*Absolument* – I'm sorry I asked."

"*Bon* – but, as I was saying, these are the birth certificates which I managed to have issued yesterday by a local vet – actually, the *type* himself is a Gryaznian Army doctor, but he moonlights as a vet and we have a long-standing and mutually-beneficial arrangement, again, never mind the details – but which you, acting as *Consul-Générale*, need to notarize. So the dogs will be properly official. Which will allow them to legally travel."

Michel-Ange could have kissed him. "That's all? *C'est tout?* Nothing more?"

"*C'est tout.*"

"Irina! Come here – how do I do this?"

She came over and whispered into his shell-like "hear",

"Chust use sém stempingks you used far de *dacumientiye* you mék for de tri gippies chust now – !"

"Of course!" And he proceeded to do just that: *bim, bang, bong,* signed everything with great flourishes, and handed it all back to *Monsieur* Lemartin.

There now occurred ornate thank-yous, assurances of mutual admiration, promises of future collaboration, not to mention sincere invitations for lavish visitations... blaaah, blah-blah... and off *he* went. Michel-Ange intercom-ed Meiavelha: "Coming through! – let 'im out!"

There being, at least for the apparently-immediate moment, no further French citizens in dire need of his dubious ministrations, Michel-Ange retreated back to the relative cool refuge of the Residence proper, trailing the faithful Irina behind him.

"*Et b'en!* – if *this* is an average morning in the life of a Consul-General I don't blame that *fripouille* of a Moitié for vanishing like yesterday's promises."

"Vat? I dunt honderstantingk – "

"Don't worry about it, *ma chérie* – Look, you go into your kitchen there and make us some *kahua,* and I'll go up and *cherche* us a new bottle of you-know-what, and then you and I will make some phone calls – you to the President's office, me to, hah hah hah, Moitié again – " *I believe this is known In The Trade as 'Making A Plan'.*

Irina thus embarked on her by-now familiar blizzard of telephonic Gryaznian, and succeeded in setting up an audience with the President for ten the next morning. "Put your best suitingks," she warned Michel-Ange, "ent vear your miédels."

"My what?"

"*Miédels, miédels – decoratsiye!*"

"You're perhaps *fouting* yourself of my *gueule*? Medals? – as if. *Dieu merçi,* I'm happy if I make it to my bed intact at night..."

Now it was his, predictably less successful, turn on the phone. Once again, no Moitié. *Leave a message.* He left a message.

"You know," he mused to Irina, "I'm not sure this – this prolonged absence of his – isn't something that we – I – shouldn't be getting seriously concerned about. Is this normal with him? I mean, for *this long*?"

"Veeeell," she turned noncommittal, "iss true Zhan-loo is likingk to be evéy – Armand vass sometimes kamplain to him – " again Michel-Ange noted – a little prissily – her disconcerting first-name-basis with the departed Excellency, "bot yes, dis time he is goingk evéy far more long time den *normalniye,* bot..." and now she got what for her passed as conspiratorial, "I sink he iss workingk on a *spétzial,* bik deal – he tolt to me, Irina, diss time I hev piérheps a deal vill creck de bank – diss vat he say, 'creck de bank'..."

"How simply formidable. Can't wait – " was all Michel-Ange could think to say.

He now sat there pondering this fax from the Quai d'Orsay: *By order of the President of the French Republic....* (then his name in Gothic lettering).... *"plenipotentiary"* – he didn't even need to look it up. It meant he had "full powers". *Is this someone's idea of a joke?*

He felt his interrupted exhaustion begin to reassert itself, but Irina cut into his incipient torpor,

"So, Misha – " *I'm "Misha" now?* "honless you vantingk to go hout to *ristaran* far diéner tonight – " Michel-Ange could only laugh at this. "Hokay, so, if you – ve – stayingk here, I shoult go to *Super-Kooperatsiya* to buyingk, mmmm, *kamestibles* – ve need do diss enyvey, iss niattingk left een *coozeena* – do you vant come viss me?"

This reminded Michel-Ange of something. "Aren't there servants for all this? Or, for that matter, a cook? A proper one, I mean?"

"*Da*, vass a chef, Chef Grisha fram Plovdiv, bot *Madama* Clothilde she fire heem de udder day – ent since den she itt outside Iémbassy ent Armand he heppy det I cook far heem."

"Of course. Why did I even ask."

"So – you kom viss me to *Super-Kooperatsiya?*"

"Shouldn't I stay here? In case there are further consular, euh, … importunings? Visitations?"

"*Niet. Konsularniye* hours iss finitch far day – *finito*, close-ed."

"*Eh b'en,* that's something, anyway. What day *is* this, by the way? I've lost track."

"Turdsdé – *zhédi* – tamarow Frydé. So, you kamingk viss me far food shop?"

"Can you manage without me?"

"Hav corse! How you tink dis Iembassié exist, day fram day, heh? Tenk you *viérié* match, Irina!"

"Well, in that case, carry on without me – *some*body should be here."

"Hokay, so pliss giff criédit cart fram Iembassié – "

"*Quoi?* How can you use that without me? How can you sign?"

"Vat you tok? I kapié *signatura* fram Armand – det iss how I olvays do – who you tink do food shoppingk here since Chef Grisha go évey? Ent how you tink I pé-ingk? Viss kesh? Hah! Giff me cart, *durak,* ent dunt be siéllié!"

Can I trust her? To not also, after buying the coffee and croissants and whatnot, nip off and buy herself a sable coat and a ticket to Tahiti? Bof, by the sound of it she's been doing the embassy's shopping with reasonable honesty for at least awhile now and, after all, she does *have the keys to the place – not to mention she's now installed in the master bedroom....*

As he fished in his jacket pocket for the Embassy Visa card, she added,

"In fect, *I* ken kapié *signatura* fram Armand, bot ken *you* kapié *signatura* fram Armand?"

"Probably not, no – at least not without practicing... good point, actually..."

"Ex-*eck-tement!* So far time beingk, et list, I hem de *honly* van ken use diss cart! Hah! ent hah!"

As she took the card and slipped it into her *faux*-Gucci, she added, "Ent pliss, keys far Wolga – "

Of course. Why the hell not. Take my Volga, please. "Here. And hey, do they sell any *pinard* at this Super-Commune place of yours?"

"Eny *vatt?*"

"*Pinard* – alcohol – *vypivka* – " *at least I can salvage* that *much from Madame Bébette's fabulous irrelevancies....*

"Ah! – hav corse, vatt you tink?"

"*Bon* – then throw in a couple of bottles of replacement *cognac*, would you please?"

"*Replace?* Egaine, hah! Dey dunt sellingk here een Laina fife-star like Armand hef – honly no-star fram Balgaria – "

"*Ca ira* – that'll do." He felt like a character out of a Gréme Grinne novel – *going native.*

As she kissed him on his forehead and sashayed out the door with "his" credit card and "his" car keys, it struck Michel-Ange with a mixture of shock/horror and amused amazement, that without him meaning to – utterly imperceptively over the past forty-eight hours or so– he'd just about gotten, *de facto*, damn near *married* to this complaisant and amazingly efficient, if 3/4-deranged, bit of Gryaznian *gonzesse...*

Fwoof! – now *this* was something he hadn't counted on when he'd kissed Jenni-faire goodbye and jokingly told her to "be good" in his absence... He felt a nagging twinge of conscience... *Pfff – alright, let's see if she's home, although unlikely at this Thursday post-lunchtime... pick up Irina's phone here and dial 0033 for France... merde, the answering machine –*

"*Allo, ma Jenni-faire,* it's me, calling during a quiet moment from our Embassy at Laina, it's two in the afternoon, *Jeudi* – well, *ma chérie,* a lot has happened in the short time since I left you and our cosy nest – not least that after a rather... unpromising start down here, the Ambassador went and fell down the stairs and *péte*-ed his *gueule,* which you'd think is also pretty unpromising – and it is! – except that it means that I'm, well... now sort of in charge here – I know, I know – *c'est fous, non*? Anyway, I'll explain later, but for now, don't worry, I'm fine – and I hope you are too – *allez,* I miss you and *je t'embrasse, mwa mwa –* "

He knew she hated long (or even short, come to that) phone messages, so he felt no extra twinge of guilt about withholding any further details. *Right – domestic duty done – what now?*

Back to bed, was what. The Ambassadorial bed, that was now "his". (And "hers".)

But Michel-Ange's body had long-since given up trying to keep up with his erratic sleep whims, so the few hours of siesta that he awarded himself turned out to be almost entirely taken up by yet another inchoate nightmare during which all his movements were inhibited, as though the air around him had the consistency of honey, against which he struggled fruitlessly... so that by the time Irina woke him by banging two large evil-looking bottles of Bulgarian "Pliska" brandy on the dresser table, he was more exhausted than ever. But he was also relieved – to escape that sisyphean torment that he'd been dreaming....

"*Feh!* Sambadié iss needingk *doucheka*! – ent I dunt meaningk secret palice," she cried, pleased with her pun, as she set about shpritzing some more of Moitié's best around the bedroom, "I vill in koosina be, mék deener," and she went clattering back downstairs.

Michel-Ange turned on the old Soviet-made "Ekran" TV set that the French had inherited when they'd bought the property and which the Duquon-Lajoies had moved into their bedroom.

He uncorked one of the new bottles of Bulgarian "Pliska" plonk and took a deep glug – *ooo-waf!* (an old gag came to him – "This stuff is awful – I can hardly wait 'till I've had enough!'") – before setting about with *le canal-zapping*. He had no interest in "France 24" 's reportage on the plight of Breton fishermen, or the repetitive and tendentious banalities of CNN... so he alighted on the evening news from the local channel – **новина за хората** *"News For The People"* – which was just reporting on the latest fresh hell from somewhere inside Serbia, involving a lot of male yelling and female crying and jerky handheld shots of slovenly and probably drunken troops in indeterminate ex-Yugo uniforms manhandling groups of civilian old men, women and even children. Michel-Ange watched this depressing *tableau* until he decided that no further elucidation would be forthcoming, nothing useful anyway, so he took another hit of *Pliska* and zapped away, eventually settling on an Italian channel, where a grinning hysteric in a shiny suit was laughing it up with a gaggle of largely-unclad leggy *ragazzas* in what was either a beauty pageant or a game show and, although certainly beyond mindless, was also certainly an improvement over the human depravity that was too often on offer back on Gryaznian "News For The People".

In due course he heard Irina calling him from downstairs, and he joined her in her little kitchen where she had put together a large amount of dinner: an unholy goulash of scrambled eggs, spaghetti bolognese and canned tuna, with crushed walnuts thrown in along with some cold leftover beets that had been hanging around the fridge for too long and which she figured he wouldn't notice.

Well, he noticed, but the whole mess turned out to be quite astonishingly tasty – "It's *délicieux, ma chérie*. But you made so much –"

"Haf *corse!* Ken eat diss far two, tri more daze more – hit dunt go biéd, hit sté goot!"

"Yes, I can see that... hmm, I wonder how the Legionnaires are getting on... d'you suppose we should take them some of this?"

"Dem? Volf ent Marteen? Hah! Dunt vorry far dem – dey téks kiér av dem-siélves *viéeerié* goot, beliff me! Liff goot lifes, dose two, far *militarniye....*"

No doubt they did, thought Michel-Ange, but nevertheless, after dinner, while Irina went upstairs to "ték bahbble-bess", he grabbed the still-mostly full *Pliska* bottle and made his way towards the gate.

He found both soldiers seated on white plastic chairs, in front of "their" bungalow – from where they could keep an eye on the gate – drinking some milky stuff which turned out to be *arak* from Turkey. They were dressed in "Legionnaire stand-down", which meant shirtless, in khaki combat shorts, but with combat boots still firmly laced up and white *képis* upon conks, weapons slung on the backs of their chairs.

They lowered the sound of France Inter on their transistor radio, beckoned him over and while Meiavelha fetched up a third chair, Schlechtermann waved off the proferred brandy and gave him a glass of this Turkish *pastis:*

"*Excellence! Monsieur le Chargé d'Affaires! Au plaisir!* Join us – out here on the perimeter of *la civilisation Gauloise!*"

"*Merçi* – most white of you – as I suspect my *patron* the colonel would say,"

"Hah hah, yes. Your colonel. A real flower, that one."

"*Ouais*, he's *spéciale...* Anyway," he patted what passed for his belly, "Irina just made me dinner... not bad... you can grab some *restes* in the kitchen if you like," he burped, "yes, I could see how one could get comfortable out here, in this little *bled of yours....*"

"*Alors*, so you and *Irène* – it's going OK, is it?"

Michel-Ange searched the German's face for a clue into the *ésprit* in which this comment might have been meant, but it betrayed nothing. So he opted for the equally non-committal:

"*Bof,* one defends oneself."

Michel-Ange, still wary, further scrutinized Schlechtermann, but when the Sgt. remained blank he was relieved and decided to divert the conversation into less eggshell-y territory –

"And so how do things pan out for *vous autres* – don't you find this to be boring duty out here?"

"*And how* it's boring – and what's wrong with a little boredom? Me, after six months of the *merde* of Somalia, a tour of *ennui* was just the thing." said Meiavehla, who'd returned with a stool.

To which his sergeant added, "And anyway, it's not *that* boring – there *is* the occasional diversion – Irène's been kind – and *sage* – enough to include us in the, ah, *v*etting and, ah, supervision of the, euh, cleaning staff. So it all stays... well, let's just say it stays *sympa* on the *domestique* side... But in any case," he interrupted himself to light a Gitane, "it's not gonna last..." (puff) "I hear from *radio tam-tam* that things are about to bloody *barder* in Rwanda, and that when it does, the two of us here should be prepared to be yanked out *ilico* and replaced by a couple of retirees – maybe even private contractors – and permit me to assure you, after a few days of trying to keep a pile of Hutu and Tutsi *énergumenes* from eating each others' *tripes*, we'll damn well wish we were back here – *allez, a la notre!*"

They threw down the first of an eclectic series of fortified potions, and called it a night about two hours later, by which time Michel-Ange was brimming with courage, happiness, confidence and fraternal love for the *2eme Régiment Etranger Parachuté*, and when he unsteadily regained his sumptuous new quarters to find Irina already asleep in "their" bed, all was fine with him as he had *no* desire for anything other than to cuddle up against her. And this time to sleep his first honest sleep since he'd left his beloved Rue Mouffetard. Back in his previous life....

24

PREZIDENT GRIB

Even if he hadn't been so informed by Irina, Michel-Ange could have *pige*-ed for himself that a visit with the President of the Gryaznian Republic was of an entirely different ceremonial magnitude than was a social call at the Minister of Sundry Whatnots....

He'd need to look extra *comme-il-faut,* and they'd need to be arriving in somewhat more style , i.e. the official Citroën, for starters, rather than the farting Volga.

So Michel-Ange scuttled back to "his" bungalow to fetch his toilet kit and his gray pin-striped St. Laurent suit, white shirt and E.N.A. tie and marveled, as he trotted along, at how he seemed to have acquired, almost literally overnight, *two domiciles...* in addition to a *de-facto,* well, "wife"....

Speaking of whom, when he returned to the Ambassadorial *salle de bain* (whose facilities *way* eclipsed the bungalow's), he found that his new *compagne* was standing before the full-length mirror, clad in one of Clothilde's slinkier numbers, and holding various of *Madame l'Ambassadrice*'s outfits in front of her, "testing" them.

"I hem vun size less smoll den her – " *"less small"? That's a novel way of putting it...* "bot I sink I ken steeal feeat," And she did. She managed to squeeze herself into a beige Hérmès suit that went nicely with her whatever-you-called-that-color hair and although it no doubt ended up higher up on her thigh than it had done on Clo, it didn't do so outlandishly. Certainly not by newly-liberated eastern European standards. In fact, *pas mal,* had to admit Michel-Ange, (although as we have by-now perhaps ascertained, he was not difficult to please.)

Even the hulking Ivan Ivanov (who Irina had finally, last night, unearthed, and alerted) had made something of a sartorial effort for the occasion – he'd affixed to the lapel of his (apparently) perpetual double-breasted tuxedo jacket a crossed-French-Gryaznian flag pin.

"Chapeau l'emblème, Ivan" said Michel-Ange, nodding at the pin, as the fellow joined them for an impromptu breakfast of coffee, bread, jam, and beet juice. Over which the two Gryaznians coached Michel-Ange:

"Dunt tok too match – smile ent say *'da, da, Frantsous pipple loff Gryaznia pipple' etciétera, etciétera, "* Irina suggested.

"Mmm 'don't talk too much' – I think I can manage that."

"He iss *viérié viérié* nice mian – ent vill far sure vantingk to mék tost – mebbe *miénié miénié* tost – so, itt djem – *mangia, mangia* – itt *bookoo* djem – *konfityur* – far liningk *stomaki. "* Sound tactical advice from Ivan.

"Ah – toast, you say? No, surely not – over *here?"* But no, nothing doing – sarcasm utterly lost on these sturdy Gryaznian *muzhiks.*

And then Irina thought to mention, almost as an afterthought, "Ah, ent dunt tok too match about *Amiérikansyie,"* Them again! "I dunt sink priézidiént iss likingk too match *Amiérikansyie* – dey makingk trabble far Siérbska, frent fram Gryaznia."

"Don't worry – I'm confident I can manage not to dwell on the subject of Americans."

After a quick final visit to the w.c. – he'd by now learned, like Boy Scouts, to "be prepared" – Michel-Ange took his seat in the back of the black Citroën. And instead of sitting up front, next to Ivan, Irina joined Michel-Ange in the back, rather as though they were Prince Bigears and Princess Diana. *Bit of culot on her part, really... but on the other hand, upon further consideration, I don't mind all that much....*

Ivan took off the black sleeve that had covered the little antenna that was affixed to the car's right front fender, unsheathing the French tricolor – which signified that this vehicle was currently on "official business". *Ho la la – quelle histoire!*

And they were off. (Michel-Ange shook off a sudden vision of the doomed WW1 Archduke Franz-Ferdinand and his consort Sophie – *Mais ça vas pas, non?)*

The Gryaznian Presidential Palace – called, of course, "The People's Palace" – was a cream-colored Stalinist/brutalist monstrosity that had been, back in the old socialist salad-days, modeled on Ceausescu's insane pipe-nightmare in Bucharest (only mercifully on a somewhat smaller scale – but still hugely excess to requirements and certainly larger than any other building in Laina). It overlooked the one Laina landmark that Michel-Ange's was familiar with, the Ghost River, albeit in a more salubrious spot than that where he'd not shed his non-tear – *Wind-induced, dammit!* – wiped away by that old *baboushka* just 2 days ago.

The street the People's Palace sat on was, of course, closed to normal traffic, and they had to negotiate a series of of blockages and barriers, manned by armed military types whose uniforms increased in Ruritania-ness at each succeeding station, so that the last lot, a pair of clanking tin soldiers who ordered Ivan to his assigned "visitors" parking slot, *exactly* resembled (if they only but knew!) drum majors of the French Lick (Indiana, USA) High School Marching Band.

At each of these interrogations-cum-holdups Michel-Ange's faxed appointment as *Chargé* and the faxed invitation from the *Prezidentzia* that Irina had coaxed out of the bureaucracy the day before, along with each of their individual ID documents, were pored over, photographed, copied – even at one point held up to the light for God knows what purpose – only to be handed back with extreme reluctance – so that it was some 40 minutes after the whole process had begun before they finally left Ivan to wait in the car.

They were escorted into the palace proper, where they passed through the usual electronical screening and were "picked up" by a pair of black leather-jacketed heavies in dark Ray-Bans who would not have been amiss as bouncers at a punk rock venue, one of whom carried a large walkie-talkie and the other a clip-board. These two "gooligan"-lookalikes ushered them into a lift.

Expecting to ascend, Michel-Ange was briefly alarmed when the lift suddenly dropped from under his feet, and they descended to at least several sub-basements. They were then shown into a room that was obviously a "waiting room" but which was so starkly empty that it might have passed for a squash court if it hadn't contained six chairs backed up against one of the walls. That was it. Six armless chairs, in a row, grimly looking as though they were awaiting the moving men to take them away.

Before any decision needed to be made regarding the depositing of posteriors upon this uninviting seating arrangement, the brute with the walkie-talkie spoke into it and almost immediately a heretofore invisible door behind them swung open, and Michel-Ange and Irina were nodded in.

President – *Prezident* – Grib came out from behind his desk to greet them – well, to specifically greet Irina, whom he seemed already to know. The two of them *mwa-mwa*-ed each other and exchanged Gryaznian pleasantries, but before he returned to his side of the desk, the Prez, almost as an afterthought, paused, came back a step, and gave Michel-Ange a brisk double hand-grasp, muttering, while still smiling, something that sounded like, "Yes yes, xhello, xhello, *bonjou', merci*, yes, *da, da!*"

The two bouncer-types had backed out and closed the door behind them, but the President was not alone in there – in the corner of the office, to the president's right, at a small table with a computer on it, sat a pretty blonde girl who looked in her early 20s – about Michel-Ange's age – and who presumably was the Presidential secretary/assistant, though God-knows-what else she might also have been. In any case, she would remain speechless throughout the entire ensuing scene.

Casting a quick *tour d'horizon,* Michel-Ange appreciated that the presidential office was quite sumptuously appointed – dark brown leather, dark brown wood, and dark red velvet predominated – while four items in particular caught his eye:

1/ A large black-and-white photograph, more prominent than all the other photos on the walls, of *Prezident* Grib with the Serbian *capo di tutti capi,* Slobodan Milosevic;

2/ An immense chandelier about the size of an upside-down crystal Christmas tree that hung dangerously low, it seemed to Michel-Ange, and which if it ever loosed its moorings, as it seemed it might easily do at any moment, would have landed right on top of his unkempt *tête*;

3/ A pair of huge upright, crossed elephant tusks standing on a sideboard by the wall to the President's left, reaching more than halfway to the ceiling, with the flag of Zimbabwe standing on a little flag-pole between them;

and finally,

4/ an immense rectangular picture-window behind the President that... *gives out onto the Ghost River itself – I can see barges moving on it! How is this even remotely possible – how can it be? I didn't goddamn* imagine *our descent into what had to be at least the second* sous-sol *just 5 minutes ago... Putain de merde, this must be some kind of jerry-built periscope-type window he's got himself installed here....*

But that was all he'd been able to quickly take in before his attention was yanked back to, and by, this President of Gryaznia, here...

This Gerasim Vladimirovich Grib. In his early 60s, one would guess. Bald, thin, of pleasant enough aspect, if a bit (Michel-Ange had been warned) given to over-ebullience occasionally bordering on mania – the man looked like a cross between the American comic Larry David and Silvio Berlusconi, before the latter "grew" back his hair, and without his nattiness.

Although like practically every employed person in the *ancien régime* he'd been a Communist Party Member, Grib was also a lawyer by training and had managed to oil, flatter and blackmail himself to the position of *Prezident* of the Supreme People's Court under the old Soviet-style set-up, a largely rubber-stamp formality of a position – indeed, a comfortable perch from which he'd been able, over the years, to alienate remarkably few and socially ingratiate himself with remarkably many.

And thus, during that period between the Berlin Wall falling in 1989 and two years later Yeltsin outgunning the KGB at the Moscow *Duma*, when all the panicked *régimes* of Eastern Europe had found themselves hastily re-painting signs and re-designing insignia while casting nervous eyes to the proverbial hills, Grib had emerged at the top of the heap pretty much by default – by lack, really, of anyone else. He'd been gratefully seized-upon and promoted, by the suddenly-at-sea and rather desperate colonels, generals and *kommissars* of the rump *DéGéBé* (who, tellingly, had grumpily resisted re-naming their ongoing racket), to the Presidency of the new "post-Communist" republic.

A position ex-Comrade and now Citizen Grib had taken to with great gusto. He loved his job, not least because, although he'd never heard of Arthur Balfour, the early 20th century British Prime Minister, he, (virtually uniquely among politicians in socialist countries), subscribed to that old *milord*'s serene creed that "Nothing matters very much, and few things matter at all."

So his conviviality was quite unforced when he now beamed at Michel-Ange and said,

"So, *mon cher ami*, zey tell me zet my good friend Ambassador Dookwon-La-La- *Armand*, enyvéy, Armand – has... gone evéy. Is ziss true? Vat happened? Vy so sodden?" The President spoke passably good English and even a bit of French, and thus what came out of his mouth was marginally less mangled than what Michel-Ange had already gotten more or less used to from Irina and

Ivan. "I vill miss zose eveningks of playing ze croquette – *most* agreeable! – and his so *very very* charmingk vife, of course, aboff all..."

Her again!

"Well, *Monsieur le Président*," came in Michel-Ange briskly, most decidedly *not* wanting things to so soon wander into any Clothilde-ian minefield, "it was a sudden... *contretemps*, rather dramatic, involving a medical evacuation, of which you are perhaps aware. He'll be alright, eventually, but I'm afraid that for now... well, I'm replacing him. As best I can, of course, hah hah. Here are my credentials...." He leaned forward and offered them to the Prez, who seemed uninterested, so Michel-Ange let them fall, plop, on the desk.

No, rather than addressing the official matters at hand, *Prezident* Grib seemed intent on pursuing more pleasing vistas,

"How is your golf, *Monsieur... Monsieur...*"

"De la Fassederad, *Monsieur le Président.*"

"*Da, da,* Dellafassra, *da* – interiésting name, Dellafassra – is zat Canadian? No? So tell me, *Monsieur* Dellafassra, are you *aristocriét*, like vass my friend Armand? And his so *very very* loffely vife?"

Huh, thought Michel-Ange, *I reckon that with dirty old Richelieu in my ancestral closet I'm closer to actual aristocracy than that old* parvenu *Duquon-Lajoie,* but he answered, "Hah hah, no I don't think so, Mister President, just a hard-working – " *hard-working? aie aie aie...* "member of the..." *pick a class, you idiot, any class...* "professional class."

"*Da, da.* Just so. Like me. And miérried?"

"Who me? No, hah hah, not yet, hah hah!" He involuntarily exchanged a quick glance with Irina, and immediately wished he hadn't.

"Too bad. *Quel dommache.* " The president sighed. "Ah, ze loffely *loffely* Clo... I tell you young Dellafassra, ze *Madame Clothilda* vass *so, so...* mégic – *bah!,* niever mind for now.... So, as I was sayingk, how is your golf?"

Michel-Ange's "golf" was, in fact, non-existent, but now that he was supposed to be a diplomat, he ventured, "Ah, yes, my golf – well, *Monsieur le Président*, my golf is not exactly of the top-notch competition quality – "

"*Ach*, too bad. Armand vass teaching me. Do you know, Dellafassra, in old *régime*, golf vass outlaw – *verboten, interditte*. First the Bolsheviks, then Mao, and then even Fidel – all Lieninist régimes, zey outlaw ze golf. But now zat we are all good *capitalistiye,* is golf OK. Is new, modern, OK actiévitié – ven I was first time playing croquette viss Armand, ve discuss golf – he is expert champion, you know – and he convince me zat for to be modern *capitalistiye* nation we must hev golf terrain – and not *pt!-pt!* minié-golf *gavno* for girls, no, but real eighteen holes golf terrain like in Scotland and Amiérica – *numéro uno*, praffiésional, like Nee-ék Faldos, Siébish Balléstrados! So I diriect canstraction of very *luxe* golf terrain on old artiellery range, out by hairport – Armand he vass help me, we finish until now fourteen holes – ze hole fifteen is still needing to take out some uniexploded bombs, but progress is good... yes, progress is good..."

Prezident Grib tailed off wistfully, and Michel-Ange felt compelled to pick up the slack, though not much leaped to mind,

"Splendid, splendid...."

"I haff an idee! I vas going to prapose zis idee to Armand, but now I will prapose to you – "

And here he picked up a picture frame from his desk and appeared to study it,

"I haff grend-chieldren, *vnutsi,* sree, all noisy, spoiled pains in ess – *bol' v zadnitse* – and zey always tellingk me – well, zeir *parents* alvays tellingk me – zat want to go wisit Paris *Diésnelant, Miékié Maus, Danald Dack, Oncle Picsou,* all zat – zey say to me I am *Priezident* of whole cantry, how I cannot arrange wisit to Paris-*Diésnelant,* so I direct our Embassy in Paris – your *mnié mnié mnié* counterpart, a, sarry to say, incompetent imbecile who also is Gryaznia representative for UNESCO, but niever mind – to send me brachure from *Diésnelant*-Paris and I see zey have viéry beautiful, viéry *luxe* golf terrain not far from park – so I have praposal for you – for Government of France – I want

you, my new good friend Dellafassra, to give *personalnyie* to *Prezident* Mitter-
and – here – wait – regard – "

And he barked something in Gryaznian to the pretty blonde in the corner who
in remarkably short order produced a document on Presidential letterhead
which Grib signed – his "signature" was little more than two large stylized "Γ"s
– and handed to Michel-Ange.

"This is *personalnyie* for my good friend and *callegua*, Frans-wa Mitterand
– it is praposal zat he inwite me to come to Paris so grand-chieldren can go
Diésnelant and I and him can play golf in nearby terrain. And after zat I vill
inwite him to come to Laina play on *my* new golf terrain fram vich, and at vich
time, all ze bombs will be taken evéy, and far sure more holes will be complete,
passible even all eighteen! Hah? Vatt you sink of those *patates*, hah, *Monsieur*
Chargé Dellafassra?"

What Michel-Ange thought about this particular *patate* was that that sedentary
old snake-in-the-grass Mitterrand played no more golf than he, Michel-Ange,
did – maybe even less, if that were possible – but he forged on, all prudence
chucked overboard,

"I think it's a formidable idea, *Monsieur le Président,* and I can think of few
things that would delight *Monsieur* Mitterrand more than this inspired proposal
of yours – I cannot wait to put it in the pipeline *protocolaire!" which means Mincemot, and I really* do *relish hearing the reaction from* that *quarter....*

Michel-Ange tucked this ludicrous bit of paper into his leather *serviette* and was
about to re-introduce the subject of his own credentials, when Grib bounced
out of his chair, went over to the side-board which bore the Zimbabwean elephant tusks, slid open a panel therein, and emerged bearing a colossal 6-litre
bottle – a "Methuselah" – of Johnnie Walker Black whiskey and barked some
more Gryaznian to the blonde girl, who nipped into another hidden door in
the wall and emerged with a tray and four cut-crystal goblets (from ex-Czecho-
slovakia).

"Zis vas gift to me – I should say to the Gryaznian People – by a dielegation fram the British Labour Party, last month, ent ve should open it – they tell me viskey goes bied if leave too long, hah hah, *nazdrovye!*"

And there followed the predictable, inevitable, relentless slam-bang, barely-pause-for-breath, bottoms-up series of "toasts" that every western visitor to a socialist or recently-ex-socialist country is eye-wateringly familiar with:

Prezident Grib: *To us! (glug glug)*

Michel-Ange: *To Franco-Gryaznian cooperation! (glou glou)*

Irina: *To peace and love! (waf)*

President Grib: *To the departed Ambassador Armand! (gulp)*

President Grib: *To golf! (glug glug)*

President Grib: *To the so loffely but tregically absent Madame Clothilde! (glug, gag, glug)*

So once again, Michel-Ange (and Irina) were six double Scotches to the good and it was not yet noon, and Michel-Ange was already beginning to feel an ominous buzzing in his ears and the last bit of whiskey was unsure whether it wanted to stay down his gullet or not.

Grib then clapped his hands, beamed "Good!" and started to half-push them out the door – with one hand, let it be recorded, firmly on Irina's left *fesse* – which the blonde girl had opened for them, when Michel-Ange uttered a strangled cry,

"Wait! My credentials!"

"Hah! Of course! Hah hah!" So more double "Γ"s were affixed to Michel-Ange's by-now almost incidental documentation that sat languishing on the Presidential desk; it was handed back to him, Irina got lavishly Presidentially kissed *again,* and this time the two were successfully shuffled out the door and back into the care of the leather-jacketed bouncers.

Michel-Ange had noticed that *Prezident* Grib's accent increased with his animation. His Excellency's parting words before he closed his door on his (and his blonde "secretary"'s) sanctum were,

"So Dellafassra, call my office when you hear fram Brother Mitterrand – I vill make priority for your call! – and you vill join us ven ve play golf! – zis I vill insist! In fact, we vill invite *Madame* Clothilde also to join, zat vey ve will be foursome! – vich reminds me, please!, please! – one last sing! – if you hev, or can find, forvarding *addresse* or better, tiéléphon namber for *Madame* Clothilde, please also call my office – for this I make *super* priority! OK, good!, good!, *vive la France!, dosvidanye!*"

"*B'en merde alors – !*" expostulated Michel-Ange to Irina and (of necessity) to Ivan Ivanov, once they were again underway in the Citroën, and re-negotiating all the checkpoints in reverse order, "*that* went rather well, don't you think?"

"Huh" grunted a clearly disgruntled Irina.

Michel-Ange chose to ignore her mood. "D'you suppose we'll be able to get him some kind of coordinates for the *misérable,* departed Clothilde? He seemed inordinately keen on *that* aspect of things...."

"I hem ashame far heem. Peeg – he iss *totalniye* peeg. Iss shame far Gryaznia. *Honte!*" She seemed pretty settled in this opinion, honking on the "H" in *Honte* to drive home the point.

"*Allez, allez,* come on now, it could have been worse – things can *al*ways be worse," Michel-Ange said, and pecked her on her Moitié-perfumed neck.

25

MOITIÉ'S BIG DEAL

It had been his intention, once he'd returned to the Embassy, to nip back underground and deliver to Mincemot a "Situation Report" (which is what the Colonel chose to call a simple update), but while opening the gate Schlechtermann made an over-his-shoulder thumb-pointing gesture, the meaning of which Michel-Ange was still wrestling with until, approaching the three aligned "bungalows", his eyes fairly popped out of his head as he saw, parked in front of "his" now-secondary dwelling, wonder of wonders, the... dusty red Lada assigned to Jean-Loup Moitié, Consul-General and Commercial Attaché of France.

Whoa! He banged the top of Ivan's chauffeur's *casquette* "Stop!" *Mincemot can damn well wait – I'm not giving this fucker the chance to disappear for* another *three days! "Hé-oh!,* I'm getting off here – Irina, you carry on – I'll catch up with you both later – "

He leaped out of the still-moving Citroën and raced into their bungalow, to find Moitié, shoe-less and in shirtsleeves, sprawled out on his bed, with an assortment of mostly-handwritten papers and what looked like the entire contents of his briefcase scattered around him, talking on his cellular phone. In Italian, Michel-Ange recognized.

The putative Consul made a vague gesture in Michel-Ange's direction which almost certainly was meant to convey "*Salut*, be with you in a minute – ", as he continued speaking, "*Guarda! – ma no! – non e posible facere cosi! – eh! – va-bé, va-bé, sono tutti bruti, eh no, non po', no –* " and so on in that vein.

Michel-Ange took the opportunity to avail himself of a long *pipi* – his body had still not quite come to grips with the six matutinal double-Johnnie Walker Blacks – and he was, in fact, still at it when Moitié poked his head through the open w.c. door to breezily declare,

"At last! Where's everybody been? I've been here an hour and there hasn't been a trace of anybody anywhere – not a *foutu* cat! *Heh!*, good thing I'm here, *hein?*, *n'est ce pas?*"

Michel-Ange could scarcely credit the fellow's *culot* – "a bit thick" didn't even come close.

"Where have *we* been? – *elle est bonne celle-la!* – where have *we* been?" Michel-Ange didn't quite sputter, but he was not far from doing so, "Where the fuck have *you* – ?" but just then, Moitié's cellular phone rang and once again he was off, this time speaking (Michel-Ange also recognized) in Arabic... and again making the airy "I'll be with you in a sec" gesture.

Rolling his eyes and anticipating what would no-doubt be a... *trying* "frank exchange of views" (the marvelous diplomat-euphemism for a good old *engueulade* that he'd laughed at when he'd first come across it) with his colleague, he decided that what the situation called for was... well, a fresh Polarnia beer, which he now fished out of Moitié's fridge – and if Moitié had any objection, fine, it might at least get him off that damn phone.

Which is what Moitié eventually got, and again turning his surprisingly (given the circumstances) languid attention to Michel-Ange, he observed, "*Eh bien*, good thing I brought in a fresh supply."

"Yes, it's undeniable – I owe you, at this point, I think at least a six-pack – "

"*Bah* – it's nothing – my *baraque es su baraque* – So tell me," Moitié said as he fished around the mess on his bed for what turned out to be his hash paraphernalia, sat back on his bed, propped himself on his pillows, and rolled a tight birthday candle-sized joint, "Brother Rat-Face, what news while I've been away – ?"

"*Eh b'en* – you may well ask – " And Michel-Ange, deciding to ignore the "Brother Rat-Face", proceeded to unload, with surprisingly few interrupted queries or even expressions of surprise out of Moitié, the series of *contretemps* that had transpired since last they'd met, back at the Post-Lenin Baccarat Café – what was it, all of two days ago? something like that.... Ending with, " – and so, *voila!* I'm just back from the *Présidence*, and – "

"So you're the new boss? You're *my* boss? *You?*" Moitié pondered this while *whsssup!* holding in a deep toke. He eventually exhaled, grimacing. "How did they *calcul* that? It appears to me *bizarre*, to say the least."

"Well yes, I can see your point – you are certainly senior to me in all apparent particulars, but... euh, how can I put this, euh, diplomatically, hah hah... you see, you appeared *not to be available*... at rather the salient moment... if you see what I mean. And by the way – " *What the hell, I'm* lançé *anyway, may as well go from one uncomfortable subject to another* "far be it for me to be old-fashioned, don't you know, but... are you... is this..." and he mimed smoking with two of his fingers "well, *cool*?" (and yes, he said "cool", in *franglais: "coole".*)

Moitié answered by offering the weed to Michel-Ange. "This? You joke? Naaa, everybody around here *s'en fous* – who's gonna give a damn, anyway? The cleaning girls? The *Légios*? Hah, right.... Not for you? OK," and he took another almighty suck.

"But," Moitié continued after he'd, *pfwooo*, exhaled, "this business of you being the new *patron* – as ridiculous as that may, in fact, be and for as long as it lasts, the truth is that it... well, it may, in fact, suit me, rather."

"Well, I'm *ravi* to hear it."

"But let's recapitulate – How's it going to work, exactly? What's the current... housekeeping situation? Has *la mère* Clothilde also removed her crazy *cul* from the premises?"

"Yes. *That* much at least seems certain – she was last heard from heading for Athens – though please don't ask me why...."

"Good riddance. And *la belle Irène* – have you taken... euh, *that* particular project in hand? Or is she being her predictable loose *balle de flipper* self? For that matter – " and here he made a comic pretense of attempting to look over into Michel-Ange's end of the bungalow, "have *you* moved into the *chateau* yet?"

Michel-Ange didn't want to be manoeuvred into sounding prissy, but on the other hand he felt it couldn't be a bad thing to maintain a modicum of *correctitude:* "Yes, I have – for the convenience, you understand – and, yes, well, Irina... Irina is being very helpful. In fact – " he added, truthfully, "I'm not sure how I would have managed without her."

Moitié refrained from asking "Managed what, exactly?" and opted instead for the even nastier "No doubt. And you're right to take advantage." (*"T'as raison d'en profiter."*)

Alright, that does it – screw the "high road" – no more Monsieur Nice Michel-Ange:

"*Bon*, listen to me *bien*, Moitié: I'm not taking any '*advantage*', as you so insinuatingly put it – I'm merely doing as I'm told. Got that? And trust me, I was happier when all I had to think about was spreading French culture – now *there*'s a laugh! – back what seems like ten years ago. Which reminds me, I had to spend half the day yesterday doing *your* job – a bunch of pluperfect cretins paraded in here needing your so-called 'consular' you-should-pardon-the-expression 'services' – Where the fuck have you been hiding these last few days and what the fuck have you been doing there? And let me add, that so-called telephone of yours may as well be a tin can with a wire stuck in it for all the *putain* use it is in getting hold of you – I must have left you a dozen messages, didn't you get any of them? And yes, I don't mind if I do – " this last referred to the latest of Moitié's Polarnias, one of which he again helped himself to.

"Alright – " Moitié inhaled his joint again, *ffffffff*... "alright, don't enervate yourself. I may as well clue you in...." and now he appeared to speak half to himself, "I had *pe-père* Duquon all on board – he was actually alright, the old snake, behind that old-school *façade* of his he was a real player – but, alright," he exhaled and re-focused on Michel-Ange, "you say he's gone, so *inshah allah*... I'll bring you on board instead..." He now pasted a serene smile on his face and made a show of studying Michel-Ange closely, "You seem like an adaptable sort of *type*...."

"Moitié – I pray you – of what are you for the love of God now talking?"

"Aha... aha... well, what I am talking about, my new friend and, I hope, collaborator, is only what I've been working on, on and off, not just over the past few days, but for the past few weeks – and on which I'm prepared to bring you in – as I'd brought in Duquon-Lajoie before you – but not before you swear to me that you will not divulge anything of what I am about to impart to you to anyone – and *certainly* not to anyone French...."

"Moitié, how can I give you such a commitment? I have no idea what you're even talking about – can you at least assure me that it's not illegal? Is it illegal? Whatever it is, this thing that you're dancing around?"

Moitié considered this for an honest second, as though encountering the notion of legality for the first time, and answered,

"Illegal? *Nnnnnon... non*, look, I'm no lawyer, of course, but for sure you could with confidence argue that it's not illegal. Not in any *strict* sense, anyway... Maybe a little *out of the ordinary*, but no, I can't see how it's... *illegal*...."

"Hmm... 'you could argue'... 'probably not'... not exactly *rassurant*, is it? But even if you're right, and it isn't illegal – then why must I not talk about it?"

"Aaah, *la discrétion,* my dear rat-face. It may not be exactly illegal, but it's certainly... well, *delicat.* But if you agree to remain *shtoum,* you'll be included to the tune of five percent."

"Listen, I didn't join the diplomatic service to enrich myself – "

Moitié first thought to retort "Easy for *you* to say – ", but didn't and instead said, with a shrug, "Nor did I – but what can you do?" He took another toke. "Anyway, this five percent that's now for you had already been allocated to Duquon, but given that he's – " and he ran a finger across his throat "*hors combat,* it's yours by default – If you don't want it, give it to charity – I *fous* myself *éperdument* – "

"Alright, let's leave that *en instance* for the moment, shall we? In any case, five percent of a question mark isn't going to get anyone very far, is it? So, *d'accord* – as long as you assure me that it's not illegal... " and now Michel-Ange looked up and affected to loudly address unseen listening devices, "AS LONG AS YOU ASSURE ME THAT IT'S NOT ILLEGAL! – I agree not to talk of whatever it is you're about to tell me, to any French person. *Bon, allez,* now *crache* – "

"Alright," said Moitié, extinguishing his joint and tucking away his stash, "so here it is: it concerns the importation of taxis. From Nice. Old ones, obsolete – although they're Mercedeses, so, heh, you can't say they're *really* obsolete – those *engins* go on forever. Anyway, a hundred of 'em, all '84 and '85 "E"-class diesels. We get 'em for five thousand US each, c.i.f., Nice to Laina, by way of the port of Constantza in Roumania, and then up-river by barge on the Ghost River. Delivered *à domicile.*"

Moitié let things hang there while Michel-Ange's soggy brain began to process. Lots of questions bubbled up, but the first one that popped out of his mouth was,

"Only five thousand *billes* US for a 10 year-old Mercedes E-Class? Seems pretty cheap, *non?*"

"And how. That's the key to the whole deal. I – we – re-sell 'em to the Laina City Council for 18 thou US each, and we clear a million three hundred US, profit, net."

" 'We'. Who's 'we'?"

"Well, at this, Gryaznian, end there's me, and there's a guy – he calls himself the 'Supervising Disburser' – at the Ministry of the Treasury, and there's the mayor of Laina. And back in Nice it's three other *mecs*: first, a guy in the office of the *Préfécture* of the Alpes Maritimes who's an old Socialist Party friend of my *papa* and whose idea this originally was and who helped me to put it together; second, there's the Mayor's *chef de cabinet* who's an Algerian and who provides us political cover in case anyone questions the selling price, and finally, third, there's the *mafieux* who's in charge of the city's procurement department. And of course you, now taking Duquon-Lajoie's five percent. That's six and a half people in all – to share out the mil-three."

"*Mais* – " Michel-Ange sat down in one of Moitié's chairs. "help me out here… the practicalities… I mean – a hundred taxis suddenly pulled out of Nice, seems a lot, *non*? Won't that, I don't know, sort of cripple things down there? What, the tourists will all suddenly be doing *le jogging* to and from the airport, will they?"

"No, it's all organized – it's about a third of the *ville*'s entire taxi fleet, but that's how the thing works, apparently – about every three years, they replace a third of the oldest cars with new ones – and when I became Commercial Attaché, my *papa* mentioned it to some of his *copains* in his card game, and that's when the guy in the *Préfét*'s office – the one I just mentioned – got the idea and he convinced me to convince the Gryaznians – "

"Who suddenly discovered they had a crying need for 100 new – well, used – taxis?"

"*Absolument* – you've been in town – did you see any taxis?"

"No, now that you mention it, I didn't – in fact, the one time I needed one I had to flag down a *privé* – a truck, as it turned out – charged me forty-five nefs – "

"Well, *paf!*, there you are. Believe me, convincing these people here that they needed some taxis in their *merdier* of a supposed capital was the easiest part of this deal. The part that was *délicat*, that I alluded to earlier, was back in Nice, getting the price set, and officially-declared, at five thousand per – and that's where the political cover from the Arab *Al Hadj* in the Nice mayor's office comes in – he's managed to contrive to fold the sale into a larger 'social action project' – don't ask! And as long as he's the one who's signed off on it, anyone who questions it gets denounced as a racist, so nobody will."

"And this whole *magouille* – sorry, this whole *merveilleux*, completely *halal*, international transaction – is all agreed, signed off, all the paperwork in place and in order?"

"Weeeell, *ouais*, yeah, there are documents that have been faxed, signed, faxed back – exchanged – so there *is* a body of *paperasse* out there that supports the deal – but I'll be honest with you, *mon vieux*, it's not any stupid paperwork that's going to keep everybody honest and *correcte* in this thing – *Non*, I'm afraid that in this *affaire* the policing, if that's the *mot juste*, of the payments and conditions will be assured less by our signatures than by, euh..." and here Moitié made a sort of Arnold Schwarzenegger gesture of double-armed muscle-flexing, "assurances of physical retribution for any, ah, backsliding."

"Well *that* sounds rather on the southern side of *idéal* – "

"*Au contraire, mon cher* – it makes things more efficient – and less costly – than legal writs and threats. Don't worry – this is how business is done in today's *ambience.*"

"Well, I wouldn't know. If you say so. But, *au fait*," Michel-Ange now stood and massaged his forehead, "can these wretched people here *afford* 100 new/old Mercedes taxis? I thought they were – and as far as I can see they *are* – poor as church mice...."

"Hah! *Détrompe-toi* – they're not as poor as you'd think – First of all, they're getting a hell of a lot of *fric* from us – from you and me – already,"

They are? "They are?"

"And how! Unimaginable amounts of 'social transformation' and 'solidarity' funds and *je n'sait quoi encore* – 'transfer payments' from the European Union – you'd shit if you knew – "

"*B'en merçi...*"

"And also – and I don't know if you know this or not – but this *bléd minable* produces some gold of its own – out in the northwest. They've got something that used to be called the Chelovyek Mining Cooperative, but which has recently been re-named the Mandela Gold Mining Expedition – it's not huge, but *sa crache* well enough – it's part of the same occurrence that they have in Bulgaria and Roumania. *Which*, in fact – "

Moitié now got off his duvet and pushed Michel-Ange aside as he knelt by the foot of his bed.

" – brings me to *this* rather pertinent detail – Here, come give me a hand – "

And Michel-Ange joined Moitié down there, kneeling, as they reached in and heaved out from under the bed two canvas mail/sail-sacks. Each sack was mostly empty, but they were damnably heavy and clanked ominously as they were dragged out.

"What the hell is this?" said Michel-Ange " – as though I need to ask...."

"*Précisément.* Eight bars of pure 24-Karat Gryaznian gold, twelve comma four kilos each. Forty nine comma six kilos in each *sac*, and ninety nine comma two kilos in all – "

"And you *trimbalé*-ed all this shit here – from God-knows-where – by *yourself*?"

"*Ouaip* – and I'm in good shape, too, but it damn near knocked me out. Actually, that old piece of shit Lada had an even harder time than I did... but *quand même*, here they are... here it is."

275

"OK – and I can't believe I'm actually saying this, but... go ahead, fill me in on how this is supposed to work – run me through it again."

"Bon, voila: to recapitulate: a hundred cars at five *briques* each, that's half a mil US. Now a cheque for that amount, from a bank in Cyprus on behalf of the Treasury of the Republic of Gryaznia – "

"A bank in *Cyprus?* Can *that* be any good?"

"Better than a check emitted by any *Gryaznian* bank, believe me... Anyway, as I was saying, said cheque, made out to the Receiver of Revenue for the *Département des Alpes Maritimes* has been delivered to the *Mairie* in Nice by DHL – I saw to this myself – and it has, *mirabile dictu,* cleared, and as a result of that miracle the hundred taxis are already, as we speak, chugging away on blue Mediterranean waves aboard the good ship *MV Marie Celeste II,* a sturdy freighter registered in Malta – the loading of said taxis having been witnessed by none other than my dear old *papa* himself.... so *that* end – the 'official' end, if you will – of the operation is assured, at least...."

Michel-Ange made a dubious face but conceded, "Alright, and – " With his foot he nudged one of the gold bars peeking out from a sack, "how does *this* stuff figure? Or, for that matter, get divided up?"

"OK, so the Gryaznians are buying each *Merce* for eighteen a pop, they've paid five, leaves thirteen – times a hundred, gives us one comma three mil to divide up. Gold today is – or at least was on the day all this was agreed – at three-eighty-seven US *la once.* Now, your standard gold bar is four hundred *onces,* or, *grosso modo,* twelve comma four kilos – that's what that bar down there weighs, twelve comma four kilos – and so it's worth a hundred and fifty five thousand dollars US. Times eight makes one million, two hundred and forty thousand *billes, Eu-ess.* And here – " he fished out an oblong bit of paper from the pile on his bed, "is the *rélicat* – the remaining sixty thousand – another cheque from the good old People's Trapeze, which, believe it or not, is what the Greeks choose to call their banks, of Cyprus. Which happens, I now realize, to coincidentally correspond, again, *grosso modo,* to your five percent."

"*Eh b'en mon p'tit con...*" Michel-Ange waved the Cypriot cheque away, "leaving that aside for the moment, you've been a busy boy, haven't you? A busy little *Consul de France*, haven't you?"

"*Eh!* – and don't forget Commercial Attaché – if this doesn't count as *commerce*, I don't know what does – "

"*Ouais,* but I'm not *entirely* sure this is what the *caïds* of the Quai had in mind when – "

"*Wou-aw,* don't come all *vieux marabout* on me – this is what the *Amerloques* call *'ween-ween'.* Where's the harm?"

"Well, I don't know... I'm sure a lawyer could find some – harm, that is – somewhere in this whole basket of crabs... But done is done, I suppose...." and Michel-Ange went to Moitié's kitchenette and started poking around, "You got any instant *kahua* here? I'm not sure another beer's *exactly* what I need at this point...."

"Here, let me," and the two made themselves useful over the coffee-organizing process. Then, returning their gaze to the booty on the floor, Michel-Ange resumed,

"So, you've got eight bars of gold that will need to be divided into – how many was it? Six?"

"That's right – the three back in Nice, me, and two guys here. And I confess, I haven't yet decided how to do the physical division, exactly. I've done counter-trade before, but gold bars is new to me."

"You've done counter-trade before? Where, here? With what?"

"Here – there – what's the diff? Perfume, condoms, whatever – that stuff's easy – but gold's definitely trickier – " *perfume, condoms...* Michel-Ange had a mental flash to Irina but it vanished as Moitié resumed, "I thought of having it melted down and re-cast into six bars, instead of eight, but that will require a level of technology, logistics, security and God knows what other *merde*, that I'm not sure I'm up to on my own... or even, now that you're on board, *à deux.... Or,* take two bars and saw each one into thirds – then you'd have six thirds, and you could give each of the six people one and a third bars...."

"Good *calcul, mon pote.*"

"*Hé,* you don't have to go to the E.N.A. to learn how to count.... Problem, is, I have no idea how easy this stuff is to saw through. Not that I even have a saw, but that's another *détail....*"

Michel-Ange suddenly had a thought, but he didn't want to tell Moitié. So instead he said, "Alright, you know what? Put this *chiasse* back under your bed, and let me think on it a bit – maybe I can help. Meanwhile, keep yourself handy for Consular duties – don't for the love of Good God *fous le camp* again... And let's make sure this place is locked up securely...."

For his part, Moitié's normal suspicion was superseded by his relief at having a collaborator in his scheme, so he agreed to go along with Michel-Ange for the time being and presently the two locked up and went their separate ways – Moitié to his Consular office, and Michel-Ange in search of Ivan Ivanov.

As Michel-Ange veered towards the garage/workshop/(commo center), he wondered whether he ought to call Mincemot and fill him in on *these* tomatoes... but decided against it, on the grounds that Moitié's venture was already well and truly locked onto the ascending roller-coaster cable, and there was nothing for it but to hope for a safe arrival at the ride's end – and having Mincemot weigh in just now with a vein-popping tirade wouldn't be conducive to *any*thing remotely helpful.

The ever-*serviable* Ivan Ivanov, only too happy to show off his array of ingeniously-amassed ironmongery, not only produced from the garage's dark oily recesses an old Yugoslav "*Čelik*" brand hack-saw, he also imparted some useful, if unbidden, info, to wit, that Irina had "borrowed" the Volga to go home to "ték care sam *personalniye* biézniéss ent she sé she ollso vill buy more foods, far you itts". *Well that's nice,* thought the otherwise preoccupied Michel-Ange as he went back to their bungalow, alone.

He got down, yanked out one of the sacks, took one of the gold bars in hand, and, having placed a dish-towel on his lap, sat cross-legged. He'd never cut gold before, and so had no idea what the process involved, shavings-wise, but in any case, he didn't want to lose even the tiniest sliver.... OK, now, ... *caaaare*fully.... he didn't want to slip and cut his damn knee, either....

And he started sawing ("hacking") off a small – one centimetre from the end – corner off the bar.

It proved even harder than he'd imagined, because it turned out that what he was cutting into wasn't "soft" gold at all, but rather... tungsten.

He had no idea, at the time, that it was, in fact, tungsten, but he could see right away that something stank, here – as he held the little pyramid in his hand and, looking at its base, gazed at what looked like a sawed-off, triangular yellow "M & M". For *effectivement*, under the thin yellow coating, this was indubitably some dark-gray metal that was *not* gold. (Michel-Ange, in his ignorance, assumed it was lead, not knowing that tungsten, having the almost identical density as gold, was, in fact, the preferred substitute for gold-fraudsters).

His mouth suddenly dry, and feeling the dead-weight of dread, Michel-Ange picked up another bar, from the other sack. Same result.

Oh, putain. Oh, boy. *Oh. Pu. Tain.*

He shoved the bars and sacks under the bed again, and, pocketing the two little tetrahedrons, headed – without even bothering to lock the bungalow door – over to the Consulate end of the Residence building.

He found Moitié in his Consul's chair, once again on his cellular phone, but this time Michel-Ange didn't wait – he interrupted,

"Hang up, *mon vieux.*"

"*Quoi?* – (sorry, I'll call you back) – what is it –?"

" '*Ustonne* – we have a *problème*' – "

26

KONFRONTATZYIA

In all candor, it cannot be reported that poor old Moitié took the news particularly well. (But who would have?):

After listening to what Michel-Ange explained to him, and turning over the little sliced-off corners in his fingers, he handed them back, did a bit of rapid blinking while staring through Michel-Ange's chestal area, and then stood up and delivered two furious blows with the base of the palm of his right hand against the metal filing cabinet that stood next to his desk. *Bam!-bam!* – they were what Michel-Ange recognized from the movies as being definitely martial-arts-derived, and they left the top part of the unoffending cabinet partly caved in.

"Ah les salauds! They got me. But *really* got me. Mother*fuck.* Fucked. *Baisé. Mais alors, baisé.* I am fucked. Fucked. Those fuckers. They – "

"Who's 'they', exactly? Who, in this whole... operation actually physically handed this *merde* off to you?"

"It was a flunky from the Ministry of The Treasury – but it was in behalf of that *con* who calls himself the 'State Surpervising Disburser'. And of course that little *salaud* of a Mayor of Laina – *he* had to be in on it too – "

"But those are, or were – if I remember your explanation correctly – *précisé-ment* two of the six who were meant to be recipients of this so-called gold... it doesn't seem *logique....*"

"*Sure* it does – now, with hindsight. Look – so they don't get any fucking gold – they don't give a shit – they still have a hundred Mercedes taxis at a third of their true value – *if that.* No, they're skating. The fucking fuckers. They must be gypsies. *Jewish* gypsies."

"*Alons, alons*, Moitié, get a hold," Michel-Ange stood up and, just to do *some-thing*, really, yanked the damaged file drawer open. To find therein an Albanian bottle of something labeled "La Capra" and two Air France plastic cups– *holy crap, this Embassy is better stocked with booze than old Manu's Macaque* – "let's not go uselessly chasing *fantasmes* – the question before us is: what is to be done?"

"Us?"

"But of course – " he smiled at his distressed colleague, "you were kind enough to 'cut me in'... to the tune of a Cypriot cheque which, by the way, I've *no* doubt is primed to bounce like *un ballon de baskette* – but anyway, ... Here, *tchin-tchin!*" he fished out and uncapped the Albanian bottle. "Because this is fraud perpetrated not just against you, but against... against... well, let's say against *French interests*... so *we* must react...."

"Well," conceded the subdued Moitié, "That's *vachement correcte* of you."

"Don't mention it." But then his smile disappeared – "Unless..."

"Unless what?"

"Unless... well, unless you... you're—*we're*... prepared to, you know... just... walk away from the thing – you know, take the loss... I mean, after all, does it *really* qualify as a loss? Rather than a, I don't know, just another... *missed opportunity*? Or, you know – just... chalk it up to experience – ?"

"*CA VAS PAS, NON?* 'Walk away'? 'Experience'? You think all those fine *go-rilles* back in Nice are gonna take this so philosophically? Listen, they just let go a million dollar *paquet* of city property for a fraction of the 'book' price – for which, depending on the *magistrat*, they could actually face some hard prison *tôle* – expecting to double their money – and you think they're gonna look kindly on little *moi* when I tell 'em 'Sorry, *les mecs*, forget it, the deal's off, back to your game of *boules'* – as the fucking taxis just disappear on the polluted waves of the Med? Well, *détrompe-toi,* my *pote* – because what they'll *really* want to do is carve me up into fish bait – !'"

"Alright, I get the point."

"And anyway, what about your *Honneur Nationale?* – You're supposed to be representing the country – in fact don't you purport to be some kind of half-arsed *aristo?* This should be an insult to you too – *especially* to you – !"

And it had to be said, the fellow had a point. For the fact was that, although he, Michel-Ange, recognized that this *farfelu* taxi scheme of Moitié's *was* pushing – to put it mildly – all manner of ethical envelopes, he nevertheless hadn't been a government *fonctionnaire* long enough yet to have had his residual patriotism *entirely* snuffed out by worldly cynicism, and he was still lucid enough to damn well recognize a national affront when he encountered one.

"You have reason, Moitié – Sorry, I mis-spoke." *I also underestimated the little bastard's survival instinct, never mind patriotism, but I'm not about to let* him *know* that... "So we agree – *la France est atteinte* and she must be defended – and if not by us, here, now – by whom, where, when? – That's alright, it's rhetorical, no need for an answer."

Those fucking pig's-bladders-in-suits at the Quai d'Orsay want to make me 'chargé d'affaires'? Well, fine, then – I'll start by taking charge of this 'affaire'....' He drained a beaker of the vile file-cabinet stuff.

"Ouf! This Albanian whatever-the-hell is truly *infecte* – "

"Ouais – it's apricot *rakia* and it was an attempted bribe from a girl who wanted a visa – She got her visa, alright, but it cost her more than a bottle of Albanian horse-piss, I can tell you – So, alright, what *are* we gonna do?"

"God, you really *are* a *salaud* – you sold a visa for a bit of *cul?* I can't believe I'm prepared to help you out of this *merdier* of yours...."

"*Hé*, choirboy – " and again he made the clam-like gesture – same one earlier used by Schlechtermann, "less *moralité* and more... ideas – "

"Yes, well... Our options aren't exactly vast, are they. Seems to me, our only move is for me to go back and strenuously – as they say – object *auprès* that President of theirs."

"You? But – shouldn't I be the one doing the complaining?"

"No, I don't think so. Look, don't take this personally – and, quite frankly, I don't believe I'm saying this myself – but I think the less you show yourself, the better. Plus, no matter how much you and I know it to be more than a bit *ridicule,* I actually *do represent France*, here. At least theoretically."

"Fine with me – believe me, I'm more than happy to *écrase*. But what can you say to the man? What, in any case, would we/you want him to *do*?"

"Well... replace this shit with real gold, *voyons*... Why not? You yourself say they grow it themselves, locally...."

"I suppose... but what if he tells you to shove the whole thing up your ass?"

"Yes, of course, he could do that – but I'll then come back and threaten him with... oh, I don't know, let's say with 'The Gravest Official Displeasure Of My Government'...."

"But that's complete bluff – you know as well as I that our government – if and when it learns of this *affaire* – will blame me, rather than the Gryaznians – "

"Of *course* it's a bluff! What d'you think? What d'you think this whole diploma-cy *guignol* is, if not a bluff? When it's not being a farce, that is..." Michel-Ange took another hit of *rakia*, gagged, and continued with a grimace " – *ack! merde,* I really need to eat something.... Anyway, look – as that old commie Danton said, *l'Audace, toujours l'audace!* – especially when you're in a hopelessly weak position. In any case, you don't know this, but I hold one small card I believe I can play to our advantage with Comrade *Prezident* Grib...."

"Oh yeah? What?"

"Clothilde – he appears to have a definite *faible* for that *horizonale regretée,* and I believe I can use her whereabouts as a carrot with the old *viçieux....* "

"But – *do* you know anything about her whereabouts?"

"Of *course* not! Again, *mon cher* Moitié, bluff – bluff, bluff *et toujours le* bluff!"

And now Michel-Ange put back the *rakia*, did his best to roll back the jammed drawer, and got down to *beez-nésse:*

"OK, Moitié, we pass to action: *primo,* I'll need you to make copies of all the relevant documents you have on this taxi affair, however bogus they turn out to be – I want something impressive to be able to wave in Grib's face. And I, for my part, will re-motivate Irina – get her to fix me another appointment – today's *foutu,* but I'll insist on tomorrow – I'll use the Clothilde card if I have to.... and meanwhile, what do you think, should we alert Paris? Who do you report to, anyway? Me, I report to that *ténébreux* colonel, and I, *ahem,* don't think I want to brief him on any of this *just now* – "

"Me? I report to the East European Division of *Affaires Etrangères* – bunch of *fonctionnaires,* and no, I don't think we need alert anyone *there* about any of this either, until and unless... we have absolutely no alternative...."

"*Bon.* So. *Allez, action!*" And with that, Michel-Ange left Moitié and re-entered the Residence, in search of Irina and, perhaps, something edible to soak up *this* morning's alcoholic marination.

But Irina appeared not yet to have returned from her errands, so he nipped into her little kitchen, found some jam and stale bread, and made himself a *tartine.* He was just swallowing the last of this when he heard his Volga clatter and fart to a halt out front, so he was at her desk to welcome Irina when she entered.

Mwa, mwa, "Hxello, boy-Chargé!"

Mwa, mwa, "Salut, my *chérie."*

But trying to fill Irina in on what Moitié had brought down on himself (and, by association, the rest of them) – even if a truncated version that did not go into too much detail regarding $ amounts – and explaining what he wanted her to immediately set about doing to help salvage something from the shambles – proved fully as vexed and migraine-inducing as he'd feared:

"Vatt? He trast dose gangksteri et Miénestrié aff *Trésor* – *Kazna? Ach,* Zhan-loo, Zhan-loo, *kak durak!"*

and

"Priézidient? Iss you kookoo, Michelangelo? I sink ven he stop to laffingk he vill be *viérié, viérié,* med, *fassé,* det you vasteingk heeis time – "

were among her more lucid comments and objections, but she brightened when he brought in the matter of their/her erstwhile nemesis, the peripatetic Dragon Lady Clothilde –

"Da!, iss goot idee! He LOFF de Clo! – he criééééié far de Clo – far *informat-zyia* aff Clo, *da,* vill sure inwite you égaine – !"

"OK, then set it up, will you please? Tell them I have the information the President asked for about *Madame l'Ambassadrice* – " and, after patting her on the rump – which she responded to by wiggling – he legged it upstairs to the Duquon-Lajoie's former quarters, hoping to discover some such information... or even an indication.

But he came up pretty much empty. Clothilde had clearly planned her de-campment thoroughly, and anyway, whatever bits of personal info that might have held clues to locating her would've been hoovered up by the Legionnaires and included in her stricken husband's bundle of personal *paperasse.*

The one thing he *did* find was an old *cotisation* from the (in English) LADIES DIPLOMATIC CIRCLE OF LAINA for an eyebrow-raising amount of nefa, made out to Madame C. Duquon-Lajoie at a quite fancy address in Neuilly, that Michel-Ange (correctly) figured to be their home back in France.

Re-descending to Irina's reception desk, he found that she was off to the *toilettes*, so he sat in her cockpit and dialed the LADIES DIPLOMATIC CIRCLE OF LAINA:

"Hello, this is de la Fassederad, the new Chargé d'Affaires at the French Embassy, and I'm calling to update the information you have on Ambassador and Madame Duquon-Lajoie – specifically their home number in Neuilly, that is to say, in Paris. They're changing their number – what number have you got for them now?"

He duly copied down the number that the Gryaznian secretary of the CIRCLE rather unthinkingly gave him, and gave her an utterly bogus one in return, thanked her and hung up. He now had Clothilde's phone number in Paris, and called *it*.

After a bit, a receiver lifted somewhere in Neuilly-sur-Seine and a definitely Iberian-accented female voice picked up.

"Si? Allo?"

"May I speak with *Madame* Clothilde Duquon-Lajoie, *s'il vous plait* –

"Pardon, but *Madama* is *actuélement* in *la République dé Gry—Gryashnie –* "

"Ah. ... Ah."

"If you like I can find you the *numero* for the *Ambassade* there, she is at the *Ambassade* there."

"Euh, no, that's alright, thank you so much – *au revoir.*"

Well, fat lot of good that *was... No, hang on, actually, it wasn't a* total *waste* – he now had something that he could plausibly pass off as Clothilde's private number. Never mind that it was useless – Michel-Ange (who was fast getting the hang of this government-service racket) reckoned that "plausible deniability" was not without some considerable currency, as he navigated these perilous diplomatic shoals. In any case, *faute de mieux,* it would have to do.

Irina returned and gave him the happy news that, although tomorrow was, in-deed, Saturday, a further audience with President Grib had been laid on, again for ten in the morning – and, yes, it was the promise of, nudge-nudge, wink-wink, some Clothilde-related intel that had done the trick. "He say he vaite *spétzialniye* far you – he say he even *rétarde* hees goff playingk far you!"

"Ah. *Sensas.*"

That evening an unusually subdued Moitié – rather like a whipped dog, ac-tually – joined Michel-Ange and Irina at her little kitchen for an impromptu dinner, consisting of a pre-boiled chicken she'd picked up at the *Hyper Co-op* with, (to Michel-Ange's silent alarm and dismay), beet *compote.* Conversation was strained. Indeed, the conversation was so virtually non-existent than mid-way through the chicken Irina turned on a little radio she kept in the counter, and they were subjected to the Evening News in Gryaznian, that she was only too happy to translate for them:

"So, *imperialisticheski* troops fram ONU, United *mnié mnié mnié* Na – *Naro-di* arriested civilist pipples in souse-west *Serbska-Krayina* viéllache, ent gavarn-ment aff Priézident Milosevic esk far *guinieralniye mobilizatsyia –* "

"What a fucking *rengaine...* " Moitié muttered.

"*Shhhhh,* Zhan-loo – you mast be knowingk off deez tings. Ent Gryaznia farénne miénestier een Novi Yorki say in *solidarnistikiye....* "

And so it went... until the meal came to a truncated, dessert-less conclusion, at which the three, clearing and washing up, agreed that, all things considered, an early night might not be amiss.

That night, Michel-Ange and Irina ended up not, actually, indulging in rum-pus-pumpus. Oh, she seemed enthusiastic enough at first – and to him she certainly remained as pneumatically and (thanks to all the Moitié-supplied wholesale perfume, which, as far as Michel-Ange was concerned, was Moitié's sole positive contribution to life) fragrantly alluring as ever. But after a bit of preliminary jockeying for position, as it were, they came to pretty much the same conclusion: that they were too preoccupied with more pressing, *ahem,* professional concerns to give any intimate proceedings the attention they required, and thus they agreed to pack things in before reaching the energy-expending phase.

"Does it derange you if we put this off... until... some other time?" is how he'd put it.

"No, I sink you har right – iss bietter not now. Iss bietter ve slipp."

And sleep they did – although, *again* he might as well not have bothered, for tonight, Michel-Ange, who normally enjoyed his dreams, had another one of these increasingly frequent ones in which he seemed to be wading, with great effort, through a vast vat of glue... so that the next morning he felt about as refreshed as if he'd spent the night doing... well, exactly that.

But *tant pis* – there was nothing for it. Onward. He thought it made good tactical sense, for the second successive Presidential audience in two days, to change attire and, it being a Saturday, he chose the tan gabardine suit with a pale blue shirt and the striped Racing Club tie.

He put into his serviette what he'd need for today's session: Clothilde's useless "co-ordinates" and his two little pyramids of gold-painted tungsten, wrapped in one of his silk handkerchiefs.

He went downstairs. Two minutes later Moitié ambled in through the front door and Irina descended the Duquon-Lajoie Memorial staircase in a new *ensemble* (another of Clothilde's, rendered all the more fetching by again being one size too small) and a cloud of Grasse's best Generic.

The three of them huddled again at the little kitchen table, this time over the apparently-permanent Lainian *petit déj*: coffee, bread and jam. (There was a large box of Russian corn flakes on the kitchen counter – *"Cukooruzhniye Klopya"* – *"кукурузные хлопья"*, to be precise – but it enticed no one and remained untouched.)

Moitié handed over a sheaf of papers that purported to be a record, of sorts, of the Great Taxi Hornswoggle, and he pointed out to Michel-Ange the names and offices of some of the guiltier parties.

The question arose as to whether Moitié should even attend this Presidential meeting or not:

The arguments against his showing his offending *gueule* were that 1/ it might be *politique* to maintain some kind of diplomatic "buffer" between offending parties, to better enable emollience, dissimulation and, if necessary, compromise, and 2/ *someone* should hold the fort back here at the Embassy, not least in case someone pitched up requiring consular services – even though technically the Consulate was closed on weekends, it was fairly well known to those parts of Laina which cared about such matters that the whole notion of a consular "schedule" was a purely notional one to the erratic *Monsieur le Consul* Moitié....

But on the other hand the finger-wagging Irina convinced them that it would be wise to have Moitié's hot and quivering body handy in case his presence was *priezidentially* demanded.

So they finally agreed that Moitié would, in fact accompany them to the meeting/confrontation with the President, but that he'd remain in a "holding", "reserve" function, i.e., waiting in the car outside with Ivan, to be available as an "expert witness", so to speak, if necessary/required. (And *tant pis* if anyone showed up wanting to see the Consul – wouldn't be the first – or last – time they'd come up empty at Moitié's Consular "Door of Chance"....)

Bon – are we ready for this... Showdown At the Grib Corral?

A somewhat grumpy Ivan Ivanov (who, after yesterday, hadn't expected another "official" trip so soon – and certainly not on a Saturday) had been summoned and coaxed into action, and presently the entire corpus of the French Embassy in Laina, Republic of Gryaznia, *sans* Legionnaires (who for now remained uninformed of the unfolding drama) rolled out of the gate. They were saluted on their way by the (speaking of whom) mildly-surprised PFC Meihavelha, who'd been about to go off duty and whose curiosity was not sufficient to overcome his grogginess and cause him to ask anyone inside the Citroën where they were going, in their Sunday finery... on this sunny Saturday morning....

27

PERSONA NON-GRATA

Once again it was Irina's overdrive mind that greased the skids, as, upon approaching the outer layer of the People's Palace's concentric protection, she produced from her magical fake-Gucci bag a faxed "hard copy" of the ad-hoc "follow-up"-invitation, that she'd had the foresight to coax out of one of her contacts in the *byurokratiya*.

As she flashed this latest bit of paper liberally about, the Citroën pretty much followed yesterday's choreography, and the added presence of Moitié in the back seat didn't seem to evoke much curiosity by the variously-uniformed *gardiens*.

Of course the two little tungsten pyramids caused the scanning booth to damn near lift off like a stage-1 rocket, but Irina talked their way through with a blast of scorn-tinged blather about *geolozhki spiécimiénskiye*, and presently they found themselves again in the barren Presidential waiting hall.

Because of the last-minute nature of this *audience*, perhaps not surprisingly they had a longer wait than yesterday. And even though it was ten on a Saturday morning in near-summer, they seemed to have arrived as what sounded like some kind of New Year's Eve party that was reaching a climax, in there, on the other side of the invisible door-in-the-wall. Laughing, folk-singing, glasses clinking, clapping – Michel-Ange and Irina exchanged glances – she shrugged and he made a wincing grimace.

Eventually, the hole in the wall opened outward, disgorging a loud troupe of ethnically-garbed "rustics", eight of them, (four women in *dirndl*-type dresses and four men in corduroy shorts, knee socks and high-top lace-up boots), still smiling and calling good-byes as they were ushered out by the Ray-Bans-and-black-leather-jacket Twins from yesterday.

Michel-Ange was expecting now to be invited in, but nothing doing – the R-b's-&-b-l-j's motioned him to keep his arse seated. More minutes went by. At one point, the blonde *nana* "assistant" also from yesterday emerged, wearing jeans that fitted her like a snake's skin, and clacked her way through and out the waiting hall on 4-inch heels – to reappear bearing some files, and back into Grib's office.

More waiting. Now a pair of high-ranking (judging by the extravagance of their chestal fruit-salad) military types appeared out of the lift and, bearing their enormous *casquettes* under their arms, entered the door-in-the-wall, which had again magically clicked itself open.

Irina attended placidly to her nails, and Michel-Ange just sat there. He was in no particular hurry, and even welcomed the opportunity to try to formulate some sort of plan.... to no great avail, it must be said....

... for, truth be told, not only did Michel-Ange not know what to expect from *Prezident* Grib, he wasn't even clear what he *hoped* for from him:

I mean, what's the old boy likely to say? 'Oh that's alright, sorry for the mix-up, here, please, accept these eight bars of genuine, un-trafiqué gold'? Ouais, sure.... Or, ... even more unlikely – 'Here, my boy, take these million three-hundred thou in green US bills, cash'? Sure, that'll be the day.... Actually, what is possible, remotely possible, is that he'll offer to make up the missing fric in stinking nefas – and what the hell I'll do if he hands me a government cheque for a gazillion nefas, God only knows – where the hell would I (or more likely that crétin Moitié) go to get that cashed, eh? And, non, no way Mincemot won't spit up blood at that, nooooooon.... *Probably on balance the best I can hope for is for this guy, the Prez, to decree the entire deal null and void, get that Maltese tub, wherever it is by now, to turn around and go back to Nice – and those* mafieux *back there will just have to return that cheque they've already pocketed for a half million US... of course, poor old Moitié, if he escapes being chopped up into, as he says, little pieces of fish food, will probably have to flee into hiding in a* couvent somewhere, *but... the important thing, as far as my – little Michel-Ange's – pathetic hide is concerned, will be that I be seen to be defending the interests and even the – and you can all just stop giggling right now – honor of France....*

Well, whatever Michel-Ange might have expected – let alone might have *hoped* for – it was never anything, even remotely, like... *this*:

The two brass hats eventually re-emerged and left, and *finally*, the head Ray-Ban-and-etc. held the door open for Michel-Ange and Irina to enter.

And, behold! – there was *Prezident* Grib bedecked in what didn't require bottomless depths of perception to deduce was meant to be his golfing outfit – *But of course, it's Saturday morning, the universally-understood Hour Of The Golf!* – but in his case the get-up was of such a fabulously retrograde idiosyncrasy that a blinking Michel-Ange had to remind himself that he wasn't in a *tableau* from the earliest *Aventures de Tintin (*although if he'd been familiar with the covers of P. G. Wodehouse's golf novels, he would have perceived an even closer approximation).

For His Maximum *Prezident*ship Gerasim Vladimirovich Grib stood, beamingly beckoning them to enter, wearing baggy brown woolen trousers that the English called "plus-fours" and the Americans called "knickerbockers", bloused above brown-red-and-yellow argyle socks, shod in lethal-looking rubber-spiked two-tone black-and-white shoes on which he clomped around his office rather after the Sicilian grape-squashing fashion. His slim torso was covered by a mustard-colored sleeveless pullover, over a pink button-down shirt with a mauve paisley *foulard* erupting flamboyantly from the open collar. And on his elegant bald conk sat a white "flat" cap. With a red *pompom* on top.

All in all, Michel-Ange had to grudgingly concede, the *mec* looked rather splendid.

And he was just now fairly shouting, with great voluble good cheer,

"Ah!, so again ve meet, *Monsieur le Chargé* from *Frantsous!,* Dellafassra!, satch a pleasure, as I am prepare for ze golf, vich lamiénted Armand taught me so nicely how to play – vich reminds me, is reason far your comingk is that you heff goot news of where is gone ze lahffly – ent my *viérié viérié* dear frent! – ze lahffly *Madame* Clothilde? ... yes?"

As Michel-Ange scrambled mentally to respond, he was gratified and relieved to notice, this morning, the (at least overt) absence of any of Squire J. Walker's products which might/could/would be toastingly used to sodden the brain and further befuddle the procedings.

"Ah, well, yes – that is to say, yes, your, *Monsieur le Président,* euh, ... yes, well, that is to say – yes and no – "

"Yes *ent* no? But your lahffly assistant Miss Vozhbuzhdena, here – " *He knew her surname, b'en* merde, *alors, even I have trouble remembering the damn thing – I guess it's not for nothing the fucking* type *became President...* "assured us zet you had found ze location of *Madame* Clothilde – "

"Well... yes, we believe we have – here, you can try this number – perhaps later – " and he handed Grib the bit of paper containing that address and phone number of the Duquon-Lajoie residence in Neuilly, "but also I have another pressing matter, *Monsieur le President,* which I feel it is my urgent duty to bring to your attention, and it is one which concerns my coll – "

'*Perhaps later*', that's *a laugh!* – the President spun abruptly around in Michel-Ange's mid-sentence and handed the paper to the blonde assistant/*nana,* with a few words in Gryaznian. And when he turned to re-face Michel-Ange his expression had changed to one of pained impatience:

"Yes? What? *Chto?* Samsing else? – zere vas samsing else? I am not sure I heff time zis morningk – paireheps you send written *pratakol* srough ze *regulyarniye* channels, and ve vill – "

But for once Michel-Ange wasn't having it. For once he just... plunged ahead. Bit the bullet, as Jenni-Faire (she of the previous life) used to say:

"Non, Monsieur le Président, I'm afraid that simply won't do." *Oh, de Dieu! – do 24 year-old Chargés d'Affaires with less than one week's total work experience tell foreign presidents 'Non, Monsieur le Président, that simply won't do'? Well, my old, we're about to find out...* "This matter is too grave to pass off to some mid-level... *fonctionnaires.* This is, I fear, a matter of great scandal on the part of some of your officials, and, quite frankly, it is a matter of national honor – " *I can't even believe these words are escaping from my mouth...* "for France! *Monsieur."*

Grib now balled his hands into fists, placed them on his hips, spread his no-longer-amusingly-spiked feet defiantly, and his eyes became downward-pointing slits that Michel-Ange hadn't seen since he'd encountered an angry King Babar as a little boy. The President took a step towards him.

"Shkandal? *Shkandal? My pipple? Your honor? Oh yes? Do, please, tell me of zis, my young... friend – I am* viérié viérié *interiested...."*

And Michel-Ange proceeded, he hoped politely, but with as much of what he'd always imagined "gravitas" might sound like as he could coax from his distressingly dry *gueule,* to lay out the tawdry facts – and even figures and not forgetting actual names of guilty parties – of the Great Gryaznian Taxi Boondoggle And Counter-Swindle of 1994. And certainly not neglecting, at the end, to dramatically brandish the two offending tungsten tetrahedrons – at which Grib's mouth curled in distaste and from which he recoiled as if they were radioactive.

(In the middle of Michel-Ange's exegesis the blonde assistant had slipped from her corner out the door, the tell-tale scrap of paper in hand, with Grib's apparent consent – at least he hadn't interrupted proceedings to stop her.)

Michel-Ange concluded his oration thus: " – and so I appeal to you, *Monsieur le Président*, to intervene in this matter and make things right – to make restitution – we are not asking that anyone be punished – " *(!)* "but rather that perhaps you can do the necessary to bring us all back to the *status quo ante.*"

The spent Michel-Ange couldn't think of anything more to add and so he stopped. And he and the simmering *Prezident* stared at each other.

Finally Grib expostulated "Is zat all? Are you finitch?"

"Yes, *monsieur,* yes – I think that concl – " and again the *Prezident* turned away before Michel-Ange had finished – stepping aside and addressing Irina, who'd been hovering near a wall, in Gryaznian.

Michel-Ange could decipher enough of his gist, and of Irina's reply, which included "*da*" and "Mwa-tee-eh" and "*v mashine*", to *pige* that his colleague, the hapless progenitor of the Great Taxi Brainstorm, was about to be summoned.

Eh b'en, this should be good – Michel-Ange, mon p'tit con, on est pas sorti d'l'aubérge!

Grib then opened his door, spoke to the Raybans-and-black-leathers again, and delivered Irina to their care – she was clearly being sent to fetch Moitié.

Which left Michel-Ange alone in the *Prezidential* office with this scowling and muttering-to-himself Gerasim Vladimirovich Grib who, by now, with his Saturday morning clearly thoroughly buggered, seemed to be weighing up the consequences of stamping his rubber-spiked foot.

Merde, what a merdique situation... rendered even more agonizing for Michel-Ange by the extreme dryness of his lips, mouth and even throat – indeed, his entire what Sgt. Schlechtermann would have called "mouth housing group" had just about shut down from acute desiccation, and reluctant as he was to broach the whole perishingly vexed matter of drink, he nevertheless forced himself, pointing to his lower face, to croak at the *Prezident*:

"*Ack! 'il vous plait* – is there? – could I ask? – drink? – water? *vody?* – *eck!*"

Grib looked at him with repugnance, but bent down and produced from his desk not, this time, Johnnie Walker's Black, or Gold or Platinum – or even Tungsten! – but rather a bottle of what turned out to be 50-nefa Serbian "Kraljika" *slivovitz,* along with what looked like a far-from-clean white plastic toothbrush cup. Apparently this stuff had been *fête*-ing the departed folk-dancing troupe, but there was still a goodish bit left.

Michel-Ange took this offering with, if possible, increased despair, but, well. again, there was nothing for it:

Hop! down the hatch – *cul sec.* The appalling stuff was about as refreshing as MiG jet-fuel, but it was at least wet... *allez* – Michel-Ange threw down a second shot.

Meanwhile, the *Prezident* stewed on. All previous happy blather about golfing with Mitterand in Paris Disneyland was as gone and forgotten as if it had never happened – irrelevant as faint echoes from another galaxy. Except that ... *'allo?, wait a sec, what's he doing now?* ... the *Prezident* clomped over to the corner behind his desk where his golf bag was propped up and extracted a club – Michel-Ange had no idea whether it was a putter, a wood, an iron or what, but he recoiled reflexively – he knew enough about golf to know that golf clubs made *trés* damn fine weapons.

At first Grib just *whoosh, whoosh* took practice swings. But he then produced from his baggy woolen trouser pocket a golf ball, placed it on the floor next to his trash basket, and gave it an almighty, un-aimed *whack!*

The ball took off like something out of an old Warner Brothers cartoon, bouncing *pok!* off the wall next to the invisible door, then back clear across the office, miraculously *through* the chandelier – making only a demure tinkling sound – to bounce *pok!* off the magical mystery "periscope"-or-whatever-it-was-"window", then back, finally coming to rest on the floor below the Zimbabwean elephant tusks.

"How you like *zat? Hah? Yah?*" demanded a half-demented *Prezident* Grib.

Though it was by no means clear that this required an answer, Michel-Ange nevertheless ventured, *"Euh...* very nice... I think – not really an expert, as I believe I mentioned in our prev – "

But Grib was already pulling another ball from his pocket – aaaand... *whack!*

This one seemed to have a kind of "slice" to it, and shot off almost directly at Michel-Ange's head – *ouiiiih!* – and by the time Michel-Ange extracted said head from under his armpit, he could see that the ball, after bouncing off two more walls, was sitting – almost quivering – on the brown leather couch next to the absent assistant's desk and chair.

"That one, on the other hand... " squeaked Michel-Ange, suddenly worried that the next shot could well greet Irina and Moitié squarely in their *gueules* if they were to suddenly just now open the door... But mercifully at this point the phone on the presidential desk rang, imposing an at least temporary quietus onto this impromptu golfing live-fire exercise. Indeed, they must have heard, out in the waiting room, what was transpiring on the *Prezidential* side of the door, because this call was from one of the Raybans-and-leathers on his cellular phone, asking for a cease-fire.

The invisible door now re-opened, and in came Irina and, judging by his hang-dog expression, a Moitié whom Irina had already brought up to speed on the trend of events – probably something like "Tings iz not goingk so *oy-oy fantastique* vis Priézidiént, Zhan-loo," – *so at least he's not joining us expecting a* fanfare *and parade....*

Prezident Grib, still gripping his semi-automatic assault golf club, advanced on Moitié and demanded, *"V etom chertov idiotiye konsulom?"* which Michel-Ange didn't even need Irina to translate as "Is this the fucking idiot of a consul?"

So he was able, as the fucking idiot's boss, to offer, *"Da, oui,* but he – "

"Ze great genius" (he pronounced it *"gué-nyoos"*) *"Frantsous* entrepreneur?" ("hantra-prinoor"?)

Again Michel-Ange attempted to speak for Moitié, (who, in truth, appeared to be struck dumb – positively calcified): "Yes, but – "

"Silence! *Zatknis!* Pliss! Zis man has kamiétted a *most* grave affiénce – *most* grave! – against me piérsonally – *piérsonally!*"

What? Wait a minute, here, I can't let that one go unchallenged.... "No, my dear *Monsieur le Président*, surely not – his intention was just to import much-needed taxis – never anything to do with you, personally or even at all – and it was, in any case, certainly not *lui* who produced the *faux* gold – !"

"Again, *zatknis!* – shad-hup! I dunt care about fockingk téxis or fockingk golt! – I *do* care about – " and here President Grib unloaded a torrent of spittle-flecked, exclamation-laced Gryaznian that left Michel-Ange in the dust, so to speak. When he finally had to pause for breath, the President nodded to Irina to do the honors:

"Priézidient say he dunt care vat deals, vat *combines* Zhan-loo make here viz comrades, sarry, viz afficials from dis or det miénestrié – but vat he care *MATCH, MATCH* about is det Zhan-loo dunt sink to giff him hees *kammissionyie* – hees *Priézidentzialnyie kammission* far satch a deal mast be *mié-nemom* – *mié-nemom* – twenty-fife partzent – he say, vot you sink? You sink satch a pasition ez Priézidient you ken hignore? Iz *beek, beek* iénsalt to heem! Diss vot he say..." she ended, rather weakly.

Michel-Ange was about to rebut, but Grib started off again, and this time the vituperation was accompanied by a lot of arm (and golf club) waving, the whole thing culminating in a most energetically-executed foot-kick, after the manner of a football goalie clearing a ball.

This time, Irina didn't translate directly, but responded to her President with some quizzical Gryaznian jabber of her own. But he shot right back, more emphatically even than before. So Irina now faced Moitié and Michel-Ange, gulped, and said,

"He say – Priézidient say – det he must make exiémple to udders, to stop satch disrespiect in *budush* – in future – so he say... det Zhan-loo mast go hout fram de cantry – he is kickingk hout – he say Zhan-loo iss, *mnié mnié mnié*, how dey say, *Persona Non Grata*. He say Zhan-loo mast go hout fram cantry in forty-height howers." She paused and looked down. "Saw sarrié, Zhan-loo, but det vat he say."

The two young Frenchmen were stunned. For perhaps five seconds all was still. But Michel-Ange willed himself back into gear, and bleated,

"But *Monsieur le Président,* surely you cannot mean this! You –" and he was aware even as the words came out that he risked sounding absurdly like that whiny American tennis player, "cannot be serious! My colleague is innocent of any wrongdoing – in fact *he/we* are the victims here – and he certainly meant no disrespect in not, ... in not, ... in not, ... euh, including you in – "

"*Pah!* I dunt vant to hear inié more about it! – *Ya nye hatchoo slyshat bolshe!* – He iss hout! *Au re-vwah!* Goot-pie! Forty-height hours – " and the President turned and clomped over to confer with his blonde assistant – who had, at some point during the just-concluded dramatic events, slipped back into the office.

Michel-Ange, Moitié and Irina just stood there, in dumb impotence, watching as the president and his girl assistant exchanged animated, if muffled, bursts of Gryaznian... The girl handed the President a piece of paper, and he, after stashing his golf club back in its bag, showed her other pieces of paper. Their exchanges became more heated (at least on his part – at one point he exclaimed *"ebanatyie pidaraz sooka!"* which Michel-Ange didn't need Irina to tell him meant something close to "fucking motherfucking whore!").

After about two minutes of this, the girl started typing furiously into her word processor, and Grib rejoined the other three, more enraged than ever. He seemed, to Michel-Ange's alarmed eye, to be actually turning purple. *I've heard of such a condition, but don't recall ever actually seeing it. Not even in Mincemot.*

Prezident Grib addressed himself directly to Michel-Ange, as he waved about this new piece of paper the girl had given him.

"And not just gengster Consul! – You too, *Monsieur le Chargé d'Affaires* – !" he dripped sarcasm on the title, "you too, go hout! You too are *Persona Non Grata!* You too heff forty-height hours to get your..." he seemed, briefly, to search for the right word, "your arrogant... *зад... cul...* arse the hells out from Gryaznia! Go! Bose of you! *Dosvydanyie!*"

"*Me?* But *why?* What –" but even now Michel-Ange fought back the reflexive use of "the hell", "in the name of God have *I* done?"

"*Why you?* Why *YOU?* Because you take me, *Prezident* of Gryaznia, for a fool! I ask you honestly, as vun man to anozzer man, for help to find location of *Madame* Clothilde – I tell you in all frankness I *viéry, viéry* much admire the *Madame* Clothilde – and vat you do? *Heh?* How do you treat my confidences? My most frank man-to-man confidences?"

Michel-Ange assumed, rightly, that these questions were rather *pro forma*, requiring no answer, so he stayed shtoom; he could think of nothing that would in the *slightest* way deflect what he could see coming with the certainty of that falling anvil in the Road-Runner cartoons:

"How?" continued Grib, "*Hah!* By making mockery of my honest sientiments. By making cruel joke – here, here! –" the seemingly-possessed President shook the paper again, "zis stupid *téléfon* number you give me, it is nossing but an old Spanish cleaning lady who tell us that *Madame* Clothilde is in... *is in Embassié in Laina!* This is cruel personal mocking of *me personally*, of the person of *Prezident* of the Republic, and so you are also *HOUT!* – Let Mitterand send me some *prapper* deeplomats, and not young gooligan vise-guys like you two –" he inhaled noisily through his nose... it was *tout juste* that his head wasn't actually smoking, "In *fect,* better – I say *fack* Mitterand! – *And* fack his golf! – he can be hieppy zat I don't cut relations *camplietely* – !"

And with that he broke off, as if to walk away, but he caught himself, turned and re-addressed Michel-Ange, this time with a nasty squinty-eyed grimace,

"*And!* – vorst of *all!* – you used zis uzeless, vorseless so-called telefon number for *Madame* Clothilde as a *blatant, trenspiérent* ruse to get back in here to kamplain of zis smellingk mish-mash téxi deal in vich you did not even see fit to include ze *Priézident* – zis is *dabble* – maybe even *treeple,* if I look closely enaff – *conspiratzyia* by you – !"

And with this he seemed to be finished, at least for the moment. He turned and strode back to his assistant's corner, from which he emerged with four pieces of paper that she'd just produced from her printer. He took them to his desk, signed all four, left two there, and rejoined the little forlorn group in the center of his office with the remaining two.

"Zese are your orders of *dis-accrediatzyia* and *expultzyia,* and zey are being faxed to your embassy here and your foreign miénestrié in Paris viss immediately effect. I am, heh, also alierting my own idiot in Paris to expect *retaliatsyia,* but never mind – impartant sing iss – you two, *HOUT!*"

Prezident Grib handed Michel-Ange and Moitié each his personalized marching orders – Michel-Ange, peering at this official, embossed Presidential expulsion decree, marveled at the speed with which the innocent-looking blonde *nana* over there had produced such handsome and portentous documents with such apparent ease – *these bloody* fumiers *must keep the template permanently handy on her word-processor.*

Grib then returned behind his desk and took his seat. From which he looked up and addressed them in his original, affable "Presidential" mode,

"So, gentlemen – I believe our affairs here are now at conclusion. I wish you a safe trip home. Oh, and Miss Vozhbuzhdena, please contact my office when these, ah, guys, these... *parenye,* have departed – you and I vill need to discuss... tings... " and he tailed off. He pushed a button under his desk which clicked the invisible door open, and the Raybans-and-black-leather-jackets hustled in to escort them out.

When they regained the Citroën – (oddly, their new pariah status seemed to, if anything, speed and ease their outward, as it were, passage) – the oblivious Ivan Ivanov chirped as he opened both passenger-side doors for them,

"Saw? Iss hokay? Everebadié ken naow enchoy rest av veek-enda, *oui*?"

Moitié still appeared incapable of speech, and Irina by now had tears dribbling down her face, so it fell to Michel-Ange to reply,

"*Ah, mon cher ami* Ivan, it's all rather *dramatique* – Irina will tell you in due course. For now, let's just get back – and now, more than ever, please endeavor to avoid any vehicular *crabouillments,* for – " and here he included the other two in his excellent *apérçu* "to tell the truth, I'm not even sure we have any *immunitée diplomatique* anymore...."

While Irina spent most of the drive back to the Embassy jabbering to Ivan in Gryaznian, pausing only to, from time to time, dab her eyes and blow her nose from a roll of bumwad that Ivan kept in the Citroën's console for purposes that didn't bear thinking about, our two young French diplomat/miscreants kept their gloomy counsel in the back seat... until, as Michel-Ange was eventually moved to place his and Moitié's expulsion orders inside his *serviette,* he fished out the two pyramids of gold-painted tungsten and said,

"Hmm, funnily enough, these *conneries* have suddenly taken on a certain sick value after all – here, *monsieur le juge,* are your Exhibits A and B – "

At which poor old Moitié, who'd been, like a sulky child, stupidly staring out the window the whole ride back, turned and looked at the offending *pièces de merde* and finally managed to give tongue,

"And *there, mon p'tit con,* you would not be wrong – I just hope those fucking *gorilles* in Nice don't make me *eat* the fucking things...."

28

A TACTICAL
RECONFIGURATION

By the time they'd been saluted through by Meiavelha and had tumbled out of the Citroën at the steps of the Residence, they'd managed, despite their varyingly dazed and confused – not to say stupefied – state, to put together a rudimentary plan of immediate action:

 * Moitié would brief the Legionnaires, and then begin packing and "organizing his affairs" – whatever that might mean and to the extent that such a thing could even be attempted on a somnolent Lainian weekend.

 * Michel-Ange would once again hie himself underground to alert "his *patron*" in Paris – a task for which his extreme reluctance was tempered by a burning desire to complain to *someone* – even as unlikely a source of sympathy as Mincemot,

and

 * Irina would get on the local blower and attempt to organize them seats on a flight to Paris before the clock ran out, i.e., (and here Michel-Ange had to double-check his expulsion order) before noon on Monday.

After yanking off his suit jacket and tie (draping them on Irina's receptionist chair), downing an entire Polarnia in the kitchen (he didn't want to overly tax the dwindling subterranean supply at this critical moment), and having a blessed *pipi (not gonna get caught out down there again)*, Michel-Ange rabitted over to the garage, backed the Façel-Vega out, and clattered down to engage the red telephone.

Oh la vache – a lot of merde'*s hit the fan since The Fierce One and I last chatted... this is gonna be some* pique-nique *of a phone call....*

And when the phone picked up at the other end – before the first ring had even finished! – Colonel Bertrand Mincemot did not disappoint:

"*Ah! Vous voila, vous!* It's about fucking time you called! Tell me, you young and useless *énergumène,* how is it even remotely possible that you have managed to so thoroughly and completely fuck things up over there in such a blindingly short time? *Hein? Hein? How?* For the love of God, man – a team of dedicated demolition sappers couldn't blow things up more efficiently than you appear to have done, you buffoonish simpleton – !"

As the colonel seemed to pause for breath, Michel-Ange seized the opportunity to venture,

"Ah – so I take it you've heard? *Mon colonel?*"

"*Of course I've fucking heard!* You *crétin fini*! I just got a 5-alarm rocket from the Quai which just got a fax from that fucking *co-co* clown who runs that fucking country, in effect shutting down our embassy there – *what did you fucking do to him?* What, fuck his wife? Piss in his *borscht*? I mean – how hard is it not to insult the president of a country? Especially when you're a snot-nosed sub-nothing who's barely old enough to be out of short trousers? *Hein? What?*... So? – what do you have to say for yourself, young *connard*?"

"May I speak, *monsieur*?"

"*Yes!,* by God! *Pute-borgne, bordelle de chiasse do bordelle de merde!* What do you think I'm... urging you to do, here? In the most gentle way I know how?"

"What I mean is, this will require perhaps a more extensive explanation than you think you might have in mind, so I pray you, *mon colonel,* to allow me to conclude my *récit.* Before you resume calling me a *connard...* "

"I *reserve* the right to call you a *connard* any damn time I please, but... alright, young man," he inhaled deeply and audibly, "Proceed...."

"Bon – Well, *mon colonel,* it begins with Moitié – "

"I *knew* it! Goddamn those useless fucking socialist incompetents at the fucking Quai, they have no eye for talent, only nepotism and stupid fucking party loyalty – "

"Mon colonel! I beg of you – you assured me – "

(sigh) "*Bon, d'accord...* go ahead.... *NO!, WAIT! –* "

"Yes?"

"You say this *farfelu* explanation is going to be long and convoluted – ?"

"I believe the word I used was, euh, 'extensive' – "

"Same thing. Alright, so hang on a sec while I switch on the recording device on my phone here – I want the lard-heads" (*"têtes de lard"*) "at the Quai to hear it direct from the source – I don't want to be accused of hyperbole or embellishment...." his voice was replaced by some clicking sounds, and then "... *bon, ça y est –* proceed – *one two three, this is de la Fassederad, our Chargé in Laina –* "

"So. Right. Well, actually, my view is that Moitié, while not *entirely* blameless in all this, is as much a victim as anyone – perhaps *more* so, as you will *constate* – but, to back up.... You'll remember that in recent days our Consul/Commercial Attaché has been persistently absent from his post, right?"

"Of course – that was the very reason that we had no choice but to elevate you to – " (cough) "Chargé d'Affaires – "

"Right. Well, the *reason* for this absence turns out to be that he was involved in finalizing – indeed receiving payment for – a scheme which...."

And Michel-Ange went on to recount:

* the whole Moitié taxi wheeze, including as best he could remember them the names and sums involved,

* his own discovery of the tungsten sting,

and

* their subsequent quandary about how best to proceed.

And then he threw in:

* the piquant Grib/Clothilde factor ("whether the infatuation was ever requited or not – this remains a mystery, *mon colonel*"),

* his rather disastrously not-thoroughly-thought-through decision to use it as an inducement to gain a second, "emergency" Saturday-morning meeting with the President,

and finally

* the latter's compounded rage at not having been cut in on the taxi deal and having been misled on a possible Clothilde contact.

Colonel Mincemot listened to all this with admirable restraint – confining his reaction to muffled grunts and the odd *"pshh!"*. And most surprising of all was that, when Michel-Ange finally came, mercifully, to an end, with the words...

"... and those forty-eight hours run out at noon on Monday, and Irina is trying to book us out of here, as I speak... and that brings us up to, well ... right now. *Mon olonel,"*

...there was an unexpected silence at the other end of the line. This was interrupted by those clicks again, which must have been the disconnection of the recording device, and then again nothing. Michel-Ange waited a few seconds more and eventually bleated into the receiver,

"*Allo, allo?* You still there, *mon colonel?*"

Only then did an extremely weary-sounding Mincemot come back on,

"*Pu-tain de merde...* I've heard a lot of bizarre *conneries* in my long life but I've got to tell you, Fassederad, none bigger than that pile of thrice-fucked *ma-gouillage* that you've just disgorged. One doesn't even know where to begin to comment – but thank God it's on the record, otherwise they wouldn't believe me... over there.... *Bon,* so now listen to me, *petit* – " and with this, his musing, almost wistful tone brusquely reverted to the old, curt, hard-arse Mincemot,

" – here's what you do: you and that imbecile truant of a colleague of yours prepare to evacuate the AO – "

"The what?"

"The AO – area of operations – *les lieus,* the premises – *ho la la.* Anyway, me, I've got some emergency calls to make, but I'll get back to you. So, what's the 'open' phone situation there? Does the official embassy line work? The one that's given out to the public?"

"Yes, *mon colonel* – it rings at the Embassy/Residence reception."

"Good. So I'll call you back on that – and from now on, that's how we'll communicate – given the, euh, circumstances, there's hardly any further need for any particular... *discrétion* and for you to have to hover around this secure phone any longer – you're underground, somewhere, is that right?"

"Yes *mon colonel* – in the garage, in a hole under the Ambassador's personal Facel Vega car – "

"Spare me – enough *extravagances Gryazniènes* for one morning. So listen further: the way these things work is, the Foreign Ministry here will issue a *pro-forma* protest, but before they do that, they'll reply to the expulsion order by automatically asking for a 'reconsideration' of the *délai* given – something that would, I don't mind saying, come in damned handy, as we – *they* – scur-ry around trying to scare up some replacements to send down to that little shit-hole, on the spur of the moment like this – but, as I say, it's all SOP – the request is probably going out already, as we speak. But now you and Moitié, while you organize yourselves, don't roam too far from that official local phone – I'll definitely be calling you back – "

"Yes, *mon colonel*."

"Oh, and Fassederad, one more thing," Like all instinctive coaches, Mincemot strove never to end a bawling-out on an irredeemably negative note.

"Yes, *mon colonel?*"

"Hang in there, kid." *("Tiens bon, fiston.")*

"Without doubt, sir." *("Sans doute, mon colonel.")*

"*Bon.* Now go – " *Click. Click.*

Michel-Ange grabbed the two remaining Polarnias, and the half-filled bottle of cognac out of Moitié's little fridge (*no sense, now, leaving* these *behind*), pulled the chain which turned off the light, and clambered out of the underground commo-hole, gratefully expecting that he'd never see its cramped funkiness again – at least not in *this* life – eased the Facel-Vega back into place, and hurried back to the Residence.

On his way in he passed Moitié, who was just leaving the Residence, heading for their bungalow, "cellphone" up against his ear but he nevertheless managed to comment to Michel-Ange, "Gotta pack – dunno how I'm gonna get all my *merde* outta here in two suitcases – somebody's gonna have to pay for some overweight – "

"*T'en fais pas* – don't sweat it – " and as he waved him airily off, it occurred to Michel-Ange that he had, in fact, very little to pack – *re*-pack, really – as he'd barely ever *un*packed (despite his having acquired two sets of living quarters), and he'd certainly not *acquired* anything.... unless you counted those little pyramids of *foutu* tungsten....

Irina was busy on her phone so Michel-Ange wandered into the kitchenette, where Sgt. Schlechtermann, an open Polarnia beside him, was making himself – what else? – a jam *tartine*. He appeared genuinely glad to see Michel-Ange:

"Ah, there he is! The man of the hour! – The Guinness record-holder as the shortest-serving Chargé d'Affaires in the history of world affairs!"

"Thank you, thank you – one does what one can…. But I'm afraid we'll be rather leaving you and Meia a bit in the lurch, here,"

"Bah! *Foutaise!*" He pronounced it Teutonically – *foo-tesse!* "We'll be fine. Here, have a beer with me, I want to *trinque* the man who singlehandedly *dévalisé*-ed the entire Embassy in, what? – three days! We must call you *l'Evacuateur* – The Evacuator!" He opened another beer and handed it Michel-Ange. "It's gonna be the *retour* of Fort Zinderneuf, around here, when you're gone – here's to your continued success, my young friend!"

"Hah hah, you're very *drole* this afternoon, *Chef*. Speaking of *drole*, remind me to leave you with the Embassy credit card before we *fous l'camp* – I still need it to organize this, euh – what's the polite military euphemism for a retreat?"

"A 'tactical reconfiguration' is the phrase I believe you're searching for…"

"Yes, *merçi* – so, we still need *le plastique* to effect Moitié's and my final, euh, evacuative payments, but after that I shall leave it with you – along with the codes and keys to get into the safes upstairs and the consular office – *allez, tchinn! –* "

They then broke it up, with Schlechtermann rejoining his guard post and Michel-Ange moving over to Irina's reception area to join her and Moitié, who'd returned from his bungalow, appearing even more uncharacteristically harassed than before. He seemed to be still preoccupied with the abundance of his *bagageries*….

"Fassederad, if you're not fully loaded, perhaps I could *confie* you one of my valises – or else, *et puis merde*, we'll just pay the excess bagage fee – "

"*Absolument*, I told you, don't worry about it – Anyway, can't we just declare the entire pile as constituting the 'diplomatic pouch', and dispense with it that way?"

Moitié made a face. "*Ho la la, non* – the diplomatic pouch is a whole other basket of crabs entirely – requires seals and all kinds of *merde* you don't want to know about – mind you, we would undoubtedly have gone that route had that fucking lead – "

"Tungsten."

" – *m'en fous!* – if it'd been *real* gold – but no, for this personal shit of ours, forget it, it's not worth all the acrobatics involved – "

"Ahem – " From her receptionist's seat, Irina gave voice, suddenly all business-like and matter-of-fact, "Chentlemens, bagages is *list* of your vorries – "

"Oh yes?" the two others said, almost in unison.

"*Da.* Becoss I heff news: I hem comingk viss iou. I vant leaf fockingk cantry Gryaznia, I vant diéfiéct to *Frantsous* – !"

"*WHAT?*" Again, the two sounded like back-up singers.

"*Da.* Ent iff you vant me help you get out fram here you vill not make trabbles far me, but vill instead help me. Pliss? Michelangelo? Zhan-loo?" And, to drive home her point, tears magically appeared, which she dramatically wiped away. *Sniff.*

The two young Frenchmen stared at each other, dumbly. Moitié folded his arms – a look of resignation had overtaken him. Indeed, he now looked as if he were awaiting arrest.

Michel-Ange slumped into the spare chair. In the stunned stillness, he scratched his head.

Now this *we need like a bullet in the* nuque. *This is surely the coup de grace de merde....*

He addressed Irina as gently as he could. "Listen, *ma chérie:* for starters, I can't imagine those people back in Paris accepting your 'defection' and granting you any such thing as 'political asylum' – what 'defect'? 'Defect' from what? You have one of the plummest jobs in the whole country – you're the Pussy Galore of the French Embassy, everyone knows you, everyone loves you – you're plugged in everywhere – "

"Dunt care. I'm tired of all little pipples here – I'm sairty years holt, ent vant see samsing else – vant see Péris. And dis iss my vun chence – so I vant you tell your boss, your *pataron* in Péris, det koronel guy, you vant he giff me palitical *asile* – "

"I'm sorry, *ma chère* Irina, but I'm just not going to do that. We've already managed to queer Franco-Gryaznian relations enough as it is, without handing out gratuitous – and bad-*publiçitaire,* not to mention *provocatif* – political asylums. I guarantee you in Paris they will refuse such a request so fast it will make you dizzy – so no, no asylum and no, I don't see you coming with us."

"Why not?" suddenly piped up Moitié, leaning his arms on her desk, "I'm with you on no asylum, but hell, *I* can give her a visa easily enough – hell, I can give her one for a year, with unlimited entries, if I like – *peuh!,* in fact, nothing would give me more pleasure...."

Irina's tears vanished as quickly as they'd appeared and she now leaped up and rushed around to hug Moitié, "Oh, senk you!, senk you!, Zhan-loo, I laff you!, you séve your leetle Irina!, *mphwa mphwa mphwa...!*" and she covered his face with kisses.

Michel-Ange felt it his duty to dampen this alarming development:

"*Oh-oh—ça vas,* you two. This is all madness – where will you stay, in France? Do you know anybody there? And, not meaning to be un-gallant, but... have you got any money? Because, *pour commencer*, there's no way we could include an air ticket for you along with ours on the Embassy *plastique* – and I must tell you, my *chèrie,* that despite – or rather because of – our socialist government,

things are *putain* expensive in France, where they certainly don't accept nefa
– "

Irina undraped herself from Moitié and chirped, "Who I know in Péris? I knows *you!* Ent Zhan-loo! Ken I stay viss *you*, Michelangelo?"

Michel-Ange blanched. "Listen, not to go too deeply into my own personal arrangements, I must tell you that I don't even *have* my own place – well, I do but I sort of share it, on a sort of permanent-ish basis, with a young American lady – who I am pretty confidently certain would not happily entertain any kind of such thing. To put it mildly..."

This news did not seem to phase Irina much – or even in the least, as far as the somewhat surprised Michel-Ange could discern. As she turned back to Moitié and half-spoke, half-licked into his ear:

"Hokays – so vat about *you*, Zhan-loo?"

Michel-Ange expected Moitié to also dismiss this outlandish proposition out of hand, but the wily embattled would-be taxi entrepreneur was already scheming ahead... and he could see the practical advantage to having Irina close to him in the rocky days that were certainly in his cards back in *la Metropole*.... Indeed, he could see her as Exhibit B (along with the Exhibit A tungsten tetra-hedrons) in his defense, both legal and moral, against the arrayed phalanxes of enraged taxi "investors", not to mention his current Quai d'Orsay employers... Of course, Moitié hadn't actually worked the practicalities *entirely* through yet, let alone could he envision how the whole wheeze might conclude... but his tactical instinct saw in her (and her photogenic allure) a potentially valu-able and above all authentic corroboration of his side in the forthcoming lurid *dénouement*.

So he utterly floored Michel-Ange (and, truth be told, Irina as well – a bit), when, grimacing slightly, he allowed as how,

"*Mwouaaii,* we'll see – perhaps we can work something out... I don't have any particular female *encombrement* awaiting me back there – You could be a *copinne* and I could set you up in the old *foyer* in Grasse... we could see how it goes... while I, *ahem,* work things out with the Ministry... But now, as for *fric* – that *is* a problem, because I certainly can't foot your air ticket, let alone – "

At this Irina banged her desk and jumped up from Moitié's lap:

"I hev anodder idee! Iz goot idee! Zhan-loo – you vill giff me wisa far *Frantsous,* you ken do, *da*? Iz iézzie, *da*? Da! – So, *you ken ollso do far odders – far manié, for pay!* I vill get – qvicklish, *miénie, miénie* pipples, dey vill pay, kesh, *bookoo* manié far *Frantsous* wisa – !"

Consul-General Moitié, of course, had not been, in the past, exactly a stranger to the deplorable practice of issuing visas in exchange for, in the case of *mecs,* various goods and favors; and in the case of *nanas,* various, euh, services – but until now he hadn't actually sold any for cold hard cash; (to the extent that you could call nefa "cold hard cash"). But, *finalement,* why not?

In the event, Moitié only had one practical question: "But are there enough people in this *foutu* country with actual passports? I've been here awhile, and they've never struck me as all that *cosmopolite....*"

"Party miémbers! – Olt Party miémbers hev *pessportyie* – ent Olt Party miémbers ollso hev manié – far vunce, *houra!* Olt Party!"

"Well then – *allons-y* – " was Moitié's verdict.

Michel-Ange felt he had to object, but his consternation was, in truth, rather *pour-la-forme* and perfunctorily-expressed. And when it was brushed aside by Moitié, who'd scoffed, "Come on, *Fassederaton!* – we're circling the fucking toilet bowl, here – it's not *le moment* for your *hautes écoles* niceties!", Michel-Ange granted his grudging assent.

After which Moitié and Irina quickly came up with a plan: 10,000 nefa, or 1,000 US$, or 6,500 FF a pop for a 3-month-er, double that for a full-year multiple-entry. They gazed upon this plan and pronounced it Good, whereupon Irina hopped-to and undertook a series of strategically-targeted phone calls to her many upscale "ex"-Communist Party friends and contacts, advertising a sudden fire-sale on French visas, to commence instanter and which would, after closing for the night, continue – *excepionnellement* – into tomorrow, Sunday.

And Moitié, for his part, would alert the Legionnaires that for the next 24 hours or so they should expect – and allow to enter – a sudden unusually large number of Gryaznian citizens requiring consular services – for which kind indulgence a handsome contribution would be duly made to the, euh, "Legionnaires' Benevolent Fund" – a philanthropic entity which had merely consisted, at least until now, of a neglected joke piggy-bank located in the "recreation bungalow".

And so this extraordinary scheme was inaugurated without delay: by mid-afternoon, Moitié was beavering away in his little Consulate, stamping and signing visas for all he was worth (if the reader will pardon the expression), while Irina assisted, directing traffic and counting and securing the incoming wherewithal.

Michel-Ange clucked and fussed nervously but inconsequentially throughout these proceedings, never wandering too far from the phone at Irina's reception desk or the fax machine...

...which, at half past five in the afternoon suddenly jumped to life, and brought forth an official document from the Presidency of the Republic of Gryaznia, addressed to the French Foreign Ministry with a copy to the French Embassy in Laina, to the effect that:

THE REQUEST FOR A RE-EXAMINATION OF THE "PERSONA NON- GRATA" EXPULSION DECREES FOR FRENCH CITIZEN-DIPLOMATS CHARGE D'AFFAIRES MICHEL-ANGE GRENIER DE LA FASSEDERAD AND CONSUL/COMMERCIAL ATTACHE JEAN-LOUP MOITIE HAS BEEN GRANTED, AND THE RESULT OF THAT RE-EXAMINATION IS THAT THE DELAY OF EXECUTION OF SAID ORDER IS REDUCED FROM 48 HOURS TO 36 HOURS: NEW HOUR AND DATE OF EXECUTION OF SAID ORDER: 2200 HOURS, SUNDAY

Putain de merde! This cannot *be happening – what the fuck next?!*

Michel-Ange grabbed the offending document and legged it through the door to the Consulate, waving it about and temporarily interrupting the flow of visa-issuance,

"*Eh!*, you guys! – they've reduced our expulsion deadline! – it's now down to twenty-two hundred tomorrow night! – Irina, these are your people, how strict are they about carrying out these orders? To the letter?"

"Viééérie viééérie siev*ier*! Efter de hower in qvestion, eef you steal here you loose *diplomiétischiye immunitet* ent dey srows you far sure een priézon – "

"*B'en voila, merde!* – Irina, you've got to knock off here, and get on the horn and get us on flights tomorrow – cancel the Monday ones – "

"Far me ollso?"

"Yes, *d'accord*, for you also – charge it all to the card and you can reimburse it by putting in the equivalent nefa into the petty cash, from this lot, here – but just get cracking – I don't care *what* else, but I'm fucked if I feel like ending up in a Gryaznian *tôle* – "

"Hokays, I go – and tenk you, my Michelangelo – " and she kissed *him* on the cheek as she handed him the cash box she'd been using to amass her (and Moitié's) new windfall, "Hier! – mék sure dey pays *fool* price – dunt allow *waa-waa* cryingk storiés, 'oh, I hem poor, I ken nat pé fool price' – dunt be soft, Michelangelo, diss iss Irina's monié, I need oll – !"

And off she whooshed, leaving the two more-beleaguered-than-ever French colleagues to get on with their *commerce douteux.*…

Meanwhile, the only useful flight going out of Laina on Sunday nights was Alitalia to Milano at 21:30 and she got all three of them on that. The ongoing flight from Milan to Paris was another Alitalia flight leaving at 0345 Monday morning (*Who the – what the hell kind of lunatic* made *these schedules?* thought Michel-Ange when he was informed) and, not surprisingly, she was able to get them seats on that as well.

The visa-selling continued on at a brisk pace into the evening until it dropped off at dinner time, at which point Moitié called the Legionnaire's guard room to tell them to halt the flow: "*Oui,* shut her down for tonight – tell 'em to come back tomorrow morning, in fact, the sooner the better – 0800, even – " upon which, after a sort of pre-valedictory drink, the three in the Residence agreed to separate:

Moitié would again go back to their bungalow to continue packing. Michel-Ange would again report back telelephonically with latest "developments" to his *patron.* And as for Irina, Michel-Ange had been wondering about what – now that she'd volunteered (and been accepted!) for Moitié-*copinne* duty – would be her choice of sleeping arrangement tonight, but she resolved this piquant little matter by declaring that she'd go to the airport with the Embassy credit card to pay for and pick up their tickets, after which she needed to go back to wherever it was she lived and "feex my affiérs, viss femily ent odders ollso, before I leavingk – Ivan vill tek me, ent bringk me back een marningk – so see you *demain,* érly, ent ve vill continue viss wisa biézniess, ent den goot-pie Laina, *bo-zhoo* Péris!"

29

"HELLO, I MUST BE GOING"

Once she'd swept herself away like a one-woman vanishing-in-a-whirlwind she-wizard in one of Squire Disney's cartoons, again leaving in her wake the wafted residue of Moitié's wholesale best, Michel-Ange found himself pondering, in this rare lull in the current end-of-days tumult, the extraordinary creature that was Irina...

Some sacré gonzesse, *that's for sure* – putain, *talk about your "easy come-easy go" – one second it's "oh I loff you too match my Michelangelo mwa mwa mwa!" and the next second she's hop!, shacked up with the appalling Moitié... but – but-but-but – having said* that, ... *yes, what* are *you saying, you idiot? I dunno – not sure... Oh she's certainly fun enough in the* plumard *for a couple of nights, but if it hadn't been for this* deus ex machina *in the unlikely form of Moitié, here, she risked becoming a real drag, I mean, a real* sparadrap *– And have you forgotten Jenni-faire so quickly, you disgusting pig? – No, no I haven't... Well there you are, then – So now, if you just stop thinking with your* bitte *for a second you'll appreciate quite how you dodged a bullet here – and a pretty unstable bullet at that... And you can be grateful that that fucking useless Moitié, whatever his other crimes against man and nature, is here to take her off your hands – in fact, you ought to kiss the wretched* mec....

And thus his thinking, like an aimlessly floating object encountering an island, bumped up against the subject of Jennifer, which he'd until now done his best to avoid. Indeed, he had to admit that he hadn't given her a proper thought since that day she'd helped propel him out of their little *foyer* on the Rue Mouffetard, but the light bulb now metaphorically appeared above his tousled head: *Hey,* tiens, *now might be perhaps an opportune time to give her a little* appelle...

So he used the phone on Irina's desk to call his own number in Paris, but all he got was his own supremely anti-climactic answering message, and he had to content himself with:

"*Salut, Jenni-faire,* my *chérie* – it's *moi!* It's Saturday night, and things are in a bit of a... a hiatus, a crossroads, just now, here in... here in... good old Laina, so I just thought I'd call to say hi. Look, *ma chérie,* I'm sorry I haven't called sooner – things have been a bit, well, *fluide* here..." and he was suddenly struck by two thoughts, one jarring and the other reassuring, viz., a/ what could or should he tell her? – was it possible, even likely, that his wretched, *minable* news has somehow not yet become "public knowledge" back in France? and b/ he remembered how much she hated recorded messages – So he decided to wrap it up with the laughably non-committal "... and well, what with one thing and another, the situation is that I may be coming back rather sooner than we'd, euh, *prévu*-ed... anyway, I'll explain later – *allez, je t'embrasse.* Bye."

This re-connection – however brief, cursory and tenuous – with his former, "normal" life back in Paris so unnerved him that he dived straight back into Irina's kitchenette for another Polarnia.

Aaah, that's better. But, ouais – *now that I think of it, just what can the situation with this expulsion* connerie *be, back "home"? Can it really, possibly be the stuff of newspaper headlines? Of those* enculés *at the News At Six O'Clock? I mean, you'd think, in a properly-ordered world, that no one outside the orbits of Mincemot and the Quai d'Orsay would give the tiniest of shits about such a piddling diplomatic occurrence as what is transpiring here, but who the hell knows?... the most surprising things become notorious these days... Meeeeeeerde, I hadn't thought of of any of this, when I was back there going* main-a-main *with that thug Grib....*

And not just Jenni-faire – Papa*'ll be not only displeased, but he might for once be moved to actual emotion – and a NEGATIVE emotion,* en plus *– might even spill his whiskey – if he learns of this while half-paying attention to that cretinous France-2... And what about me? – what'll become of me?... and not in some distant future, either, but in a few fucking days? Will I be a "national scandal"? An object of national derision? Will I still be employed – I can't imagine I will – but more realistically, will I even be employ*able? *One thing's for* damn *sure – my comfortable little life as the happy amateur* farniente *Enarque-égaré Michel-Ange will never – EVER – be the same....*

Michel-Ange wasn't entirely comfortable with these thoughts and felt it better to put them aside – *do something with yourself....*

But what? The evening and night stretched unenticingly out before him. Irina was gone, preparing her own *départ*, as was Moitié....

So he pocketed the keys to the Ambassadorial safes, gathered up a few further Polarnias and wandered down the driveway towards the Legionnaire's guardhouse, passing his/Moitié's bungalow along the way ("*Ca vas* in there?" "*Ouais!* Fuck me...!"). He found Sgt. Schlechtermann on duty, alone – Meihavelha had taken their jeep and gone to do something in town.

"*Salut, Chef.* Here, I brought you a cold one – " he shovel-passed a beer at Schlechtermann, "Although I'm sure you've heard by now, I'm here to officially announce to you, in the words of the noted social critic *Groocheaux* Marx, 'Hello, we must be going!' – Oh, and before I forget, here are the keys to the Ambassador's safes – the new *mec* will bring with him the codes, or, *in extremis*, somebody'll call 'em into you on *'le rouge'* – but, as we'll no doubt need the credit card at the – hah! – airport, I'll pass that over to you guys there, at the last moment... *Ah la la, Chef,* I must say, I'm sorry to be leaving you and Meia alone, here, holding the bag... well, holding the fort... so to speak."

"*Bah, pas de problème* – they'll send a replacement quickly enough. But, speaking personally, I'll – we'll – be sorry to see you go. We've had worse than you around here, believe me."

"Well, that's – to use your own expression of not so long ago – white of you to say…. *Effectivement,* my career, hah hah, as a diplomat, hah hah hah, appears to have *démarre*-ed in a decidedly… curious fashion… In fact, I doubt I'll remain one much longer…."

"*Ouais.* Your career. As a diplomat. Listen, *petit,* I don't know – what do I know? I'm just a simple soldier and not even properly French, yet – but speaking as a friendly observer I'd suggest that, after this little *guignol à la con* here, you might want to give a thought to perhaps doing something else with your… considerable, euh, talents…."

"Yes, well… I'm not so sure what those talents, if they indeed exist, might point towards – "

"Hell, you could always join the military."

"Hah hah. Good one."

"No, I'm serious. Do a spell at St. Cyr, become an officer. You'd be fine – believe me, not only I've served under worse diplomats than you, I've served under worse officers as well. *Lots* worse – in fact, if you ever need an endorsement, track me down – I'm the only Schlechtermann in the *Légion* – and I'll be happy to support your *candidature* – "

And after this short but fraternal exchange, and feeling noticeably bucked, Michel-Ange returned to the Residence.

He dumped the empty Polarnias in the kitchen (for who to clean up – Ivan? No, he remembered, there was still Irina's team of cleaning girls on the payroll…), made himself yet another jam sandwich and, lodging the box of stale – indeed, practically antique – Russian Corn Flakes under his arm, headed upstairs. He'd spend the night here, where it at least still smelled Irina-bulk-perfume-from-Grasse good.

But he still wasn't quite ready to sleep, so he deposited his *goûter* onto *Madame l'Ambassadrice*'s dressing table, to be dealt with later, and… continued to fuss and *tripotte… I mean, for the love of God, I'm in charge of this stupid*

Embassy and I'm being kicked out tomorrow – isn't there some *God-forsaken* connerie *that I can or should be occupying myself with?*

He searched his beleaguered and increasingly sodden brain: having turned over the keys to Schlechtermann, he couldn't think of any "official" duty that remained, and was addressing himself to the still-not-empty bottle of cognac on the Ambassador's dresser – when, suddenly feeling rather as he imagined Napoleon might have as he prepared to sail for Elba, he came up with the quaint notion of penning a "Note" to his "Successor", to perhaps bequeath such wisdom as he'd gleaned during his short but, (ahem), tumultuous incumbency as "Chargé d'Affaires". So, pulling out a sheet of Embassy stationery he wrote out in his elegant Lycée Janson de Sailly script,

1/ For *ad hoc* banking/cash-acquisition needs, one can do much worse than the services of our own Mr. I. Ivanov, who accords excellent exchange rates.

2/ Do not expect a rapturous – or indeed any – appreciation for French culture. Golf, however (and of all things), appears to be something of a door-opener in higher Gryaznian social circles.

3/ For quick and efficient (if no-star) restauration, the "Roky Balbao! Campion Pizza!", just down the road on 3 Oktobr Prospekt, is surprisingly acceptable, and I recommend it. In exigencies.

4/ If any commercial activity whatsoever is contemplated by any member of the Embassy Staff, it is absolutely imperative to "remember" the President – otherwise dire doom is ensured.

... before realizing the full fatuity of what he was in the process of doing, and... gave it up. (He did not, however, crumple up and throw this plaintive testament into the *poubelle,* but rather slid it into the Ambassador's desk drawer. One never knew....)

He sighed. Was there anything else he could usefully do here before he was chased out, tomorrow, like a whipped dog? How about securing sensitive documents into the safe? *Mais non* – he quickly banished the thought as quixotic – not to say idiotic – as anything of conceivable interest had already been hoovered up and thrown into the Ambassador's personal travel bag by the Legionnaires.

So instead he gave up and resignedly grabbed the box of Russian Corn Flakes (the contents of which, on closer inspection, resembled – and tasted like – tree bark) and switched on the tube:

The TV was tuned to the late night news on RT-Gryaznia-1 and Michel-Ange's attempts to switch channels on this Cyrillic remote-control "gun" were abruptly frozen in mid-jab as he saw appear on the screen *his own passport picture!* – and then that of the gibbering fool Moitié – and distinctly in the Gryaznian jibber-jabber which accompanied these horrifying images could be heard the words *"... dosvidanye k' Frantsouski Chargé d'Affaires Fassdratte i diplomatski-prestoopnik Mwateeyé..."*

Aaaagh! – his thumbs manically stabbed at the black plastic lump in his hands until his and Moitié 's hideous *poires* had been replaced by... the, (of all people), feckless members of the Bundy family, as Michel-Ange's frantic exertions landed him in the witless sub-imbecilities of the *seet-comme Americain* "Married With Children", whose dubious charms were further enhanced by being dubbed into Gryaznian. But that was alright – under the circumstances, that would do nicely, *merci beaucoup....*

So on this last "official" night he washed down his jam *tartine* with superfluous 4-star cognac, and nodded off half-clothed to troubled half-sleep, the TV softly babbling as the defeated Bundy family gave way to even greater televised irrelevancies, with the lights still on... and only Irina's lingering generic perfume hanging above and around the bed to remind the dozing Michel-Ange of happier times... not so very long ago....

30

"PLIER BAGAGES"

Unbeknownst to Michel-Ange (who'd finally fallen asleep by then), at precisely midnight the electricity was cut off to the French Embassy in Laina, so that he was able to pursue the final hours of his *sommeil* undisturbed by the annoying televisual white noise, which had eventually come on.

But even he could figure out that something was amiss when the bathroom light didn't work as he brushed his teeth and concluded his other matutinal *préparatifs* in the non-electric gray morning light, before trotting down the stairs.... to discover Irina and Ivan hovering around the Legionnaires, who were in the process of what was quickly revealed to Michel-Ange to be the installation and *mise en marche* of a nifty little MAN auxiliary generator.

Michel-Ange's Tissot watch told him it was 8:15, and as the four saw him descend they all seemed to want to speak to him simultaneously, but eventually he managed to discern a certain order to the chatter:

Pfc. Meiavelha informed him that "Those vindictive shits at the *Présidence* have cut off the current until you guys fuck off out of here tonight – "

To which Irina added, "I *telefon* to *Prezidentsyia* ent dey say vill ollso cut *telefon* soon, bat who cares, dey dunt knows about red *telefon* een garatch, so *merda* to dem!"

At this point Moitié ambled in and added, "*Ooof!*, well, I'm more or less packed... but *putain* have I got a lot of excess *merde....*"

"No problem," Michel-Ange told him, "I've got very little – between us it'll even out."

"Very *chic* of you, my brother. So what's with this cutting the *courant bordelle?* – is it gonna affect... our little operation? – *Chef*, is my Minitel there in the Consulate branched onto your *engin*, here – ?"

Schlectermann nodded *yes, it is*, and so the three civilians repaired briefly to the kitchenette for coffee – before resuming the Great Visa Sale in Moitié's Consulate...

... which duly continued throughout the morning and, while eating lunch (Irina-made chicken sandwiches) *in situ,* into the early afternoon.

Michel-Ange observed, and occasionally assisted, Moitié and Irina at their dubious, to not say almost certainly criminal, commerce with a disinterested, quasi-Solomonic, detachment:

Was it to be deplored? Certainly.

Then was he wrong to condone it? No, he didn't think so:

By his moral calculus, Michel-Ange judged it sufficient that he had noted the deplorability of this specific, narrowly-focused, visa-shopping session – yes, it was objectively wrong, there was no denying that. But on the other side of his moral ledger he also made note of the peculiar financial exigencies of the current situation. And this inclination towards leniency was reinforced when he thought of who the "victims" of this, (technically speaking), malfeasance actually were, viz., pretty much all, until very recently, members of the Gryaznian Communist Party... *well,* tant pis *for your* gueules, *comrades – time to pay some back, you venal bastards....* And back in France? The Quai? *Le publique?* Pah! These visas were a tiny fraction of a drop in the ocean... and for "refugees from a war zone", to boot...

... so he was more or less un-fussed by the whole ethical aspect of the thing.

What *did* preoccupy him, however, was the clock, and the absolute imperative of his getting their collective *culs* to the airport in time to avoid the dreaded cut-off hour... and a spell in Grib's insalubrious *tôle*.

Somewhere in all this *angst* Michel-Ange realized that he himself had not yet packed, so he set about that not-terribly involved task, trotting back and forth between "his" bungalow (in which, he noted drily, he'd only spent one night) and the Residence, gathering together his few, if dispersed, things.

For their 21:30 flight, Michel-Ange reckoned they ought to *fous le camp* from the Compound at 18:30, at the latest – maybe closer to 18:00. After all, although as still-diplomats, they ought to have a relatively easy passage out of the country, they *were* being accompanied by the un-diplomatic Irina – plus, they were leaving under an official "cloud", so it would be wise to plan for... *imponderables.*

Though the managing of the *horaire* was summarily taken out of his – their – hands when Pfc. Meiavelha came chuffing into the Consulate/Visa Sales Office to announce,

"Hé – just so you know – a couple of BTR-80s" (Soviet-made armored personnel carriers) "just rolled up at the gate – I can't really talk to the *cons,* but by their gestures and watch-pointing it's clear they're here to, euh, escort you to the airport, euh, on time – which is high-handed enough, you ask me, but you should also know that it's put a sharp *halte* to anyone entering *les lieus –* " He helped himself to a gulp of the Polarnia that Moitié happened to have on his desk, "so I'd pack up this *bordelle* if I were you – you know, *Banco! Rien ne vas plus!"*

So that was that. But it was time, anyway – the clock was ticking...

Nevertheless... by the time they shut down "Opération Visa", at 16:05 on that Sunday afternoon, they'd amassed enough multi-currencied cash for:

1/ The reimbursement of Irina's round-trip ticket,

2/ Sufficient (presumably tax-free) funds for her to live modestly in France for at least six months, if not more (depending on how things panned out with Moitié),

3/ A contribution to the Legionnaire's Benevolent Fund that would keep them and the cleaning girls happy – certainly until the soldiers got replaced and shipped off to Bosnia... or... Rwanda,

4/ A handsome gratuity for the brave Ivan for being the one to stay behind, keeping the *locaux* ship-shape until a replacement team arrived and, most crucially, to remain *shtoom* about the whole potentially explosive affair,

and finally, far from least,

5/ Moitié to pay for some reasonably robust bodyguarding for when he returned and had to break the bad news to his, ah, business associates in the notoriously recriminatory *midi* of France.

There was nothing allocated for Michel-Ange, but that was fine with him – in fact he was already trying to blot the whole *douteux* episode from his frazzled mind. But certainly, it *had* been quite a success for about 13 hours' work. (Well, Moitié *was* a "Commercial" Attaché, after all....)

So now they were faced with a great pile of US$, FF and a surprising amount of Deutschmarks. (They'd refused six offers of Russky roubles and all offers of nefa.) And the sorting, counting, and allocating of all this stuff (including inevitably residual amounts of nefa), and its preparation for crossing international borders now occupied them for the better part of an hour. The question arose (rather belatedly, thought Michel-Ange in some alarm) concerning whether or not nefa were convertible abroad – but Moitié eased their fears:

"Look, as Commercial Attaché and Consul, if there's anything I know, it's about this money stuff. Now the *foutu* nef is still a controlled currency by this idiot Gryaznian government and as a result you're not supposed to take any out of the country – but the situation is quite schizophrenic abroad, and banks in Europe – France, for instance – will exchange it. It's a weird, paradoxical situation, but it's the same with roubles and South African rands. In any case, you, Fassederad, as senior, euh, diplomat – we're still diplomats, *merde!* – you should carry all the different denominations in your suitcase – it makes sense to keep it all together in one place."

"Thank you very much – "

"Don't make yourself worries – you're not *quite* a diplomatic pouch, but we still have diplomatic immunity – or at least we can loudly claim we do – which ought to suffice."

For once Moitié seemed to be making sense, so the others let him carry on, and he concluded,

"So most of the nefs we leave for Ivan, the Legios and the cleaning girls, but you should keep some to surrender to the *gorilles* at the airport – and make it enough to dissuade 'em from being too inquisitive for more."

So they placed the money in different plastic bags, according to currency, and Michel-Ange hand-wrote, and signed, a list of the numerical totals – with no explanatory text – of which he made copies for Moitié and Irina. He put Ivan's and the girls' cuts in envelopes for Irina to deal with, and gathered up the rest, including an envelope with the contribution to the "Legionnaire's Benevolent Fund" which he dropped off with Meiavelha and which was enthusiastically received: *"Merci mon frère! – t'est pas aussi con que l'on dit!"* *("Thank you my brother! – your not as big an asshole as everyone says!")*, before stowing the considerable balance in his Vuitton.

Irina went off with Ivan again in the Citroën to take care of some last minute business of hers – *the poor girl's changing her whole life on the spur of the moment, here, after all* – while Moitié continued to struggle with his complicated baggage situation.

Michel-Ange thought he might invest some of his dwindling minutes into hazarding one last call to Mincemot. So he re-gained the wretched red-phone-in-the-hole, which he was heartily grateful he'd never have to endure again, and cranked it up. (*How the hell was it powered now, with the electricity cut? The*

Legionnaires' little generator? Rodents on a wheel, somewhere? Qui *the fuck knew....)*

Anyway, probably mercifully for all concerned, there was no answer on Mincemot's line, and Michel-Ange left a terse message,

"*Mon colonel* – it's about 17:30 on Sunday here in Laina, and Moitié and I – " he thought it best not to mention Irina – not yet, anyway, and *certainly* not on an answering machine, "are about to evacuate the compound. Things are as under control as can be hoped, and I, euh... am looking forward to speaking with you soon. *Términé.* Michel-Ange de la Fassederad."

Feeling slightly cheated, somehow, he hitched up his courage and decided that, *bof!, w*hat the hell, *puisque on y est,* to try *Mlle.* Bergère. It being a late Sunday afternoon, he did so *pour la forme,* really, with not expectation... But to his amazement and no small shock, she actually picked up.

"Ah – you're there?" he found himself saying, by way of greeting.

"Who is this on the phone?" He distinctly detected intimations of indignation.

"*Mlle.* Bergère – it's *moi,* de la Fassederad, from Laina – I was trying to get hold of the colonel, yet again, but he doesn't answer – "

"Of course he doesn't. His Sundays are sacrosant. As are mine, come to that – what exactly was it you wanted, young *Monsieur* de la Fassederad?"

"*Eh bien...* I just wanted to keep him *au courant* – Things have become a little... how can I put this... *constrained,* down here. In fact, I'm minutes away from being *foutu* out the door – "

"I know. *He* knows. We *all* know, Michel-Ange."

"*Bon* – "Was this really *bon?* Hardly. "Well *that*'s cleared up at least. But still, I would like to, ah, go over a thing or two with him as a matter of some urgency. So could you get word to the Colonel that I'll try to call him again, if I can – I suppose that would be from Milan Airport – it'll probably be about midnight tonight – can you get that word to him? *Mademoiselle?*"

She sighed. And resumed, "Do you know, Michel-Ange, that of all the colonel's many agents – "

Agents? "Agents?" He hadn't even meant to blurt this out – it just happened.

"Alright, *adjoints* if you prefer – that the colonel has, here and there, that he is responsible for – and who, excuse me for saying, are of considerably more geo-strategic importance than you – Well, of all of them, not *one*, that I know of, in the past ten days, has tied up his valuable time and generally *emmerde*-ed him more than you. I offer this merely as a passing observation."

"Yes, no, I didn't know that, and I'm desolated to have been – and to continue to be – an *emmerdement*... It's just that... well... it's hard to explain how all this happened, *Mademoiselle*, really – it's just that one thing just seemed to lead to another...."

"Hmmm. Just like that." ("Hmmm. *Comme-ça.*")

"Yes, really." Now it was his turn to feel a spark of indignation and he decided he was prepared to take a somewhat firmer tone with her than with her *patron,*

"Look, I'm not saying I'm beyond reproach, but – as I look back on events, it's not so much that I didn't do anything *wrong,* but rather that I don't seem to have done anything *at all* – right *or* wrong. Nothing. I was just... *there,* and things just... *happened*. It's all rather extraordinary, really."

"No doubt. No doubt. Well, the important thing is that you're alive and well, isn't it."

"Ha ha. A good one, *Mademoiselle.*"

"Thank you – I thought so. Well, I'll alert the *patron* that you'll be calling him late tonight – something he'll be absolutely ravished to hear, by the way... *Bon,* you and I will be seeing each other again soon enough – *A bientot,* young man – " *Click.*

He sat there, no more encouraged or even enlightened than before he'd made these calls, but, *pffff...*

He glanced at his Tissot and noticed that H-hour was just about upon him.

Michel-Ange escaped the perishing garage for the last time and hustled to the Residence and upstairs to the ambassador's bedroom, where he donned a pale blue shirt and his Enarque tie. And his white linen suit, *(Being officially evicted from the foreign country to which one is accredited is surely one of those moments in life that calls for an extra bit of* je ne sait quoi*),* with a red silk square in the breast pocket. *("Bleu-blanc-rouge").*

He clapped his Vuitton shut, drained what remained of the cognac bottle – *ooof!* – and clattered down the Duquon-Lajoie Memorial staircase *also* one last time... to join the just-barely still-serving totality of the French Embassy, Laina, (minus half its military auxiliary support team), who'd mustered in the drive-way between the Residence and the three bungalows.

"Allez! Temps de plier bagages!" he declared rather redundantly, as he surveyed the assembled expedition.

Irina's considerable *patatras* already filled the official Citroën, so the Legion-naire's P4 jeep, with Meiavelha at the wheel, had been pressed into emergency airport service and loaded up with Moitié's even more extensive accumulation of appurtenances, on top of which Michel-Ange tossed his Vuitton.

As they were about to climb aboard – Michel-Ange in the jeep with Meiavel-ha, Irina and Moitié in the Citroën with Ivan Ivanovich – Michel-Ange cried "Stop! Has anyone got a camera?" It emerged that Moitié did – a newfangled Bulgarian "digital" one.

"Our departure must somehow be immortalized for posterity – and I know exactly where I want to do it – ", and he shepherded them all the short distance to the garage, where he pulled open the sliding front door and had Ivan pho-tograph them all posed in front of, and draped upon – smiling and waving as though it were *la libération de Paris* – the Ambassador's immortal Facel-Vega.

"Make sure we get copies," Michel-Ange ordered Moitié, as they regained their vehicles, "specially me – otherwise I'll have no proof that I was ever here at all – "

"There's always your expulsion order," offered Moitié helpfully.

"*Aie*, well played – *That*'ll be on my wall with my other diplomas – in fact, in the center."

As they reached the guard house at the gate, again Michel-Ange stood up in the topless jeep and, like a caricature of De Gaulle on the Champs Elysées, raised an imperious hand. "Wait!"

"Oh vat now?" grumped Irina through her open window in the Citroën.

What it was was Michel-Ange striding to the flagpole, on the southeastern corner of the erstwhile croquet pitch/helicopter-LZ *gazon*, and lowering the national *Tricolor*. He folded it and handed it to Sgt. Schlechtermann,

"Here, *Chef*, please present this to my replacement – with my compliments and my wishes for the best of luck."

"*A vos ordres, monsieur!*" And Schlechtermann saluted one last time. After which Michel-Ange then shook his hand and said "Thanks for everything, *Chef*. Really."

With that, the two French vehicles finally moved out to join the two Gryaznian Army BTR-80 armored personnel carriers, (one fore, one aft), that had been waiting for them in increasing impatience, and the ad hoc mini-convoy rather ponderously rumbled out on the 3 Oktobr Prospekt towards Laina International Airport.

My own parade, it occurred to Michel-Ange, as they passed bemused Lainians on the sidewalks, who (always attuned to random militarized displacements) looked up briefly to wonder "what fresh hell is this?" – before resuming their daily grind, having decided, quite rightly, that... it was nothing.

The wholly unwarranted sense of "occasion" that Michel-Ange weirdly felt became even more pronounced when they rolled up at the airport's not-too (at this late hour) but-still-somewhat shambolic departure hall – so much so that Michel-Ange almost – *almost* – regretted not having unfurled the little French flag on the front fender of the Citroën.

Although once they actually made their bulky, luggage-laden way into the building itself, any such fatuous sense quickly dissipated and, indeed, turned a bit sour – as they were immediately faced with an obligatory division, with "Diplomats, VIPs and other Personalities" (which Michel-Ange and Moitié still technically were) required *to go here,* and the rest of humanity *to go there.*

Ivan and Meiavelha left their vehicles flagrantly but "legally" dumped right at the airport entrance, that had been "cleared" by the lumbering BTR-80 beasts, and helped their three passengers lug their *merde* as far as they were allowed to, (with the Legionnaire producing a "professional" trolley from God-knows-where – *Did he* really *hold up some poor Gryaznian porter for it? Not* entirely *impossible...*), but now even they had to *exeunt* the stage. So in a final flurry of handshaking, saluting, and even, as the individual case required, hugging and kissing on both cheeks, Ivan and Meiavelha bowed out. Michel-Ange's last act as Chargé d'Affaires was to hand over the Embassy credit card to the Legionnaire. "Here, Meia – knock yourselves out."

Although Moitié appeared eager to plow on with things, Michel-Ange hesitated, caught in a minor moral quandary – he was reluctant to abandon the technically "undiplomatic" Irina to check in on her own with the *hoi polloi,* and was trying to figure out a way of *baratin*-ing her way in with them, as a "diplomat", but she would hear none of it and shushed away his demurrals:

"Dunt vorries far me, Michelangelo, dese are my pipples – I hef kaniéctions viss Halitalia boy here ent ollso viss Diépart guys, I vill be *viéry* hokays – vill see you on plane – "

"Alright, if you insist... but I don't like it – I'd feel better if...."

"*Pah!* I hem more vorried far *you!* Listen, Michelangelo, dunt mék fass in dere – Zhan-loo, dunt let Michelangelo mék fass! – Dunt argue viss dem, ent pay baksheesh if niécessaire. Iff vorse kom to vorse, you cry *viéry* loud 'Irina!', 'Irina!', ent I vill come help you – so, now, go – !" and, pushing her maximum allowable baggage along with her shapely but deceptively muscular leg, she disappeared into the small, but noisy and smelly, crowd that had gathered in front of the Alitalia check-in desk.

31

"WOW, THAT WAS QUICK"

So the two young French barely-still-diplomats, along with about two-camels'-worth of baggage piled onto a trolley, made their way into "their" enclosure. A surprisingly elegant (given the condition of the rest of the airport) and largely empty room – Alitalia to Milan was the last outgoing flight on this Sunday, and the only other "customers" (as the airline-wallahs had recently and un-accountably decided it made public-relations sense to start calling their pas-sengers) entitled to the "VIP" area were an Italian army brigadier-general in a sickly pea-green uniform and a young Oriental fellow in a too-large gray suit who turned out to be a junior political officer at the Red Chinese embassy.

A quite attractive Gryaznian Alitalia girl with "Galina" pinned onto a small but provocatively-revealed breast, checked them in, all smiley and accommo-dating – it was almost as though their "disgrace" had bestowed upon them a sort of weirdly dangerous allure – but before they could turn to the inviting open bar (which came with crisps, peanuts and dainty little beet sandwiches with the crusts cut off), they were minded to address themselves to the mat-ter of their considerable *équipement* – upon which a team of young *Douchka* border guards were now gazing interestedly, with one of them tapping the top-most valise – Michel-Ange's Vuitton – with a clip-board.

This fellow, assuming (not entirely mistakenly) that Michel-Ange's white suit either meant that he was in charge or that he was looking for trouble, looked him directly in the eye and asked, in an unnerving repetition of the very first words ever spoken to him in this country (it seemed a century but was barely a week ago), "You hev nefa?"

Remembering not to look *Douchka*-man in the eyes, Michel-Ange answered by fishing a few fifty-nefa notes out of his arse pocket. "Just this", he said.

"Dey stays here," the fellow said as he took and clipped them to his board, and now nodded at the bags, "Ent vot's to declare, in oll ziss staffs?"

Michel-Ange was most relieved when Moitié, who seemed positively eager to take the lead in dealing with these customs *cons*, suddenly and seemingly confidently leaned in to interrupt, and assured the *Douchka* customs guys, in a part French/part English/part Gryaznian pidgin, "*Izvinitsye*, unlike my colleague, I have no nefa, *nitchevo*. And all this *merde* here is merely personal effects – there's quite a lot of it because we're regrettably not coming back, do you see?"

"No *nationalniye* triéasures?"

Both Frenchmen thought of the sawn bits of tungsten "evidence" and managed to keep straight faces.

"No," continued Moitié placidly, "but I do have these...." and he pulled out of one of his several canvas bags a couple of gigantic (250ml) *flacons* of generic perfume from Grasse which went under the ludicrous name of *"Rêves de Nuits"* ("Night Dreams") but which smelled alright and which had "Made in France" prominently spelled-out in raised glass letters on the bottoms.

One-each of these presented to the *Douchka mecs* – and a third handed to the beaming Galina for good measure – was more than sufficient to do the trick, and *pouf!* all their clobber was duly tagged and shuffled off plane-wards.

"You're a *putain* of a genius, you know that?" muttered Michel-Ange when they finally got to the bar and helped themselves to large whiskeys-and-soda, "You may be an *escroc* but for sure you're *my kind* of *escroc* – "

"Hah hah. Back home *chez moi* that stuff's cheaper than a good *pinard* – *à vrais dire,* one of the smartest things I ever did was to have a shitload sent out to me here – it's come in handy, I don't mind telling you...."

"I can imagine. By the way – speaking of clandestine substances – what the hell did you do with your... *shnouff*? I hope to God you didn't pack it – "

"My *what*?"

"Your... you know – " Michel-Ange made a two-fingered toke-smoking gesture, "I don't know what the latest *au courant* term is for the stuff – "

"Oh – hah hah! – my *cam*? – I gave it to Ivan. Well, ... 'gave'... I *sold* it to Ivan – but he got a good deal, I gave him a good deal. Of course it was a good deal for me, too...."

"A good deal for *both* of you? How did *that* work, exactly?"

Moitié gave him a sour little smile. "It's called capitalism – but you *aristos* wouldn't know anything about that – "

"No, but you socialists do – "

"We observe." With this, Moitié made an eyebrow-arched grimace and knocked back his whiskey. And re-filling his glass, he continued,

"*Ouais, bof!*, socialism – you know, it's more a fairy tale than anything – although," *(gulp)* "mind you, I'm gonna need a lot of help from Papa's socialist *copains* to save my *cul* from my, euh... my, euh... *investors*...."

They underwent a cursory "security check" wanding during which it was revealed that Michel-Ange was still in possession of the key to the magnificent Duquon-Lajoie Facel-Vega. *Merde! – and with all the other* conneries *that were going down, I never even got to properly drive the damn thing – would've loved to* drague *in downtown Laina in that 'tumbapantis' – Now I'll have to give the damn key to Mother Superior to send back to the Legionnaires pronto – they'll have difficulty getting to the 'rouge' without the key to shift the car....*

As they passed out of the "VIP" departure hall to board the Alitalia 737, Moitié handed Galina his card (which, of course, included his French-based cellular phone number) and whispered in her ear – loudly enough for Michel-Ange to hear – "Whenever you're in France, give me a call – "

Not for the first time, Michel-Ange marveled at the sheer single-minded audacity of the little blond *spécimène* Moitié. Even though the little fucker was directly the cause of their current *salade*, you had to hand it to him – he was, like one of those rats furiously on his tread-wheel, always *fonce*-ing... always driving on, regardless. Again, *"L'audaçe, toujours l'audaçe!"* – and would the old lunatic Danton have approved of his fellow-socialist Moitié? Probably not....

But speaking of audacity, when they finally got on the plane, what did they find but a/ Irina not only already on board (it seemed that under the old socialist system, the "VIPs" boarded last, rather than first), and b/ she was already smilingly seating and making herself quite comfy (although she'd been assigned a toilet-class seat) next to the Italian general up there in first class.

Michel-Ange smiled at her and gave her a thumb-up as they shuffled past, but she barely acknowledged them – "Oh... yes, xhello..." and just the twinge of a sheepish smirk... was all she accorded them.

The Laina-Milan hop was only an hour and a half, and it passed uneventfully – all the more so because, it being less than full – and first class practically empty – Moitié and Michel-Ange were each able to secure isolated aisle seats for themselves.

(At one point Michel-Ange leaned over and asked Moitié if he was going to give his card also to "their" stewardess, a stern-looking matron with manly calves and a face like Anna Magnani's father, as she, first class or no, slapped down their requested Campari-and-sodas. Moitié hissed back *"Arrète ton char* – anyway, what's your *maman* doing working for Alitalia?")

Back at Laina Airport the lubricious "VIP" Galina had told them that because their connection in Milan would involve a plane change, they should, while staying in the *Concessioni* sector of the airport, claim and "re-direct" their baggage. Even at the time that had all sounded more than a little improbable to Michel-Ange, but he'd been at that moment so singlemindedly preoccupied with getting their stuff past *Douchka*-customs that he hadn't questioned it. But *now* was time to question it.

The three of them had re-convened in the corridor at the end of the "de-plane-ment" chute.

"Irina, where's your generalissimo?" Moitié wanted to know.

"Hah! He giff me hees téléfon namber!"

Michel-Ange ignored them and rather addressed himself to a middle-aged and disabused-looking Alitalia *tuttofare* who was standing idly around manning a wheelchair,

"*Buonasera*, my dear fellow, but we are on the 0345 Alitalia flight to Paris – "

Wheelchair-Man silently pointed to a large DEPARTURES/PARTENZE board above their heads – and sure enough, even though it was almost 4 hours away, their Paris flight was already posted.

"Yes, *grazie mille*, but we are wondering about our *bagagi* – ?"

Wheelchair-Man, still silent, now pointed them to an office that gave off from the corridor where most of the passengers was headed anyway, that had a sign saying BAGAGLIO PERSO. So they went there.

On the way, Irina announced that she had to "mék *pipi*" and, after Michel-Ange told her "*D'accord*, re-join us in here –", she peeled off on her own.

As they approached the salient door, Michel-Ange said to Moitié, "One thing of two – either it'll be an utter *bordelle* in here, or it'll be completely empty – want to bet?" Moitié just motioned with his chin that he should just get on with it, so in they went. "Empty" would have won the bet.

Michel-Ange's delight at it being, indeed, empty was tempered by experienced suspicion (*an empty place of business almost invariably means I'm in the wrong place*), but he approached the one seated functionary who appeared in charge of this particular operation – an extravagantly-mustachioed black-haired officer of some kind who wore a gray beret decorated by a huge raging flame of a badge which had the effect of making it seem as though his headgear was actually on fire. The flamboyant figure gave voice,

"Sì? Co'sè? Waad can I for you do?"

Michel-Ange, again drawing on the dialogue of the many films he'd seen – in this case Italian ones, obviously – and fashioning from them a sort of Franco-Italian pidgin, related the gist of their baggage situation, and Flame-Head started to bang away on a huge Olivetti computer. From behind which he eventually announced,

"Ecco! Ho trovato! So! *I* yora baggagas issa onna itsa way! – holready! – to Parigi! *Ecco, vabè –* !"

"What – ?" expostulated Michel-Ange, "How can this be? On what flight?"

"Ah. These I cannot e-say. And to tell you de troose, I donna even know. But even iffa I a-know, cannot a-tell-a you – " and here the extraordinary fellow flicked his front tooth conspiratorily with his thumb, "Issa question of-a security."

"*What?*" Michel-Ange had never heard such a *connerie* in his life. He turned to Moitié, "I've never heard such a *connerie* in my life – If there's one thing I know about this *soi-disant* security game it's that passengers and bags always must travel together, on the same plane – "

"Don't tell me, tell *him.*"

Michel-Ange turned back to do so, but Flame-Head pre-empted him, evidently trying to sound emollient,

"Waad issa problema any-ways? You all-a going to Parigi *any*-ways-a, no? So – ééééh – *va che* – be happy, *va bè*, go!, *buon viaggio....*"

"But hang on – where are our baggage stubs?"

"Your e-wat?"

"Our – these things, these *putain de trucs* with which one claims one's baggage –" and he produced the ones they'd been given by Galina back in Laina –

"Uh, Fassederad, I'm afraid – "

What does the bloody con *Moitié want now?* "What, what is it?"

"There, see? Our bags are *already* tagged all the way to Paris – there, see?"

And so they were. *Well I'll be buggered.... Galina!*

Michel-Ange felt slightly faint. "Well I give up," he said softly, "I don't think I can deal with this *merde* much longer...."

Flame-Head now clotured procedings: "So, all issa good, *si? Si!* So, tank you, *grazie,* now, good-bye, please – !"

Irina (who had at some point rejoined them) pulled Michel-Ange by the hand as the three re-gained the corridor, with Michel-Ange still mumbling, "But how will we know where to claim the *putain de* bags? We don't know which flight...."

"Kam, Michelangelo, dunt vorries, ve vill find dems – *ho!*, you mék yourself vorries for nassingk – kam, let us to drink samsingk! – dere, I hem seeingk...."

And what she was "seeingk" were the pastel neon lights of the only establishment in any visible radius that appeared still open, one

Lombardia Internazionale Volo-Bar I Caffé

to which they now stumbled. It was a kind of half-arsed "self-service" affair, so Moitié offered,

"At this point I don't know which of you two's got the Embassy *plastique,* but hand it over and I'll get us something – what do *vous-autres* want?"

The seated Michel-Ange wearily told him "I had to leave the credit card with the Legionnaires – here take this," and he handed Moitié some $US that he fished out of his nearby Vuitton, "and I'll have a whiskey and soda with my change." Irina said she wanted a Campari also with soda and, having placed her order, wandered off to look at the duty-free boutiques, even though they were closed.

As Moitié turned to go, Michel-Ange added "And perhaps you could *file*-me that cellular phone *bidule* of yours – I need to call Paris, and I cannot *begin* to *emmerde* myself with acquiring the necessary lire for a pay-phone – not to mention I don't even *see* any public phones around here – I take it this thing of yours can reach Paris?"

"Yes, it can, but don't go on in your usual *Enarque* blather – minutes on these things cost the skin of your *fesses* – So, *there*... you push *that,* then compose the number, then you push *that* – and when you're done, you push *that*. Welcome to the Bronze Age, *mon seigneur* – "

"Go *fous* yourself – and as long as we're wasting money, here, make mine a *double* whiskey and bring me a beer with it – and of course don't neglect to get something for yourself, my good man...."

So Michel-Ange now found himself alone, and he dialed his own number at the Rue Mouffetard. It rang so long he thought it would again go to the recording, but eventually a strangely breathless, yet soft – almost "strangled"-sounding – Jennifer answered,

"H-hello?"

"Jenni-faire! It's *moi* –!"

"*Michel?* My God, where are you? – What's happened – ?"

"I'm in Milan! – and I'm coming back! – I'll be back tomorrow! Practically later today, in fact!"

"Wh-what?" Pause. "What do you mean 'coming back'? Like, *back* back – ?"

"Yes! – Didn't you get my message? Anyway, it's a long story, I'll explain when I see you – but the whole thing, there, in Gryaznia, has gone rather, as you say, bellied-up – *c'est fini* – *pffftt!* – I'll explain when I see you – !"

"Wow, *that* was quick. You've barely been gone a week, if that – " she seemed to be trying to clear her throat, "but that's great... *great*... uh... look, Michel, I've got to run to the bathroom – call me when you land in Paris, OK? Bye, *ciao* – "

Hmm... Had he detected a suspiciously-long silence when he'd said he'd be returning tomorrow? Yes, he definitely thought so.... And a little slow on the spontaneous celebration uptake... a bit long to produce the *youpiiii*....

Does that indicate that I might have interrupted some in-flagrante affaire*? That she now suddenly needs to, euh, clean up? Or – even worse – not clean up? Well, the Universal Odds would certainly favor that likelihood, but if that turns out to be the case, the real question is – do I care?*

Yes, he undoubtedly did. Care, that is. But not, he realized to his surprise, *quite as much* as he probably should have... Curious, that...

But I mean, what the hell – what, after all, was I myself doing with Irina not three nights ago? And had that 'meant' anything? No, it hadn't – not much, anyway... or even at all, really – So why should Jenni-faire's having a fling (if that's what she's doing) be any different? Good point... although, you know, ... women... Yes, and? – 'women' what? – Nothing... Just,... nothing –

Young Michel-Ange was not an immensely complicated fellow, and excessive jealousy and possessiveness scarcely put in appearances in his emotional inventory. So, cause for alarm? *Bof... maybe yeah but probably naah... one way or the other, this'll likely* also *turn out alright... eventually....Still, how about that Jenni-faire, eh? You had to hand it to her...* sacré *piece of work....*

Moitié now pitched up, staggering under a tray laden with enough booze to sink the aircraft carrier *Charles De Gaulle,* and he dumped it and himself down. He threw a tumbler of some brown liquid down himself and belched,

"*Brrrrk!* Drink up, peasants – *à la notre* – *vive* us! – Here's your change, Sun King, not that there *is* much....*"

Michel-Ange, who'd already started dialing Mincemot's number, waved him off, "*Shh!* – I'm calling my *patron* – "

"Give the old *fasho* my love –"

"*Ta gueule, imbecile – Allo? Allo? Mon colonel –* ?"

"Yes, Fassederad, *Mlle.* Bourgeois warned me to expect your call. Where are you? – not that I particularly want to know – and what can I do for you at this hour? – which I also don't particularly want to know – "

"Well, *mon colonel*, I just wanted to keep you up to speed on events – Moitié and I – " he still instinctively felt disinclined to mention Irina, "are currently between planes in Milan. We'll be in Paris later, on Monday."

"Alright. And is there anything else we need to discuss *just now?*"

"Well, there *are* just a few, euh, administrative details which are nagging at me, and which I'd hope would not get lost in the, euh, *événements* to come – "

"Such as?"

"Well, *mon colonel*, for example – the Legionnaires were rather insistent, as I left them, that I plead with you, or with anyone else who controls such matters, that they not be forgotten – like so many Japanese soldiers marooned on nameless islands after '45 – and that a replacement for Ambassador Duquon-Lajoie, or me, come to that – or, really, *anyone* – be sent there *asappe-illico* –"

It sounded as though the Colonel was taking a deep breath. "Don't make yourself worries on that score. The Quai will see to it, believe me – indeed, I can affirm with confidence that after your little bravura performance there, the Quai is not likely to forget our Embassy in Laina anytime soon. I expect they'll have some warm body – even if just an emergency *pompier* – down there by Tuesday, or Wednesday at the latest."

"Well that's good, at least. But now another thing – Moitié tells me that when we get to Paris he'll be reporting to the East European Desk at the Quai – I have no idea who those people are, or even where they sit – is that where I should go as well?"

"No, under no circumstances. No, when you get back to Paris, you say *au re-voir* to your truant *copain,* and come back to us, here."

"Ah."

"You sound... underwhelmed, *jeune homme.* Do you have any problem with such a plan?"

"Non, mon colonel. It's just that... well, don't I... fall under – if that's the phrase that I'm *cherche*-ing – the Quai? As Moitié does? You know, the... Diplomatic Corps?"

"Non, you don't. You are *spéciale.* Well, not *you* particularly, but your status – your status is *spéciale.* You belong to me/us. Here. Whole separate department. Not the Quai at all."

Michel-Ange said nothing as he tried to... *process* this. The colonel barked,

"You still there? Fassederad, *bon sang* – !"

"W-oui. Mon colonel."

"So, you got that? Your colleague, there, the *crétin* Consul, will face some kind of 'internal' Quai 'inquiry', but he'll be fine – his *syndicat* will see that no harm comes to him and he'll be kicked comfortably sideways. But not you – you'll just... disappear – administratively, that is. As I said, you're, believe it or not, *spéciale.* Hah! – my *'cas spéciale'.*"

"D'accord, mon colonel, if you say so... But... well, just *now* may not be the ab-solute best time to be asking this, but... as long as you bring it up – how did it happen that I became, as you say, *'speciale'?"*

"Well, I suppose there's no harm in telling you: your *papa.* A good element, so I'm told." *And if I haven't gleaned anything else from this whole mess it's that the damn colonel's definitely partial to "good elements".* Mincemot continued, "And in fact, you weren't meant to get involved with the actual diplomatic side of things at all – but we didn't foresee that priapic imbecile Duquon tripping over his own *quéquette* or the young mafioso Moitié so utterly queering relations with HostGov and your subsequent rocketing up to prominence. So to speak."

"Well, alright, *mon colonel,* again, if you say so – I suppose. I mean, I have all confidence in you, *mon colonel.* But I have no idea, really, what any of this means. Or where matters now stand.... For example, are you... going to fire me? Or – for all I know – am I fired already?"

"Certainly not. Why would you think such a thing?"

"Well... as you so vividly just pointed out – things have suddenly become – if I may permit myself the phrase – such an almighty shit-in-the-bed" *("chie-en-lit")* "there, in Laina, and since, by whatever concatenation of un-planned events, I ended up in charge of *it* – *things,* I mean – I am rather supposing that the way these things work – *le protocole* – is that I should be the one held responsible, and therefore it should be me who would be... *couiiiiic!"*

"Weeeell, not necessarily... not necessarily..." The colonel trailed off and then suddenly affected expansiveness, "I do agree with you that... 'things' as you left them down there *do* look rather appalling – but there are sometimes... *mitigating circumstances.* So, no, young Fassederad, don't go jumping to conclusions."

"Well, so – again – where does that leave me/us? If I may permit myself to ask? *Mon colonel....*"

"As I say – *demerde* yourself to get back here more or less intact – and we'll see where we go – ".

"Yes, *d'accord, mon colonel.* And so what you're saying is that it's, in effect, premature of me to ask... 'what next?'"

Now, the truth was – and Michel-Ange would not have guessed this in a million years – that Col. Mincemot *had* been surprised at, and even somewhat impressed by, Michel-Ange's seemingly phlegmatic *sang-froid* during his past week's Gryaznian ordeal. Indeed, the boy had proved himself to be a not entirely un-resourceful young "element", and one who, with perhaps not too much further training and molding, might conceivably prove useful in other circumstances... Yes, yes, the Colonel was already planning ahead....

Not, of course, that he'd ever intimate as much to young Fassederad....

So instead, the old boy continued, rather *comme-ça*:

"Yes. Premature would be the word. But tell me, *petit* – speaking theoretically, you understand... would you have any objections to our, euh, well.... *éventuellement* changing your name?"

"My name? What an idea. I don't know. Hard to say, *sur le champ* – it depends *to what*, I suppose... But, now that I think of it, it would present one problem, at least – I'd have to throw out all my shirts. They're monogrammed, you see...."

"We could always give you the same initials."

"Well, then, that would be alright."

"Yes. And, as long as we're speaking theoretically here, of course – we might be wanting to make you look different, as well."

"Pardon? Mon colonel?"

"Nothing crippling, don't worry – more cosmetic than anything – like, let's say... give you a haircut... perhaps add a *moustache*...."

"Oh-oh-oh!, hep-la!, mon colonel – let's not get carried away – do anything rash – don't want to start looking like a *pédé*, here..."

"Don't worry, my boy – I wouldn't let that happen. Heh, we like to think we're pretty *mondain* around here, but no, not that. Not yet, anyway – *that* sort of thing is still the purvieu of the *foutu* Quai..."

"Well thank you for that, *mon colonel*.... So – it seems I'm to live another day, then?"

"Well, you know what they say, don't you?"

"No, I don't. Well, I mean yes, *en principe* I do, but – let's say I don't – What *do* they say? *Mon colonel*?"

"Well, my boy, they say: 'As one door closes, another manhole opens'."

"Ah! Hah hah. *Mon Colonel*. It's a good one."

"Yes, isn't it. *Bon*. Well, enough for now, I think. *A bientot,* then, young man. *Execution!* Out. – *NO, WAIT! –* "

"Mon colonel?"

"One last quick thing – The Americans – In the end, you never *did* manage to find out what the Americans are up to while you were down there, did you?"

"The Americans?" *The Americans?* "Euh, *non, mon colonel,* regrettably not."

"Ah." Amazingly, (to Michel-Ange), Mincemot seemed unconvinced. So Michel-Ange felt he should add,

"The sad reality is, *mon colonel,* that in fact, during the hah hah less than a week I was even *in* that country, I didn't actually run into *any*one, much," – *except Irina – who it'll be interesting, to put it mildly, to see your reaction to, when I eventually reveal her to you, mon colonel....* "never mind Americans...."

"*D'accord,* then. Well, as I said, – *execution!*" *Click.*

Michel-Ange snapped shut this unpleasant and still-alien little apparatus and tossed it back to Moitié, who rather amazingly (given his half-sozzled condition) caught it in one hand – and made the universal "money" gesture with the thumb and first two fingers of his other hand...

Get stuffed, you little maniac, you owe me a good deal more than I owe you....

But nevertheless, as Michel-Ange watched the cellular telephone disappear into his ex-Consul's pocket, he pondered with gloomy apprehension the likelihood that, like it or not, he wouldn't be able to escape getting, as Irina liked to put it, *viéry, viéry match* more acquainted with these *foutue* things in the looming and probably not-untroubled, near future....

FIN – THE END

www.ingramcontent.com/pod-product-compliance
Lightning Source LLC
Chambersburg PA
CBHW071246250626
47163CB00002B/353